I remembered pain. Not merely the agony of flesh searing and splitting open, steaming and cooking even as our eyes were burned away, but the torture of being torn apart forever from the one woman in all the universes whom I loved.

The whip cracked against my bare back again.

"Harder! Pull harder, you whoreson, or by the gods I'll sacrifice *you* instead of a bullock once we make landfall!"

He leaned over me, his scarred face red with anger, and slashed at me again with the whip. The pain of the lash was nothing. What was the sting of his whip compared to the agony of death, the hopelessness of loss?

We rowed around the rocky headland and saw a calm sheltered inlet. A mile or so inland, up on a bluff that commanded the beach, stood a city or citadel of some sort. The young men at the stern seemed to get tenser at the sight of the walled city. Their voices were low, but I heard them easily enough.

"There it is," one of them said to his companions. His voice was grim.

The youth next to him nodded and spoke a single word.

"Troy."

Other works by Ben Bova
published by Tor Books

Altair
The Astral Mirror
Battle Station
Colony
Escape Plus
The Kinsman Saga
The Multiple Man
Orion
Out of the Sun
Privateers
Prometheans
The Starcrossed
Test of Fire
Voyagers II: The Alien Within

BEN BOVA
VENGEANCE OF
ORION

A TOM DOHERTY ASSOCIATES BOOK
NEW YORK

VENGEANCE OF ORION

Copyright © 1988 by Ben Bova

A TOR Book
Published by Tom Doherty Associates, Inc.
49 West 24 Street
New York, NY 10010

Cover art by Boris Vallejo

ISBN: 0-812-53161-2   Can. ISBN: 0-812-53162-0

Library of Congress Catalog Card Number: 87-50879

First edition: February 1988

First mass market edition: February 1989

Printed in the United States of America

0 9 8 7 6 5 4 3 2 1

To the kindly, courteous, cheerful, and always-helpful staff of the West Hartford Library, with my thanks.

The great invasions which destroyed late Bronze Age civilization came from two directions. From the northwest a variety of tribes, called by the Egyptians the "sea peoples," began raiding the eastern coasts of the Mediterranean . . . [by] 1200 B.C. the Hittite empire was destroyed. . . . While these invasions from the northwest swept over Greece, Asia Minor, and the Mediterranean coasts, other hordes of invaders came from the southeast, from the fringes of the Arabian desert . . . The movement began early: the Israelites were already in Palestine before 1220 B.C.

—*The Columbia History of the World*, 1972

Prologue

I am not superhuman.

I do have abilities that are far beyond those of any normal man's, but I am just as human and mortal as anyone of Earth.

Yet I am a solitary man. My life has been spent alone, my mind clouded with strange dreams and, when I am awake, half memories of other lives, other existences that are so fantastic that they can only be the compensations of a lonely, withdrawn subconscious mind.

As I did almost every day, I took my lunch hour late in the afternoon and made my way from my office to the same small restaurant in which I always ate. Alone. I sat at my usual table, toying with my food and thinking about how much of my life is spent in solitude.

I happened to look up toward the front entrance of the restaurant when she came in—stunningly beautiful, tall and graceful, hair the color of midnight and lustrous gray eyes that held all of eternity in them.

"Anya," I breathed to myself, even though I had no idea who she was. Yet something within me leaped with joy, as if I had known her from ages ago.

She seemed to know me as well. Smiling, she made her way directly to my table. I got up from my chair, feeling elated and confused at the same time.

"Orion." She extended her hand.

I took it in mine and bent to kiss it. Then I held a chair for her to sit. The waiter came over and she asked for a glass of red wine. It trundled off to the bar.

"I feel as if I've known you all my life," I said to her.

"For many lifetimes," she said, her voice soft and melodious as a warm summer breeze. "Don't you remember?"

I closed my eyes in concentration and a swirl of memories rushed in on me so rapidly that it took my breath away. I saw a great shining globe of golden light and the dark brooding figure of a fiercely malevolent man, a forest of giant trees and a barren windswept desert and a world of unending ice and snow. And her, this woman, clad in silver armor that gleamed against the darkness of infinity.

"I . . . remember . . . death," I heard myself stammer. "The whole world, the entire universe . . . all of space-time collapsed in on itself."

She nodded gravely. "And rebounded in a new cycle of expansion. That was something that neither Ormazd nor Ahriman foresaw. The continuum does not end; it begins anew."

"Ormazd," I muttered. "Ahriman." The names touched a chord in my mind. I felt anger welling up inside me, anger tinged with fear and resentment. But I could not recall who they were and why they stirred such strong emotions within me.

"They are still out there," she said, "still grappling with each other. But they know, thanks to you, Orion, that the continuum cannot be destroyed so easily. It perseveres."

"Those other lives I remember—you were in them."

"Yes, as I will be in this one."

"I loved you, then."

Her smile lit the world. "Do you love me now?"

"Yes." And I knew it was so. I meant it with every atom of my being.

"And I love you, too, Orion. I always have and I always will. Through death and infinity, my darling, I will always love you."

"But I'm leaving soon."

"I know."

Past her shoulder I could see through the restaurant's window the gaudy crescent of Saturn hanging low on the horizon, the thin line of its rings slicing through its bulging middle. Closer to the horizon the sky of Titan was its usual smoggy orange overcast.

The starship was parked in orbit up there, waiting for us to finish our final preparations and board it.

"We'll be gone for twenty years," I said.

"To the Sirius system. I know."

"It's a long voyage."

"Not as long as some we've already made, Orion," she said, "or others we will make someday."

"What do you mean?"

"I'll explain it during the voyage." She smiled again. "We'll have plenty of time to remember everything then."

My heart leaped in my chest. "You're going too?"

"Of course." She laughed. "We've endured the collapse and rebirth of the universe, Orion. We have shared many lives and many deaths. I'm not going to be separated from you now."

"But I haven't seen you at any of the crew briefings. You're not on the list . . ."

"I am now. We will journey out to the stars together, my beloved. We have a long and full lifetime ahead of us. And perhaps even more than that."

I leaned across the table and kissed her lips. My loneliness was ended, at last. I could face anything in the world now. I was ready to challenge the universe.

BOOK I

TROY

Chapter 1

THE slash of a whip across my bare back brought me to full awareness.

"Pull, you big ox! Stop your daydreaming or you'll think Zeus's thunderbolts are landing on your shoulders!"

I was sitting on a rough wooden bench along the gunwale of a long, wallowing boat, a heavy oar in my hands. No, not an oar. A paddle. We were rowing hard, under a hot high sun. I could see the sweat streaming down the emaciated ribs and spine of the man in front of me. There were welts across his nut-brown skin.

"Pull!" the man with the whip roared. "Stay with the beat."

I wore nothing but a stained leather loincloth. Sweat stung my eyes. My back and arms ached. My hands were callused and dirty.

The boat was like a Hawaiian war canoe. The prow rose high into a grotesquely carved figurehead; some fierce demonic spirit, I guessed, to protect the boat and its crew. I glanced swiftly around as I dug my paddle into the heaving dark sea and counted forty rowers. Amidships there were bales of goods, tethered sheep and pigs that squealed with every roll of the deck.

The sun blazed overhead. The wind was fitful and light. The boat's only sail was furled against its mast. I could smell the stench of the animals' droppings. Toward the stern a brawny bald man was beating a single large mallet on a well-worn drum, as steady as a metronome. We drove our paddles into the water in time with his beat—or took a sting from the rowing master's whip.

Other men were gathered down by the stern, standing, shading their eyes with one hand and pointing with the other as they spoke with one another. They wore clean knee-length linen tunics and cloaks of red or blue that went down to midcalf. Small daggers at their belts, more for ornamentation than combat, I judged. Silver inlaid hilts. Gold clasps on their cloaks. They were young men, lean, their beards light. But their faces were grave, not jaunty. They were looking toward something that sobered their youthful spirits. I followed their gaze and saw a headland not far off, a low treeless rocky rise at the end of a sandy stretch of beach. Obviously our destination was beyond that promontory.

Where was I? How did I get here? Frantically I ransacked my mind. The last firm memory I could find was of a beautiful, tall, gray-eyed woman who loved me and whom I loved. We were . . . a shudder of blackest grief surged through me. She was dead.

My mind went spinning, as if a whirlpool had opened in the dark sea and dragged me down into it. Dead. Yes. There was a ship, a very different ship. One that traveled not through the water but through the vast emptiness between stars. I had been on that ship with her. And it exploded. She died. She was killed. We were both killed.

Yet I lived, sweaty, dirty, my back stinging with welts, on this strangely primitive oversized canoe heading for an unknown land under a brazen cloudless sky.

Who am I? With a sudden shock of fright I realized that I could remember nothing about myself except my name. I am Orion, I told myself. But more than that I could not recall. My memory was a blank, as if it had been wiped clean, like a classroom chalkboard being prepared for a new lesson.

I squeezed my eyes shut and forced myself to think about that woman I had loved and that fantastic star-leaping ship. I could not even remember her name. I saw flames, heard screams. I held her in my arms as the heat blistered our skins and made the metal walls around us glow hell-red.

"He's beaten us, Orion," she said to me. "We'll die together. That's the only consolation we will have, my love."

I remembered pain. Not merely the agony of flesh searing and splitting open, steaming and cooking even as our eyes were burned away, but the torture of being torn apart forever from the one woman in all the universes whom I loved.

The whip cracked against my bare back again.

"Harder! Pull harder, you whoreson, or by the gods I'll sacrifice *you* instead of a bullock once we make landfall!"

He leaned over me, his scarred face red with anger, and slashed at me again with the whip. The pain of the lash was nothing. I closed it off without another thought. I always could control my body completely. Had I wanted to, I could have snapped this hefty paddle in two and driven the ragged end of it through the whipmaster's thick skull. But what was the sting of his whip compared to the agony of death, the hopelessness of loss?

We rowed around the rocky headland and saw a calm sheltered inlet. Spread along the curving beach were dozens of ships like our own, pulled far up on the sand. Huts and tents huddled among their black hulls like shreds of paper littering a city street after a parade. Thin gray smoke issued from cook fires here and there. A pall of thicker, blacker smoke billowed off in the distance.

A mile or so inland, up on a bluff that commanded the beach, stood a city or citadel of some sort. High stone walls with square towers rising above the battlements. Far in the distance, dark wooded hills rose and gradually gave way to mountains that floated shimmering in the blue heat haze.

The young men at the stern seemed to get tenser at the sight of the walled city. Their voices were low, but I heard them easily enough.

"There is it," one of them said to his companions. His voice was grim.

The youth next to him nodded and spoke a single word.

"Troy."

Chapter 2

WE landed, literally, driving the boat up onto the beach until its bottom grated against the sand and we could go no farther. Then the whipmaster bellowed at us as we piled over the gunwales, took up ropes, and—straining, cursing, wrenching the tendons in our arms and shoulders—we hauled the pitch-blackened hull up onto the beach until only its stern and rudder paddle touched the water.

Hardly any tide to speak of, I knew. When they finally sail past the Pillars of Herakles and out into the Atlantic, that's when they'll encounter real tides.

Then I wondered how I knew that.

I did not have time to wonder for long. The whipmaster allowed us a scant few moments to get our breath back, then he started us unloading the boat. He roared and threatened, shaking his many-thonged whip at us, his cinnamon-red beard ragged and tangled, the scar on his left cheek standing out white against his florid frog's-eyed face. I carried bales and bleating sheep and squirming, foul-smelling pigs while the gentlemen in their cloaks and linen tunics and their fine sandals walked down a gangplank, each followed by two or more slaves who carried their goods, mostly arms and armor, from what I could see.

"Fresh blood for the war," grunted the man next to me, with a nod toward the young noblemen. He looked as grimy as I felt, a stringy old fellow with skin as tanned and creased as weather-beaten leather. His hair was sparse, gray, matted with perspiration; his beard, mangy and unkempt. Like me, he wore nothing but a loincloth; his skinny legs and knobby knees barely seemed strong enough to tote the burdens he carried.

There were plenty of other men, just as ragged and filthy as we, to take the bales and livestock from us. They seemed delighted to do so. As I went back and forth from the boat I saw that this stretch of beach was protected by an earthenwork rampart studded here and there with sharpened stakes.

We finished our task at last, unloading a hundred or so massive double-handled jugs of wine, as the sun touched the headland we had rounded earlier in the day. Aching, exhausted, we sprawled around a cook fire and accepted steaming wooden bowls of boiled lentils and greens.

A cold wind blew in from the north as the sun slipped below the horizon, sending sparks from our little fire glittering toward the darkening sky.

"I never thought I'd be here on the plain of Ilios," said the old man who had worked next to me. He put the bowl to his lips and gobbled the stew hungrily.

"Where are you from?" I asked him.

"Argos. My name is Poletes. And you?"

"Orion."

"Ah! Named after the Hunter."

I nodded, a faint echo of memory tingling the hairs at the back of my neck. The Hunter. Yes, I was a hunter. Once. Long ago. Or—was it a long time *from now*? Future and past were all mixed together in my mind. I remembered . . .

"And where are you from, Orion?" asked Poletes, shattering the fragile images half-forming in my mind.

"Oh," I gestured vaguely, "west of Argos. Far west."

"Farther than Ithaca?"

"Beyond the sea," I answered, not knowing why, but feeling instinctively that it was as honest a reply as I could give.

"And how came you here?"

I shrugged. "I'm a wanderer. And you?"

Edging closer to me, Poletes wrinkled his brow and scratched at his thinning pate. "No wanderer I. I'm a storyteller, and happy was I to spend my days in the agora, spinning tales and watching the faces of the people as I talked. Especially the children, with their big eyes. But this war put an end to my storytelling."

"How so?"

He wiped at his mouth with the back of his grimy hand. "My lord Agamemnon may need more warriors, but his faithless wife wants *thetes.*"

"Slaves?"

"Hah! Worse off than a slave. Far worse," Poletes grumbled. He gestured to the exhausted men sprawled around the dying fire. "Look at us! Homeless and hopeless. At least a slave has a master to depend on. A slave belongs to someone; he is a member of a household. A *thes* belongs to no one and nothing; he is landless, homeless, cut off from everything except sorrow and hunger."

"But you were a member of a household in Argos, weren't you?"

He bowed his head and squeezed his eyes shut, as if to block out a painful memory.

"A household, yes," he said, his voice low. "Until Queen Clytemnestra's men booted me out of the city for repeating what every stray dog and alley cat in Argos was saying—that the queen has taken a lover while her royal husband is here fighting at Troy's walls."

I took a sip of the rapidly cooling stew, trying to think of something to say.

"At least they didn't kill you," was all I could come up with.

"Better if they had!" Poletes replied bitterly. "I would be dead and in Hades and that would be the end of it. Instead, I'm here, toiling like a jackass, working for wages."

"That's something, anyway," I said.

His eyes snapped at me. "You are eating your wages, Orion."

"This . . . this is our payment?"

"For the day's work. Exactly. Show me a *thes* with coin in his purse and I'll show you a sneak thief."

I took a deep breath.

"Lower than slaves, that's what we are, Orion," said Poletes, in a whisper that was heavy with overdue sleep. "Vermin under their feet. Dogs. That's how they treat us. They'll work us to death and let our bones rot where we fall."

With a heavy sigh Poletes put his empty bowl down and stretched out on the sandy ground. It was getting so dark that I could barely see his face. The pitiful little fire had gone down to nothing but embers. The wind blowing in from the water was cold and sharp. I automatically adjusted my blood flow to keep as warm as possible. There were no blankets or even canvas tarpaulins among the sprawled bodies of the exhausted *thetes*. They slept in their loincloths and nothing else.

I lay down beside the old man, then found myself wondering how old he could truly be. Forty, perhaps. I doubted that anyone lived much past fifty in this primitive time. A pair of mangy dogs snarled at each other over some bones by the fire, then settled down side by side, better protected against the night than we were.

Just before I closed my eyes to sleep, I caught sight of the beetling towers of Troy bulking dark against the deepening violet sky.

Agamemnon. Troy. How did I get here? How long could I survive as something lower than a slave?

Falling asleep was like entering another world. My dream was as real as life. I thought perhaps it *was* life, a different life on a different plane of existence.

I stood in a place that had neither time nor dimension. No land, no sea, no sky. Not even a horizon. A great golden glow surrounded me, stretching away to infinity on every side, warm and so bright that it dazzled my eyes. I could see nothing except its radiance.

Without knowing why, I began to walk. Slowly at first, but soon my pace quickened, as if I knew where I was heading and why. Time was meaningless here, but I walked endlessly, my bare feet striking something firm beneath me, though when I looked down all I could see was the gleaming golden light.

And then, far, far off, I saw a brilliance that outshone everything else. A speck, a spot, a source of radiance that blazed pure gold and drew me forward like a magnet draws a sliver of iron, like the fiery sun draws a falling comet.

I ran, I flew toward that burning golden glow. Breathlessly I raced to it, my eyes painfully dazzled, my heart thundering wildly, the breath rasping in my throat.

I stopped. As if an invisible wall had risen before me. As if my body had suddenly become paralyzed.

I stopped and slumped to my knees.

A human form sat before me, elevated above my level, resting on nothing more substantial than golden light. He was the source of all the radiance. He shone so beautifully that it hurt my eyes to look upon him. Yet I could not look away.

He was splendid. Thick mane of golden hair, gold-flecked eyes. Skin that glowed with life-giving radiance. Utterly handsome face, masculine yet beautiful, calm and self-assured, the hint of a smile curling his lips. Broad shoulders and wide hairless chest. Bare to the waist, where draperies of gleaming gold enfolded him.

"My poor Orion." His smile turned almost mocking. "You are certainly in a sorry state."

I did not know what to reply. I could not reply. My voice froze in my throat.

"Do you remember your Creator?" he asked, tauntingly.

I nodded dumbly.

"Of course you do. That memory is built so deeply into you that nothing but final destruction can erase it."

I knelt before my Creator, my mind whirling with faint half memories, struggling to find my voice, to speak, to ask him . . .

"Do you remember my name?" he asked.

Almost, I did.

"No matter. For the present you may call me Apollo. Your companions on the plain of Ilios refer to me by that name."

Apollo. The Greek god of light and beauty. Of course. The god of music and medicine—or is it biotechnology, I wondered. But I seemed to recall that he had another name, another time. And there were other gods, as well. And a goddess, the one whom I loved.

"I am being harsh with you, Orion, because you disobeyed me in the matter of Ahriman. You deliberately twisted the course of the continuum, out of sentiment."

"Out of love," I replied. My voice was weak, gasping. But I spoke.

"You are a creature, Orion," he sneered. "What can you know of love?"

"The woman," I pleaded. "The goddess . . ."

"She is dead."

His voice was as coldly implacable as fate. I felt ice freezing my veins.

"You killed her," I said dully.

His sneering smile faded into grim solemnity. "In a sense,

Orion, it was *you* who killed her. By daring to love a goddess, by tempting her to assume a human form, you sealed her doom."

"You blame me . . ."

"Blame? A god does not blame, Orion. A god punishes. Or rewards. You are being punished—for the while. Accept your fate and your punishment will cease."

"And then?"

His smile returned. "I have other tasks for you, my creature, after the Trojans have beaten off these Greek barbarians. Don't be afraid, I don't plan on letting you die again, not for a while. There is much work for you to do in this era."

I began to ask him what he meant, but a sandaled foot prodded my ribs and I opened my eyes to see that I was on the beach among the Greeks who were besieging Troy, a *thes,* the lowest of the low.

"On your feet! There's work to be done!" shouted the whipmaster.

I looked up at him but saw instead the blinding radiance of the morning sun. I winced and bowed my head.

Chapter 3

WE were given a bowl of thin barley gruel and then set to work with wooden shovels on the earthworks defending the beach.

While the warriors ate a leisurely breakfast of mutton and flat bread, and their men-at-arms yoked horses to chariots and sharpened swords and spears, we lumbered out through one of the makeshift gates in the low rampart that had been heaped up along the beach. Our task this fine, windy morning was to deepen the trench in front of the mound and pile the diggings atop it. This would make it even harder for Trojan troops or chariots to reach the ships.

We worked a good part of the morning. The sky was a sparkling bowl of wondrously clear, cloudless blue, dotted by screeching white gulls soaring above us. The sea was an even deeper blue, restless with flecks of white-foamed waves. Grayish brown humps of islands rose above the distant horizon. In the other direction, Troy's towers and beetling walls seemed to glower down at us from across the plain. Beyond it the distant hills were dark with trees and beyond them rose the hazy mountains.

The wind strengthened into a brisk gusting breeze as the sun rose higher, helping to keep us cool as we dug and emptied our shovels of sandy soil into woven baskets that were carried to the top of the mound by other *thetes*.

As I dug and sweated, I thought about my memories of the night. It was no dream, I was certain of that. The Golden One really existed, whether he called himself Apollo or some other name from an earlier existence. I dimly remembered knowing him from another time, another era—him, and a dark, brooding hulking presence. The one he called Ahriman, I thought. And the goddess, the woman I loved. The woman who was dead. The Golden One said I was responsible for her death. Yet I knew that he had set in motion the train of events that ended with our starship exploding. He had killed her, killed us both. Yet somehow he had revived me, placed me here in this time and place, alone and bereft of memory.

But I *did* remember. A little, anyway. Enough to know I hated the Golden One for what he had done to me. And to her. I tightened my callused hands on the shovel, anger and the hollow empty feeling of heartsickness driving me. None of the other *thetes* were pushing themselves and the work went slowly, mainly because the whipmaster and the other overseers ignored us, spending their time at the top of the mound where they could ogle the camp and the noblemen in their splendid bronze armor.

Achaians, they called themselves. I heard it from the men laboring around me. It would be another thousand years before they began to think of themselves as Greeks. They were here besieging Troy, yet they seemed worried that the Trojans would break through these defenses and attack the camp. There is trouble among the Achaians, I thought.

And the Golden One said that the Trojans were going to beat off their besiegers.

Poletes had been picked to carry baskets of dirt from down where we were digging up to the top of the rampart. At first I thought this was too much of a burden for his skinny old legs, but the baskets were small and carried only a light load, and the overseers were lax enough to let the load-carriers meander up the slope slowly.

The old man spotted me among the diggers and came to me.

"All is not well among the high and mighty this morning," he whispered to me, delighted. "There's some argument between my lord Agamemnon and Achilles, the great slayer of men. They say that Achilles will not leave his tent today."

"Not even to help us dig?" I joked.

Poletes cackled with laughter. "The High King Agamemnon has sent a delegation to Achilles to beseech him to join the battle. I don't think it's going to work. Achilles is young and arrogant. He thinks his shit smells like roses."

I laughed back at the old man.

"You there!" The whipmaster pointed at us from the top of the mound. "If you don't get back to work I'll give you something to laugh about!"

Poletes hoisted his half-filled basket up to his frail shoulders and started climbing the slope. I turned back to my shovel.

The sun was high in the cloudless sky when the wooden gate nearest me creaked open and the chariots started streaming out, the horses' hooves thudding on the packed-earth ramp that cut across the trench. All work stopped. The overseers shouted for us to come up out of the trench and we scrambled eagerly up the slope of the rampart, happy to watch the impending battle.

Bronze armor glittered in the sun as the chariots arrayed themselves in line abreast. Most were pulled by two horses, though a few had teams of four. The horses neighed and stamped their hooves nervously, as if they sensed the mayhem that was in store. There were seventy-nine chariots, by my count. Quite a bit short of the thousands that the poets sang about.

Each chariot bore two men, one handling the horses, the other armed with several spears of different weights and length. The longest were more than twice the height of a warrior, even in his bronze helmet with its horse-hair plume.

Both men in each chariot wore bronze breastplates, helmets, and arm guards. I could not see their legs but I guessed that they were sheathed in greaves, as well. Most charioteers carried small round targes strapped to their left forearms. Each warrior held a figure-eight shield that was nearly as tall as he was, covering him from chin to ankles. Every man bore a sword on a baldric that looped over his shoulder. I caught the glitter of gold and silver on the handles of the swords. Many of the charioteers had bows slung across their backs or hooked against the chariot rail.

A shout went up as the last chariot passed through the gate and along the trodden-smooth rampway that crossed our trench. The four horses pulling it were magnificent matched blacks, glossy and sleek. The warrior in it seemed stockier than most of the others, his armor filigreed with gold inlays.

"That's the High King," said Poletes, over the roar of the shouting men. "That's Agamemnon."

"Is Achilles with them?" I asked.

"No. But that giant there is Great Ajax," he pointed, excited despite himself. "There's Odysseus, and . . ."

An echoing roar reached us from the battlements of Troy. A cloud of dust showed us that a contingent of chariots was filing out of a gate to the right side of the city, winding its way down an incline that led to the plain before us.

Ground troops were hurrying out of our gates now, men-at-arms bearing bows, slings, axes, cudgels. A few of them wore armor or chain mail, but most of them had nothing more protective than leather jerkins, some studded with bronze pieces.

The two armies assembled themselves facing each other on the windswept plain. A fair-sized river formed a natural boundary to the battlefield on our right, while a smaller stream defined the left flank. Beyond their banks on both sides the sandy ground was green with tussocks of long-bladed grass, but the battlefield had been worn bare by chariot wheels and the tramping feet of soldiery.

For nearly a half hour, nothing much happened. Heralds went out and spoke with each other while the dust drifted away on the wind.

"None of the heroes are challenging each other to single combat today," explained Poletes. "The heralds are exchanging offers of peace, which each side will disdainfully refuse."

"They do this every day?"

"So I'm told. Unless it rains."

"Did the war really start over Helen?" I asked.

Poletes shrugged elaborately. "That's the excuse. And it's true that Prince Aleksandros abducted her from Sparta while her husband's back was turned. Whether she came along with him willingly or not, only the gods know."

"Aleksandros? I thought his name was Paris."

"He is sometimes called Paris. But his name is Aleksandros. One of Priam's sons." Poletes laughed. "I hear that he and Menalaos, the lawful husband of Helen, fought in single combat a few days ago and Aleksandros ran away. He hid behind his foot soldiers! Can you believe that?"

I nodded.

"Menalaos is Agamemnon's brother," Poletes went on, his voice dropping lower, as if he did not want others to overhear.

"The High King would love to smash Troy flat. That would give him clear sailing through the Hellespont into the Sea of Black Waters."

"Is that important?"

"Gold, my boy," Poletes whispered. "Not merely the metal that kings adorn themselves with, but golden grain grows by the far shores of that sea. A land awash in grain. And no one can pass through the straits to get at it unless they pay a tribute to Troy."

"Ahhh." I was beginning to see the real forces behind this war.

"Aleksandros was on a mission of peace to Mycenae, to arrange a new trade agreement between his father Priam and High King Agamemnon. He stopped off at Sparta and wound up abducting Helen instead. That was all the excuse Agamemnon needed. If he can conquer Troy he can have free access to the riches of the regions beyond the straits."

I was about to ask why the Trojans would not simply return Helen to her rightful husband, when a series of bugle blasts ended the quiet on the plain below us.

"Now it begins," Poletes said, grimly. "The fools rush to the slaughter once again."

We watched as the charioteers cracked their whips and the horses bolted forward, carrying Achaians and Trojans madly toward each other.

I focused my vision on the chariot nearest us and saw the warrior in it setting his sandaled feet in a pair of raised sockets, to give him a firm base for using his spears. He held his body-length shield before him and plucked one of the lighter, shorter spears from the handful rattling in their holder on his right.

"Diomedes," said Poletes, before I asked. "The prince of Argos. A fine young man."

The chariot approaching his swerved suddenly and the warrior in it hurled a spear. It sailed past harmlessly.

Diomedes threw his spear and hit the rump of the farthest of his opponent's four horses. The horse whickered and reared, throwing the other three so off stride that the chariot skewed wildly, tumbling the warrior onto the dusty ground. The charioteer either fell or ducked behind the chariot's siding.

Other combats were turning the worn-bare field into a vast cloud of dust, chariots wheeling, spears hurtling through the air, shrill battle cries and shouted curses ringing everywhere. The foot soldiers seemed to be holding back, letting the noblemen fight their single encounters for the first few moments of the battle.

One voice pierced all the other noises, a weird screaming cry like a seagull gone mad.

"The battle cry of Odysseus," Poletes said. "You can always hear the King of Ithaca above all others."

But I was still concentrating on Diomedes. His charioteer reined in his team and the warrior hopped down to the ground, two spears gripped in his left hand, his massive figure-eight shield bumping against his helmet and greaves.

"Ah, a lesser man would have speared his foe from the chariot," Poletes said admiringly. "Diomedes is a true nobleman. Would that he had been in Argos when Clytemnestra's men put me out!"

Diomedes approached the fallen warrior, who clambered back to his feet and held his shield before him, drawing his long sword from its scabbard. The prince of Argos took his longest and heaviest spear in his right hand and shook it menacingly. I could not hear what the two men were saying to each other, but they shouted something back and forth.

Suddenly both men dropped their weapons, rushed to each other, and embraced like a couple of long-lost brothers. I was stunned.

"They must have relatives in common," Poletes explained. "Or one of them might have been a guest in the other's household sometime in the past."

"But the battle . . ."

He shook his gray head. "What has that to do with it? There are plenty of others to kill."

The two warriors exchanged swords, then they both got back onto their chariots and drove in opposite directions.

"No wonder this war has lasted ten years," I muttered.

But although Diomedes and his first encounter of the day ended nonviolently, that was the only bit of peace I saw amid the carnage of the battle. Chariots hurtled at each other, spearmen driving their fourteen-foot weapons into their enemies like medieval knights would use their lances nearly two thousand years later. The bronze spear points were themselves the length of a man's arm. When all the energy generated by a team of four galloping horses was focused on the gleaming tip of that sharp spear point, it was if a high-velocity cannon shell tore into its target. Armored men were lifted off their feet, out of their chariots, when those spears found them. Bronze armor was no protection against that tremendous force.

The warriors preferred to fight from the chariots, I saw, although here and there men had alighted and faced their opponents afoot. Still the infantry soldiers hung back, skulking and squinting in the swirling clouds of dust, while the noblemen faced each other singly. Were they waiting for a signal? Was there some tactic in this bewildering melee of individual combats? Or was it that the foot soldiers knew that they could never face an armored nobleman and those deadly spears?

Here two chariots clashed together, the spearman of one driving his point through the head of the other's charioteer. There a pair of armored noblemen faced each other on foot, dueling and parrying with their long spears. One of them whirled suddenly and rammed the butt of his spear into the side of his opponent's helmet. The man dropped to the ground and his enemy drove his spear through his unprotected neck. Blood gushed onto the thirsty ground.

Instead of getting back into his chariot, or stalking another enemy, the victorious warrior dropped to his knees and began unbuckling the slain man's armor.

"A rich prize," Poletes explained. "The sword alone should buy food and wine for a month, at least."

Now the foot soldiers came forward, on both sides, some to help strip the carcass, others to defend it. A comical tug-of-war started briefly, but quickly turned into a serious fight with knives, axes, cudgels, and hatchets. The armored nobleman made all the difference, though. He cut through the enemy foot soldiers with his long sword, hacking limbs and lives until the few who could ran for their lives. Then his men resumed stripping the corpse while the warrior stood guard over them, as effectively out of the battle for the time being as if he himself had been killed.

Most of the chariots were overturned or empty of their warriors by now. Men were fighting on foot with long spears or swords. I saw armored noblemen pick up stones and throw them, to good effect. Archers—many of them charioteers who fired from the protection of their cars' leather-covered side paneling—began picking off unprotected infantry. I saw an armored warrior suddenly drop his spear and paw, howling, at an arrow sticking in his beefy shoulder. A chariot raced by and the warrior in it spitted an archer on his spear, lifting him completely out of his chariot and dragging him in the dust until his dead body wrenched free of the spear's barbed point.

All this took only a few minutes. There seemed to be no order to the battle, no plan, no tactics. The noble contestants seemed more interested in looting the bodies of the slain than defeating the enemy forces. It was more like a game than a war. A game that soaked the ground with blood and filled the air with screams of pain and terror.

The one thing that stood out above all others was that to turn and attempt to flee was much more dangerous than facing the enemy and fighting. I saw a charioteer wheel his team about to get away from two chariots converging on him. Someone threw a spear that caught him between the shoulder blades. His team ran wild, and while the warrior in the chariot attempted to take the reins from the dead hands of his companion and get the horses under control, another spearman drove up and killed him with a thrust in the back.

Foot soldiers who turned away from the fighting took arrows in the back or were cut down by chariot-mounted warriors who swung their swords like scythes.

It was getting difficult to see, the dust was swirling so thickly. But I heard a fresh trumpet blast and the roar of many men shouting in unison. Then the thunder of horses' hooves shook the ground.

Through the dust came three dozen chariots, heading straight toward the place where we stood atop the earthworks rampart.

"Prince Hector!" said Poletes, with awe in his voice. "Look how he slices through the Achaians."

Hector had either regrouped his main chariot force or had held them back from the opening melee of the battle. Whichever, he was now driving them like shock troops through the Achaian forces, slaughtering left and right. Hector's massive long spear was stained with blood halfway up its fourteen-foot length. He carried it as lightly as a wand, spitting armored noblemen and leather-jerkined foot soldiers alike, driving relentlessly toward the rampart that protected the beach, the camp, and the ships.

For a few minutes the Achaians fought back, but when Hector's chariot broke past the ragged line of Greek chariots and headed for the gate in the rampart, the Achaian resistance crumbled. Noblemen and foot soldiers alike, chariots and infantry, they all ran screaming for the safety of the earthworks.

Hector and his Trojan chariots wreaked bloody havoc among the panicked Achaians. With spears and swords and arrows they killed and killed and killed. Men ran hobbling, limping, bleeding toward us. Screams and groans filled the air.

An Achaian chariot rushed bumping and rattling to the gate, riding past and even over the fleeing footmen. I recognized the splendid armor of the squat, broad-shouldered warrior in it: Agamemnon the High King.

He did not look so splendid now. His plumed helmet was gone. His armor was coated with dust. An arrow protruded from his right shoulder and blood streaked the arm.

"We're doomed!" he shrieked in a high girlish voice. "Doomed!"

Chapter 4

THE Achaians were racing for the safety of the rampart, with the Trojan chariots in hot pursuit, closely followed by the Trojan infantry brandishing swords and axes. Here and there a foot soldier would stop for a moment to sling a stone at the retreating Achaians or drop to one knee to fire an arrow.

An arrow whizzed past me. I turned and saw that Poletes and I were alone on the crest of the rampart. The other *thetes*, even the whipmaster, had gone down into the camp.

A noisy struggle was taking place at the gate. It was a ramshackle wooden affair, made of planks taken from some of the ships. It was not a hinged door but simply a wooden barricade that could be lifted and wedged into the opening in the earthworks.

Some men were frantically trying to put the gate in place, while others were trying to hold them back until the remainder of the fleeing Achaians could get through. I saw that Hector and his chariots would reach the gate in another minute or less. Once past that gate, I knew, the Trojans would slaughter everyone in the camp.

"Stay here," I said to Poletes. Without looking to see if he obeyed, I dodged among the stakes planted in the rampart's crest, heading toward the gate.

Out of the corner of my eye I saw a light spear hurtling toward me. My senses seemed to be heightened, sharpened. The world around me went into slow-motion as my body surged into hyperdrive. The javelin came floating lazily through the air, flexing slightly as it flew. I skipped back a step and it struck the ground at my feet, quivering. I yanked it loose and raced toward the gate.

Hector's chariot was already pounding up the sandy ramp that cut across the trench in front of the rampart. There was no time for anything else, so I leaped from the rampart's crest onto the ramp, right in front of Hector's charging horses. I yelled and threw up both arms, and the startled horses reared up, neighing.

For an instant the world stopped, frozen as in a painting on a vase. Behind me the Achaians were struggling to put up the barricade that would hold the Trojans out of the camp. Before me Hector's team of horses reared high, the unshod hooves of their forelegs flashing inches from my face. I stood crouched slightly, holding the light javelin in both my hands at chest level, ready to move in any direction.

The horses shied away from me, their eyes bulging white with fear, twisting the chariot almost sideways along the pounded-earth ramp. I saw the warrior in the chariot still standing, one hand on the rail, the other raised over his head, holding a monstrously long blood-soaked spear.

Aimed at my chest.

I looked into the eyes of Hector, prince of Troy. Brown eyes they were, calm and deep. No anger, no battle lust. He was a cool and calculating warrior, a thinker among hordes of adrenaline-soaked brutes. I noticed that he wore a small round shield buckled to his left arm instead of the massive body-length type most of the other nobles carried. On it was painted a flying heron, almost in a style that would be called Japanese in millennia to come.

He jabbed the spear at me. I sidestepped and, dropping the javelin I had been carrying, grabbed the hefty ash wood shaft and pulled Hector clear over the railing of his chariot. Wrenching the spear from his one-handed grasp, I swung it against the charioteer's head, knocking him over the other side of the car.

The horses panicked and stumbled over each other in the narrow passage of the ramp. One of them started sliding along the steep edge of the trench. Whinnying with fear, they backed away and turned, trampling the poor charioteer as they bolted off back down the ramp and toward the distant city, dragging the empty chariot with them.

Hector scrambled to his feet and came at me with his sword. I parried with the spear, holding it like an elongated quarterstaff, and knocked his feet out from under him again.

By this time more Trojans were rushing up the ramp on foot, their chariots useless because Hector's panicked team had scattered the others.

I glanced behind me. The barricade was up now, and Achaian archers were firing through the slits between its planks. Others were atop the rampart, hurling stones and spears. Hector held his shield up to protect himself against the missiles and backed away. A few Trojan arrows came my way, but I avoided them easily.

The Trojans retreated, but only beyond the distance of a bowshot. There Hector told them to stand their ground.

And just like that the morning's battle was ended. The Achaians were penned up in their camp, behind the trench and rampart, the sea at their backs. The Trojans held the corpse-strewn plain.

I clambered up the barricade and threw a leg over its top. Hesitating for a second, I glanced back at the battlefield. How many of those youthful lords who had come on our boat were now lying out there, stripped of their splendid armor, their jeweled swords, their young lives? I saw birds circling high above in the clean blue sky. Not gulls: vultures.

Poletes called to me. "Orion, you must be a son of Ares! A mighty warrior to best Prince Hector!"

Other voices joined the praise as I let myself over the rickety barricade and dropped lightly to the ground. They surrounded me, clapping my back and shoulders, smiling, shouting. Someone offered me a wooden cup of wine.

"You saved the camp!"

"You stopped those horses as if you were Poseidon himself!"

Even the whipmaster looked on me fondly. "That was not the action of a *thes*," he said, looking me over carefully, perhaps for the first time, out of his bulging frog's eyes. "Why is a warrior working as a paid man?"

Without even thinking about it, I replied, "A duty I must perform. A duty to a god."

They edged away from me. Their smiles turned to awe. Only the whipmaster had the courage to stand his ground before me. He nodded and said quietly, "I understand. Well, the god must be pleased with you this morning."

I shrugged. "We'll know soon enough."

Poletes came to my side. "Come, I'll find you a good fire and hot food."

I let the old storyteller lead me away.

"I knew you were no ordinary man," he said as we made our way through the scattered huts and tents. "Not someone with your shoulders. Why, you're almost as tall as Great Ajax. A nobleman, I told myself. A nobleman, at the very least."

He chattered and yammered, telling me how my deeds looked to his eyes, reciting the day's carnage as if he were trying to set it firmly in his memory for future recall. Every group of men we passed offered us a share of their midday meal. The women in the camp smiled at me. Some were bold enough to come up to us and offer me freshly cooked meats and onions on skewers.

Poletes shooed them all away. "Tend to your masters' hungers," he snapped. "Bind their wounds and pour healing ointments over them. Feed them and give them wine and bat your cow-eyes at them."

To me he said, "Women cause all the trouble in the world, Orion. Be careful of them."

"Are these women slaves or *thetes*?" I asked.

"There are no women *thetes*. It's unheard of. A woman, working for wages? Unheard of!"

"Not even prostitutes?"

"Ah! In the cities, yes, of course. Temple prostitutes. But they are not *thetes*. It's not the same thing at all."

"Then the women here . . ."

"Slaves. Captives. Daughters and wives of slain enemies, captured in the sack of towns and farms."

We came to a group of men sitting around one of the larger cook fires, down close beside the black-tarred boats. They looked up and made room for us. Up on the boat nearest us a large canvas had been draped to form a tent. A helmeted guard stood before it, with a well-groomed dog by his side. I stared at the carved and painted figurehead of the boat, a grinning dolphin's face against a deep blue background.

"Odysseus's camp," Poletes explained, in a low voice, as we sat and were offered generous bowls of roasted meat and goblets of honeyed wine. "These are Ithacans."

He poured a few drops of wine on the ground before drinking, and made me do the same. "Reverence the gods," Poletes instructed me, surprised that I did not know the custom.

The men praised me for my performance at the barricade, then fell to wondering which particular god had inspired me to such heroic action. The favorites were Poseidon and Ares, although Athene was a close runner and Zeus himself was mentioned now and then. Being Greeks, they soon fell to arguing passionately among themselves without bothering to ask me about it.

I was happy to let them speculate. I listened, and as they argued I learned much about the war.

They had not been camped here at Troy for ten years, although they had been campaigning in the region each summer for nearly that long. Achilles, Menalaos, Agamemnon, and the other warrior kings had been ravaging the eastern Aegean coast, burning towns and taking captives, until finally they had worked up the nerve —and the forces—to besiege Troy itself.

But without Achilles, their fiercest fighter, the men thought that their prospects were dim. Apparently Agamemnon had awarded Achilles a young woman captive and then taken her back for himself, and this insult was more than the haughty warrior could endure, even from the High King.

"The joke of it all," said one of the men, tossing a well-gnawed lamb bone to the dogs hovering beyond our circle, "is that Achilles prefers his friend Patrokles to any woman."

They all nodded and murmured agreement. The strain between Achilles and Agamemnon was not over a sexual partner; it was a matter of honor and stubborn pride. On both sides, as far as I could see.

As we ate and talked the skies darkened and thunder rumbled from inland.

"Father Zeus speaks from Mt. Ida," said Poletes.

One of the foot soldiers, his leather jerkin stained with spatters of grease and blood, grinned up at the cloudy sky. "Maybe Zeus will give us the afternoon off."

"Can't fight in the rain," someone else agreed.

Sure enough, within minutes it began pelting down. We scattered for whatever shelter we could find. Poletes and I hunkered down in the lee of Odysseus's boat.

"Now the great lords will meet and arrange a truce, so that the women and slaves can go out and recover the bodies of the dead. Tonight their bodies will be burned and a barrow raised over their bones." He sighed. "That's how the rampart began, as a barrow to cover the remains of the slain heroes."

I sat and watched the rain pouring down, turning the beach into a quagmire, dotting the sea with splashes. The gusting wind drove gray sheets of rain across the bay, and it got so dark and misty that I could not see the headland. It was chill and miserable and there was nothing to do except wait like dumb animals until the sun returned.

I crouched as close to the boat's hull as I could, feeling cold and utterly alone. I knew I did not belong in this time and place. I had been exiled here by the same power that had killed my love.

I serve a god, I had told these gullible Achaians. Yes, but not willingly. Like a poor witless creature blundering through a fathomless forest, I am reacting to forces beyond my comprehension.

Who did inspire my heroics? I wondered. The golden figure in my dream called himself Apollo. But from what the men around the campfire had said, Apollo supported the Trojans in this war, not the Achaians. I found myself dreading sleep. I knew that once I fell asleep I would again have to face that . . . god. I had no other word for him.

Suddenly I realized a man was standing in front of me. I looked up and saw a sturdy, thick-torsoed man with a grizzled dark beard and a surly look on his face. He wore a wolf's skin draped over his head and shoulders. The rain pounded on it. Knee-length tunic, with a sword buckled to his hip. Shins and calves muddied. Ham-sized fists planted on his hips.

"You're the one called Orion?" he shouted over the driving rain.

I scrambled to my feet and saw that I stood several inches taller than he. Still, he did not look like a man to be taken lightly.

"I am Orion."

"Come with me," he snapped, and started to turn away.

"To where?"

Over his shoulder he answered, "My lord Odysseus wants to see what kind of man could stop Prince Hector in his tracks. Now move!"

Poletes came with me around the prow of the boat, through the soaking rain, and up a rope ladder to its deck.

"I *knew* Odysseus was the only one here wise enough to make usc of you," he cackled. "I knew it!"

Chapter 5

W HICH god do you serve?" Odysseus asked.
I stood in the presence of the King of Ithaca, who was sitting on a wooden stool, flanked on either side by other noblemen. He did not appear to be a very tall man; his legs seemed stumpy, but heavily muscled. His chest was enormous, broad and deep like that of a man who had swum every day since boyhood. Thick strong arms, circled by leather wristbands and a bronze armlet above his left elbow that gleamed with polished onyx and lapis lazuli even in the gloom inside his shipboard tent. White scars from old wounds stood out against the dark skin of his arms, parting the black hairs like roads through a forest.

There was a fresh gash on his right forearm, as well, red and still oozing blood slightly.

The rain drummed against the canvas, scant inches above my head. The tent smelled of dogs, musty and damp. And cold. Odysseus wore a sleeveless tunic, his legs and feet bare, but he had a sheep's fleece thrown across his wide shoulders.

His face was thickly bearded with dark curly hair. Only a trace of gray in that beard. His heavy mop of ringlets came down to his shoulders and across his forehead almost down to his black eyebrows. Those eyes were as gray as the sea outside on this rainy afternoon, probing, searching, judging.

He had asked his question the instant Poletes and I were

ushered into his tent, without any preliminaries or formal greetings.

"Which god do you serve?"

Hastily I replied, "Athene." I was not sure why I picked the warrior goddess, except that Poletes had said she favored the Achaians against the Trojans.

Odysseus grunted and motioned for me to sit on the only unoccupied stool in the tent. The two other men sitting on either side of him were dressed much as he was. One of them seemed about Odysseus's age, the other much older: His hair and beard were entirely white and his limbs seemed withered to bones and tendons. He had wrapped a blue cloak around himself. They all looked weary and drained by the morning's battle even though neither of them bore fresh wounds as Odysseus did.

Odysseus seemed to notice Poletes for the first time. "Who is he?" he asked, pointing.

"My friend," I said. "My companion and helper."

He nodded, accepting the storyteller. Behind Poletes, barely inside the tent and out of the pelting rain, stood the officer who had summoned us to this audience with the King of Ithaca.

"You did us a great service this morning," said Odysseus. "Such service should be rewarded."

The frail old man at Odysseus's right spoke up in a surprisingly deep, strong voice. "We are told that you arrived as a *thes* aboard the boat that came in last night. Yet you fought this morning like a warrior born and bred. By the gods! You reminded me of myself when I was your age. I was absolutely fearless then! As far away as Mycenae and even Thebes I was known! Let me tell you . . ."

Odysseus raised his right hand. "Please, Nestor, I pray you forego your reminiscences for the moment."

The old man looked displeased, but sank back in silence.

"What reward would you ask?" Odysseus said to me. "If it is in my power I will gladly grant it."

I thought for half a moment only, then replied, "I ask to be made a warrior in the service of the King of Ithaca." Then, sensing a slight shuffling of bare feet behind me, I added, "And to have my friend here as my servant."

For several seconds Odysseus said nothing, although Nestor bobbed his white-bearded head vigorously and the younger warrior on the king's left smiled at me.

"You are both *thetes,* without a household?" Odysseus asked.

"Yes."

He stroked his beard. Then a slow smile spread across his face. "Then welcome to the household of the King of Ithaca. Your wish is granted."

I was not certain of what I should do, until I saw Nestor frown slightly and prompt me by motioning with both hands, palms down. I knelt before Odysseus.

"Thank you, great king," I said, hoping it was the right degree of humility. "I shall serve you to the best of my abilities."

Odysseus took the armlet from his biceps and clasped it on my arm. "Rise, Orion. Your courage and strength will be a welcome addition to our forces." To the officer at the tent's entrance he commanded, "Antilokos, see that he gets some decent clothing —and weapons."

Then he nodded a dismissal at me. I turned. Poletes was beaming at me. Antilokos, his wolfskin cape still dripping, looked at me as if measuring me, not for clothing, but as a fighter.

As we left the tent and went back into the pouring rain, I could hear King Nestor's vibrant voice. "Very crafty of you, Odysseus! By bringing him into your household you gain the favor of Athene, whom he serves. I couldn't have made a wiser move myself, although in my years I've made some very delicate decisions, let me tell you. Why, I remember the time when Dardanian pirates were raiding the coast of my kingdom and nobody seemed to be able to stop them, since King Minos's fleet had been destroyed in the great tidal wave. Well then, the pirates captured a merchant ship bearing a load of copper from Kypros. Worth a fortune it was, because you know that you can't make bronze without copper. No one knew what to do! The copper was . . ."

His voice, strong as it was, was finally drowned out by the heavy rain and moaning wind.

Antilokos led us past several Ithacan boats to a lean-to made of logs lashed together and then daubed with the same black pitch that caulked the boats. It was the largest structure I had seen in the camp, big enough to hold a couple of dozen men, I estimated. There was only one doorway, a low one with a sheet of canvas tacked over it to keep out the rain and wind.

Inside, the shed was a combination of warehouse and armory that made Poletes whistle with astonishment. Chariots were stored there, tilted up with their yoke poles pointing into the air. Stacks of helmets and armor were neatly piled along one wall, while racks of spears, swords, and bows lined the other, with chests full of clothes and blankets along the back wall between them.

"So much!" Poletes gasped.

Antilokos, who was not a man given to humor, made a grim smile. "Spoils from the slain."

Poletes nodded and whispered, "So many."

A wizened old man stepped across the sand floor from his hideaway behind a table piled with clay tablets.

"What now? Haven't I enough to do without you dragging in strangers?" he whined. He was a lean and sour-faced old grump, his hands gnarled and twisted into claws, his back stooped.

"A new one for you, scribe. My lord Odysseus wants him outfitted properly." And with that, Antilokos turned and ducked through the shed's low doorway.

The scribe shuffled over close enough almost to touch me and peered up at me with squinted eyes. "Big as a Cretan bull! How does he expect me to find proper clothing for someone your size?"

He grumbled and muttered as he led Poletes and me past tables laden with bronze cuirasses, arm protectors, greaves, and plumed helmets. I stopped and reached for a helmet.

"Not that!" the scribe screeched. "Those are not for the likes of you!"

He sank one of those clawlike hands into my forearm and tugged me to a pile of clothes on the ground, close by the entrance to the shed.

"Here," he said. "See what you can find among those."

It took a while, but I eventually dressed myself in a stained linen tunic, a leather skirt that reached my knees, and a sleeveless leather jerkin that did not feel so tight across the shoulders that it would hamper my movements. While the scribe scowled and grumbled, I made certain that Poletes found a tunic and a wool shirt. For weapons I took a plain short sword and strapped a dagger to my right thigh, beneath the skirt. Neither one of them had precious metals or jewels in their hilts, although the sword's crosspiece bore an intricate design engraved in its bronze.

The scribe could not find any kind of helmet that would fit me, so we finally settled on a hooded mantle of bronze chain mail.

Sandals and bronze-studded leather greaves completed my array, although my toes hung out over the edges of the sandals noticeably.

The scribe resisted fiercely, but I insisted on taking two blankets apiece. He screeched and argued and threatened that he would call the king himself to tell what a spendthrift I was. It was not until I lifted him off his feet with a one-fisted grab at his tunic that he shut up and let me take the blankets. But his scowl would have curdled milk.

By the time we left the shed the rain had stopped and the westering sun was rapidly drying off the beach. Poletes led the way back to the fire and the men with whom we had shared our midday meal. We ate again, drank wine, and laid out our newly acquired blankets in preparation for sleeping.

Then Poletes fell to his bony knees and grasped my right hand in both of his, tightly, with a strength I would not have guessed was in him.

"Orion, my master, you have saved my life two times this day."

I wanted to pull my hand loose.

"You have saved the whole camp from Hector's spear and his vengeful Trojans, but in addition you have lifted me out of a life of misery and shame. I will serve you always, Orion. I will always be grateful to you for showing such mercy to a poor old storyteller."

He kissed my hand.

I reached down and lifted him by his frail shoulders to his feet.

"Poor old windbag," I said lightly, "you're the first man I've ever seen grateful to become a slave."

"*Your* slave, Orion," he corrected. "I am happy to be that."

I shook my head, uncertain of what to do or say. Finally I groused, "Well, get some sleep."

"Yes. Certainly. May Phantasos send you happy dreams."

I did not want to close my eyes. I did not want to dream of the Creator who called himself Apollo—if my encounter with him could be called a dream.

I lay on my back staring at the star-studded blackness, wondering which star our ship had been traveling to, and whether the light of its explosion would ever be seen in Earth's night skies. I saw her face again, lovely beyond belief, dark hair gleaming in the starlight, gray eyes sparkling with desire.

He had killed her, I knew. The Golden One. Apollo. Killed her and blamed it on me. Killed her and exiled me to this primitive time. Killed her, but saved me for his own amusement.

"Orion?" a voice whispered.

I sat up and automatically put out a hand for the sword resting on the ground beside me.

"The king wants you." It was Antilokos kneeling beside me.

I scrambled to my feet, gripping the sword. It was black night, with just enough light from the dying fire for me to recognize the man's face.

"Better bring your helmet, if you have one," Antilokos said.

I reached down and took my chain-mail mantle. Poletes's eyes opened.

"The king wants to speak to me," I told the old man. "Go back to sleep."

He smiled and snuggled happily into his blankets.

I followed Antilokos past the sleeping bodies of our comrades to the prow of Odysseus's boat.

As I had suspected, the king was much shorter than I. The plume of his helmet barely reached my chin. He nodded a greeting to me and said simply, "Follow me, Orion."

The three of us walked silently through the sleeping camp and up to the crest of the rampart, not far from the gate where I had gained their respect earlier that day. Soldiers stood on guard up there, gripping long spears and eyeing the darkness nervously. Beyond the inky shadow of the trench the plain was dotted with Trojan campfires.

Odysseus gave a sigh that seemed to wrench his mighty chest. "Prince Hector holds the plain, as you can see. Tomorrow his forces will storm the rampart and try to break into our camp and burn our ships."

"Can we hold them?" I asked.

"The gods will decide, once the sun comes up."

I said nothing. I suspected that Odysseus was trying to come up with a plan that might influence the gods his way.

A strong tenor voice called from the darkness below us. "Odysseus, son of Laertes, are you counting the Trojan campfires?"

Odysseus smiled grimly. "No, Big Ajax. They are too many for any man to count."

He motioned to me and we went back down into the camp. Ajax was indeed something of a giant among these men: He towered over them and even topped me by an inch or two. He was big across the shoulders, as well, and his arms were as thick as young tree trunks. He stood bareheaded under the stars, dressed only in a tunic and leather vest. His face was broad, with high cheekbones and a little pug of a nose. His beard was thin, new-looking, not like the thick curly growth of Odysseus and the other chieftains. With a bit of a shock, I realized that Big Ajax was very young, probably no more than nineteen or twenty.

A much older man stood beside him, hair and beard white, wrapped in a dark cloak.

"I brought Phoenix along," said Big Ajax. "Maybe he can appeal to Achilles better than we can."

Odysseus nodded his approval.

"I was his tutor when Achilles was a lad," said Phoenix in a slightly quavering voice. "He was proud and touchy even then."

Ajax shrugged his massive shoulders. Odysseus said, "Well, let us try to convince Achilles to rejoin the army."

We started off for the far end of the camp, where Achilles's boats were beached. Half a dozen armed men trailed behind the three nobles, and I fell in with them.

The wind was blowing in off the water, cold and sharp as a knife. I almost envied Poletes the blankets he had wrapped around himself, and began to wonder why I had not taken cloaks for the two of us from the tight-fisted old scribe.

Once we entered Achilles's portion of the camp, we passed several sentries on duty, fully armed and armored, with helmets strapped on tightly and spears in their hands. They wore cloaks, which the wind plucked at and whipped around their suits of bronze armor. They recognized the giant Ajax and the squat but powerful King of Ithaca, of course, and let the rest of us pass unchallenged.

Finally we were stopped by a pair of guards whose armor glittered even in the faint starlight, within a few yards of a large cabin, built of planks.

"We are a deputation from the High King," said Odysseus, his voice deep and grave with formality, "sent to see Achilles, prince of the Myrmidones."

The guard saluted by clasping his fist to his heart and said, "Prince Achilles has been expecting you and bids you welcome."

He stepped aside and gestured us to the door of the cabin.

Chapter 6

MIGHTY warrior though he was, Achilles apparently enjoyed his creature comforts. The cabin's interior was draped with rich tapestries, and the floor was covered with more carpets. Couches and pillows were scattered across the spacious room. In one corner a hearth fire smoldered red, keeping out the cold and damp. I could hear the wind moaning through the hole in the roof, but inside it was reasonably snug and warm.

Three women sat by the fire staring at us with great dark eyes. They were slim and young, dressed modestly in sleeveless gray chemises. Iron and copper pots stood on tripods at the hearth, faint wisps of steam issuing from them. I smelled spiced meat and garlic.

Achilles himself sat on a wide couch against the far wall of the cabin, his back to a magnificent arras that depicted a gory battle scene. The couch was up on a dais, raised above the floor of the cabin like a king's throne.

My first sight of the great warrior was a surprise. He was not a mighty-thewed giant, as Ajax. His body was not broad and powerful, as Odysseus's. He seemed small, almost boyish, his bare arms and legs slim and virtually hairless. His chin was shaved clean and the ringlets of his long black hair were tied up in a silver chain. He wore a splendid white silk tunic, bordered with a purple key design, cinched at the waist with a belt of interlocking gold crescents.

He wore no weapons, but behind him a half-dozen long spears rested against the arras, within easy reach.

His face was the greatest shock. Ugly, almost to the point of being grotesque. Narrow beady eyes, lips curled in a perpetual snarl, a sharp hook of a nose, skin pocked and cratered. In his right hand he gripped a jeweled wine cup; it seemed to me that he had already drained it more than once.

At his feet sat a young man who was absolutely beautiful, gazing not at us but up at Achilles. It was Patrokles, I knew without being told. His tightly curled hair was reddish brown, rather than the usual darker tones of the Greeks. I wondered if it was his natural color. Like Achilles, Patrokles was beardless. But he seemed young enough not to need to shave. A golden pitcher of wine stood on the carpet beside him.

I looked at Achilles again and understood the demons that drove him to be the greatest warrior of his age. A small ugly boy born to a king. A boy destined to rule, but always the object of taunts and derisive laughter behind his back. A young man possessed with fire to silence the laughter, to stifle the taunting. His slim arms and legs were iron-hard, knotted with muscle. His eyes were absolutely humorless. There was no doubt in my mind that he could outfight Odysseus or even powerful Ajax on sheer willpower alone.

"Greetings, Odysseus the Ever-Daring," he said, in a calm, clear tenor voice that was close to mocking. "And to you, mighty Ajax, King of Salamis and champion of the Achaian host." Then his voice softened. "And to you, Phoenix, my well-loved tutor."

I glanced at the old man. He bowed toward Achilles, but his eyes were on the beautiful Patrokles.

"We bring you greetings, Prince Achilles," said Odysseus, "from Agamemnon the High King."

"The bargain-breaker, you mean," Achilles snapped. "Agememnon the gift-snatcher."

"He is our High King," Odysseus said, his tone barely suggesting that they were all stuck with Agamemnon and the best they could do was try to work with him.

"So he is," admitted Achilles. "And well beloved by Father Zeus, I'm sure."

It was going to be a difficult parley, I could see.

"Perhaps our guests are hungry," Patrokles suggested in a soft voice.

Achilles tousled his curly mop of hair. "Always the thoughtful one."

He bade us sit and told the serving women to feed us and bring wine cups. Odysseus, Ajax, and Phoenix took couches arranged near Achilles's dais. Patrokles filled their cups from his pitcher of gold. We underlings sat on the floor, by the entrance. The women passed trays of broiled lamb with onions among us and filled our wooden cups with spiced wine mixed with honey.

After a round of toasts and polite banter, Achilles said, "I thought I heard the mighty Agamemnon bawling like a woman, earlier today. He breaks into tears quite easily, doesn't he?"

Odysseus frowned slightly. "Our High King was wounded today. A cowardly Trojan archer hit him in the right shoulder."

"Too bad," said Achilles. "I see that you did not escape the day's fighting without a wound, yourself. Did it bring you to tears?"

Ajax burst out, "Achilles, if Agamemnon cries, it's not from pain or fright. It's from shame! Shame that the Trojans have penned us up in our camp. Shame that our best fighter sits here on a soft couch while his comrades are being slaughtered by Hector and his troops."

"Shame is what he *should* feel!" Achilles shouted back. "He's robbed me! He's treated me like a slave or even worse. He calls himself the High King but he behaves like a thieving whoremaster!"

And so it went, for hours. Achilles was furious with Agamemnon for taking back a prize he had been awarded, some captive girl. He claimed that he did all the fighting while Agamemnon was a coward, but after the battle was won the High King parceled out the spoils to suit himself and even then reneged on what Achilles felt was due him.

"I have sacked more towns and brought the Achaians more captives and loot than any man here, and none of you can say I haven't," he insisted hotly. "Yet that fat lard-ass can steal my proper rewards away from me and you—all of you!—just let him do it. Did any of you stick up for me in the council? Do you think I owe you anything? Why should I fight for you when you won't even raise your voices on my behalf?"

Patrokles tried to soothe him, without much success. "Achilles, these men aren't your enemies. They've come here on a mission of reconciliation. It isn't proper for a host to bellow at his guests so."

"I know," Achilles replied, almost smiling down at the young man. "It's not your fault," he said to Odysseus and the others. "But I'll see myself in Hades before I'll help Agamemnon again. He's not trustworthy. You should be thinking about appointing a new leader for yourselves."

Odysseus tried tact, praising Achilles's prowess in battle, downplaying Agamemnon's failures and shortcomings. Ajax, as blunt and straightforward as a shovel, flatly told Achilles that he was helping the Trojans to murder the Achaians. Old Phoenix appealed to his former student's sense of honor, and recited childhood homilies at him.

Achilles remained unmoved. "Honor?" he snapped at Phoenix. "What kind of honor would I have left if I put my spear back in the service of the man who robbed me?"

Odysseus said, "We can get the girl back for you, if that's what you want. We can get a dozen girls for you."

"Or boys," Ajax added. "Whatever you want."

Achilles got to his feet, and Patrokles scrambled to stand beside him. I was right, he was terribly small, although every inch of him was hard with sinew. Even the slender Patrokles topped him by a few inches.

"I will defend my boats when Hector breaks into the camp," Achilles said. "Until Agamemnon comes to me personally and apologizes, and begs me to rejoin the fighting, that is all that I will do."

Odysseus rose, realizing that we were being dismissed. Phoenix stood up and, after glancing around, Ajax finally understood and got up too.

"What will the poets say of Achilles in future generations?" Odysseus asked, firing his last arrow at the warrior's pride. "That he sulked in his tent while the Trojans slaughtered his friends?"

The shot glanced off Achilles without penetrating. "They will never say that I humbled myself and threw away my honor by serving a man who has humiliated me."

We went to the doorway, speaking polite formal farewells. Phoenix hung back and I heard Achilles invite his old mentor to remain the night.

Outside, Ajax shook his head wearily. "There's nothing we can do. He just won't listen to us."

Odysseus clapped his broad shoulder. "We tried our best, my friend. Now we must prepare for tomorrow's battle without Achilles."

Ajax trudged off into the darkness, followed by his men. Odysseus turned to me, a thoughtful look on his face.

"I have a task for you to perform," he said. "If you are successful you can end the war."

"And if I am not?"

Odysseus smiled and put his hand on my shoulder. "No man lives forever, Orion."

Chapter 7

I N less than an hour I found myself picking my way across the trench that fronted our rampart and heading into the Trojan camp. A white cloth knotted above my left elbow proclaimed that I was operating under a flag of truce. The slim willow wand in my right hand was the impromptu symbol of a herald.

"These should get you past the Trojan sentries without having your throat slit," Odysseus had told me. He did not smile as he said those words, and I did not find his reassurances very reassuring.

"Get to Prince Hector and speak to no one else," he had commanded me. "Tell him that Agamemnon offers a solution to this war: If the Trojans will return Helen to her rightful husband, the Achaians will return to their own lands, satisfied."

"Hasn't that offer been made before?" I asked.

Odysseus smiled at my naiveté. "Of course. But always with the demand for a huge ransom, plus all the fortune that Helen brought with her. And always when we were fighting under the walls of Troy. Priam and his sons never believed we would abandon the siege without breaking in and sacking the city. But now that Hector is besieging us, perhaps they will believe that we are ready to quit, and merely need a face-saving compromise to send us packing."

"Returning Helen is nothing more than a face-saving compromise?" I blurted.

He looked at me curiously. "She is only a woman, Orion. Do you think Menalaos has been pining away in celibacy since the bitch ran off with Aleksandros?"

I blinked at him, so taken aback by his attitude that I had no reply. I wondered, though, if Odysseus felt the same way about his own wife, waiting for him back in Ithaca.

He made me repeat my instructions and then, satisfied, led me to the top of the rampart, not far from where I had gained my moment of glory earlier in the day. I gazed out into the darkness. In the silvery moonlight a mist had risen, turning the plain into a ghostly shivering vapor that rose and sank slowly like the breath of some living thing. Here and there I could make out the glow of Trojan campfires, like distant faint stars in the shrouding fog.

"Remember," said Odysseus, "you are to speak to Prince Hector and no one else."

"I understand," I said.

I scrambled down the slope of the rampart, into the inky shadows of the trench, and finally made my way through the slowly drifting tendrils of mist toward the Trojan camp, guided by the fires that flickered and glowed through the fog. The mist was cold on my skin, like the touch of death.

Peering through the moon-silvered haze, I saw one campfire that seemed larger, brighter, than all the others. That must be where Hector's tent is, I told myself. I headed toward it, tense with the expectation of being challenged by a sentry at any moment. I hoped I would be challenged, and not merely speared out of the darkness before any questions were asked. My senses were hyper-alert; I think I could have heard a dagger being drawn from its sheath, or seen a man stalking behind me out of the back of my head. But I heard and saw nothing. It was as if the fog had enveloped the whole camp, muffled every sound, mummified every man there except me.

The fire seemed to be growing, as if someone were feeding it, turning it from a dying campfire into a great welcoming beacon. But it no longer flickered like a fire. It was a steady bright glare, growing more brilliant by the moment. Soon it was so bright that I had to throw my arm across my brow to shield my eyes from its burning intensity. I felt no heat from it, but its brilliance exerted a force of its own. I felt myself *pressed* by that blinding glare, forced to my knees by its overpowering golden radiance.

Then I heard a man's laughter, and knew at once who it was.

"On your feet, Orion!" said the Golden One. "Or do you enjoy crawling like a worm?"

Slowly I rose to my feet. The Golden One stood bathed in a warm glow that seemed to separate us from the mist-shrouded plain. It remained night beyond us. No one in the camp stirred. No sentries saw us or heard us.

"Orion," he said, his smile mocking, "somehow you continually find ways to displease me. You saved the Achaian camp."

"That displeases you?" I asked.

He scratched at his chin, a strangely human gesture in so godlike a person. "As Apollo, the sun god, the one who brings light and beauty to these people, I seek victory for the Trojans over these barbarians from Achaia."

"And the other . . ." I groped for a word, settled on, "gods? Not all of them favor Troy, do they?"

His smile withered.

"There are others," I said. "Godlike beings like yourself?"

"There are," he admitted.

"Greater than you? Is there a Zeus, a Poseidon?"

"There are several . . . beings such as I, Orion," he said, waving a hand vaguely. "The names that these primitive people call them are irrelevant."

"But are they more powerful than you? Is there a Zeus? A king among you?"

He laughed. "You're trying to find a way of fighting against me!"

"I'm trying to understand who and what you are," I said. Which was truth, as far as it went.

The Golden One eyed me carefully, almost warily. "Very well," he said at last, "if you want to see some of the others . . ."

And gradually, like a night fog slowly burning away under the morning sun, I saw images beginning to form all around me. Slowly they emerged, materialized, took on solidity and color. Living, breathing men and women surrounded me, peered down at me, inspected me as a scientist might examine some species of insect or bacterium.

"This is rash," said one of them in a deep godly voice.

"He is my creature," the Golden One retorted. "I can control him."

Yes, I thought. You can control me. But one day your control will slip.

I could see dozens of faces peering at me: beautiful women with flawless skin and eyes that glowed like jewels; men who radiated youth and yet spoke with the gravity and knowledge of millennia, eons, eternity itself.

I felt like a little boy in the midst of vastly wiser adults, like a child confronted by giants.

"I brought him here from the plain of Ilios," said the Golden One, almost as if daring them to complain.

"You grow bolder," said the one who had spoken first. He was dark of hair and eye, as solemn as a high craggy mountain. I thought of him as Zeus, even though there were no lightning bolts in his grip and his beard was neatly trimmed and barely touched with gray.

The Golden One laughed carelessly.

Around that circle of vast unsmiling faces I searched, looking for one that would be familiar, the goddess I had loved, or even the dark Ahriman whom I had hunted. I saw neither.

One of the women spoke. "You still intend to allow the Trojans to win their war?"

The Golden One smiled at her. "Yes, even though that displeases you."

"The Greeks have much to offer your creatures," she said.

"Pah! Barbarians."

"They will not always be so. In time they will build a beautiful civilization . . . if you let them."

With a shake of his golden mane, "The civilization of Troy will be even more beautiful, I promise you."

"I have studied the time-tracks," said one of the males. "The Greeks should be allowed to win."

"No!" shouted the Golden One. "Damn the time-tracks! I am creating a new track here, one that will please all of us, if you'd only stop interfering with my plans."

"We have as much right to manipulate these creatures as you do," said the woman. "I really have very little confidence in your plans."

"Because you don't understand," the Golden One insisted. "I want Troy to win because Troy will then become the most important nexus in this phase of human history. The city will grow into a mighty empire that spans Europe and Asia. Think of it! The energy and vigor of the Europeans combined with the wisdom and patience of the East. The wealth of both worlds will be commingled into a single, unified Ilian empire that will span from the British Isles to the Indian subcontinent!"

"What good will that do?" asked one of the other men. Like the others, he was as handsome as a human face can be, flawless in every detail. "Your creatures will still have to face the ultimate crisis. Unity among them may be less desirable than a healthy amount of competition."

"Yes," said the woman. "Remember the Neanderthal-dominated track that you sent this creature to destroy. You ended by nearly destroying all of *us*."

The Golden One glared down at me. "That was a mistake that will not be repeated."

"No, not with Ahriman and his tribes safely in their own continuum now."

"That is done and we survived the crisis," said the one I called Zeus. "The question at hand is what to do about the particular nexus at Troy."

"Troy must win," insisted the Golden One.

"No, the Greeks should . . ."

"The Trojans will win," the Golden One stated flatly. "They will win because I will *make* them win."

"So that you can create this Ilian empire that appears to be so dear to your heart," said Zeus.

"Exactly."

"Why is that so important?" asked the woman.

"It will unify all of Europe and much of Asia," he replied. "There will be no separation of East and West, no dichotomy of the human spirit. No Alexander of Macedon with his semibarbaric lusts, no Roman Empire, no Constantinople to act as a barrier between Asia and Europe. No Christianity and no Islam to fight their twenty-century-long war against each other."

They listened and began to nod. All but the skeptical woman and the one I called Zeus.

It is a game to them, I realized. They are manipulating human history the way a chess player moves pieces across his board. And if a civilization is utterly destroyed, it means as little to them as if a pawn or a rook is captured and removed from the board.

"Does it really make that much difference?" asked one of the dark-haired men.

"Of course it does!" the Golden One replied. "I seek to unite the human race, to bring all the many facets of my creatures into harmony and unity . . ."

"So that they can help us to face the ultimate crisis," said Zeus, almost in a mutter.

The Golden One nodded. "That is my goal. We need all the help we can get."

"I am not certain that your way is the best method," Zeus said.

"I'm certain it's *not*," said the woman.

"I'm going ahead with it whether you approve or not," the Golden One retorted. "These are my creatures and I will bring them to the point where they can be of true assistance to us."

The others in the circle murmured and nodded or shook their heads. There was no unanimity among them. As I watched, they began to fade away, to blur and dissolve until only the Golden One and I stood facing each other against the all-pervasive glow of a place that had no location, no time, in any world that I knew.

"Well, Orion, you have met the others. Some of them, at least."

"You spoke of us as your creatures," I said. "Do the others have creatures of their own, as well?"

"Some do. Others seem more interested in meddling with my creatures than in creating their own."

"Then . . . the men and women of Earth—you created them?"

"You were one of the first of them, Orion," he answered. "And, in a sense, you then created us."

"What? I don't understand."

"How could you?"

"You created the human race so that we can help you," I said, repeating what I had heard.

"Ultimately, yes."

"But while the others think you will bring us humans to their aid, you actually plan to have us help you *against them*," I realized.

He stared at me.

"And that will make you the mightiest of all the gods, won't it?"

He hesitated for a moment before replying. "I *am* the mightiest of all the Creators, Orion. The others may not recognize that fact, but it is so."

Now I felt my lips twisting into a sardonic smile.

He knew my thought. "You think I do this out of egomania? Out of lust for worship by creatures I myself created?" He shook his head sadly. "How little you understand. Do you have any great desire for your sandals to adore you, Orion? Is it necessary for your happiness to have your sword or the knife hidden under your kilt to proclaim you as the greatest master they have ever known?"

"I don't understand . . ."

"How could you? How could you dream of the consequences that I am dealing with? Orion, I created the human race out of necessity, truly—but not the necessity to be adored! The universes are wide, Orion, and filled with dangers. I seek to protect the continuum, to keep it from being torn apart by forces that you could not even imagine. While the others dither and bicker, I *act*. I create. I command!"

"And to accomplish your goal it is necessary for Troy to win this war?"

"Yes!"

"And it was necessary to destroy the starship we were riding? Necessary to kill the woman I loved? The woman who loved me?"

For a moment he looked almost startled. "You recall that?"

"I remember the starship. The explosion. She died in my arms. We both died."

"I revived you. I returned you to life."

"And her?"

"She was a goddess, Orion. I can only revive creatures whom I myself have created."

"If she was a goddess, how could she die?"

"Gods and goddesses can die, Orion. Tales of our immortality are rather exaggerated. As are the pious recitations of our goodness and mercy."

I felt my heart thudding in my chest, the blood roaring in my ears. My head swam. I could barely breathe. I hated this man, this golden self-styled god, this murderer. Hated him with every fiber of my being. He claims to have created me, I told myself. Yet I will destroy him.

"I did not want to kill her, Orion," he said, and it almost sounded sincere. "It was beyond my control. She chose to make herself human. For your sake, Orion. She knew the risks and she accepted them for your sake."

"And died." A murderous rage was burning inside me. Yet when I tried to take a step toward him, I found I could not move. I was frozen, immobilized, unable even to clench my fists at my sides.

"Orion," said the object of my hatred, "you cannot blame me for what *she* did to herself."

How wrong he was!

"You must serve me whether you like it or not," he insisted. "There is no way for you to avoid your destiny, Orion." Then he added, muttering, almost to himself, "No way for either of us to avoid our destinies."

"I can refuse to serve you," I said stubbornly.

He lifted one golden eyebrow and considered me, the haughty, mocking tone back in his voice. "While you live, my angry creature, you will play your part in my plans. You cannot refuse because you can never know which acts of yours serve me and which do not. You stagger along blindly in your time-bound linearity, going from day to day, while I perceive space-time on the scale of the continuum."

"Grand talk," I spat. "You sound almost as grandiloquent as old Nestor."

His eyes narrowed. "But I speak the truth, Orion. You see time as past and present and future. I *create* time and manipulate it to keep the continuum from being torn asunder. And while you live, you will help me in this mighty task."

"While I live," I repeated. "Is that a threat?"

He smiled again. "I make no threats, Orion. I have no need to. I created you. I can destroy you. You have no memory of how many times you have died, do you? Yet I have revived you each time, so that you could serve me again. That is your destiny, Orion. To serve me. To be my Hunter."

"I want to be free," I shouted. "Not your puppet!"

"Pah! I waste my time trying to explain myself to you. No one is free, Orion. No creature can ever be free. Not as long as you live."

He clasped his arms together across his chest and disappeared as abruptly as a candle snuffed out by a sharp gust of wind. Suddenly I was alone in the fog-wrapped darkness of the plain before Troy.

As long as I live, I thought silently, I will struggle to reach your throat. It was a mistake to tell me that you are not immortal. I am the Hunter, and now I know the prey I seek. I will kill you, golden Apollo, Creator, whatever your true name and shape may be. While I live I will seek your death and nothing less. Just as you killed her, I will kill you.

Chapter 8

"**Y**OU there! Hold!"

I was standing in the Trojan camp again, a sudden sharp wind gusting in from the sea and shredding the mist that had covered the plain. Campfires dotted the darkness, and off in the distance the beetling towers of Troy bulked black and menacing against the moon-bright sky.

I tottered on unsteady feet, like a man who has drunk too much wine, like a man who has suddenly been pushed through a door that he had not seen. The Golden One and the other Creators were gone as completely as if they had been nothing more than a dream. But I knew they were real. They were out there in another plane of existence, toying with us, arguing over which side should win this wretched war. My hands clenched into fists as the memory of their faces and their words fueled the rage burning within me.

A pair of sentries approached me warily, heavy spears in their hands. I gulped down a deep breath of chill night air to calm myself.

"I am an emissary from the High King Agamemnon," I said, slowly and carefully. "I have been sent to speak to Prince Hector."

The sentries were an unlikely pair, one short and squat with a dirty, tangled black beard and a pot belly bulging his chain mail corselet, the other taller and painfully thin, either clean-shaven or too young to start a beard.

"Prince Hector the Tamer of Horses he wants to see," said the pot-belly. He laughed harshly. "So would I!"

The younger one grinned and showed a gap where a front tooth was missing.

"An emissary, eh?" Pot-belly eyed me suspiciously. "With a sword at his side and a mantle of chain mail across his shoulders. More likely a spy. Or an assassin."

I held up my herald's wand. "I have been sent by the High King. I am not here to fight. Take my sword and mantle, if they frighten you." I could have disabled them both before they knew what had happened, but that was not my mission.

"Be a lot safer to ram this spear through your guts and have done with it," said Pot-belly.

The youngster put out a restraining hand. "Hermes protects messengers, you know. I wouldn't want to draw down the anger of the Trickster."

Pot-belly scowled and muttered, but finally satisfied himself by taking my sword and chain mail. He did not search me, and therefore did not take the dagger strapped to my right thigh. He was more interested in loot than security.

Once Pot-belly had slipped my baldric across his shoulder and fastened my mantle under his quivering chins, the two of them led me to their chief.

They were Dardanians, allies of the Trojans who had come from several miles up the coast to fight against the invading Achaians. Over the next hour or so I was escorted from the chief of the Dardanian contingent to a Trojan officer, from there to the tent of Hector's chief lieutenants, and finally past the makeshift horse corral and the silently waiting chariots, tipped over with their long yoke poles poking into the air, to the small plain tent and guttering fire of Prince Hector.

At each stop I explained my mission again. Dardanians and Trojans alike spoke a dialect of the Greek spoken by the Achaians, different but not so distant as to be unintelligible. I realized that the city's defenders included contingents from many areas up and down the coast. The Achaians had been raiding their towns for years, and now they had all banded together under Trojan leadership to resist the barbarian invaders.

That was the Golden One's aim: to have the Trojans beat back the Achaians and gain supremacy over the Aegean. Eventually they would establish an empire that would span Europe, the Middle East, and India.

If that was his goal, then mine must be to prevent it from being achieved. If Odysseus was offering a compromise that would allow the Achaians to sail away without burning Troy to the ground, then I must sabotage the offer. I felt a momentary pang of conscience. Odysseus trusted me. Or, I asked myself, had he sent me on this diplomatic mission because he could better afford to lose me than one of his own people?

With those thoughts swirling in my head, I was brought before Hector.

His tent was barely large enough for himself and a servant. A pair of armored noblemen stood by the fire outside the tent's entrance, their bronze breastplates gleaming against the night. Insects buzzed and darted in the firelight. No slaves or women in sight. Hector himself stood at the entrance flap to the tent. He was a big man for these people, nearly my own height.

Hector wore no armor, no badge of his rank. Merely a soft clean tunic belted at the waist, with an ornamental dagger hanging from the leather belt. He had no need to impress anyone with his grandeur. He possessed that calm inner strength that needs no outward decorations.

In the flickering light of his campfire he studied me silently for a moment. Those same grave brown eyes. His face was handsome, intelligent, though there were lines of weariness around his eyes, furrows across his broad brow. Despite the fullness of his rich brown beard I saw that his cheeks were becoming hollow. The strain of this war was taking its toll on him.

"You are the man at the gate," he said finally. His words were measured, neither surprise nor anger in them.

I nodded.

He looked me over carefully. "Your name?"

"Orion."

"From where?"

"Far to the west of here. Beyond the seas where the sun sets."

"Beyond Okeanus?" he asked.

"Yes."

He puzzled over that, brow knitted, for a few moments. Then he asked, "What brings you to the plain of Ilios? Why are you fighting for the Achaians?"

"A duty I owe to a god," I said.

"Which god?"

"Athene."

"Athene sent you here to fight for the Achaians?" He seemed concerned at that, almost worried.

With a shake of my head, I answered, "I arrived at the Achaian camp the night before yesterday. I had never seen Troy before. Suddenly, in the midst of the fighting, I acted on impulse. I don't know what made me do what I did. It all happened in the flash of a moment."

Hector smiled tightly. "Battle frenzy. A god took control of your spirit, my friend, and inspired you to deeds no mortal could achieve unaided. It has happened to me many times."

I smiled back at him. "Yes, perhaps that is what happened to me."

"Have no doubt of it. Ares or Athene seized your spirit and filled you with battle frenzy. You could have challenged Achilles himself in such a state."

Slaves came out of the darkness to set up chairs of stretched hides and offer fruit and wine. Following Hector's lead, I sat and took a little of each. The quality of the Trojan wine was far superior to that of the Achaians.

"You carry the wand of a herald and say that you are here as an emissary of Agamemnon," Hector said, leaning back tiredly in his creaking chair.

"I bring an offer of peace."

"We have heard such offers before. Is there anything new in what Agamemnon proposes?"

I noticed that his two aides stepped closer, eager to hear what I had to say. I thought briefly of Odysseus, who trusted me. But I said: "The High King repeats his earlier offer of peace. If you will restore Helen and the fortune she brought from Sparta with her, and pay an indemnity for the costs the Achaians have incurred, Agamemnon will lead his ships away from Ilios and Troy."

Hector glanced up at his two standing lieutenants, who muttered grimly.

Then to me he said, "We did not accept these terms when the Achaians had us penned up inside our city walls, without allies. Now that we outnumber them and have *them* penned in their own camp, why should we even consider such insulting terms?"

I had to make it sound at least halfway convincing, I thought. "In the view of the Achaians, Prince Hector, your success today was helped greatly by the fact that Achilles did not enter the battle. He will not remain on the sidelines forever."

"One man," Hector countered.

"The best warrior in the Achaian host," I pointed out. "And his Myrmidones are a formidable fighting unit, I am told."

"True enough," admitted Hector. "Still, this offer of peace is no different than all the others, even though we now hold the upper hand."

"Then what am I to tell the High King?"

Hector got to his feet. "That is not my decision to make. I command the army, but my father is still king in Troy. He and his council must consider your offer."

I rose too. "King Priam?"

"Polydamas," he called, "conduct this herald to the king. Aeneas, spread the word to the chiefs that we will not attack until King Priam has considered the latest peace offering from Agamemnon."

A surge of elation swept through me. The Trojans will not attack the Achaian camp as long as I am dickering with their king! I can give Odysseus and the others a day's respite from battle, at least.

And then I realized that this is exactly what Odysseus had planned. The King of Ithaca had sent an expendable hero—one whom Hector would recognize, yet not someone important to the Achaian strength—into the Trojan camp in a crafty move to gain a day's recuperation from this morning's disaster.

I had thought that I was betraying Odysseus, but he had outsmarted both Hector and me.

Trying to look properly grave and not let my emotions show, I followed the Trojan nobleman called Polydamas through the camp on the plain and to the walls of Troy.

Chapter 9

I entered the fabled city of Troy in the dead of night. The moon was up, but still it was so dark that I could see practically nothing. The city walls loomed above like ominous shadows. I saw feeble lanterns lighting a gate as we passed a massive old oak tree, tossing and sighing in the night breeze, leaning heavily, bent by the incessant wind of Ilios.

To approach the gate we had to follow a road that led alongside the beetling walls. Just before the gate a second curtain wall extended on the other side of the road, so that anyone coming up to the gate was vulnerable to fire from both sides, as well as ahead.

The gate itself seemed only lightly defended. Virtually the entire Trojan force was camped down by the beach, I realized. A trio of teenagers were lounging in the open gateway, their inevitable long spears resting against the stone wall. A few more stood on the battlements above.

Inside, a broad packed-earth street led between buildings that seemed no more than two stories tall. The moon's pale cold light only made the shadows of their shuttered fronts seem deeper and darker. It must have been well past midnight. Hardly anyone was stirring along this main street or in the black alleyways leading off it, not even a cat.

Polydamas was not a wordy fellow. In virtually total silence he led me to a low-roofed building and into a tiny room lit by the fluttering yellow-blue flame of a small copper oil lamp sitting on a three-legged wooden stool. There was a single narrow bed and a chest of cedarwood, nothing else. A rough woolen blanket covered the bed.

"You will be summoned to the king's presence in the morning," said Polydamas, his longest speech of the night. With not another word he left me, closing the wooden door softly behind him.

And bolting it.

With nothing better to do, I undressed, pulled back the scratchy blanket, and stretched out on the bed. It was springy; a thin mattress of feathers atop a webbing of ropes.

As I started to drowse off I suddenly realized that the Golden One might invade my dreams once again. For a while I tried to stave off sleep, but my body got the better of my will, and inevitably my eyes closed. My last waking thought was to wonder how I might make contact with some of the other Creators, with the Zeus who regarded the Golden One's plans so questioningly, with the woman who openly opposed him.

But if I did dream, I had no memory of it when I was awakened by the door bolt snapping back. I sat up, immediately alert, and reached for the dagger that I had unstrapped, but left on the bed between my body and the wall.

A serving woman backed into the room, carrying a basin and a jug of water. When she turned and saw me sitting there naked, she smiled, made a little curtsy, and deposited the pottery atop the cedarwood chest. Then she backed out of the room and shut the door. Outside, I could hear the giggling of several women.

A Trojan man entered my room after a single sharp rap on the door. He seemed more a courtier than a warrior. He was fairly tall but round-shouldered, soft-looking, with a bulging middle. His beard was quite gray, his pate balding, his tunic richly embroidered and covered with a long sleeveless robe of deep green.

"I am to conduct you to King Priam's audience chamber, once you have had your morning meal."

Diplomacy moved at a polite pace; I was glad of it. The Trojan courtier led me to the urinals in the back of the house, then back to my room for a quick washup. Breakfast consisted of fruit, cheese, and flat bread, washed down with goat's milk. We ate in the large kitchen that fronted the house. Half the room was taken up by a big circular hearth, under an opening in the roof. It was cold and empty except for a scattering of gray ashes that looked as if they had been there a long time.

Through the kitchen's open window I could see men and women going about their morning chores. Serving women attended us, eyeing me curiously. The courtier ignored them, except to give orders for more figs and honey.

Finally we walked out along what seemed to be Troy's only major street, sloping gently uphill toward a majestic building of graceful fluted columns and a steeply pitched roof. Priam's palace, I guessed. Or the city's main temple. Perhaps both. The sun was not high yet, but still it felt much warmer here in the street than out on the windy plain.

"Is that where we're going?" I pointed.

The courtier bobbed his head. "Yes, of course. The king's palace. A more splendid palace doesn't exist anywhere in the world—except perhaps in Egypt, of course."

I was surprised at how small the city actually was. And crowded. Houses and shops clustered together tightly. The street was unpaved, and sloped like a V so that water would run down its middle when it rained. Cart wheels had worn deep grooves in it. The men and women bustling about their morning's work seemed curious yet courteous. I received bows and smiles as we strolled up toward the palace.

"The royal princes, such as Hector and Aleksandros and their brothers, live in the palace with the king." My courtier was turning into a tour guide. He gestured back down the street. "Nearer the Scaean gate are the homes of the lesser princes and nobility. Fine homes they are, nevertheless, far finer than you will find in Mycenae or even Miletus."

We were walking through the market area now. Awning-shaded stalls lined the two-story high brick homes here, although I saw precious little merchandise on sale: bread, dried vegetables, a skinny lamb that bleated mournfully.

Yet the merchants, men and women both, seemed smiling and happy.

"You bring a day of peace," the courtier told me. "Farmers can bring their produce to market this morning. Wood-cutters can go out to the forest and bring back fuel before night falls. The people are grateful for that."

"The siege has hurt you," I murmured.

"To some extent, of course. But we are not going hungry. There is enough grain stored in the royal treasury to last for years! The city's water comes from a spring that Apollo himself protects. And when we really need firewood or cattle or anything else, our troops escort the necessary people on a foray inland." He lifted his gray-bearded chin a notch or two. "We will not starve."

I said nothing.

He took my silence for an argument. "Look at those walls! The Achaians will never be able to scale them."

I followed his admiring gaze down a crooked alley and saw the towered walls that rose above the houses. They did indeed look high and solid and strong.

"Apollo and Poseidon helped old King Laomedon build those walls, and they have withstood every assault made on them. Of course, Herakles once sacked the city, but he had divine help and even he didn't dare try to breach those walls. He attacked over on the western side, where the oldest wall stands. But that was long ago."

I perked up my ears. The western wall was weaker? But, as if sensing that he had said too much, my guide lapsed into a red-faced silence. We walked the rest of the way to the palace without further words.

Men-at-arms held their spears stiffly upright as we passed the crimson-painted columns at the front of the palace and entered its cool interior. I saw no marble, which somehow surprised me. The columns and the thick palace walls were made of a grayish, granitelike stone, polished to gleaming smoothness. Inside, the floors were covered with brightly colored polished tiles. The walls were plastered and painted in bright yellows and reds, with blue or green borders running along the ceilings.

The interior was cold. Despite the sun's heat, those thick stone walls insulated the palace so well that I almost imagined I could see my breath frosting in the shaded air.

The hall beyond the entrance was beautifully decorated with painted landscapes on its plastered walls. Scenes of lovely ladies and handsome men in green fields rich with towering trees. No battles, no hunting scenes, no proclamations of imperial power or bloodthirstiness.

Statues lined this corridor, most of them life-size, some smaller, several so large that their heads or outstretched arms scraped the polished beams of the high ceiling.

"The city's gods," my courtier explained. "Most of these statues stood outside the city's four main gates, before the war. Of course we brought them in here for safekeeping from the despoiling Achaians."

"Of course," I agreed.

The statues seemed to be marble. To my surprise, they were brightly painted. Hair and beards were deep black, with bluish highlights. Gowns and tunics were mostly gold, and real jewels adorned them. The flesh was delicately colored, and the eyes were painted so vividly that they almost seemed to be watching me.

I could not tell one from another. The gods all seemed broad-shouldered and bearded, the goddesses ethereally beautiful. Then I recognized Poseidon, a magnificently muscular figure with a deep curly beard who bore a trident in his right hand.

We stepped out of the chilly entrance hall and into the warming sunlight of a courtyard. A huge statue, much too large to fit indoors, stood just before us. I craned my neck to see its face against the crystal-blue morning sky.

And felt my knees give way.

It was the Golden One. Perfect in every detail, as if he had sat for a portrait. Every detail except one: The Trojan artist had painted his hair black, as all the other gods. But the face, the slight curl of the lip, the *eyes*—they stared down at me, slightly amused, slightly bored. I trembled. I fully expected the statue to move, to speak.

"Apollo," said the courtier. "The protector of our city." If he noticed how the statue affected me, he was too polite to mention it. Or perhaps it was reverence for the god.

I pulled my gaze away from the Golden One's painted eyes. My insides fluttered with anger and the frustration that comes with hopelessness. How could I even think of working against his wishes, of defying him, of killing him? Yet I will do it, I told myself. With an effort of will that seemed to wrench at the soul within me, I promised myself afresh that I would bring the Golden One to dust.

We started across the sunny courtyard. It was decked with blossoms and flowering shrubs. Potted trees were arranged artfully around a square central pool. I saw fish swimming there lazily.

"We also have our statue of Athene," the courtier said, pointing across the pool to a small wooden piece, scarcely three feet tall. "It is very ancient and very sacred."

The statue was facing away from us as we crossed the courtyard and entered the other wing of the palace. Instantly, as we stepped into the shade of the wide entrance hall, the temperature dropped precipitously.

More soldiers stood guard in this hallway, although I got the feeling that their presence was a matter of pomp and formality, not security. The courtier led me to a small chamber comfortably furnished with chairs of stretched hide and gleaming polished tables inlaid with beautiful ivory and silver. There was one window, which looked out on another, smaller, courtyard, and a massive wooden door decorated with bronze strapping. Closed.

"The king will see you shortly," he said, looking nervously toward the closed door.

I took a chair and willed my body to relax. I did not want to appear tense or apprehensive in front of the Trojan king. The courtier, whom I had assumed spent much of his life in this palace, seemed to be wound up tight. He paced the small chamber worriedly. I pictured him with a cigarette, puffing like an expectant father.

Finally he blurted, "Do you truly bring an offer of peace, or is this merely another Achaian bluff?"

So that was it. Beneath his confidence in the walls built by gods and the food and firewood gathered by their army and the eternal spring that Apollo himself protects—he was anxious to have the war ended and his city safe and at peace once more.

Before I could reply, though, that heavy door creaked open. Two men-at-arms pushed at it, and an old man in a green cloak similar to my courtier's motioned me to come to him. He leaned heavily on a long wooden staff topped with a gold sunburst symbol. His beard was the color of ashes, his head almost totally bald. As I ducked through the doorway and approached him, he squinted at me nearsightedly.

"Your proper name, herald?"

"Orion."

"Of?"

I blinked, wondering what he meant. Then I replied, "Of the House of Ithaca."

He frowned at that, but turned and took a few steps into the audience chamber, then banged his staff on the floor three times. I saw that the stone floor was deeply worn at that spot.

He called out, in a voice that may have once been rich and deep but now sounded like a cat yowling, "Oh Great King—Son of Laomedon, Scion of Scamander, Servant of Apollo, Beloved of the Gods, Guardian of the Hellespont, Protector of the Troad, Western Bulwark of the Hatti, Defender of Ilios—an emissary from the Achaians, one Orion by name, of the House of Ithaca."

The chamber was spacious, wide and high-ceilinged. Its middle was open to the sky, above a circular hearth that smoldered a dull red and sent up a faint spiral of gray smoke. Dozens of men and women stood among the painted columns on the far side of the hearth: the nobility of Troy, I supposed, or at least the noblemen who were too old to be with the army. And their ladies. Their robes were rich with vibrant colors and flashing jewels.

I stepped forward and beheld Priam, the King of Troy, sitting on a splendid throne of carved ebony inlaid with gold set upon a three-step-high dais. To my surprise, he was flanked on his right by Hector, who must have come up from the camp by the beach. On his left sat a younger man, and standing behind him—

She was truly beautiful enough to launch a thousand ships. Helen was blonde, golden curls falling past her shoulders. A small, almost delicate figure except for magnificent breasts covered only by the sheerest blouse. A girdle of gold cinched her waist, adding emphasis to the bosom. Even from across the wide audience chamber I could see that her face was incredible, sensuous yet wide-eyed with an appearance of innocence that no man could resist.

She leaned against the intricately carved back of Aleksandros's chair; the young prince on Priam's left had to be Aleksandros, I realized. Darker of hair and beard than Hector, almost prettily handsome. Helen rested one hand on his shoulder. He looked up at her and she smiled dazzlingly at him. Then they both turned their gaze toward me as I approached. Helen's smile disappeared the instant Aleksandros looked away from her. She regarded me with cool, calculating eyes.

Priam was older than Nestor, and obviously failing. His white beard was thin and ragged, his long hair also, as if some wasting disease had hold of him. He seemed sunk into his robes of royal purple as he sat slumped on his gold-inlaid throne, too tired even this early in the morning to sit upright or lift his arms out of his lap.

The wall behind his throne was painted in a seascape of blues and aquamarines. Graceful boats glided among sporting dolphins. Fishermen spread their nets into waters teeming with every kind of fish.

"My lord king," said Hector, dressed in a simple tunic, "this emissary from Agamemnon brings another offer of peace."

"Let us hear it," breathed Priam, as faintly as a sigh.

They all looked to me.

I glanced at the assembled nobility and saw an eagerness, a yearning, a clear hope that I carried an offer that would end the war. Especially among the women I could sense the desire for peace, although I realized that the old men were hardly firebrands.

I bowed deeply to the king, then nodded in turn to Hector and Aleksandros. I caught Helen's eye as I did so, and she seemed to smile slightly at me.

"O Great King," I began, "I bring you greeting from High King Agamemnon, leader of the Achaian host."

Priam nodded and waggled the fingers of one hand, as if urging me to get through the preliminaries and down to business.

I did. I told them not of Odysseus's offer to leave with Helen and nothing else, but of *my* elaboration: Helen, her fortune, and an indemnity for Agamemnon to distribute to his army.

I could feel the air in the chamber change. The eager expectation died. A somber reaction of gloom settled on them all.

"But this is nothing more than Agamemnon has offered in the past," wheezed Priam.

"And which we have steadfastly refused," Hector added.

Aleksandros laughed. "If we refused such insulting terms when the Achaians were pounding at our gates, why should we even consider them now, when we have the barbarians penned up at the beach? In a day or two we'll be burning their ships and slaughtering them like the cattle they are."

"I am a newcomer to this war," I said. "I know nothing of your grievances and rights. I have been instructed to offer the terms for peace, which I have done. It is for you to consider them and make an answer."

"I will never surrender my wife," Aleksandros snapped. "Never!"

Helen smiled at him and he reached up to take her hand in his.

"A newcomer, you say?" Priam asked, his curiosity pricked

enough to light his eyes. "Yet you claim to be of the House of Ithaca. When you first ducked your head past the lintel of our doorway I thought you might be the one they call Great Ajax."

I replied, "Odysseus has taken me into his household, my lord king. I arrived on these shores only a few days ago . . ."

"And singlehandedly stopped me from storming the Achaian camp," Hector said, somewhat ruefully. "Too bad that Odysseus has adopted you. I wouldn't mind having such a fearless man at my side."

Surprised by his offer, and wondering what it might imply, I answered merely, "I fear that would be impossible, my lord."

"Yes," Hector agreed. "Too bad, though."

Priam stirred on his throne, coughed painfully, then said, "We thank you for the message you bring, Orion of the House of Ithaca. Now we must consider before making answer."

He gestured a feeble dismissal. I bowed again and went back to the anteroom. The guards closed the heavy door behind me.

I was alone in the small chamber; the courtier who had guided me earlier had disappeared. I went to the window and looked out at the lovely garden, so peaceful, so bright with flowers and humming bees intent on their morning's work. No hint of war there: merely the endless cycle of birth, growth, death, and rebirth.

I thought about the words the Golden One had spoken to me. How many times had I died and been reborn? To what purpose? He wanted Troy to win this war, or at least survive the Achaian siege. Therefore my desire was the same as Agamemnon's: to crush Troy, to burn it to the ground, to slaughter its people and destroy it forever.

Destroy that garden? Burn this palace? Slaughter Hector and aged Priam and all the rest?

I clenched my fists and squeezed my eyes tight. Yes! I told myself. Just as the Golden One would slaughter Odysseus and old Poletes. Just as he burned my love to death.

"Orion of Ithaca."

I wheeled from the window. A single soldier stood at the doorway, bareheaded, wearing a well-oiled leather harness rather t' an armor, a short sword at his hip.

"Follow me, please."

I followed him down a long hallway and up a flight of stairs, then through several rooms that were empty of people, although richly furnished and decorated with gorgeous tapestries. They will burn nicely, I found myself thinking. Up another flight we went, and finally he ushered me into a comfortable sitting room, with undraped windows and an open doorway that looked out on a terrace and the distant sea. Lovely murals decorated the walls, scenes of peaceful men and women in a pastel world of flowers and gentle beasts.

The soldier closed the door and left me alone. But not for long. Through the door on the opposite side of the room, a scant few moments later, stepped the beautiful Helen.

Chapter 10

SHE was breathtaking, there is no denying it. She wore a flounced skirt of shimmering rainbow colors with golden tassels that tinkled as she walked toward me. Her corselet was now as blue as the Aegean sky, her white blouse so gauzy that I could see the dark circles of the areolae around her nipples. She wore a triple gold necklace and more gold at both wrists and earlobes. Jeweled rings glittered on her fingers.

She was tiny, almost delicate, despite her hour-glass figure. Her skin was like cream, unblemished and much lighter than the women I had seen in the Achaian camp. Her eyes were as deeply blue as the Aegean, her lips lush and full, her hair the color of golden honey, with ringlets falling well past her lovely shoulders. One stubborn curl hung down over her forehead. She wore a scent of flowers: light, clean, yet beguiling.

Helen smiled at me and gestured toward a chair. She took a cushioned couch, her back to the open windows. I sat and waited for her to speak. In truth, just looking at her against the background of the blue sky and bluer sea was a feast that seemed too good for mere words.

"You say you are a stranger to this land." Her voice was low, melodious. I could understand how Aleksandros, or any other man, would dare anything to have her. And keep her.

I nodded and found that I had to swallow once before I could speak. "My lady, I arrived on a boat only a few days ago. Before then, all I knew of Troy was . . . stories told by wayfarers."

"You are a sailor, then?"

"Not really," I said. "I am a . . . traveler, a wanderer."

She looked at me with a hint of suspicion in those clear blue eyes. "Not a warrior?"

"I have been a warrior, from time to time, but that is not my profession."

"Yet it may be your destiny."

I had no answer for that.

Helen said, "You serve the goddess Athene." It was not a question. She had excellent intelligence sources, apparently.

Nodding, I replied, "That is true."

She bit her lower lip. "Athene despises me. She is the enemy of Troy."

"Yet her statue is honored . . ."

"You cannot fail to honor so powerful a goddess, Orion. No matter how Athene hates me, the people of this city must continue to placate her as best they can. Certain disaster will overtake them if they do not."

"Apollo protects the city," I said.

She nodded. "Yet I fear Athene." Helen looked beyond me, looking into the past, perhaps. Or trying to see the future.

"My lady, is there some service you wish me to do for you?"

Her gaze focused on me once again. A faint smile dimpled her cheeks. "You wonder why I summoned you?"

"Yes."

The smile turned impish. "Don't you think that I might want a closer look at such a handsome stranger? A man so tall, with such broad shoulders? Who stood alone against Hector and his chariot team and turned them away?"

I bowed my head slightly. "May I ask you a question, my lady?"

"You may—although I don't promise to answer."

"All the world wonders: Did Aleksandros actually abduct you, or did you leave Sparta with him willingly?"

Her smile remained. It even grew wider, until she threw her head back and laughed a hearty, genuinely amused laugh.

"Orion," she said at last, "you certainly don't understand the ways of women."

I may have blushed. "That's true enough," I admitted.

"Let me tell you this much," Helen said. "No matter how or why I accompanied Aleksandros to this great city, I will not willingly return to Sparta." Before I could reply she quickly added, "Not that I harbor ill feelings for Menalaos, my first husband. He was kind to me."

"But Aleksandros is kinder?"

She spread her arms. "Look about you, Orion! You have eyes, use them. What woman would willingly live as the wife of an Achaian lord when she could be a princess of Troy?"

"But Menalaos is a king . . ."

"And an Achaian queen is still regarded less than her husband's dogs and horses. A woman in Sparta is a slave, be she wife or concubine, there is no real difference. Do you think there would be women present in the great hall at Sparta when an emissary arrives with a message for the king? Or at Agamemnon's Mycenae or Nestor's Pylos or even in Odysseus's Ithaca? No, Orion. Here in Troy women are regarded as human beings. Here there is civilization."

"Then your preference for Aleksandros is really a preference for Troy," I said.

She put a finger to her lips, as if thinking over the words she wished to use. Then, "When I was wed to Menalaos I had no say in the choice. The young lords of Achaia all wanted me—and my dowry. My father made the decision. If, the gods forbid, the Achaians should win this war and force me to return to Sparta with Menalaos, I will again be chattel."

"Would you agree to return to Menalaos if it meant that Troy would be saved from destruction?"

"Don't ask such a question! Do you think Agamemnon fights for his brother's honor? The Achaians are intent on destroying this city. I am merely their excuse for attacking."

"So I have heard from others, in the Achaian camp."

"Priam is near death," Helen said. "Hector will die in battle; that is foretold. But Troy itself need not fall, even if Hector does."

And, I thought, if Hector dies Aleksandros will become king. Making Helen the queen of Troy.

She fixed me with her eyes and said, "Orion, you may say this to Menalaos: If he wants me to return to him, he will have to win me by feats of battle. I will not go willingly to a man as the consolation prize for losing this war."

I took in a deep breath. She was far wiser than I had assumed. She unquestionably wants Troy to win this war, wants to remain in this city so that one day she can be its queen. Yet she wants to tell her former husband that she will come back to him—if he wins! She's telling him, through me, that she will return to Sparta and be the docile Achaian wife—if and when Troy is burned to the ground.

Clever woman! No matter who wins, she will protect her own lovely skin.

We chatted for a few moments more, but it was clear that Helen had imparted the message she wanted me to bear back to the Achaians. Finally she rose, signaling that our meeting was ended. I got to my feet and went to the door by which I had entered the chamber. Sure enough, the guard was outside waiting to escort me back to the king's audience hall.

No one was there except the courtier who had been with me earlier in the morning. The columned hall was empty, echoing.

"The king and royal princes are still deliberating on your message," he whispered. "You are to wait."

I waited. We strolled through several of the palace's halls and chambers and finally out into the big courtyard we had come through that morning. The hot sun felt good on my bare arms.

Out of curiosity I walked across the garden to the small statue of Athene. It was barely the length of my arm, and obviously very old, weathered by many years of rain and wind. Unlike the other, grander statues, it was unpainted. Or, rather, the original paint had long since worn away and had never been replaced.

Athene. The warrior goddess was dressed in a long robe, yet carried a shield and spear. A plumed helmet rested on the back of her head, pushed up and away from her face.

I looked at that face and the breath gushed out of me. It was *her* face, the face of the woman I had loved. The face of the goddess that the Golden One had killed.

Chapter 11

S O it was true. The gods are not immortal. Just as the Golden One had told me. And I knew that he had not lied about the rest: The gods are neither merciful nor beneficent. They play their games and make up their own rules while we, their creatures, try to make sense of what they do to us.

The rage burned in me. They are not immortal. The gods can be killed. I can kill the Golden One. And I will, I promised myself anew. How, I did not know. When, I had no idea. But by the flames that burned inside me I swore that I would destroy him, no matter how long it took and no matter what the cost.

I swung my gaze around the graceful flowered courtyard of Priam's palace. Yes, this is where I would start. *He* wants to save Troy, to make it the center of an empire that spans Europe and Asia. Then I will destroy it, crush it, slaughter its people, and burn its buildings to the ground.

"Orion."

I blinked, as though waking from a dream. Hector stood before me. I had not seen him approaching.

"Prince Hector," I said.

"Come with me. We have an answer for Agamemnon."

I followed him into another part of the palace. As before, Hector wore only a simple tunic, almost bare of adornment. No weapons. No jewelry. No proclamation of his rank. He carried his nobility in his person, and anyone who saw him knew instinctively that here was a man of merit and honor.

Yet, as I matched him stride for stride through the halls of the palace, I saw again that the war had taken its toll of him. His bearded face was deeply etched by lines around the mouth and eyes. His brow was creased and a permanent notch of worry had worn itself into the space between his eyebrows.

We walked to the far side of the palace and up steep narrow steps in murky darkness lit only by occasional slits of windows. Higher and higher we climbed the steep, circling stone steps, breathing hard, around and around the stairwell's narrow confines until at last we squeezed through a low square doorway onto the platform at the top of Troy's tallest tower.

"Aleksandros will join us shortly," said Hector, walking over to the giant's teeth of the battlements. It was almost noon, and hot in the glaring sun despite the stiff breeze from the sea that huffed at us and set Hector's brown hair flowing.

From this high vantage I could see the Achaian camp, dozens of long black boats drawn up on the beach behind the sandy rampart and trench I had helped to dig barely forty-eight hours earlier. The Trojan army was camped on the plain, tents and chariots dotted across the worn-bare soil, cook fires sending thin tendrils of smoke into the crystalline sky. A fair-sized river flowed across the plain to the south and emptied into the bay. A smaller stream passed to the north. The Achaian camp's flanks were anchored on the two riverbanks.

Beyond the gentle waves rolling up onto the beach I saw an island near the horizon, a brown hump of a worn mountain, and beyond that another hovering ghostlike in the blue hazy distance.

"Well, brother, have you told him?"

I turned and saw Aleksandros striding briskly toward us. Unlike Hector, his tunic looked as soft as silk and he wore a handsome royal-blue cloak over it. A jeweled sword was at his hip, and more jewels flashed on his fingers and at his throat. His hair and beard were carefully trimmed and gleamed with sweet-smelling oil. His face was unlined, though he was not that many years younger than his brother.

"I was waiting for you," said Hector.

"Good! Then let me give him the news." Smiling nastily, Aleksandros said to me, "You may tell fat Agamemnon that King Priam rejects his insulting offer. Moreover, by this time tomorrow our chariots will be riding through your camp, burning your boats and slaying your white-livered Achaians until nothing is left but ashes and bones. Our dogs will feast well tomorrow night."

I kept my face immobile.

Hector made the tiniest shake of his head, then laid a restraining hand on his brother's blue-cloaked shoulder. "Our father is not feeling well enough to see you again. And although my brother's hot words may seem insulting, the answer that we have for Agamemnon is that we reject his offer of peace."

"And any offer that includes returning my wife to the barbarian!" Aleksandros snapped.

"Then we will have war again tomorrow," I said.

"Indeed we will," said Aleksandros.

"Do you really think you are strong enough to break through the Achaian defenses and burn their fleet?"

"The gods will decide," Hector replied.

"In our favor," added Aleksandros.

I was beginning to dislike this boastful young man. "It is one thing to fight from chariots on this plain," I gestured toward the battlefield bounded by the beach, the two rivers, and the bluff on which the city stood. "It is another to break into the Achaian camp and fight their entire host on foot. That will not be a battle of hero against hero. Every man in the Achaian camp will be fighting for his life."

"Don't you think we're fighting for our lives?" Aleksandros retorted. "And the lives of our wives and children?"

"I don't think you can wipe out the Achaians," I insisted. "Not with the forces I see camped on the plain."

Aleksandros laughed. "You are looking in the wrong direction, barbarian. Look *there*, instead!"

He pointed inland, toward the distant wooded hills and the mountains that bulked beyond them, "There lies the empire of the Hatti," Aleksandros said. "It spreads from this shore far to the east and south. The Hatti High King has fought wars with the Egyptians, Orion. And won them! He is our ally."

I drew the obvious conclusion. "You expect help from him."

"It is already on the way. We put up with the Achaian raids on the farms and towns nearby, but when pompous Agamemnon landed his army here, we sent a delegation to the High King of the Hatti, in his capital at Hattusas."

Hector said calmly, "I saw that city when I was a lad, Orion. It could swallow Troy ten times over. It is immense, and the power of the Hatti makes it so."

I said nothing.

"So far we have fought the Achaians only with the help of our neighbors, the Dardanians and other peoples of the Troad," Aleksandros resumed. "But when the Hatti send their troops to aid us, Agamemnon's army will be utterly crushed."

"Why are you telling me this?" I asked.

Before Aleksandros could answer, Hector said, "Because we have decided to make Agamemnon a counter offer, Orion. We did not seek this war. We prefer peace, and the gentler arts of commerce and trade, to the blood and fire of battle."

"But we don't fear battle!" Aleksandros insisted.

Silencing his brother with a stern glance, Hector continued, "King Priam offers a simple plan for peace. If Agamemnon will remove his army and return to Achaia, my father the king offers to negotiate a new treaty of friendship and trade that will allow Mycenae free passage of the Hellespont."

"Mycenae?" I asked. "What about the other Achaian cities: Ithaca, Nestor's Pylos, Tiryns . . ."

"Mycenae," repeated Hector. "As High King, Agamemnon can make his own agreements with the other Achaian cities. As long as the trade is carried in Mycenaean boats, Troy will make no objection."

A masterful stroke of diplomacy! Dangle the carrot of free passage through the straits to Agamemnon, and to him alone, so that he will have a commanding position among the other Achaian powers. At the very least, it should set up an argument among the various Achaian petty kings that will destroy their ability to make a united war against Troy. Masterful.

"I will take this message to Agamemnon," I lied.

"Do that," snapped Aleksandros. "And tell the greedy High King that if he does not accept our offer by dawn tomorrow, his body will be feeding kites and dogs by sunset."

I stared at him. He tried to meet my gaze, but after a moment he looked away.

"We will expect an answer by sunrise tomorrow," Hector said. "If our offer is not accepted, we will force the Achaian camp. Even if we are not successful in that, it is only a matter of a few days before the Hatti army reaches us."

"We've had messages from smoke signals," Aleksandros boasted. "Their army has been seen within a three-day march of our walls."

I looked back to Hector. He nodded and I believed him.

"There has been enough killing," Hector said. "It is time to make peace. Agamemnon can return to Mycenae with honor. We make him a generous offer."

"But Helen stays with me!" Aleksandros added.

I had to smile at that. I could hardly blame him for wanting to keep her.

Hector gave me a four-man guard of honor that escorted me out the same Scaean gate I had entered the night before. Now I could see the massive walls of Troy close-up. Almost I could believe that gods had helped to build them. Immense blocks of stone were wedged and fitted together to a height of more than nine meters, with high square towers surmounting them at the major gates and corners. The walls sloped outward, so that they were thickest at ground level.

Since the city was built on the bluff overlooking the plain of Ilios, the attacking army would have to fight its way uphill before ever reaching the walls.

I returned to the Achaian camp to find old Poletes waiting at the makeshift gate for me.

"What news do you bring?" he asked me eagerly. I realized that his voice, though thin and grating, had none of the rasping and wheezing quality that had afflicted Priam.

"Nothing good," I said. "There will be battle tomorrow."

Poletes's skinny shoulders slumped beneath his worn tunic. "The fools. The bloody fools."

I knew better, but I did not reveal it. There would be battle tomorrow because I would not let the two sides know that each side was prepared to make peace.

I went straight to Odysseus, with Poletes skipping beside me, his knobby legs working overtime to keep pace with me. Soldiers and noblemen alike stared at me, reading in my grim face the news I brought from Troy. The women looked too, then turned away, knowing that tomorrow would bring blood and carnage and terror. Many of them were natives of this land, and hoped to be freed of bondage by the Trojan soldiery. But they knew, I think, that in the frenzy and bloodlust of battle, their chances of being raped and put to the sword were much more likely than their chances of being rescued and returned to their rightful households.

Odysseus's quarters were on the deck of his boat. He received me alone, dismissing his aides and servants to hear my report. He was naked and wet from his morning swim, rubbing himself briskly with a rough towel. Sitting on a three-legged stool, he rested his back against the boat's only mast. The musty canvas that had served as a tent when it had been raining was folded back now that the hot sun was shining, but his bearded face was as dark and foreboding as any storm cloud as I told him that Priam and his sons rejected the Achaian peace terms.

"They offered no counter terms?" he asked, once I had finished my report.

Without hesitating, I lied, "None. Aleksandros said he would never surrender Helen under any circumstances."

"Nothing else?"

"He and Prince Hector told me that a Hatti army is marching to their assistance."

Odysseus's eyes widened. "What? How far are they from here?"

"A few days' march, from what Aleksandros said."

He tugged at his beard, real consternation in his face. "That cannot be," he muttered. "It *cannot* be!"

I waited in silence, and looked out across the rows of beached boats. Each of them had its mast in place, as if the crews were making ready to sail. The masts had not been up the day before.

Finally Odysseus jumped to his feet. "Come with me," he said urgently. "Agamemnon must hear of this."

Chapter 12

"**T**HE Hatti are marching here? To aid Priam?" Agamemnon piped in his high squeaking voice. "Impossible! It can't be true!"

The High King looked startled, even frightened. He sat at the head of the council, his right shoulder swathed in strips of cloth smeared with blood and some oily poultice.

He was broad of shoulder and body, built like a squat turret, round and thick from neck to hips. He wore a coat of gilded mail over his tunic, and a harness of gleaming leather over that, with silver buckles and ornaments. A jeweled sword hung at his side. Even his legs were encased in elaborately decorated bronze greaves, buckled in silver. His sandals had gold tassels on their thongs.

All in all, Agamemnon looked as if he were dressed for battle rather than a council of his chief lieutenants, the kings and princes of the various Achaian tribes.

But, knowing the Achaians and their penchant for argument, perhaps he hoped to awe them with his panoply. Or perhaps he thought he *was* going into a battle.

Thirty-two men sat in a circle around the small hearth fire in Agamemnon's hut, the leaders of the Achaian contingents. Every group allied to Agamemnon and his brother Menalaos was there, although the Myrmidones were represented by Patrokles, rather than Achilles. I sat behind Odysseus, who was placed two seats down on the High King's right, so I had the opportunity to study Agamemnon closely.

There was precious little nobility in the features of the High King. Like his body, his face was broad and heavy, with a wide stub of a nose, a thick brow, and deep-set eyes that seemed to look out at the world with suspicion and resentment. His hair and beard were just beginning to turn gray, but they were well combed and glistening with fresh oil perfumed so heavily that it made my nostrils itch, even from where I sat.

He held a bronze scepter in his left hand; his right rested limply on his lap. The one rule of sanity and order in the council meeting, apparently, was that only the man holding the scepter was allowed to speak.

"I have the sworn word of Hattusilis himself, High King of the Hatti, that he will not interfere in our war against Troy," Agamemnon said petulantly. "In writing!" he added.

"I have seen the agreement," vouched Menalaos, his brother.

Several of the kings and princes nodded their heads in acceptance, but big, blunt Ajax, sitting halfway down the circle, spoke up.

"Many of us have never seen the document sent by the Hatti High King."

Agamemnon sighed, almost girlishly, and turned to the servant hovering behind his chair. He immediately went to a far corner of the hut, where a table and several chests had been clustered together to form something like an office.

The High King's hut was larger than Achilles's, but not as luxurious. The log walls were bare, for the most part, although the king's bed was hung with rich tapestries. For all his bluster, Agamemnon kept no dais. He sat at the same level with the rest of us. The loot of dozens of towns was scattered around the hut: armor, jeweled swords, long spears with gleaming bronze points, iron and bronze tripods, chests that must have contained much gold and jewelry. The High King had cleared the hut of women and other slaves. None were here except the council and a few scribes and servants.

The servant produced a baked clay tablet covered with cuneiform inscriptions. Agamemnon passed it around the full circle of councilmen. Each man inspected it carefully, although it seemed to me that hardly any of them could read it. As if to prove my suspicion, Agamemnon had the servant read it aloud once it had returned to his hands.

The document was a masterpiece of diplomatic phrasing. It greeted Agamemnon as a fellow High King, and I could see his chest swell pridefully as the words were spoken. The High King of the Hatti, ruler of all the lands from the shore of the Aegean to the ancient walls of Jericho (by his own humble admission), recognized the justice of the Achaian grievance against Troy and promised not to interfere in its settlement. Of course, the wording was much more roundabout than that, but the meaning seemed clear enough. Even a Trojan would have to agree that Hattusilis had promised Agamemnon that he would not help Troy.

"Yet the Trojans claim that a Hatti army is within a few days' march, coming to their aid," said Odysseus.

"Pardon me, King of Ithaca," said old Nestor, sitting between Odysseus and Agamemnon, "but you do not have the scepter and therefore you are speaking out of turn."

Odysseus smiled at the whitebeard. "Neither do you, King of Pylos," he said mildly.

"What are they saying?" shouted one of the princes on the other side of the circle. "I can't hear them!"

Agamemnon handed the scepter to Odysseus, who stood up and repeated his statement in a clear voice.

Ajax blurted, "How do we know this is true?"

They argued back and forth, then finally commanded me to tell them exactly what had been told to me. I got to my feet and repeated the words of Aleksandros and Hector.

"Aleksandros said it?" Menalaos spat on the sandy floor. "He is the prince of liars."

"But Hector agreed with the story," Nestor said, hastily taking the scepter from my hands. As I sat, he rose and said, "If this tale of a Hatti army had been told our herald merely by Aleksandros, I would agree with King Menalaos . . ." On and on Nestor rambled, secure in the possession of the scepter. The gist of his statement was that Hector was an honorable man: If *he* said that the Hatti army was approaching Troy, that meant it was true. Hector was a man who could be believed, unlike his brother.

"That means disaster for us!" Agamemnon cried, his narrow

little eyes actually brimming with tears. "The Hatti army could annihilate us *and* the Trojans at the same time!"

Everyone seemed to agree.

"They have fought battles against the Egyptians!"

"They conquered Akkad."

"And sacked Babylon!"

"Hattusilis marched on Miletus and the city opened its gates to him, rather than have his army batter down its walls."

The fear that spread around the council circle was palpable, like a cold wind that snuffs out a candle and leaves you in darkness.

None of them seemed to know what to do. They dithered like a herd of antelope that sees a pride of lions approaching and cannot make up its mind which way to run.

Finally Odysseus asked for the scepter. Rising, he said calmly, "Perhaps Hector and his wicked brother are wrong in their belief that the Hatti are marching to their aid. Perhaps the Hatti troops are nearby for reasons of their own, reasons that have nothing to do with our war against Troy."

Mumbles and mutters of dissent. "Too good to be true," said one voice out of the grumbling background.

"I suggest we send a herald to meet the Hatti commander and ask what his intentions are. Let our herald carry with him some sign of the agreement between Hattusilis and our own High King, to remind the Hatti commander that his king has promised not to interfere in our war."

"What good would that do?" Agamemnon wrung his hands, wincing and clutching his shoulder.

"If they mean to war on us, we might as well pack up now and sail back home."

Everyone agreed with that.

But Odysseus held the scepter aloft until they fell silent. "If the Hatti are coming to Troy's aid, would Hector be preparing to attack our camp tomorrow?" he asked.

Puzzled glances went around the circle. Much scratching of beards.

Odysseus continued, "He is making preparations to attack us, that we know. Why would he risk the lives of his own people—and his own neck—if there's a Hatti army on its way to fight at his side?"

"For glory," said Patrokles. "Hector is like my lord Achilles: his life means less to him than honor and glory."

With a shake of head, Odysseus replied, "Perhaps that is true. But I am not convinced of it. I say we should at least send a herald to show the Hatti general his king's sworn agreement with us, and to determine if the Hatti really will come to Troy's relief."

It took another hour or so of wrangling, but eventually they agreed to Odysseus's plan. They really had no other option, except to sail away.

The herald they picked, of course, was me.

When at last the council meeting ended, I asked Odysseus for permission to approach Menalaos with a private message from his wife. The King of Ithaca looked at me solemnly, his mind playing out the possible consequences of such a message. Then, with a nod, he called out Menalaos's name and caught up with the Spartan king as he turned at the door of Agamemnon's hut.

"Orion has a message for you, from Helen," he said simply, his voice low so that the other departing council members could not easily hear him.

"What is it?" he asked eagerly, clutching my arm as we stepped through the doorway and out onto the beach.

Odysseus stayed tactfully inside the hut. Menalaos and I walked a few paces along the sand before I spoke. He was a handsome man, with a full black beard and thick curly hair. Menalaos was many years younger than his brother, and where Agamemnon's features were heavy and almost coarse, the same general structure gave Menalaos's face a sort of strength and nobility. He was much slimmer than the High King, not given to feasting and drinking.

"Your wife sends you greetings," I began, "and says that she will return willingly with you to Sparta . . ."

His face lit up anew.

I finished, ". . . but only if you succeed in conquering Troy. She said she will not leave Troy as a consolation prize for the loser of this war."

Menalaos took a deep breath and threw his head back. "Then by the gods," he murmured, "by Ares and Poseidon and mighty Zeus himself, I will climb Troy's high walls and carry her back with me, no matter how much blood it takes!"

I understood how he felt, having seen Helen and spoken with her. And I felt inside myself a vicious sense of satisfaction. I had done everything I could to encourage the Achaians to press on with their war. There would be no peace with Troy. Not if I could help it.

Then I remembered that there was an army on the march to come to Troy's aid, and I was supposed to find them and stop them, somehow.

Chapter 13

I brought Poletes with me.

We waited until nightfall, then went to the southern end of the camp where the larger river, the Scamander, anchored both our right flank and the flank of the Trojan forces camped on the plain.

Odysseus saw to it that we obtained a flimsy reed boat, and I paddled across the river's strong current while Poletes bailed. It was a race to see if the leaky reed vessel would sink before we could reach the far shore. We made it, but just barely.

The night was dark; the moon had not yet risen. Wisps of fog were drifting in from the sea.

"A night for ghosts and demons," Poletes whispered.

But my eye was on the far bank of the river, where the Trojan campfires gleamed.

"Never mind ghosts and demons," I whispered back to him. "Be on the lookout for Trojan scouts and foragers."

I had a new sword at my side, and a dark blue cloak across my shoulders. Poletes carried only a small hunting knife; he was no good with weapons, he said. He too had a cloak for warmth against the night chill, and he bore a small knapsack of dried meat and bread and a leather sack of wine.

On my left wrist was a copper band that bore a copy of the Hatti High King's agreement with Agamemnon. It looked like an ordinary wristband, but the cuneiform symbols were etched into it. Roll it across a slab of wet clay and the document would reproduce itself.

We spent the darkest hours of the night skirting along the riverbank, moving inland past the plain of Ilios and the city of Troy. In the darkness the thick bushes tangled against our feet, slowing us. We tried to move silently, but often we had to hack the leafy branches out of our way. By the time the moon came up over the distant mountains, we were climbing the steady slope of the first of the foothills. I could see the edge of the woods ahead, lofty oak and ash trees, beech and larch, silvery and silent in the moonlight. Farther uphill, dark pines and spruce rose straight and tall. The bushes were thinner here and we could make better time.

Poletes was puffing hard, but he did his best to keep up with me. As we plunged into the darker shadows of the trees an owl hooted, as if to challenge us.

"Athene welcomes us," Poletes panted.

"What?"

He grabbed at my shoulder. I stopped and turned around. He bent over, hands on knobby knees, wheezing and gasping for breath.

"We don't need . . . forest demons," he panted. "You have . . . your own demon . . . inside you."

I felt a pang of conscience. "I'm sorry," I said. "I didn't realize I was going too fast for you."

"Can we . . . rest here?"

"Yes."

He slung the knapsack off his shoulder and collapsed to the mossy ground. I took in a deep breath of clean mountain air, crisp with the tang of pine.

"What was that you said about Athene?" I asked, kneeling beside him.

Poletes waved a hand vaguely. "The owl . . . it is Athene's symbol. Its hooting means that she welcomes us to the safety of these woods. We are under her protection."

I felt my jaw clenching. "No, old man. She can't protect anyone, not even herself. Athene is dead."

Even in the darkness I could see his eyes go round. "What are you saying? That's blasphemy!"

I shrugged and squatted on the ground beside him.

"Orion," Poletes said earnestly, propping himself on one elbow, "the gods cannot die. They are immortal!"

"Athene is dead," I repeated, feeling the hollow ache of it in my guts.

"But you serve her!"

"I serve her memory. And I live to avenge her murder."

He shook his head in disbelief. "It is impossible, Orion. Gods and goddesses cannot die. Not as long as one mortal remembers them. As long as *you* revere Athene, and serve her, she is not dead."

"Perhaps so," I said, to placate him and calm his fear. "Perhaps you are right."

We stretched out for a few hours' sleep, wrapped in our cloaks. I was afraid to close my eyes so I lay there listening to the subtle night sounds of the forest, the soft rustling of the trees in the cool dark breeze, the chirrup of insects, the occasional hoot of an owl.

She is dead, I told myself. She died in my arms. And I will kill the Golden One someday.

The moon peeked down at me through the swaying branches of the trees. Artemis, sister of Apollo, I thought. Will you defend your brother against me? Or was that you arguing against him? Will the other gods fight against me or will I find allies among you in my vengeance against the Golden One?

I must have fallen asleep, for I dreamed that I saw her again: Athene, standing tall and radiant in gleaming silver, her long dark hair burnished like polished ebony, her beautiful gray eyes regarding me gravely.

"You are not alone, Orion," she said to me. "There are allies all around you. You have only to find them. And lead them to your goal."

I reached out to her, only to find myself sitting upright on the mossy forest floor, the fresh yellow light of sunrise slanting between the trees. Birds were singing a welcome to the new day.

Poletes stirred before I tried to wake him. We ate a cold breakfast washed down with warm wine, then resumed our march.

We cut northward now, toward the main road that led from Troy inland. Over two rows of wooded hills we climbed, and as we reached the crest of the third, we saw spread out below us a broad valley dotted with cultivated fields. A river meandered gently through the valley, and along its banks tiny villages huddled.

An ugly column of black smoke rose from one of the villages. I pointed. "There's the Hatti army."

We hurried down the wooded slope and out across the fields of chest-high grain, wading through the golden crop like shipwrecked sailors staggering to the safety of an unknown shore.

"Why would a Trojan ally be burning a Trojan village?" Poletes asked.

I had no answer. My attention was fixed on that column of smoke, and the pitiful cluster of burning huts that produced it. I could see wagons and horses now, and men in armor that glittered under the morning sun.

We breasted the ripening grain until we came to the edge of the field. Poletes tugged at my cloak.

"Perhaps we'd better lie low until we find out what's going on here."

"No time for that," I said. "Hector must be attacking the beach by now. If these are Hatti troops, we've got to find out what they're up to."

I plunged ahead and within a dozen strides broke out of the cultivated field. I could clearly see the troops now. They were taller and fairer than the Achaians. And, man for man, better armed and equipped. Each soldier wore a tunic of chain mail and a helmet of polished black iron. Their swords were long, and their blades were iron, not bronze. Their shields were small and square and worn across their backs, since there was no fighting going on.

A half-dozen soldiers were herding a peasant family out of their hut: a man, his wife, and two young daughters. They looked terrified, like rabbits caught in a trap. They fell to their knees and raised their hands in supplication. One of the soldiers tossed a torch onto the thatched roof of the hut, while the others gathered around the pleading, crying family with drawn swords and ugly smiles.

"Stop that!" I called, striding toward them. I could hear the rustling behind me of Poletes diving into the stalks of grain to hide himself.

The soldiers turned toward me.

"Who the hell are you?" their leader shouted.

"A herald from High King Agamemnon," I said, stepping up to him. He was slightly shorter than I, well built, scarred from many battles. His face was as hard and fierce as a hunting falcon's, his eyes glittering with suspicion, his nose bent hawklike. His sword was in his hand. I kept mine in my scabbard.

"And who in the name of the Nine Lords of the Earth is High King Aga . . . whatever?"

I extended my left hand. "I bear a message from your own High King, a message of peace and friendship he sent to Agamemnon."

The Hatti soldier grinned sourly. "Peace and friendship, eh?" He spat at my feet. "That's how much peace and friendship are worth." To the five men behind him he said, "Slit the farmer's throat and take the women. I'll deal with this one myself."

My body went into hyperdrive instantly, every sense so acute that I could see the pulse throbbing in his neck, just below his ear, and hear the slight swish of his iron blade swinging through the air. Beyond him I saw one of the other soldiers grab the kneeling farmer by the hair and yank his head back to bare his throat. The wife and daughters drew in their breaths to scream.

I easily ducked under the swinging sword blade and launched myself at the soldier who was about to slaughter the farmer. My flying leap knocked both of them to the ground. I rolled to my feet and kicked the soldier in the head. He went over on his back, unconscious.

Everything happened so quickly that my reactions seemed automatic, not under my conscious control. I disarmed the two nearest soldiers before their partners could move. When they did stir, it seemed to be in slow motion. I could see what they intended to do by the movement of their eyes, the bunching of muscles in their biceps or thighs. It was a simple matter to ram a fist into a solar plexus and bring my other hand up into the jaw of the next man, fracturing bone.

I stood before the huddled, kneeling family, five Hatti soldiers on the ground behind me and their leader facing me, sword still in his right hand. His mouth hung agape, his eyes bulged. There was no fear in his face, just an astonishment that made his breath catch in his throat.

For an instant we stood facing each other, poised for combat. Then, with a roaring curse, he pulled back his sword arm for what I thought would be a charging attack at me.

Instead, he threw the sword. I saw its point flying straight for my chest. No time for anything but a slight sidestep. As the blade slid past my leather vest I grabbed at its hilt. The momentum of the sword and my own motion turned me completely around. When I faced the Hatti warrior again I had his sword in my hand.

He stood rooted to the ground. I am sure he would have run away if he could have commanded his feet, but the shock of what he had just seen froze him.

"Get your men together and take me to your commanding officer," I said, gesturing with his sword.

"You . . ." he gaped at the sword, not lifting his eyes to look me in the face, "you're not . . . human. You must be a god."

"He serves Athene!" piped Poletes, coming up from his hiding place in the grain field, a gap-toothed smile on his wrinkled old face. "No man can stand against Orion, servant of the warrior goddess."

I handed him back his sword. "What is your name, soldier?"

"Lukka," he answered. It took him three tries to get his sword back into its scabbard, his hands were shaking so.

"I have no quarrel with you, Lukka, or with any Hatti soldier. Take me to your commander; I bear a message for him."

Lukka was totally awed. He gathered up his men: One had a broken jaw; another seemed dazed and glassy-eyed with a concussion.

The farmer and his family crawled on their hands and knees to me and began to kiss my sandaled feet. I pulled the man up roughly by his shoulders and told the women to stand up.

"May all the gods protect you and bring you your every desire," said the farmer. His wife and daughters kept their heads down, their eyes on the ground. But I could see tears streaming from each of them.

I felt bile in my throat. May all the gods protect me! In his ignorance he thought that the gods actually cared about human beings, actually could be moved by prayers or sacrifices. If this simple man knew what the gods really were he would puke with disgust. Yet, when I looked into his brimming eyes, I could not bring myself to disillusion him. What good would it do, except to fill his days with agony?

"And may the gods protect you, farmer. You bring life from the bosom of Mother Earth. That is a far higher calling than warring and slaying."

Having offered their thanks, they dashed inside their hut to put out the fire that the soldiers had started. I followed Lukka and his limping, wounded men through the burning village in search of the Hatti commander. Poletes skipped along beside me, reciting a blow-by-blow account of what had just happened, rehearsing it for later storytelling.

It seemed clear to me that this was far too small a contingent to be the Hatti army. Yet there were no other troops in the valley, as far as Poletes and I were able to see from the hilltop earlier in the day. Could this small unit be the force that Hector and Aleksandros expected to help them?

And if these soldiers were allies of the Trojans, why were they burning a Trojan village?

In the village square—nothing more than a clearing of bare earth among the dried-brick huts—a procession of soldiers wound its way past a line of wagons and chariots. The Hatti commander was standing in one of the chariots, parceling out loot for his officers and men. The soldiers were carrying the villagers' pitiful possessions up to the chariot in a long, ragged line: a two-handled jug of wine, a blanket, a squawking flapping pair of chickens, a clay lamp, a pair of boots. It was not a rich village.

In the distance I could hear women's screams and crying. Apparently the soldiers were not taking female captives with them; they raped them and left them to their lamentations.

The commander was a short, swarthy, thickset man, more like the Achaians than Lukka and his men. His hair and thick beard were so deeply black that they seemed to cast bluish highlights. A brutal white scar slashed down the left side of his face from cheek to jawline, parting his beard. Like the other Hatti soldiers, he wore chain mail. His leather harness, though, was handsomely tooled, and the sword at his side was set with ivory inlays along its hilt.

Lukka stood at a respectful distance with me at his side and Poletes behind me, while his five men limped off to tend to their bruises and wounds. The commander glanced our way questioningly, but continued dividing the loot his soldiers brought before him: About half of everything went into a growing pile at the foot of his chariot; the soldiers carried away the other half for themselves. I folded my arms over my chest and waited, the stench of burning huts in my nostrils, the wailing of the women in my ears.

Finally the last clay jugs and bleating goats were parceled out, and the commander gestured to a pair of barefoot men dressed in rough jerkins to pick up his share of the loot and load it onto the nearby wagons. Slaves, I thought. Or possibly *thetes*.

The commander stepped tiredly down from his chariot and summoned Lukka with a crook of his finger.

Watching me as we approached him, he said, "This man isn't a shit-eating farmer."

Lukka clasped his fist to his chest and replied, "He claims to be a herald from some High King, sir."

The commander looked me over. "My name is Arza. What's yours?"

"Orion," I said.

"You look more like a fighter than a herald."

I tapped the wristband on my left arm. "I carry a message from the High King of the Hatti to the High King of the Achaians, a message of peace and friendship."

Arza glanced at Lukka, then focused his deep brown eyes back on me. "The High King of the Hatti, eh? Well, your message isn't worth the clay it was written on. There is no High King of the Hatti. Not anymore. Old Hattusilis is dead. The great fortress of Hattusas was in flames the last time I saw it."

Poletes gasped. "The Hatti have fallen?"

"The great nobles of Hattusas fight among themselves," said Arza. "Hattusilis's son may be dead, we've heard rumors to that effect."

"Then what are you doing here?" I asked.

He snorted. "Surviving, herald. As best we can. Living off the land and fighting off other bands of soldiers and marauders who try to take what we have."

I looked around the village. Dirty black smoke stained the clear sky. Dead bodies lying on the bare ground drew clouds of flies.

"You're nothing but a band of marauders yourselves," I said.

Arza's eyes narrowed. "Harsh words from a *herald*." He sneered at the last word.

But my mind was racing ahead. "Would you care to join the service of the Achaian High King?" I asked.

He laughed. "I'll serve no barbarian king or anyone else. Arza's band serves itself! We go where we want to go and take what we want to take."

"Mighty warriors," I replied scornfully. "You burn villages and rape helpless women who have no soldiers to protect them. Very brave of you."

From the corner of my eye I saw Lukka pale and take half a step away from me. I sensed Poletes backing off too.

Arza wrapped his hand around the ivory-inlaid hilt of his sword. "You look like a soldier," he snarled. "Do you want to protect what's left of this village? Against me?"

Lukka said, "Sir, I should warn you—this man is a fighter such as I've never seen before. He serves Athene and . . ."

"The bitch goddess?" Arza laughed. "The one they claim to be a virgin? *My* god is Taru, the god of storm and lightning, and he'll conquer your dainty little virgin goddess every time! She won't be a virgin for long if she fights against Taru!"

He was trying to goad me into a fight. I shook my head and turned to walk away.

"Lukka," he commanded loudly. "Slit his cowardly throat."

Before the agonized Lukka could reply, I wheeled back to face Arza and said, "Do it yourself, mighty attacker of women."

He broke into a wide grin as he pulled his sword from its well-worn scabbard. "With pleasure, herald," he said.

I took out my sword, and Arza laughed again. "Bronze! You poor fool, I'll slice that toy in half with my iron."

As he advanced toward me, holding his sword in front of him, my senses went into overdrive again. Everything slowed to a dreamlike pace. I could see the rise and fall of his chest as he breathed, the trickle of a bead of perspiration forming on his brow and starting down his cheek. Lukka was standing like a statue, unable to decide whether he should try to stop his commander or join his attack against me. Poletes was wide-eyed, his mouth slightly open, his hands clutching the air at his sides.

Arza advanced a few steps, then retreated back to his chariot and, without taking his eyes from me, reached back and took up his shield with his left hand. I stayed where I was and let him fix the shield on his arm. He grinned at me again and, seeing I was not moving to attack him, he grabbed his iron helmet and pulled it on. It was polished to a brilliant gleam, and its flaps protected the sides of his face. I could see that his scar ran exactly along the edge of the iron flap.

He was a professional soldier and he would take any advantage I allowed him. For my part, I had no real desire to kill him. But if the only way to gain his respect was to best him in a fight, I was more than ready to do that.

He advanced on me confidently, crouching slightly, peering at me through the narrow gap between the rim of his helmet and the top of his shield. It bore a lightning flash symbol crudely painted on its stretched hide. I waited for him, watching. The shield covered most of his body when he crouched, making it difficult to see which way he intended to move. Still, I waited.

He feinted with the shield, jabbing it toward my face and simultaneously starting a sword cut at my midsection.

I parried his swing with my bronze blade, then slashed backhand and cracked the metal frame of his shield. But the blow snapped my sword in half.

With an exultant cry Arza flung his broken shield away and leaped at me. I could have spitted him easily on the jagged stump of my blade, but instead I stepped into him, grabbed his sword wrist in my left hand, and rapped him sharply on the head with the pommel of my broken sword.

He went to his knees, rolled over, and shook his head. I saw a nice dent in his polished helmet.

Arza got to his feet and lunged at me again. I dropped my sword, took his arm in both my hands, and twisted the weapon out of his hand.

With a snarl of rage he yanked his dagger from his belt and came at me again.

I backed away, open-handed. "I have no desire to kill you," I told him.

He bent down and scooped his sword from the dusty ground. By now more than a dozen of his troops had gathered around us, gaping.

"I'll kill you, herald, despite your tricks," he growled.

He came at me again, sword and dagger, slashing and cursing at me, spittle flying from his mouth. I danced away lightly, wondering how long this game could last.

"Stand and fight!" he screamed.

"Without a weapon?" I smiled as I said it.

He charged again and, instead of running, I ducked under and tripped him. He fell heavily.

But got to his feet, snarling, "I'll kill you!"

"You can't," I said.

"I will! You men—hold him fast!"

The soldiers hesitated just a moment, long enough for me to decide that if I did not kill this maddened animal, he would have me killed.

Before they could lay hands on me, I picked up the shattered stump of my bronze sword and advanced toward Arza. He grinned wickedly at me and lunged with his sword, ready to counter with the dagger once I tried to parry the sword thrust. Instead of parrying, I sidestepped his lunge and drove the jagged end of my blade into his chest just below the armpit.

Arza looked very surprised. His mouth dropped open, then filled with blood. For a moment I carried all his weight on my extended sword arm. I let go of the weapon and he dropped to the dusty ground, his hands still clutching his useless sword and dagger.

I looked toward Lukka. He gazed down at his fallen commander, then up to me. A word from him and the entire squad of soldiers would be on me.

Before he could speak, I shouted to the soldiers, "This man led you to little victories over farmers' villages. How would you like to join in the loot of a great city, filled with gold? Who will follow me to help conquer Troy?"

They raised their hands and cheered. All of them.

Chapter 14

THERE were forty-two men in the Hatti band, and I led them back across the Scamander and down toward the beach where the Achaians were camped—if they had not been wiped out in the meantime by Hector and his Trojans.

Lukka accepted me as their leader. He kept his hawklike face impassive, but I thought I saw a hint of awe at my fighting prowess glimmering in his dark eyes. The others went along with him. There was no great affection for the fallen Arza among them. He had been their commander when the civil strife had broken out among the various Hatti factions. Like professional soldiers everywhere, they had followed their commanding officer even though they thoroughly disliked him. As long as he kept them together, and ensured their survival by raiding helpless villages, they were willing to put up with his petty tyrannies and nasty disposition.

"We've been living like dogs," Lukka told me as we climbed across the wooded ridges that ran between the high road and the river. "Every man's hand is raised against every other's. There's no *order* in the land of the Hatti anymore, not since the old king died and his son was driven off by the nobles. Now they fight for the kingdom and the army is split into a thousand little bands like ours, without discipline, without respect, without any pay at all except what we can steal from farmers and villagers."

"When we get to the Achaian camp," I promised him, "King Odysseus will be happy to welcome you into his service."

"Under your command," Lukka said.

I glanced at him. He was completely serious. He took it for granted that the man who slew Arza would take command of the troop.

"Yes," I said. "Under my command."

He grinned wolfishly. "There's much gold in Troy, that I know. We guarded a tribute caravan from the Troad to Hattusas once. A lot of gold."

So we marched toward the plain of Ilios. I was now the leader of a unit of professional soldiers who dreamed of looting the gold of Troy. The army that Hector expected to come to Troy's rescue no longer existed; it had split into a thousand marauding bands, each intent on its own survival.

Lukka became my lieutenant automatically. He knew the men and I did not. He regarded me as little less than a god. It made me feel uneasy, but it was useful for the moment. He was a strong, honest professional soldier, a man of few words. Yet his hawk's eyes missed nothing, and the men respected him totally.

We slept in the same woods where Poletes and I had spent the previous night. I stretched out, sword and dagger on either side of me, and willed my mind to make contact with the gods. No, they are not gods, I reminded myself. Creators, yes. But not gods.

I closed my eyes and strained with every nerve and sinew in me to see them again, speak with them. Utterly in vain. All I got for my effort was a set of tension-stiffened muscles that made my back and neck ache horribly and kept me awake through most of the night.

The next morning we found a ford in the river, crossed it, and marched toward the sea.

It was well past noon before we saw the beetling walls of Troy, up on its bluff. Trojan tents no longer dotted the plain. Instead, the debris of battle littered the worn ground between the Achaian rampart and the walls of Troy. Broken chariots and tattered remains of tents were scattered everywhere. Black-clad women and half-naked slaves moved slowly, mournfully, among scores of bodies lying twisted and stripped of armor under the high sun. Vultures circled patiently above. Dark humps of dead horses lay here and there. The battle must have been ferocious, I told myself.

But the Achaian ships were still lined up along the beach, I saw, their black hulls intact, unburnt. Somehow, Agamemnon, Odysseus, and the others had survived Hector's onslaught.

Poletes stared at the carnage across the river with wide, tearful eyes. Lukka and the other Hatti soldiers seemed to be giving the area a professional evaluation.

"That is Troy," Lukka said, pointing, as we marched along the riverbank.

"That is Troy," I agreed.

He eyed the high walls appreciatively. "It won't be easy to breach those defenses."

"Can it be done at all?"

He smiled grimly. "If the great walls of Hattusas could be overthrown, that city can be taken."

We waited in the shade of the trees along the river's edge while Poletes and one of the Hatti soldiers rowed the leaky little reed boat across the current and beached it in the Achaian camp. My orders to Poletes were to report to Odysseus and no one else.

An hour passed. Then two. The sun glittered on the sea; the afternoon was hot and still. Finally I saw a dolphin-headed galley gliding toward us, its oars moving in smooth rhythm. We splashed out waist-deep in the cool water and clambered aboard the Ithacan warship. Lukka insisted that I go first. He brought up the rear.

Poletes was at the gunwale, reaching out his skinny arms to help me aboard. His scraggly bearded face was grim.

"What's the news?" I asked, dripping water onto the deck and the rowers.

"A great battle was fought yesterday," he said.

"That I can see."

He took me by the elbow and led me back toward the stern, away from the rowers. "Hector and his brothers broke through the defenses and into the camp. Still Achilles refused to fight. Patrokles put on his master's golden armor and led the Myrmidones in a counterattack. They drove the surprised Trojans out of the camp and back to the very walls of Troy."

"They must have thought it was Achilles," I muttered.

"Perhaps they did. A god filled Patrokles with battle frenzy. Everyone in the camp thought he was too soft for fighting, yet he drove the Trojans back to their own gates and slew dozens with his own hand."

I cocked an eyebrow at "dozens." War stories grow with each telling, and this one was already becoming exaggerated, scarcely twenty-four hours after it had happened.

"But then the gods turned against Patroklos," the old storyteller said mournfully. "Hector spitted him on his spear and stripped Achilles's golden armor from his dead body."

I felt my own face harden. The gods play their games, I thought. They let Patrokles have a moment of glory and then take their price for it.

"Now Achilles wails in his hut and covers his head with ashes. He swears a mighty vengeance against Hector and all of Troy."

"So he will fight," I said, wondering if one of those who opposed the Golden One had not arranged all this, manipulated Patrokles into his death as a way of making Achilles return to the battle.

"Tomorrow morning," Poletes told me, "Achilles will meet Hector in single combat. It has been arranged by the heralds. There will be no fighting until then."

Single combat between Hector and Achilles. Hector was much the bigger of the two, an experienced fighter, cool and intelligent even in battle. Achilles was no doubt faster, though smaller, and fueled on the kind of rage that drove men to impossible feats. Only one of them would walk away from the fight, I knew.

Even before our galley was beached I could hear the wailing and keening from the Myrmidones camp. I knew it was a matter of form, that Prince Achilles had ordered the women to mourn. But there were men's deep voices among the cries of the women. And a drum beating a slow, unhappy dirge. A huge bonfire blazed at that end of the camp, sending a sooty black smoke skyward.

"Achilles mourns his friend," Poletes said. But I could see that the excess of grief unnerved him slightly.

Yet despite the mourning rites among the Myrmidones, the rest of the camp was agog with the impending match between Achilles and Hector. There was almost a holiday mood among the men. They were placing bets, giving odds. They laughed and made jokes about it, as if it had nothing to do with blood and death. I realized that they were trying to drive away the dread and fear that they all felt. The lamentations from the Myrmidones's camp continued unabated. It sent shivers up my spine. But slowly it came to me that the others all felt that this battle between the two champions would settle the war, one way or the other. They thought that no matter which champion fell, the war would be over and the rest of them could finally go home.

Odysseus inspected the Hatti contingent as soon as they disembarked from his galley. Lukka drew them up in a double line, while I stood at their head, the throb of the funeral drum and the keening of the mourners hanging over us all like the chilling hand of death.

The King of Ithaca tried to ignore the noise. He smiled at me. "Well, Orion, you have brought your own army with you."

"My lord Odysseus," I replied, "like me, these men are eager to serve you. They are experienced soldiers, and can be of great help to you."

He nodded, eyeing the contingent carefully. "I will accept their service, Orion. But not before I speak with Agamemnon. It wouldn't do to make the High King jealous—or fearful."

"As you wish," I said. He knew the politics and personalities of his fellow Achaians much better than I. Odysseus was not called "the crafty" for nothing.

As we walked back to the boat on which Odysseus kept his own quarters, I explained to him that there was no Hatti army marching to the relief of Troy, telling him what Arza and Lukka had told me about the death of the old High King and the civil war that was tearing the Hatti empire to pieces.

Stroking his beard thoughtfully, Odysseus murmured, "I thought that the High King was losing his power when he agreed to allow Agamemnon to settle his quarrel against Priam. Always in the past the Hatti have protected Troy and marched against anyone who threatened the region."

I saw to it that my Hatti soldiers were fed and given tenting and bedding for the coming night. They sat in a circle around their own fire, not mixing with the Achaians. For their part, the Ithacans and others of the camp looked on the Hatti with no little awe. They especially ogled their uniform outfits of chain mail and tooled leather. No two Achaians dressed the same or carried the same equipment. To see forty-some men outfitted alike was a novelty to them.

To my surprise, the Achaians did not seem impressed or even interested in the iron swords that the Hatti carried. I myself bore the blade that Arza had carried; I had seen firsthand how much tougher the iron blade was than a bronze one.

As the sun was setting, turning the sea to a deep wine red, Lukka approached me. I was sitting apart from the men, taking my supper with Poletes by my side. Lukka stopped on the other side of our little cook fire, nervously fingering the straps of his harness, his face contorted into a deep scowl. I thought he had come to complain about the Myrmidones's lamentations; I couldn't blame him for that, even though there was nothing I could do about it.

There was no other chair for him to sit on, so I got to my feet and beckoned for him to come to me.

"My lord Orion," he began, "may I speak to you frankly?"

"Of course. Speak your mind, Lukka. I want no thoughts hidden away where they can cause misunderstandings between us."

He puffed out a pent-up sigh of relief. "Thank you, sir."

"What is it, then?"

"Well, sir . . . what kind of a siege is this?" He was almost indignant. "The army sits here in camp, eating and drinking, while the people in the city open their gates and go to gather food and firewood. I don't see any engines for battering down the gates or surmounting the city walls. This isn't a proper siege at all!"

I smiled at him. Patrokles's funeral lamentations had nothing to do with what was bothering him. He was a professional soldier, and the antics of amateurs irked him.

"Lukka," I said, "these Achaians are not very sophisticated in the arts of warfare. Tomorrow you will see two men fight each other from chariots, and that may well settle the whole issue of this war."

He shook his head. "Not likely. The Trojans won't let these barbarians inside their walls willingly. I don't care how many champions fall."

"You may be right," I agreed.

"Look now." He pointed at the city up on the bluff, bathed in reddish gold by the setting sun. "See that course of wall, the stretch where it is lower than the rest?"

It was the western side of the city, where the garrulous courtier had admitted that the defenses were weaker.

"My men can build siege towers and wheel them up to that part of the wall, so the Achaian warriors could step from their topmost platforms right onto the battlements."

"Wouldn't the Trojans try to destroy the towers as they approached their wall?"

"With what?" he sneered. "Spears? Arrows? Even if they shoot flaming arrows at them, we'll have them covered with wetted horsehides."

"But they'll be able to concentrate all their men at that one point and beat you off."

He scratched at his thick black beard. "Maybe so. Usually we try to attack two or three spots along a wall at the same time. Or create some other diversions that keep their forces busy elsewhere."

"It's a good idea," I said. "I'll speak to Odysseus about it. I'm surprised none of the Achaians have thought of it themselves."

Lukka made a sour face. "These aren't real soldiers, my lord. The kings and princelings fancy themselves great warriors, and maybe they are. But my own unit could beat five times their number of these people."

We spoke for a little while longer, and then he left me to see that his men were properly bedded in their new tents.

Poletes, who had sat quietly through our conversation, got to his feet. "That man is too greedy for victory," he said, in a whisper that was almost angry. "He wants to win everything, and leave nothing for the gods to decide."

"Men fight wars to win them, don't they?" I asked him.

"Men fight wars for glory, and spoils, and for tales to tell their grandchildren. A man should go into battle to prove his bravery, to face a champion and test his destiny. *He* wants to use tricks and machines to win his battles." Poletes spat on the sand to show how he felt about it.

"Yet you yourself have scorned these warriors and called them bloodthirsty fools," I reminded him.

"That they are! But at least they fight fairly, as men should fight."

I laughed. "Where I come from, old man, there is a saying, 'All is fair in love and war.'"

For once, Poletes had no answer. He grumbled to himself as I left him by the fire and sought out Odysseus.

In the musty tented quarters of the King of Ithaca I explained the possibilities of building siege towers.

"They can be put on wheels and pulled up to the walls?" This was a new idea to Odysseus.

"Yes, my lord."

"And these Hatti troops know how to build such machines?"

"Yes, they do."

In the flickering light of the lone copper lamp on his work table I could see Odysseus's eyes gleaming with the possibilities of it. Absently, he patted the thickly furred neck of the dog at his feet as he thought over the possibilities.

"Come," he said at last, "now is the moment to tell Agamemnon about this!"

The High King seemed half-asleep when we were ushered into his hut. Agamemnon sat drowsily in a camp chair, a jewel-encrusted wine goblet in his right hand. Apparently his shoulder had healed enough for him to bend his elbow. No one else was in the hut but a pair of women slaves, dark-eyed and silent in thin shifts that showed their bare arms and legs.

Odysseus sat facing the High King. I squatted on the floor at his side. We were offered wine. It was thick with spiced honey and barley meal.

"A tower that moves?" Agamemnon muttered after Odysseus had explained it to him twice. "Impossible! How could a stone tower . . ."

"It would be made of wood, son of Atreus. And covered with hides for protection."

Agamemnon looked down at me blearily and let his chin sink to his broad chest. The lamps cast long shadows across the room that made his heavy-browed face look sinister, even threatening.

"I had to return the captive Briseis to that young pup," he grumbled. "And hand him over a fortune of booty. Even with his lover slain by Hector the little snake refused to reenter the war unless his 'rightful' spoils were returned to him." The scorn he put on the word "rightful" could have etched steel.

"Son of Atreus," soothed Odysseus, "if this plan of mine works, we will sack Troy and gain so much treasure that even overweening Achilles will be happy."

Agamemnon said nothing. He waved his goblet slightly, and one of the slaves came to fill all three. Odysseus's was made of gold, like the High King's. Mine was wooden.

"Three more weeks," Agamemnon muttered. He slurped at his

wine, spilling some of it over his already stained tunic. "Three more weeks is what I need."

"Sire?"

Agamemnon let his goblet slip from his fingers and plonk onto the carpeted ground. He leaned forward, a sly grin on his fleshy face.

"In three more weeks my ships will bring the grain harvest from the Sea of Black Waters through the Hellespont to Mycenae. And neither Priam nor Hector will be able to stop them."

Odysseus made a silent little "oh." I saw that Agamemnon was no fool. If he could not conquer Troy, he would at least get his ships through the straits and back again, loaded with grain, before breaking off the siege. And if the Achaians had to sail away from Troy without winning their war, at least Agamemnon would have the year's grain supply in his own city of Mycenae, ready to use it or sell it to his neighbors as he saw fit.

Odysseus had the reputation of being cunning, but I realized that the King of Ithaca was merely careful, a man who considered all the possibilities before he made his move. Agamemnon was the crafty one: sly, selfish, and grasping.

Recovering quickly from his surprise, Odysseus said, "But now we have the chance of destroying Troy altogether. Not only will we have the loot of the city, and its women, but you will have clear sailing through the Hellespont for all the years of your kingship!"

Agamemnon slumped back on his chair. "A good thought, son of Laertes. A good thought. I will consider it and call a council to decide upon it. After tomorrow's match."

With a nod, Odysseus said, "Yes, after we see whether Achilles remains among us or dies on Hector's spear."

Agamemnon smiled broadly.

Chapter 15

I slept fitfully that night.

I had a tent of my own now, as befits a commander of soldiers. And I had expected the heavy honeyed wine to act as a drug on my mind. But it did not. I tossed on my pallet of straw and every time I managed to doze off my inner vision filled with the faces of the Creators. They were arguing, bickering among themselves, placing wagers about who would win the coming battle.

Then I saw Athene, my beloved, standing silent and alone, far removed from the laughing uncaring gods who toyed with men's lives. She regarded me gravely, without a smile, without a sound. As still as a statue made of frozen flesh. She gazed into my eyes for endless moments, as if she were trying to impart some knowledge to me telepathically.

"You are dead," I said to her.

Instead of her voice, I heard Poletes's scratchy, rasping words, "As long as *you* revere Athene, and serve her, she is not dead."

Fine sentiment, I thought. But that does not allow me to hold her in my arms, to feel her warmth and her love.

Instead, I told myself, I will take the Golden One in these hands and crush the life out of him. Just as I once . . .

I remembered something. Someone. A dark, brooding man, a hulking gray-skinned shape that I had hunted down through the centuries and the millennia. Ahriman! I remembered him, his harsh, tortured, whispering voice.

I heard him now. "You fool," he whispered. "You seek for strength and find only weakness."

I thought I woke up. I thought I propped myself on an elbow and passed a weary hand over my cobwebbed eyes. But I heard, as distinctly as if he had been standing next to me, the clear cold voice of the Golden One: "Stop fighting against me, Orion. If a goddess can die, think how easily I can send one of my own creations to the final destruction."

I sat bolt upright and saw a gleam of gold seeping through the flaps of my tent. Scrambling outside, naked except for the sword I grabbed, I saw that it was only the morning sun starting the new day.

The morning dawned clear and bright and windy.

Although the single combat between Achilles and Hector was what everyone looked forward to, still the whole army prepared to march out onto the plain. Partly they went out because a single combat can degenerate into a general melee easily enough. Mostly they went out to get a close look at the fight.

I instructed Lukka to keep his men out of the fighting. "This will not be your kind of battle," I said. "There's no point in risking the men."

"We could be starting to fell the trees we need for the siege towers," he said. "I saw enough good ones across the river for it."

"Wait until this combat is over," I said. "Stand by the gate to the rampart here and be prepared to defend it from the Trojans if necessary."

He clasped his fist to his breast in acknowledgment.

Virtually the entire Achaian force drew itself up, rank upon rank, on the windswept plain before the camp. By the walls of the city the Trojans were drawing themselves up likewise, chariots in front, foot soldiers behind them, swirls of dust blowing into the cloudless sky. I could see pennants fluttering along the battlements on the city walls, and even imagined glimpsing Helen's golden bright hair on the tallest tower of Troy.

Odysseus had ordered me to stand at the left side of his chariot. "Protect my driver if we enter the fray," he said. And he saw to it that I was outfitted with one of the figure-eight body shields that extended from chin to ankle. It weighed heavily on my left arm, but the weight was almost a comfort. Five plies of hides stretched across a thin wooden frame and bossed with bronze studs, the shield would stop almost anything except a spear driven with the momentum of a galloping chariot behind it.

Poletes was up on the rampart with the slaves and *thetes,* straining his old eyes for a view of the fight. He would interrogate me for hours this night, I knew, dragging every detail of what I had seen out of my memory. Then I thought, if either of us is still alive after today's fighting.

As I stood on the windy plain, squinting against the bright sun, a roar went up from the Trojans. I saw Hector's chariot, pulled by four magnificent white horses, kicking up a cloud of dust as it sped from the Scaean gate and drove toward the head of the arrayed ranks of soldiery. Hector stood tall and proud, his great shield at his side, four huge spears in their holder, pointing heavenward.

For many minutes nothing more happened. Muttering started among the Achaian foot soldiers. I glanced up at Odysseus, who merely smiled tolerantly. Achilles was behaving like a self-appointed star, as usual, making everyone anxious for his appearance. I thought that it would have been good psychology on any opponent except Hector. That man will use the time to study every rock and bump on the field, I said to myself. He is no child to be frightened by waiting.

Finally an exultant roar sprang up among the Achaians. Turning, I saw four snorting, spirited, matched midnight-black horses, heads tossing, groomed so perfectly that they seemed to glow, pounding across the earthen ramp that cut across our trench. Achilles's chariot was inlaid with ebony and ivory, and his armor—only his second-best since Hector had stripped Patrokles's dead body—gleamed with burnished gold.

With his plumed helmet on, there was little of Achilles's face to be seen. But as his chariot swept past me I saw that his mouth was a grim tight line and his eyes burned like furnaces.

He did not stop for the usual prebattle formalities. He did not even slow down. His charioteer cracked his whip over the black horses' ears and they plunged forward at top speed as Achilles took a spear in his right hand and screamed loud enough to echo off the walls of Troy: "PATROKLES! PA . . . TRO . . . KLES!"

His chariot aimed straight for Hector's. The Trojan driver, startled, whipped his horses into motion and Hector hefted one of his spears.

The chariots pounded toward each other, and both warriors cast their spears simultaneously. Achilles's struck Hector's shield and staggered him. He almost tumbled out of the chariot, but he regained his balance and reached for another spear. Hector's shaft passed between Achilles and his charioteer, splintering the wooden floor of the chariot.

A chill went through me. Achilles had not raised his shield when Hector's spear drove toward him. He had not even flinched as the missile passed close enough to shave his young beard. Either he did not care what happened to him or he was mad enough to believe himself invulnerable.

The chariots swung past each other and again the two champions hurled spears. Hector's bounced off the bronze shoulder of Achilles's armor. Again the man made no move to protect himself. His own spear caught Hector's charioteer in the face. With an awful shriek he fell over backward, both hands pawing at the shaft that had turned his face into a bloody shambles.

The Achaians shouted and surged a few steps forward. Hector, knowing he could not control his horses and fight at the same time, jumped lightly from his chariot, two spears gripped in his left hand. The horses raced on, their reins slack, heading back for the walls of the city.

Achilles had the advantage now. His chariot drove around Hector, circling the stranded warrior again and again, seeking an advantage, a momentary dropping of his guard. But Hector held his shield firmly before him, crouching slightly, and pivoted smoothly to present nothing more to Achilles than a bronze plumed helmet, the body-length shield, and the greaves that protected his ankles.

Achilles cast another spear at him, but it went slightly wide. Hector remained in place, or seemed to. I noticed that each time he wheeled to keep his front to Achilles's chariot, he edged a step or two closer to his own ranks.

Achilles must have noticed this, finally, and jumped out of his chariot. A great gusting sigh of expectation went through both armies. The two champions were going to face each other on foot, at spear's length.

Hector advanced confidently toward the smaller Achaian. He spoke to Achilles, who spat out a reply. They were too far away for me to make out their words.

Then Achilles did something that wrenched a great moaning gasp from the Achaians. He threw his shield down clattering on the bare ground and faced Hector with nothing but his body armor and his spear.

The fool! I thought. He must actually believe that he's invulnerable. Achilles gripped his spear in both hands and faced Hector without a shield.

Dropping the shorter of his two spears, Hector drove straight at Achilles. He had the advantage of size and strength, and of experience, and he knew it. Achilles, smaller, faster, seemed to be absolutely crazy. He did not try to parry Hector's spear thrust or run out of its reach. Instead he dodged this way and that, avoiding Hector's spear by scant inches, keeping his own spear point aimed straight at Hector's eyes.

It is a truth of all kinds of hand-to-hand combat that you cannot attack and defend yourself at the same time. The successful fighter can switch from attack to defense and back again at the flick of an eye. Hector knew this, and his obvious aim was to keep the shieldless Achilles on the defensive. But Achilles refused to defend himself, except for dodging Hector's thrusts. I began to see method in his madness; Achilles's great advantages were speed and daring. The heavy shield would have slowed him.

He gave ground, and Hector moved steadily forward, but even there I soon saw that Achilles was edging around, moving to stand between Hector and the Trojan ranks, maneuvering Hector closer and closer to our own side.

I saw the look on Achilles's face as they sweated and grunted beneath the high sun. He was smiling. Like a little boy who enjoys pulling the wings off flies, like a man who was happily looking forward to driving his spear through the chest of his enemy, like a madman intent on murder. I had seen that smile before. On the lips of the Golden One.

Hector realized that he was being maneuvered. He changed his tactics and tried to engage Achilles's spear, knowing that his superior strength could force his enemy's point down, and then he could drive his own bronze spearhead into Achilles's unguarded body.

Achilles feinted and Hector followed the motion for a fraction of an instant. It was enough. Launching himself completely off his feet like a distance jumper, Achilles drove his spear with all the strength in both his arms into Hector's body. The point struck Hector's bronze breastplate; I could hear the screech as it slid up along the armor, unable to penetrate, and then caught under Hector's chin.

The impact knocked Hector backward but not off his feet. For an instant the two champions stood locked together, Achilles ramming the spear upward with both his hands white-knuckled against its haft, his eyes blazing hatred and bloodlust, his lips pulled back in a feral snarl. Hector's arms, one holding his long spear, the other with the great shield strapped to it, slowly folded forward, as if embracing his killer. The spear point went deeper into his throat, up through his jaw, and buried itself in the base of his brain.

Hector went limp, hanging on Achilles's spear point. Achilles wrenched it free and the Trojan prince's dead body slumped to the dusty ground.

"For Patrokles!" Achilles shouted, holding his bloodied spear aloft.

A triumphant roar went up from our ranks, while the Trojans seemed frozen in gasping horror.

Achilles threw down his bloody spear and pulled his sword from its scabbard. He hacked at Hector's neck once, twice, three times. He wanted the severed head as a trophy.

The Trojans screamed and charged at him. Without a word of command we charged too. In the span of a heartbeat the single combat turned into a general brawling battle.

I raced behind Odysseus's chariot, thinking that the very men who had hoped this fight between the champions would end the war were now racing into battle themselves, unthinking, uncaring, like murderous lemmings responding to some mysterious urge deep inside them.

"You enjoy fighting," I remembered the Golden One telling me once, long ago. "I built that instinct for killing into my creatures."

And then there was no time for thought. My sword was in my hand and enemies were charging at me, blood and murder in their eyes. Like Achilles, I slid my left arm free of the cumbersome shield. I did not need it; my senses went into overdrive and the world around me became a slow-motion dream.

My iron sword served me well. Bronze blades chipped or broke against it. Its sharp edge slashed through bronze armor. I caught up with Odysseus's chariot. He and several other mounted warriors had formed a screen over the body of Hector as Achilles and his Myrmidones stripped the corpse down to the skin. I saw the brave prince's severed head bobbing on a spear, and turned away in disgust. Then someone tied his ankles to a chariot's tail and tried to fight through the growing melee and make his way with the body back toward the Achaian camp.

Instead of being dispirited by these barbarities, the Trojans seemed infuriated. They fought with a rage born of desecration and battled fiercely to recover Hector's body before it could be dragged back behind our rampart.

While this struggle grew in fury, I realized that none of the Trojans were protecting their line of retreat, or even thinking about guarding the gate from which they had left the city.

I rushed to Odysseus's chariot and shouted over the cursing and clanging of the battle, "The gate! They've left the gate unprotected!"

Odysseus's eyes gleamed. He looked up toward the city walls, then back at me. He nodded once.

"To the gate!" he called in a voice that roared across the plain. "To the gate before they can close it!"

Screaming his eerie battle cry, Odysseus fought his way clear of the struggle around Hector's corpse, followed by two more chariots. I ran ahead, slashing my way clear until there was nothing between me and the walls of Troy but empty bare ground.

"To the gate!" I heard behind me, and a chariot clattered past, its horses leaning hard into their harnesses, nostrils blowing wide, eyes white and bulging.

Within seconds Hector's corpse was forgotten. The battle had turned into a race for the Scaean gate. Odysseus led the Achaians who were trying to get there before the Trojans could close it. The Trojan army streamed toward it so that they could get inside the protection of the city walls before the gate was closed and they were cut off.

Achilles, back in his chariot, was cutting a bloody path through the Trojans, hacking with his sword until the foot soldiers and chariot-riding noblemen alike gave him a wide berth. Then he snatched the whip from his driver's hands and lashed his horses into a frenzied gallop toward the city gate.

I saw Odysseus fling a spear into the chest of a Trojan guarding the gate. More Trojans appeared at the open gateway, graybeards and young boys armed with light throwing javelins and swords. From up on the battlements that flanked the gate on both sides others were firing arrows and hurling stones. Odysseus was forced to back away.

But not Achilles. He drove straight for the gate, oblivious to the bombardment from above. The rear guard scattered before him, ducking behind the massive wooden doors. From behind, some- one started pushing them closed. Seeing that the gap between the doors was too small for his chariot to pass through, Achilles jumped to the ground, his bloodstained great spear in his hand, and charged at the gate. He met a hedgehog of spear points but dived at them headlong, jabbing and slashing two-handed with his own spear.

Odysseus and another chariot-mounted warrior, whom I later learned was Diomedes, rushed up to help him, their great shields strapped on their backs, protecting them from neck to heel from the stones and arrows being aimed at them from above. I saw the main mass of the Trojan troops not far behind us, a wild tangled melee battling with the rest of the Achaians, fighting its way to the protection of the city's walls.

I pushed my way between Achilles and Odysseus, hacking with my sword at the spears sticking out from the gap between the doors. I grabbed one spear with my left hand and pulled it out of the hands of the frightened boy who had been holding it. Flinging it to the ground, I reached for another.

Somewhere deep inside my mind I heard myself asking why I should be killing Trojans. They are men, human beings, creations of the Golden One just as I am. What they do they do because the Golden One drives them, manipulates them, just as he drives and manipulates me.

But I answered myself: All men die, and some of us die many times over. The goal of life is death, and as long as these creatures serve the Golden One, even unknowingly, unwittingly, then they are my enemies. Just as they would kill me, I will kill them.

And I did. I pulled on the spear in my left hand, dragging the graybeard holding it, until he was within reach of my sword. He saw the blow coming and released the spear, raising his arms over his head and screaming, as if that would protect him. My blade bit through both his arms and buried itself in his skull.

A teenager thrust his spear at me while I worked my sword free. I dodged it, wrenched the blade from the dead man's bloody head, and swung it at the youth. But there was little purpose in my swing, except to scare him off. He backed away, but then came forward again. I did not give him a second chance.

The struggle at the gate seemed to go on for an hour, although common sense tells me it took only a few minutes. The rest of the Trojans came up, still battling furiously with the main body of the Achaians. Chariots and foot soldiers hacked and slashed and cursed and shouted and screamed their final cries in that narrow passage between the walls that flanked the Scaean gate. Dust and blood and arrows and stones filled the deadly air. The Trojans were fighting for their lives, desperately trying to get inside the gate, just as our own Achaians had been trying to escape from Hector's spear a few days earlier.

Despite our efforts, the Trojans still held the gate ajar and kept us from entering it. Only a few determined men were needed to keep an army at bay, and the Trojan rear guard at the gate had the determination born of sheer desperation. They knew that once we forced that gate their city was finished; their lives, their families, their homes would be wiped out. So they held us at bay, new men and boys taking the place of those we killed, while the main body of their army began to slip through the open doors, fighting as they retreated to safety.

Then I saw the blow that ended the battle. Everything still seemed to move in slow-motion for me. Arrows flew through the air so lazily that I thought I could snatch one in my bare hand. I could tell where warriors were going to send their next thrust by watching their eyes and the muscles bunching and rippling beneath their skin.

Still fighting at the narrowing entrance to the gate, I had to turn almost ninety degrees to deal with the Trojan warriors who were battling their way to the doors in their effort to reach safety. I saw Achilles, his eyes burning with bloodlust, his mouth open with wild laughter, hacking at any Trojan who dared to come within arm's length. Up on the battlements a handsome man with long flowing golden hair leaned out with a bow in his hands and fired an arrow, fledged with gray hawk feathers, toward Achilles's unprotected back.

As if in a dream, a nightmare, I shouted a warning that was

drowned out in the cursing, howling uproar of the battle. I pushed past a half-dozen furiously battling men and reached for Achilles as the arrow streaked unerringly to its target. I managed to get a hand on his shoulder and push him out of its way.

Almost.

The arrow struck him on the back of his left leg, slightly above the heel. Achilles went down with a high-pitched scream of pain.

Chapter 16

FOR an instant the world seemed to stop.

Achilles, the seemingly invulnerable champion, was down in the dust, writhing in agony, an arrow jutting out from the back of his left ankle.

I stood over him and took off the head of the first Trojan who came at him with a single swipe of my sword. Odysseus and Diomedes joined me and suddenly the battle had changed its entire purpose and direction. We were no longer trying to force the Scaean gate; we were fighting to keep Achilles alive and get him back to our camp.

Slowly we withdrew, and in truth, after a few moments the Trojans seemed glad enough to let us go. They streamed back inside their gate and swung its massive doors shut. I picked Achilles up in my arms while Odysseus and the others formed a guard around us and we headed back to the camp.

For all his ferocity and strength, he was as light as a child. His Myrmidones surrounded us, staring at their wounded prince with round, shocked eyes. Achilles's unhandsome face was bathed with sweat, but he kept his lips clamped together in a painful white line as I carried him past the huge windblown oak just beyond the gate.

"I was offered a choice," he muttered, behind teeth clenched with pain, "between long life and glory. I chose glory."

"It's not a serious wound," I said.

"The gods will decide how serious it is," he replied, in a voice so faint I hardly heard him.

Halfway across the bloody plain six men carrying a stretcher of thongs laced across a wooden frame met us, and I laid Achilles on it as gently as I could. He grimaced, but did not cry out or complain.

Odysseus put a heavy hand on my shoulder. "You saved his life."

"You saw?"

"I did. The arrow was meant for his heart."

"How bad a wound do you think it is?"

"Not too bad," said Odysseus. "But he will be out of action for many days."

We trudged across the dusty plain side by side. The wind was coming in off the water again, blowing dust in our faces, forcing us to squint as we walked toward the camp. Every muscle in my body ached. Blood was crusted on my sword arm, my legs, spattered across my tunic.

"You fought very well," Odysseus said. "For a few moments there I thought we would force the gate and enter the city at last."

I shook my head wearily. "We can't force a gate that is defended. It's too easy for the Trojans to hold the narrow opening."

Odysseus nodded agreement. "Do you think your Hatti troops can really build a machine that will allow us to scale their walls?"

"They claim they have done it before, at Ugarit and elsewhere."

"Ugarit," Odysseus repeated. He seemed impressed. "I will speak with Agamemnon and the council. Until Achilles rejoins us, we have no hope of storming one of their gates."

"And little hope even with Achilles," I said.

He looked at me sternly, but said nothing more.

Poletes was literally jumping up and down on his knobby legs when I returned to the camp.

"What a day!" he kept repeating. "What a day!"

As usual, he milked me for every last detail of the fighting. He had been watching from the top of the rampart, of course, but the mad melee at the gate was too far and too confused for him to make out.

"And what did Odysseus say at that point?" he would ask. "I saw Diomedes and Menalaos riding side by side toward the gate; which of them got there first?"

He set out a feast of thick barley soup, roast lamb and onions,

flat bread still hot from the clay oven, and a flagon of unadulter-
ated wine. And he kept me talking with every bite.

I ate, and reported to the storyteller, as the sun dipped below
the western sea's edge and the island mountaintops turned gold,
then purple, and then faded into darkness. The first star gleamed
in the cloudless violet sky, so beautiful that I understood why
every culture named it after its love goddess.

There was no end of questions from Poletes, so finally I sent him
to see what he could learn for himself of Achilles's condition.
Partly it was to get rid of his pestering, partly to soothe a strange
uneasiness that bubbled inside me. Achilles is doomed, a voice in
my head warned me. He will not outlive Hector by many hours.

I tried to dismiss it as nonsense, battle fatigue, sheer nerves. Yet
I sent Poletes to find out how bad his wound really was.

"And find Lukka and send him to me," I called to his retreating
back.

The Hatti officer looked grimly amused when he came to my fire
and saluted by clenching his fist against his breast.

"Did you see the battle?" I asked.

"Some of it."

"What do you think?"

He made no attempt to hide his contempt. "They're like a
bunch of overgrown boys tussling in a town square."

"The blood is real," I said.

"Yes, I know. But they'll never take a fortified city by storming
defended gates."

I agreed.

"There are enough good trees on the other side of the river to
build six siege towers, maybe more," Lukka said.

"Start building one. Once the High King sees that it can be
done, I'm sure he'll grasp the possibilities."

"I'll start the men at first light."

"Good."

"Sleep well, sir."

I almost gave a bitter laugh. Sleep well, indeed. But I controlled
myself enough to reply, "And good sleep to you, Lukka."

Poletes came back soon after, his face solemn in the dying light
of our fire, his gray eyes sad.

"What's the news?" I demanded as he sank to the ground at my
feet.

"My lord Achilles is finished as a warrior," said Poletes. "The arrow has cut the tendon in the back of his heel. He will never walk again without a crutch."

I felt my mouth tighten grimly.

Poletes reached for the wine, hesitated, and cast me a questioning glance. I nodded. He poured himself a heavy draft and gulped at it.

"Achilles is crippled," I said.

Wiping his mouth with the back of his hand, Poletes sighed. "Well, he can live a long life back in Phthia. Once his father dies he will be king, and probably rule over all of Thessaly. That's not so bad, I think."

I nodded agreement, but I wondered how Achilles would take to the prospect of a long life as a cripple.

As if in answer to my thoughts, a loud wail sprang up from the Myrmidones's end of the camp. I jumped to my feet. Poletes got up more slowly.

"My lord Achilles!" a voice cried out. "My lord Achilles is dead!"

I glanced at Poletes.

"Poison on the arrowhead?" he guessed.

I threw down the wine cup and started off for the Myrmidones. All the camp seemed to be rushing in the same direction. I saw Odysseus's broad back, and huge Ajax outstriding everyone with his long legs.

Spear-wielding Myrmidones guards held back the crowd at the edge of their camp area, allowing only the nobles to pass them. I pushed up alongside Odysseus and went past the guards with him. Menalaos, Diomedes, Nestor, and almost every one of the Achaian leaders were gathering in front of Achilles's hut.

All but Agamemnon, I saw.

We went inside, past weeping soldiers and women tearing their hair and scratching their faces as they screamed their lamentations.

Achilles's couch, up on a slightly raised platform at the far end of the hut, had turned into a bier. The young warrior lay on it, left leg swathed in oil-soaked bandages, dagger still gripped in his right hand, a jagged red slash from just under his left ear to halfway across his windpipe still dripping bright red blood.

His eyes stared sightlessly at the mud-chinked planks of the ceiling. His mouth was open in a rictus that might have been a final smile or a grimace of pain.

Odysseus turned to me. "Start your men building the siege tower."

I nodded.

Chapter 17

O DYSSEUS and the other leaders headed for Agamemnon's hut for a council of war. I went back to my own tent. The camp was wild with the news: Achilles dead by his own hand. No, it was a poisoned arrow. No, a Trojan spy had done it. No, the god Apollo had slain him personally in vengeance for killing Hector and then despoiling his body.

The god Apollo.

I crawled into my tent and stretched out on the straw pallet. Lacing my fingers behind my head, I thought that for once I *wanted* to sleep, I wanted to go into that other existence and meet the Creators again. I had things to tell them, questions to ask, answers to demand.

But how could I pass through to their dimension? The Golden One had brought me to them. I could not do it myself.

Or could I? Closing my eyes, I cast my thoughts back to the "dreams" I had gone through before. I slowed their moments down to ultra slow-motion in my mind, stretching each second into hours, peering deeper and deeper into the scene until I could almost visualize the individual atoms that made up our bodies and see them scintillating and vibrating in their eternal dance of energy.

A pattern. I sought a pattern. There must be some arrangement of energies, some alignment of particles, that forms a gate between one world and the other. They are linked, I knew, part of what the

Golden One called a continuum. Where is the link? How does the gate operate?

Outside my little tent, I knew, insects buzzed and the stars turned on their spheres. The moon rose and climbed up the night sky. Midnight came and went. Still I lay there as in a trance, my eyes closed, my vision focused on the times when the Golden One had pulled me through the gate that linked his world with mine.

I saw a pattern. I replayed each moment when the Golden One had summoned me before him, and saw the same pattern of energies arrange themselves in the atoms around me. I visualized the pattern, froze it in my memory, and then poured every gram of mental energy I had into that image. I felt perspiration trickling across my brow, my chest, my arms and legs. Still I concentrated until it felt as if my brain was on fire.

I will not stop, I told myself. I will break through or kill myself. There is no third way.

A flash of cryogenic cold swept through me and then, with the abruptness of a light being switched on, I felt a gentle warming glow.

I opened my eyes and saw myself standing in the middle of a circle of the same gods and goddesses I had met before. But this time I was on their level, in their midst. And they looked shocked.

"How dare you!"

"Who summoned you?"

"You have no right to intrude here!"

I grinned at their surprise. They were truly splendid, robed and gowned in rich fabrics and glittering metallics. I had on nothing except my leather kilt, I realized.

"The insolence of this creature!" said one of the women.

I searched their faces for the Golden One. He pushed past two other men and confronted me.

"How did you get here?" he demanded.

"You showed me the way."

Anger flared in his gold-flecked eyes. But the older, bearded one I thought of as Zeus stepped forward to stand beside him.

"You show remarkable abilities, Orion," he said to me. Then, turning to the Golden One, "You should be congratulated for making him so talented."

I thought I saw a trace of an ironic smile on Zeus's bearded face. The Golden One bowed his head slightly in acknowledgment.

"Very well, Orion," he said, "so you've found your way here. To what purpose? What do you want?"

"I want to know if you have decided to make Troy win this war or not."

They glanced back and forth at one another without answering.

"That's not for you to know," said the Golden One.

I looked around at all their faces, so flawlessly beautiful, so unable to hide their inner feelings.

"By that," I said, "I take it that you are still arguing among yourselves about what the outcome should be. Good! The Achaians will attack Troy one more time. And this time they will take the city and burn it to the ground."

"Impossible!" snapped the Golden One. "I won't permit it."

"You think that by killing Achilles you've ruined any chance the Achaians had of winning. Well, you're wrong. We'll win. And on our next attack."

"I'll destroy you!" he raged.

I regarded him calmly. Strangely enough, I actually felt serene within myself. Not a trace of fear.

"You can destroy me, certainly," I said. "But I have learned something about you self-styled gods and goddesses. You cannot destroy all of your creatures. You can influence us, manipulate us, but you haven't the power to destroy us, one and all. You may have created us, but now we exist and act on our own. We are beyond your control—not totally, I know, but we have much more freedom of action than you like to admit."

Zeus said softly, like the warning rumble of distant thunder, "Be careful, Orion. You are tempting a terrible wrath."

"Your powers are limited," I insisted. And suddenly I understood why. "You can't destroy us! If you did, you would be destroying yourselves! *You* exist only as long as your creatures exist. Our destinies are linked throughout time."

One of the goddesses, a cruel smile on her beautiful lips, stepped toward me. "You flatter yourself, arrogant creature. You can be destroyed utterly, and very painfully, too."

The Golden One agreed. "We don't have to destroy all of you creatures. Merely striking a city with plague or sending a devastating earthquake is usually enough to get what we want from you pitiful little worms."

The goddess reminded me of what the Achaians had said of

Hera, the wife of Zeus: beautiful, wily, and a relentless, implacable enemy.

"Personally, I favor the Achaians," she said, tracing a fingernail down my bare chest hard enough to draw blood. "But if your conceited interference is what we have to look forward to, I will gladly switch my loyalty to agree with our Apollo, here."

The Golden One took her hand and kissed it. "You see, Orion," he said to me, "you are dealing with forces far beyond your scope. Perhaps it would be better if I eliminated you now, once and for all."

"As you eliminated the one called Athene?" I snarled.

"More insolence!"

"Destroy him now and be done with it," said one of the other males.

The Golden One nodded, a half-reluctant smile on his lips. "I'm afraid you've outlived your usefulness, Orion."

"Leave him alone."

The words were spoken in a hissing, rasping whisper, but they froze all the gods and goddesses ringed around me.

They stepped aside to make room for a burly, massive figure who walked slowly toward me. It was as if they were afraid to touch him, afraid that his powerful arms would crush them if he merely reached out. His shoulders were rounded, but broad and thick with muscle. His body was heavy and deep, his legs shorter than I would have expected, but equally massive and powerful. His face was wide, with eyes that burned red beneath thick brows.

Unlike the others in their splendid robes, he wore a black leather vest and knee-length kilt of forest green. His skin was gray, the hair of his head black and pulled straight back. Despite his slightly bent posture he loomed over me and all the others there.

He came straight up to me, glowering before me like a smoldering volcano.

"Do you remember me?" His voice was a harsh, labored whisper.

"Ahriman," I said, awed by his presence.

He closed his eyes for a moment. Then, "We have been enemies for long, long ages, Orion. Do you remember that?"

I looked deep into those red burning eyes and saw pain and hatred and a hunt that spanned fifty thousand years. I saw a battle in the snow and ice of a bygone era, and a struggle between us in other places, other times.

"It's . . . all confused," I said to him.

"Go back to your world, Orion," said Ahriman. "Once you did me a good turn and now I repay the debt. Go back to your world and don't tempt your destiny any further."

"I'll go back to my world," I said. "And I'll help the Achaians to conquer Troy."

The gods and goddesses remained silent, although I could feel the anger radiating from the Golden One.

Chapter 18

I awoke with the first light of day, as one of the camp's roosters raised his raucous cry of morning. As I went to pull my gray linen tunic over my head, I noticed the long thin slice of a cut oozing blood down my chest. I willed the capillaries to clamp themselves down and the bleeding stopped.

So the physical body is actually transported to the other realm, I said to myself. It's not merely a trick of the mind, a projection of one's mentality. The body moves from one universe to the other, as well.

Lukka and his men were already heading off toward the river to cut down the trees from which they would build our siege tower. I spoke briefly with him before he left, then went to Odysseus's quarters, up on his boat, to learn what had transpired in the council meeting.

The Trojans had sent a delegation to ask for the return of Hector's dismembered body. Try as they might to keep Achilles's death a secret, the Achaians were unable to prevent the Trojan emissaries from finding out the news: The whole camp was buzzing with it. The council met with the Trojan delegation, and after some debate agreed to return Hector's body, and suggested a two-day truce in which both sides could properly honor their slain.

Once the Trojans had departed with the corpse of their prince, Agamemnon told the council about the siege tower. They swiftly decided to use the two days of truce to build the machine in secret.

I spent those two days with my Hatti troops, on the far side of the Scamander river, screened from Trojan eyes by the riverbank's line of trees and shrubbery. Odysseus, who above all the Achaians appreciated the value of scouting and intelligence-gathering, spread a number of his best men along the riverbank to prevent any stray Trojan scouts from getting near us. I hoped that our hammering and sawing, which I was certain the Trojans could hear when the wind blew inland, would be taken as a shipbuilding job and nothing more.

We commandeered dozens of slaves and *thetes* to do the dogwork of hewing trees and carrying loads. Lukka was a born engineer, and directed the construction with dour efficiency. The tower took shape swiftly, and on the evening of the last day of truce Agamemnon, Nestor, and the other leaders came across the river to inspect our work.

We had built it horizontally, laying it along the ground, partly because it was easier to do that way but mainly to keep it hidden behind the tree line. Once it got dark enough, I had several dozen slaves and *thetes* haul on ropes to pull it up into its true vertical position.

Agamemnon peered up at it. "It's not as tall as the city walls," he complained.

While Lukka and his men had been building, I had been planning how best to use the tower. We had time only for one of them, if we were to strike as soon as the truce ended. So we needed to strike where it would do us the most good.

"It is tall enough, my lord king," I replied, "to top the western wall. That is the weakest section. Even the Trojans admit that that section of their walls was not built by Apollo and Poseidon."

Nestor bobbed his white beard. "A wise choice, young man. Never defy the gods, it will only bring you to grief. Even if you seem to succeed at first, the gods will soon bring you low because of your hubris. Look at poor Achilles, so full of pride. Yet a lowly arrow wound has been his downfall."

As soon as Nestor took a breath, I rushed to continue, "I have been inside the city. I know its layout. The west wall is on the higher side of the bluff. Once we get past that wall we will be on the high ground, and very close to the palace and temple."

Odysseus agreed. "I too have served as an emissary, if you recall, and I studied the city's streets and buildings carefully.

Orion is right. If we broke through the Scaean gate, for example, we would still have to fight through the streets, uphill every step of the way. Breaking in over the west wall is better."

"Can we get this thing up the hill to the wall there?" Agamemnon asked.

"The slope is not as steep at the west wall as it is to the north and east," I said. "The southern side is the easiest, where the Scaean and Dardanian gates are located. But it's also the most heavily defended, with the highest walls and tall watchtowers alongside each gate."

"I know that!" Agamemnon snapped. He poked around the wooden framework, obviously suspicious of what was to him a new idea.

Before he could ask, I said, "It would be best to roll it across the plain tonight, after the moon goes down. There should be a fog coming in from the sea. We can float it across the river on the raft we've built and roll it over the plain on its back, so that the mist will conceal us from any Trojan watchmen on the walls. Then we raise it . . ."

Agamemnon cut me off with a peevish wave of his hand. "Odysseus, are you willing to lead this . . . this maneuver?"

"I am, son of Atreus. I plan to be the first man to step onto the battlements of Troy."

"Very well then," said the High King. "I don't think·this will work. But if you're prepared to try it, then try it. I'll have the rest of the army ready to attack at first light."

We got no sleep that night. I doubt that any of us could have slept even if we had tried. Nestor organized a blessing for the tower. A pair of aged priests sacrificed a dozen rams and goats, slitting their throats with ancient stone knives as they lay bound and bleating on the ground, then painting their blood on the wooden framework. They fretted that there were no bulls or human captives to sacrifice; Agamemnon did not think enough of the project to allow such wealth to be wasted on it.

Lukka supervised rafting the tower across the river, once the night fog began blowing in from the sea. We waited, crouched in the chilling mist, the tower's framework looming around us like the skeleton of some giant's carcass, until the moon finally disappeared behind the islands and the night became as black as it would ever be.

I had hoped for cloud cover, but the stars were watching as we slowly, painfully, pulled the tower on big wooden wheels across the plain of Ilios and up the slope that fronted Troy's western wall. Slaves and *thetes* strained at the ropes, while others slathered animal grease on the wheels to keep them from squeaking.

Poletes crept along beside me, silent for once. I strained my eyes for a sight of Trojan sentries up on the battlements, but the fog kept me from seeing much. Straight overhead I could make out the Dippers and Cassiopeia's lopsided W. The constellation Orion, my namesake, was rising in the east, facing the V-shaped horns of Taurus the Bull. The Pleiades gleamed like a cluster of seven gems on the Bull's neck.

The night was eerily quiet. Perhaps the Trojans, trusting in the truce the Achaians had asked for, thought that no hostilities would start until the morning. True, the *fighting* would start with the sun's rise. But were they fools enough not to post lookouts through the night?

The ground was rising now, and what had seemed like a gentle slope felt like a cliff. We all gripped our hands on the ropes and put our backs into it, trying not to cry out or groan with the pain. I looked across from where I was hauling and saw Lukka, his face contorted with the effort, his booted heels dug into the mist-slippery grass, straining like a common laborer, just as all the rest of us were.

At last we reached the base of the wall and huddled there, waiting. I sent Poletes scampering around to the corner where the wall turned, to watch the eastern sky and tell me when it started to turn gray with the first hint of dawn. We all sat sprawled on the ground, letting our aching muscles relax until the moment for action came. The tower lay lengthwise along the ground, waiting to be pulled up to its vertical position. I sat with my back against the wall of Troy and counted minutes by listening to my heartbeat.

I heard a rooster crow from inside the city, and then another. Where is Poletes? I wondered. Has he fallen asleep, or been found by a Trojan sentry?

Just as I was getting to my feet, the old storyteller scuttled back through the mist to me.

"The eastern sky is still dark, except for the first touch of faint light between the mountains. Soon the sky will turn milk-white, then as rosy as a flower."

"Odysseus and his troops will be starting out from the camp," I said. "Time to get the tower up."

We almost got the job done before the Trojans realized what we were about.

The fog was thinning slightly as we hauled on the ropes that raised the tower to its vertical position. It was even heavier than it looked, because of the horse hides and weapons we had secured to its platforms. Lukka and his men stood on the other side, bracing the tower with poles as it rose. There was no way we could muffle the noise of the creaking and our own gasping, grunting exertions. It seemed to take an hour to get the thing standing straight, although actually only a few strenuous minutes had elapsed.

Still, just as the tower tipped over and thumped against the wall in its final position, I heard voices calling confusedly from the other side of the battlements.

I turned to Poletes. "Run back to Odysseus and tell him we're ready. He's to come as fast as he can!"

The plan was for Odysseus and a picked team of fifty Ithacans to make their way across the plain on foot, because chariots would have been too noisy. I was beginning to wonder if that had been the smartest approach.

Someone was shouting from inside the walls now, and I saw a head appear over the battlements, silhouetted for a brief instant against the graying sky.

I pulled out my sword and swung up onto the ladder that led to the top of the tower. Lukka was barely a step behind me, and the rest of the Hatti soldiers swarmed up the sides, unrolling the horsehide shields to protect the tower's sides against spears and arrows.

"What is it?" I heard a boy yelling from atop the wall.

"It's a giant horse!" a fear-stricken voice answered. "With men inside it!"

Chapter 19

reached the topmost platform of the tower, sword in hand. Our calculations had been almost perfect. The platform reared a foot or so higher than the wall's battlements. Without hesitation I jumped down onto the parapet and from there onto the stone platform behind it.

A pair of stunned Trojan youths stood there, mouths agape, eyes bulging, long spears in their trembling hands. Lukka rushed past me and cut one of them nearly in half with a savage swing of his sword. The other dropped his spear and, screaming, jumped off the platform to the street below.

The sky was brightening. The city seemed asleep. But across the angle of the wall I could see another sentry on the platform, his long spear outlined against the gray-pink of dawn. Instead of charging at us, he turned and ran toward the square stone tower that flanked the Scaean gate.

"He'll alarm the guard," I said to Lukka. "They'll all be at us in a few minutes."

Lukka nodded wordlessly, his hawk's face showing neither fear nor anticipation.

It was now a race between Odysseus's Ithacans and the Trojan guards. We had won a foothold inside the walls; now our job was to hold it. As Lukka's men swiftly broke out the spears and shields that we had roped to the tower's timbers, I looked out over the parapet. Fog and darkness still shrouded the plain. I could not see Odysseus and his men in the shadows—if they were there.

Trojan guards spilled out of the watchtower, an even dozen of them. And I saw more Trojans coming at us from the other side, running along the north wall, spears leveled. The battle was on.

The Hatti were professional soldiers. They had faced spears before, and they knew how to use their own. We formed a defensive wall by locking our shields together, and put out a bristling hedgehog front with our long spears. I too gripped a spear in my right hand and held my shield butted against Lukka's. My senses went into overdrive once more and the world around me slowed. Still I felt my heart pounding and my palms becoming slippery with sweat.

The Trojans attacked us with desperate fury, practically leaping on our spear points. They fought to save their city. We fought for our lives. I knew there was no way for us to retreat without being butchered. We either held our beachhead on the wall or we died.

Our shield wall buckled under their savage attack. We were forced a step back, and then another. A heavy bronze spear point crashed over the top of my shield, passed my ear, and plunged into the man behind me. As he died I thrust my spear into the belly of the man who had killed him. His face went from triumph to surprise to the final agony of death in the flash of a second.

More Trojans were pouring up the stairs to the platform, buckling armor over their nightclothes as they ran. These were the nobility, the cream of their fighting strength; I could tell from the gaudy plumes of their helmets and the gold that glinted in the light of the new day against the bronze of their breastplates.

Archers were leaning across the battlements, too, firing flaming arrows at our tower. Others fired at us. An arrow chunked into my shield. Another hit the man on my right in his leg; he staggered and went down. Instantly a Trojan spear drove through the unprotected back of his neck.

The archers were lofting their shots now, to get over our shield wall. Flaming arrows fell among us; men screamed and fell to the stone flooring, their clothes and flesh on fire.

The barrage of arrows would quickly break our shield wall, and then what was left of my men would go down individually under the weight of Trojan numbers. I felt a burning fury rising inside me, a rage against these men who were trying to kill us and against the gods that drove us to such murderous games. Call it battle frenzy, call it bloodlust, I felt the civilized compunctions, the veneer of morality burning away; and out of that flame of hatred and fear there arose an Orion who was beyond civilization, a barbarian with a spear in his hand that thirsted for blood.

"Hold here," I said to Lukka. Before he could do more than grunt I drove forward, surprising the Trojans in front of me. Holding my spear in two hands, level with the floor, I pushed four of them off their feet and slipped between the others, dodging their clumsy thrusts as they turned in dreamlike slow-motion to cut me down. I killed two of them; Lukka and his men killed several more, and the others quickly turned back to face the Hatti soldiers.

I dashed toward the archers. Most of them turned and ran, although two stood their ground and fired arrows at me as rapidly as they could. I picked them off with my shield as I ran. I caught the first archer on my spear, a lad too young to have more than the wisp of a beard. His companion started to pull out the sword at his side but I knocked him spinning with a swipe of my shield. He toppled off the platform to the ground below.

The other archers had retreated out of range of my Hatti troops, who were still battling to hold their foothold on the wall. For the span of a heartbeat I was alone. But only for that long. The Trojan nobles were rushing along the platform toward me, a dozen of them, with more behind them. I hefted my long spear in one hand and threw it at the closest man. Its heavy weight drove it completely through his shield and into his chest. He staggered backward into the arms of his two nearest companions.

I threw my shield at them to slow them down further, then picked up the bow from the archer I had slain. It was a beautiful, gracefully curved thing of horn and smooth-polished wood. But I had no time to admire its construction. I fired every arrow in the dead youth's quiver, forcing the nobles to cower behind their bodylength shields, holding them at bay for a precious few minutes.

Once the last arrow was gone and I threw down the useless bow, their leader dropped his shield enough for me to recognize him: Aleksandros, a sardonic smile on his almost-pretty face.

"So the herald is a warrior, after all," he called to me.

Sliding my sword from its sheath, I responded, "Yes. Is the stealer of women a warrior, as well?"

"A better one than you," Aleksandros said.

"Prove it then," I stalled. "Face me man to man."

He glanced at the Hatti battling behind me. "Much as I would enjoy that, today is not the day for such pleasures."

"Today is the last day of your life, Aleksandros," I said.

As if on cue, a piercing, blood-curdling war cry came from behind me. Odysseus!

Aleksandros looked startled for a moment, then he screamed to his followers, "Clear the wall of them!"

The Trojans charged. They had to get past me before they could reach Lukka and Odysseus. I faced a dozen long spears with nothing but my sword. They ran at me in slow-motion, bronze spear points glinting in the dawning light, bobbing slightly with each pounding step they took. I noticed that Aleksandros slid toward the rear and let others come at me first.

I moved a step toward the edge of the platform, then dived between the two nearest spears and got close enough to use my sword. Two Trojans went down, and the others turned toward me. I barely avoided one point jamming toward my belly as I hacked at another spear haft and cut it in two with my iron blade. I ducked another thrust and stepped back—onto empty air.

As I tottered on the edge of the platform, another spear came thrusting at me. I banged its bronze head with the metal cuff around my left wrist, deflecting it enough to save my skin. But the motion sent me tumbling off the platform.

I turned a full somersault in midair and landed on my feet. The impact buckled my knees and I rolled on the bare dirt of the street. A spear thudded into the ground next to my shoulder. Turning, I saw a pair of arrows heading my way. I dodged them and ducked behind the corner of a house.

Aleksandros and his men rushed toward the battle still raging farther along the platform, at the top of the wall: my Hatti contingent and Odysseus's Ithacans against the growing numbers of Trojans roused so rudely from their sleep. We needed a diversion, something to draw off the Trojan reinforcements.

I sprinted down the narrow alley between houses until I found a door. I kicked it open. A woman screamed in sudden terror as I stamped in, sword in hand. She crouched in a corner of her kitchen, her arms around two small children huddling against her. As I strode toward them they all shrieked and ran along the wall, screeching and skittering like mice, then bolted for the open door. I let them go.

A small cooking fire smoldered in the hearth. I yanked down the flimsy curtains in the doorway that separated the kitchen from the next room and tossed them onto the fire. It flared into open flame. Then I smashed the wooden table and fed it to the blaze. Striding into the next room, I grabbed straw bedding and blankets and added them to the fire.

Two houses, three, then the whole row of them I set ablaze. People were screaming and shouting. Men and women alike raced toward the fire with buckets of water drawn from the fountain at the end of the street.

Satisfied that the fire would keep them busy, I started up the nearest flight of steps to return to the battle on the platform.

Achaians were pouring over the parapet now and the Trojans were giving way. I leaped on them from the rear, yelling out to Lukka. He heard me and led his contingent to my side, cutting a bloody swath through the defending Trojans.

"The watchtower by the Scaean gate," I said, pointing with my reddened sword. "We've got to take it and open the gate."

We fought along the length of the wall, meeting the Trojan warriors as they came up in groups of five or ten or a dozen and driving away those few we did not kill. The fires I had started were spreading to other houses now, and a pall of black smoke hid the palace from our sight.

The watchtower was only lightly guarded; most of the Trojan strength was being thrown against Odysseus on the western wall. We broke into the guard room, the Hatti using their spear butts to batter the door down, and slaughtered the men there. Then we raced down to the ground and started to lift the heavy beams that barricaded the Scaean gate. A wailing scream arose, and I saw that Aleksandros and the other nobles were racing down the stone steps from the parapet toward us.

We had them on the horns of uncertainty now. If they allowed Odysseus to hold the wall, the rest of the Achaians would enter the city that way. But if they concentrated on clearing the wall, we would open the gate and allow the Achaian chariots to drive into the city. They had to stop us at both places, and stop us quickly.

Archers began shooting at us, but despite them the Hatti tugged and pushed to open the massive gate. Men fell, but the three enormous beams were slowly lifting, swinging up and away from the doors.

I ducked an arrow and saw Aleksandros rushing toward me across the open square behind the gate.

"You again!" he shouted at me.

They were his last words. He charged at me with his spear. I dodged sideways, forced it down with my left forearm, and drove my iron sword through his bronze breastplate up to the hilt. As I yanked it out, bright red blood spattered over the golden inlays and I felt a mad surge of pleasure, battle joy that I had taken the life of the man who had caused the war.

Aleksandros sank to the ground. I saw the light go out of his eyes. But in that moment an arrow struck me in my left shoulder. Pain flared for an instant before I reacted automatically and shut it down. I pulled the arrow out, its barbed head tearing at my flesh. Blood spurted, but I consciously clamped down those vessels and willed the wound to clot.

Even as I did so, the other Trojans came at me. But they stopped in their tracks as a great creaking groan of huge bronze hinges told me that the Scaean gate was swinging open at last. A roar went up and I turned to see chariots plunging through the open gate, bearing down directly on me.

The Trojans scattered and I dived out of the way. Agamemnon was in the first chariot. His horses pounded over Aleksandros's dead body and the chariot bumped, then clattered on, chasing the fleeing Trojan warriors.

I stepped backward, dust from the charging chariots stinging my eyes, coating my skin, my clothes, my bloody sword. The battle lust began to ebb and I watched Aleksandros's mangled body tossed and crushed by chariot after chariot. Lukka came up beside me, a gash on his cheek and more on both his arms. None of them looked serious, though.

"The battle is over," he said. "The slaughter begins."

I nodded, suddenly bone weary.

"You are hurt," he saw.

"It's not serious."

He examined the wound, shaking his head and muttering. "It looks halfway healed already."

"I told you it's not serious."

The men gathered around us, looking uneasy. Not frightened, but edgy, nervous.

"This is the time when soldiers collect their pay," Lukka told me.

Loot, he meant. Stealing everything you can carry, raping the women, and then putting the city to the torch.

"Go," I said, remembering that the first fires had been set by me. "I'll be all right. I'll see you back at the camp."

Lukka touched his fist lightly to his chest, then turned to what was left of his men. "Follow me," he commanded. "And remember, don't take any chances. There are still plenty of armed men left alive. And some of the women will try to use knives on you."

"Any bitch tries to cut me will regret it," said one of the men.

"Any bitch who sees your ugly face will probably use her knife on herself!"

They all laughed and marched off together. I counted thirty-five of them. Seven had been killed.

For a while I stood there near the wall and watched Achaian chariots and foot soldiers pouring through the open, undefended gate. The smoke was getting thicker. I squinted up at the sky and saw that the sun had barely topped the wall. It was still early in the morning.

So it is done, I said to myself. Your city has fallen, Apollo. Your plans are ruined.

I felt no exultation, no joy at all. This is not revenge, I realized. Killing a thousand or so men and boys, burning down a city that had taken centuries to build, raping women and carrying them off into slavery—that is not triumph.

Slowly I pulled myself to my feet. The square was empty now, except for the mangled body of Aleksandros and the other slain men. Behind the first row of columned temples I could see flames rising into the sky, smoke billowing toward heaven. A sacrifice to the gods, I thought bitterly.

Raising my bloody sword over my head I cried out, "I want *your* blood, Golden One! Your blood!"

There was no answer.

I looked down at what was left of Aleksandros. We all die, prince of Troy. Your brothers have died. Your father is probably dying at this very moment. Some of us die many times. The lucky ones, only once.

Then a thought struck me, like a telepathic message beamed into my brain. Where is Helen, the beautiful Helen who was the reason for this slaughter, the calculating woman who had tried to use me as a messenger?

Chapter 20

I strode up the main street of burning Troy, sword in hand, through a morning turned dark by the smoke of fires I had started. Women's screams and sobs filled the air, men bellowed and laughed raucously. The roof of a house collapsed in a shower of sparks, forcing me back a few steps. Perhaps it was the house I had slept in; I could not be sure.

Up the climbing avenue I walked, my face blackened with dust and soot, my arms spattered with blood—most of it Trojan. I saw that the gutter running along the center of the dirt street also ran red.

A pair of children ran shrieking past me, and a trio of drunken Achaians lurched laughingly after them. I recognized one of them: giant Ajax, lumbering along with a huge wine jug in one hand.

"Come back!" he yelled drunkenly. "We won't hurt you!"

The children fled into the smoke and disappeared down an alley.

I climbed on, toward the palace, past the market stalls that now blazed hot enough to singe the hair on my arms, past a heap of bodies where some of the Trojans had tried to make a stand. Finally I reached the steps at the front of the palace. They too were littered with fallen bodies.

Sitting on the top step, leaning against one of the massive stone pillars, was Poletes. Weeping.

I rushed to him. "Are you hurt?"

"Yes," he said, bobbing his old head. "In my soul."

I almost felt relieved.

"Look at the desolation. Murder and fire. Is this what men live for? To act like beasts?"

"Yes," I replied. Grabbing him by his bony shoulder, I said, "Sometimes men do act like beasts. Sometimes they behave like angels. They can build beautiful cities and burn them to the ground. What of it? Don't try to make sense out of it, just accept us as we are."

Poletes looked up at me through eyes reddened by tears and smoke. "So we should accept the whims of the gods, and dance their dance whenever they pull our strings? Is that what you tell me?"

"There are no gods, Poletes. Only vicious bullies who laugh at our pain."

"No gods? That cannot be. There *must* be some reason for our existence, some order in the world."

"We do what we have to do, old moralizer," I said gruffly. "We obey the gods when we have no other choice."

"You speak in riddles, Orion."

"Go back to the camp, old man. This is no place for you. Some drunken Achaian might mistake you for a Trojan."

But he did not move, except to lean his head against the pillar. I saw that its once-bright red paint was now blackened and someone had scratched his name into the stone with the point of a sword: Thersites.

"I'll see you back at the camp," I said.

He nodded sadly. "Yes, when mighty Agamemnon divides the spoils and decides how many of the women and how much of the treasure he will take for himself."

"Go to the camp," I said, more firmly. "Now. That's not advice, Poletes, it is my command."

He drew in a long breath and sighed it out, then raised himself slowly to his feet.

"Take this sign." I handed him the armlet Odysseus had given me. "It will identify you to any drunken lout that wants to take off your head."

He accepted it wordlessly. It was much too big for his frail arms, so he hung it around his skinny neck. I had to laugh at the sight.

"Laughter in the middle of the sack of a great city," Poletes said. "You are becoming a true Achaian warrior, my master."

With that he started down the steps, haltingly, like a man who really did not care which way he went.

I went through the columned portico and into the hall of statues, where Achaian warriors were directing slaves to take down the gods' images and carry them off toward the boats. Into the open courtyard that had been so lovely I went. Pots were overturned and smashed, flowers trampled, bodies strewn everywhere staining the grass with their blood. The little statue of Athene was already gone. The big one of Apollo had toppled and broken into several pieces. I smiled grimly at that.

One wing of the palace was afire. I could see flames crackling in the windows. I closed my eyes momentarily, picturing in my mind the chamber where Helen had spoken to me. It was there where the fire blazed.

From a balcony overhead I heard shouts, then curses. The clash of metal on metal. A fight was still going on up there.

"The royal women have locked themselves into the temple of Aphrodite," I heard a man behind me yell. "Come on!" He sounded like someone rushing to a party, or hurrying to get back to his seat before the curtain rose on the final act of the drama.

I snatched my sword from its scabbard and rushed up the nearest stairs. A handful of Trojans were making a last-ditch defense of the corridor that led to the royal temples, fighting desperately against a shouting, bellowing mob of Achaian warriors. Behind the doors locked at the Trojans' backs waited aged Priam and his wife, Hecuba, together with their daughters and grandchildren, I realized.

Helen must be there too, I thought. I saw Menalaos, Diomedes, and Agamemnon himself thrusting their spears at the few desperate Trojan defenders, laughing at them, taunting them.

"You sell your lives for nothing," shouted Diomedes. "Put down your spears and we will allow you to live."

"As slaves!" roared Agamemnon.

The Trojans fought bravely, but they were outnumbered and doomed, their backs pressed against the doors they tried so valiantly to defend, as more and more Achaians rushed up to join the sport.

I sprinted down the next corridor and pushed my way through rooms where soldiers were tearing through chests of gorgeous robes, grabbing jewels from gold-inlaid boxes, and pulling silken tapestries from the walls. This wing of the palace would also be in flames soon, I knew. Too soon.

I found a balcony, swung over its ballustrade, and, leaning as far forward as I dared, clamped one hand on the edge of a window in the otherwise blank rear wall of the temple wing. I swung out over thirty feet of air and pulled myself up onto my elbows, then hoisted a leg onto the windowsill. Pushing aside the beaded curtain, I peered into a small, dim inner sanctuary. The walls were bare, the tiles of the floor old and worn to dullness. Small votive statues stood lined on both sides of the room, some of them still decked with rings of withered flowers. The palace smelled of incense and old candles. Standing by the door, her back to me, her hands clasped in fear, stood Helen.

I could hear the sounds of the fighting from outside the temple. I dropped lightly to my feet and walked quietly toward her.

"Helen," I said.

She whirled to face me, her fists pressed against her mouth, her body tense with terror. I saw her eyes recognize me, and she relaxed a little.

"The emissary," she whispered.

"Orion," I reminded her.

She stood there for an uncertain moment, wearing her finest robes, decked with gold and jewels, more beautiful than any woman had a right to be. Then she ran to me, three tiny steps, and pressed her golden head against my grimy, bloodstained chest. Her hair was scented like fragrant flowers.

"Don't let them kill me, Orion! Please, please! They'll be crazy with bloodlust. Even Menalaos. He'd take my head off and then blame it on Ares. Please protect me!"

"That's why I came to you," I said. As I spoke the words, I knew they were true. It was the one civilized thing I could do in this entire mad, murderous day. Having slain the man who had abducted her, I would now see to it that her rightful husband took her back.

"Priam is dead," she said, her voice muffled and sobbing. "His heart broke when he saw the Achaians coming over the western wall."

"The queen?" I asked.

"She and the other royal women are in the main temple, just on the other side of that door. The guards outside have sworn to go down to the last man before allowing Agamemnon and his brutes to enter here."

I held her and listened to the clamor of the fight. It did not last long. A final scream of agony, a final roar of triumph, then a thudding as they pounded against the locked doors. A splintering of wood, then silence.

"It would be better if we went in there, rather than letting them break in and find you," I suggested.

She pulled herself away from me and visibly fought for self-control. Lifting her little chin like the queen she had hoped to be, Helen said, "Yes. I am ready to face them."

I went to the connecting door, unlatched it, and opened it a crack. Agamemnon, his brother Menalaos, and dozens of other Achaian nobles were crowding into the temple. Gold-covered statues taller than life lined its walls, and the floor was of gleaming marble. At the head of the temple, behind the marble altar, loomed a towering marble statue of Aphrodite, gilded and painted, decked with flowers and offerings of jewels. Hundreds of candles burned at its base, casting dancing highlights off the gold and gems. But the Achaians ignored all the temple's treasures. Instead they stared at the richly draped altar, and the old woman on it.

I had never seen Hecuba before. The aged, wrinkled woman lay on the altar, arms crossed over her breast, eyes closed. Her robes were threaded with gold; her wrists and fingers bore turquoise and amber, rubies and carnelian. Heavy ropes of gold necklaces and a jewel-encrusted crown had been lovingly placed upon her. Seven women, ranging in age from gray-haired to teenaged, stood trembling around the altar, facing the sweating, bloodstained Achaians, who gaped at the splendor of the dead Queen of Troy.

One of the older women was saying quietly to Agamemnon, "She took poison once the king died. She knew that Troy could not outlive this day, that my prophecy had finally come true."

"Cassandra," whispered Helen to me. "The queen's eldest daughter."

Agamemnon turned slowly from the corpse to the gray-haired princess. His narrow little eyes glared anger and frustration.

Cassandra said, "You will not bring the Queen of Troy back to Mycenae in your black boat, mighty Agamemnon. She will never be a slave of yours."

A leering smile twisted Agamemnon's lips. "Then I'll have to settle for you, princess. You will be my slave in her place."

"Yes," Cassandra said, "and we will die together at the hands of your faithless wife."

"Trojan bitch!" He cuffed her with a heavy backhand swat that knocked her to the marble floor.

Before any more violence erupted, I swung wide the door of the sanctuary. The Achaians turned, hands gripping the swords at their sides. Helen stepped through with regal grace and an absolutely blank expression on her incredibly beautiful face. It was as if the most splendid statue imaginable had taken on the power of life.

She went wordlessly to Cassandra and helped the princess to her feet. Blood trickled from her cut lip.

I stood by the side of the altar, my left hand resting on the pommel of my sword. Agamemnon and the others recognized me. Their faces were grimy, hands stained with blood. I could smell their sweat even from this distance.

Menalaos, who seemed to be stunned with shock for a moment, suddenly stepped forward and gripped his wife by her shoulders.

"Helen!" His mouth seemed to twitch, as if he were trying to say words that would not leave his soul.

She did not smile, but her eyes searched his. The other Achaians watched them dumbly.

Every emotion a human being can show flashed across Menalaos's face. Helen simply stood there, in his grip, waiting for him to speak, to act, to make his decision on whether she lived or died.

Agamemnon broke the silence. "Well, brother, I promised you we'd get her back! She's yours once again, to deal with as you see fit."

Menalaos swallowed hard and finally found his voice. "You are my wife, Helen," he said, more for the ears of Agamemnon and the others than hers, I thought. "What has happened since Aleksandros abducted you was not of your doing. A woman captive is not responsible for what happens to her during her captivity."

I kept myself from smiling. Menalaos wanted her back so badly he was willing to forget everything that had happened. For now.

Agamemnon clapped his brother on the back gleefully. "I'm

only sorry that Aleksandros didn't have the courage to face me, man to man. I would have gladly spitted him on my spear."

"Where is Aleksandros?" Menalaos asked suddenly.

"Dead," I answered. "His body is in the square at the Scaean gate."

The women started to cry, sobbing quietly as they stood by their mother's bier. All but Cassandra, whose eyes blazed with unconcealed fury.

"Odysseus is going through the city to find all the princes and noblemen," said Agamemnon. "Those that still live will make noble sacrifices to the gods." He laughed at his own pun.

So I left Troy for the final time, marching with the Achaian victors through the burning city as Agamemnon led seven Trojan princesses back to his camp and slavery, and Menalaos walked side by side with Helen, his wife once more. A guard of honor marched alongside us, spears held stiffly up to the blackened sky. Wailing and sobs rose all around us; the air was filled with the stench of blood and smoke.

I trailed behind and noted that Helen never voluntarily touched Menalaos, not even to take his hand. I remembered what she had told me when we had first met: that being a wife among the Achaians, even a queen, was little better than being a slave.

She never touched Menalaos, and he hardly looked at her, after that first emotion-charged meeting in the temple of Aphrodite at dead Hecuba's bier.

But she looked over her shoulder more than once, looked back at me, as if to make certain I was not far from her.

Chapter 21

THE Achaian camp was one gigantic orgy of feasting and roistering all that day and far into the night. There was no semblance of order and no attempt to do anything but drink, wench, eat, and celebrate the victory. Men staggered drunkenly around, draped in precious silks pillaged from the burning city. Women cowered and trembled—those that were not beaten or savaged into insensibility.

Fights broke out. Men quarreled over a goblet or a ring or, more often, a woman. Blood flowed, and several Achaians who thought they were safe now that the war had ended learned that death could find them even in the midst of triumph.

"Tomorrow will be the solemn sacrifices of thanksgiving to the gods," Poletes told me as we sat beside our evening cook fire. "Many men and beasts will be slaughtered, and the smoke of their pyres offered to heaven. Then Agamemnon will divide the major spoils."

I looked past his sad, weatherbeaten face to the smoldering fire of the city, still glowing a sullen red against the darkening evening sky.

"You will be a rich man tomorrow, master Orion," said the old storyteller. "Agamemnon cannot help but give Odysseus a great slice of the spoils, and Odysseus will be generous with you—far more generous than Agamemnon himself."

I shook my head wearily. "It makes no difference, Poletes. Not to me."

He smiled as if to say, Ah, but wait until Odysseus heaps gold and bronze upon you, and iron tripods and pots. Then you will feel differently.

I got to my feet and went out among the riotous Achaians, looking for Lukka and my other Hatti soldiers. I did not have to look far. They had made their own little encampment around their own fire. The area was heaped with their loot: fine blankets and boots, beautiful bows of bone and ivory, and a couple of dozen women who huddled together, clinging to each other, staring at their captors with wide fearful eyes.

Lukka scrambled to his feet when he saw me approaching out of the raucous darkness.

"Is that what you've taken from the city?" I asked.

"Yes, sir. The custom is for the leader to pick his half and the men to divide the rest. Do you want to pick your half now?"

I shook my head. "No. Divide it all among yourselves."

Lukka frowned with puzzlement. "All of it?"

"Yes. And you've done well to stick together like this. Tomorrow Agamemnon divides the major spoils. The Achaians may want a share of your booty."

"We've already put aside the king's share," he said. "But your own . . ."

"You take it, Lukka. I don't need it."

"Not even a woman or two?"

I smiled at him. "Where I come from, women are not taken as slaves. They come freely or not at all."

For the first time since I had met him, the doughty Hatti warrior looked surprised. I laughed and bid him a pleasant night.

As I crawled into my tent I thought that the howling and screaming of the camp would keep me awake. But almost as soon as I stretched out on the pallet, my eyes closed and I fell asleep.

To find myself standing in that golden emptiness once more, in the realm of the Creators. I peered into the all-pervasive glow and made out, dimly, strange shapes and masses far, far off, like the towers and buildings of a distant city seen in the dazzle of an overpoweringly bright sun.

I had not willed myself to make contact with the Creators, I knew. It must be that the Golden One had summoned me once again.

"No, Orion, he has not summoned you. I have."

A human form materialized about twenty yards from me. The dark-haired one with the precisely trimmed beard, the one I thought of as Zeus. Instead of godly robes, though, he wore a simple one-piece suit with trousers and sleeves and a high collar that buttoned at his throat. It was sky-blue, and it shimmered strangely as he walked toward me.

"Be glad that our Apollo has not called you," he said, his expression halfway between amused curiosity and serious concern. "He is furious with you. He blames you for the fall of Troy."

"Good," I said.

Zeus shook his head in a neat, economical move. "Not good, Orion. In the rage he's in now, he would destroy you utterly. I called you here to protect you against him."

"Why?"

He cocked an eyebrow at me. "Orion, you are supposed to thank the gods for the blessing they bestow on you."

I bowed my head slightly. "I do thank you, whatever your true name is . . ."

"You may call me Zeus." He seemed delighted at the idea. "For the time being."

"I thank you, Zeus."

His smile widened. "The most grudging thanks a god has ever received, I'll bet."

I shrugged my shoulders.

"Nevertheless, the truth is that you have wrecked Apollo's plans—for the moment."

"I doubt that I could have done anything at all without the help of some of you other Creators," I said. "Several of you opposed his plan for Troy."

He sighed. "Yes, we were not united about it. Not united at all."

"Is the one I call Hera actually your wife?" I asked.

He looked surprised. "Wife? Of course not. No more than she's my sister. We don't have such things here."

"No wives?"

"Nor sisters," he said. "But that's not important. The real question is, how do we continue our work in the face of Apollo's intransigence? He's quite enraged. We can't have an open split among us, it would be catastrophic."

"Just what is your work?" I asked.

"I doubt that you could understand it," Zeus said, staring hard at me. "The capacity was never built into you."

"Try me. Perhaps I can learn . . ."

But he shook his head, more vigorously this time. "Orion, you can't visualize the universes. When you freed Ahriman and allowed him to tear down that continuum, you never thought that a new continuum would establish itself out of all that liberated energy, did you?"

His words struck a dim chord of memory in me. "I freed Ahriman," I said slowly. "After tracking him down in the time before the Ice Age."

"Before, after, it makes little difference," Zeus said impatiently. "Ahriman's people now live peacefully in their own continuum, safely out of the stream that we are trying to protect. But you . . ."

"The Golden One—Apollo—did he truly create me?"

Zeus nodded. "And the entire human race. There were five hundred of you, originally."

Faint images were shimmering in my mind like ghosts, blurred and indistinct, but almost within touch. "We were sent to destroy Ahriman's race, to prepare the Earth for our own kind."

He waved a hand impatiently. "That's of little consequence now. That's all been resolved." He did not like to think about our task of genocide. He had agreed to it, obviously, but did not want to be reminded of it.

"And a few of us survived to establish the human race on Earth."

"That is true," said Zeus.

"And we evolved, over the millennia, to eventually produce . . ." I remembered now, "to eventually produce *you,* a race of advanced humans, so advanced that you seem like gods."

"And *we* created *you,*" Zeus said. "The one you call Apollo headed that project. Then we sent you back in time to make the Earth habitable for us."

"By killing off its original inhabitants: Ahriman's race."

"They're safe enough," he said, showing that trace of irritability again. "Thanks to you."

"And Ahriman now has the same powers you do."

"Virtually."

I saw it all now. Or most of it. "But what's Troy got to do with this?" I asked.

Zeus smiled thinly, as if savoring his superior knowledge. "Once you begin altering the continuum, Orion, you create all sorts of side effects that must either be deliberately controlled or allowed to run their natural course until they damp down of themselves. Apollo seeks to control events, to make deliberate adjustments to the continuum wherever and whenever they can be altered to our advantage. Others among us feel that this is self-defeating, that every change we make engenders more side effects and makes it more difficult to protect the continuum."

I almost understood. "He sent me to Troy, then, to help the Trojans win."

"Yes. Most of us wanted the war to run its natural course, without our interference. Apollo defied us and sent you to that spot in the continuum. I believe his plan was to have you slay the Achaian leaders in their camp."

Almost, I laughed. But then a wisp of memory made me blurt, "He said something about dangers from beyond the Earth, and even you spoke of universes—plural."

Zeus made an effort to control the surprise and fear that my words struck in him. He controlled his face and made it almost expressionless, but not quickly enough to totally mask his emotions.

"There are others, elsewhere in the universe?" I asked. "Other universes?"

"That was something we had not expected," he admitted. "Our continuum impinges on others. When we make changes in this space-time, it affects other universes. And their manipulations affect us."

"And what does this mean?"

He made a deep sighing breath. "It means that we must struggle not only to maintain this continuum, but to protect it against outsiders who would manipulate it for their own purposes."

"And I? Where do I fit in?"

"You?" He regarded me with frank puzzlement, as if a sword or a computer or a starship had asked what its purpose might be. "You are a tool of ours, Orion, to be used where and when we see fit. But you are a stubborn tool; you disregarded Apollo's commands, and now he seeks to destroy you."

"He killed the woman I loved. She was one of you: the one I call Athene."

"Don't blame him for that, Orion."

"I do blame him."

Zeus shook his head. "It's sad that you should blame the gods and regard *us* as the source of your troubles. It was your own actions that have brought you worse sufferings than any you were intended to bear."

"Yet you protect me from Apollo's anger."

"You may still be useful to us, Orion. It is wasteful to destroy a tool that can still be used."

I felt the anger rising in me. His cool smugness, his air of superiority, was beginning to infuriate me. Or was I seething because I knew he was superior, far more powerful than I could ever hope to be?

"Give the golden Apollo a message for me," I said. "Tell him that I am learning. My memories are coming back to me. One day, whatever he knows, I will know. Whatever he can do, I will be able to do. And on that day I will destroy him."

Zeus smiled at me, pityingly, the way a father smiles at a naughty child. "He will destroy you long before that day arrives, Orion. You are living on borrowed time."

I wanted to reply, but he faded into nothingness. The distant city, the golden aura all around me, they all disappeared like the thread of smoke from a candle. I was in my tent again, and the sun was rising on the day when the spoils of Troy would be divided, and the gods would receive their sacrifices of beasts and men.

Chapter 22

THE day dawned gray and dreary. The Achaians, aching and sick from their revelries of the night, were quiet and solemn as the sun climbed slowly behind banks of scudding clouds. The wind from the sea hinted rain, and the chill of approaching autumn.

Neither I nor my Hatti band took part in the sacrifices. Poletes was puzzled at that.

"But you serve the goddess," he said.

"She is dead. Regardless of what they offer, she won't be able to receive it."

Muttering "sacrilege," Poletes wandered off toward the tall pyres of driftwood and timber that the slaves and *thetes* were piling up in the center of the camp. I remained near our own fire, close by Odysseus's boats, and watched.

Nestor led the priests in a procession around the camp, followed by Agamemnon and the other chiefs—all in their most splendid armor and carrying long glittering spears that seemed to me more ornamental than battle weapons.

While they paraded through the camp, singing hymns of praise to Zeus and all the other immortals, the sacrificial victims were being assembled by the pyres. There was a regular herd of goats and bulls and sheep, hundreds of them, kicking up enough dust to obscure the blackened remains of Troy up on the bluff. Their bleatings and bellowings made a strange counterpoint to the chanting and singing of the Achaians.

Standing off to one side of them were the human sacrifices, every man over the age of twelve who had been captured alive, their hands tightly bound behind their backs, their ankles hobbled. Even from the distance where I stood, I could recognize the old courtier who had escorted me in the palace. They stood silently, grimly, knowing full well what awaited them but neither begging for mercy nor bewailing their fate. I suppose they each knew that nothing was going to alter their destiny.

The whole long day was spent in ritual slaughter. First the animals, from a few doves to raging, bellowing bulls that thrashed madly even though their hooves were firmly lashed together, arching their backs and tossing their heads until the priest's stone ax cut through their throats with a shower of hot blood. Even horses were sacrificed, dozens of them.

Then came the men. One by one they were led to the blood-soaked altar, made to kneel and bow their heads. The lucky ones died in a single stroke. Many were not so fortunate.

By the time it was ended and the pyres were lit, the priests were covered with blood and the camp stank of entrails and excrement. As the sun went down the pyres blazed across the darkening landscape, sending up smoke that was thought to be pleasing to the gods.

Then the whole camp swarmed toward Agamemnon's boats, in the center of the beach, where the spoils of Troy had been heaped high. Hundreds of women and children stood near the pile of loot, guarded by a grinning handful of warriors.

Agamemnon climbed up onto a beautifully carved chair pillaged from the city. It had been set up on a makeshift platform, to turn it into a rough sort of throne. Then he began to divide the spoils, so much to each chieftain, starting with white-bearded old Nestor.

The Achaians crowded around, greed and envy shining in their eyes. I stayed by Odysseus's boat and watched from afar. I noticed that Lukka and his men stayed with me.

"Your own goods are safe?" I asked him.

He grunted affirmatively. "They wanted to take our women for the High King to divide out, but we convinced them to leave us alone."

I almost smiled, picturing Lukka and his disciplined soldiers forming a phalanx against a gaggle of hung-over Achaian warriors.

Far into the night the ceremony went. Agamemnon parceled out bronze armor and weapons, gold ornaments, beautiful urns and vases, porphyry and onyx, glittering jewels, kitchen implements of copper, iron tripods and cooking pots, robes, silks, blankets, tapestries—and women, young boys and girls.

Half of everything he kept for himself: the High King's prerogative. But as some of the chieftains and men passed me, carrying their loot back to their boats, I heard them complain of the High King's meanness.

"He's got the generosity of a dung beetle."

"He knew we had done the hardest fighting, up on the wall. And what do we get for it? Less than his brother."

"Those women should have been ours, I tell you. The fat king is too greedy."

"What can you do? He takes what he wants and we get his leavings."

I thought that even Odysseus looked less than pleased when he approached me. The pyres smoldered in the distance, but our campfires lit his darkly bearded face with flickers of red.

"Orion," he called to me. I went to him.

"Your servant Poletes is digging a grave for himself," Odysseus said. "He is mocking the High King's generosity."

I looked into Odysseus's dark eyes. "Isn't everyone?" I asked mildly.

His answering smile told me how he felt. "But not everyone is speaking so loosely within earshot of Nestor and Menalaos and others who will report his words to Agamemnon. You'd better see to it. The old storyteller is swimming in dangerous waters."

"Thank you, my lord. I will see to it."

I hurried over toward Agamemnon's part of the camp, passing a stream of disgruntled Achaians toting their loot.

Poletes was sitting on the sand by a small campfire, practically under the nose of one of the High King's boats, surrounded by a mob of squatting, standing, grinning, laughing Achaian men. None of them were of the nobility. Off in the shadows, though, I noticed Nestor standing with his skinny arms folded across his chest, frowning in Poletes's direction.

". . . and do you remember when Hector drove them all back inside our own gates, here, and he came in with an arrow barely puncturing his skin, crying like a woman, 'We're doomed! We're doomed!' "

The crowd around the fire roared with laughter. I had to admit that the old storyteller could mimic Agamemnon's high voice almost perfectly.

"I wonder what Clytemnestra will do when her brave and noble husband comes home?" Poletes grinned. "I wonder if her bed is high enough off the ground to hide her lover?"

Men rolled on the ground with laughter. Tears flowed. I started to push my way through the crowd to get to him.

But I was too late. A dozen armed men tramped in, and Poletes's audience scrambled out of their way. I recognized Menalaos at their head.

"Storyteller!" he snapped. "The High King wants to hear what you have to say. Let's see if your scurrilous tales can make him laugh."

Poletes's eyes went wide with sudden fear. "But I only . . ."

Two of the armed guards grabbed him under his armpits and hauled him to his feet.

"Come along," said Menalaos.

I stepped in front of him. "This man is my servant. I will take care of him."

Before Menalaos could reply, Nestor bustled up. "The High King has demanded to see this teller of tales. No one can interfere!" It was the shortest speech I had ever heard the old man make.

With a small shrug, Menalaos headed off toward Agamemnon's quarters, his guards dragging Poletes after him, followed by Nestor, me, and all of the men who had been rollicking at the storyteller's gibes.

Agamemnon still sat on his makeshift throne, fat, flushed with wine, flanked by the treasures of Troy. His chubby fingers gripped the chair arms as he eyed Poletes being hauled before him. Rings glittered on each finger and both his thumbs.

The old storyteller knelt trembling before the High King, who glared down at his skinny, shabby presence.

"You have been telling lies about me," Agamemnon snarled.

Poletes drew himself together and lifted his chin to face the High King. "Not so, your royal highness. I am a *professional* storyteller. I do not tell lies, I speak only of what I see with my own eyes and hear with my own ears."

"You speak filthy lies!" Agamemnon screamed, his voice rising shrilly. "About my wife!"

"If your wife were an honest woman, sire, I would not be here at all. I'd be in the marketplace at Argos, telling stories to the people, as I should be."

"I'll listen to no calumnies about my wife," Agamemnon warned.

But Poletes insisted, "The High King is supposed to be the highest judge in the land, the fairest and most impartial. Everyone knows what is going on in Mycenae—ask anyone. Your own captive Cassandra, a princess of Troy, has prophesied . . ."

"Silence!" roared the High King.

"How can you silence the truth, son of Atreus? How can you turn back the destiny that fate has chosen for you?"

Now Agamemnon trembled, with anger. He hauled himself up from his chair and stepped down to the ground before Poletes.

"Hold him!" he commanded, drawing out the jeweled dagger at his belt.

The guards gripped Poletes's frail arms.

"I can silence you, magpie, by separating you from your lying tongue."

"Wait!" I shouted, and pushed my way toward them.

Agamemnon looked up as I approached, his piggish little eyes suddenly worried, almost fearful.

"This man is my servant," I said. "I will punish him."

"Very well then," said Agamemnon, pointing his dagger toward the iron sword at my side. *"You* take out his tongue."

I shook my head. "That is too cruel a punishment for a few joking words."

"You refuse me?"

"The man's a storyteller," I pleaded. "If you take out his tongue you condemn him to starvation or slavery."

Slowly, Agamemnon's flushed, heavy features arranged themselves in a smile. It was not a joyful one.

"A storyteller, eh?" He turned to Poletes, who knelt like a sagging sack of rags in the grip of the two burly guards. "You only speak what you see and what you hear, you claim. Very well. You will see and hear—*nothing*! Ever again!"

My guts churned as I realized what he intended to do. I reached for my sword, only to find ten spears surrounding me, almost touching my skin.

A hand clasped my shoulder. I turned. It was Menalaos, his face grave. "Be still, Orion. The storyteller must be punished. No sense getting yourself killed over a servant."

Poletes was staring at me, his eyes begging me to do something. I moved toward him, only to be stopped by the points of the spears against my flesh.

"My wife has told me how you protected her during the sack of the temple," Menalaos said, low in my ear. "I owe you a debt of gratitude. Don't force me to repay it with your blood."

"Then run to Odysseus," I begged him. "Please. Perhaps he can soothe the High King's anger."

Menalaos merely shook his head. "It will all be over before I could reach the Ithacans' first boat. Look."

Nestor himself carried a glowing brand from one of the pyres, a wicked, perverse smile on his aged face. Agamemnon took it from him as the guards yanked on Poletes's arms while one of them put a knee in his back. Agamemnon grabbed the old storyteller by the hair and pulled his head back. Again I felt the spear points piercing my clothes.

"Wander through the world in darkness, cowardly teller of lies."

Poletes screamed in agony as Agamemnon burned out first his left eye and then his right. The old man fainted. The smile of a madman still twisting his thick lips, Agamemnon tossed the brand away, took out his dagger again, and slit the ears off the unconscious old man's head.

The guards dropped Poletes's limp body to the sand.

Agamemnon looked up and said in his loudest voice, "So comes justice to anyone who maligns the truth!" Then he turned, grinning, to me. "You can take your servant back now."

The guards around me stepped back, but still held their spears leveled, ready to kill me if I moved on their king.

I looked down at Poletes's bleeding form, then up to the High King.

"I heard Cassandra's prophecy," I said. "She is never believed, but she is never wrong."

Agamemnon's half-demented smile vanished. He glared at me.

For a long wavering moment I thought he would command the guards to kill me on the spot.

But then I heard Lukka's voice calling from a little way behind me. "My lord Orion, are you all right? Do you need help?"

The guards turned their gaze toward his voice. I saw that Lukka had brought his entire contingent, fully armed and ready for battle: thirty-five Hatti soldiers armed with shields and iron swords.

"He needs no help," Agamemnon answered, "except to carry away the slave I have punished."

With that he turned and hurried back toward his hut. The guards seemed to breathe one great sigh of relief and let their spears drop away from me.

I went to Poletes, picked up his bleeding, whimpering body, and carried him back to our own tents.

Chapter 23

I tended Poletes through the remainder of that night. There was only wine to ease his pain, and nothing at all to ease the anguish of his mind. I laid him in my own tent, groaning and sobbing. Lukka found a healer, a dignified old graybeard with two young women assistants, who spread salve on his burns and the bleeding slits where his ears had been.

"Not even the gods can return his sight," the healer told me solemnly, in a whisper so that Poletes could not hear. "The eyes have been burned away."

I knew what that felt like. I remembered my whole body being burned alive.

"The gods be damned," I growled. "Will he live?"

If my words shocked the healer, he gave no sign of it. "His heart is strong. If he survives the night he will live for years to come."

The healer mixed some powder into the wine cup and made Poletes drink. It put him into a deep sleep almost at once. His women prepared a bowl of poultice and showed me how to smear it over a cloth and put it on Poletes's eyes. They were silent throughout, instructing me by showing, rather than speaking, as if they were mute, and never dared to look directly into my face. The healer seemed surprised that I myself wanted to act as Poletes's nurse. But he said nothing and maintained his professional dignity.

I sat over the blinded old storyteller until dawn, putting fresh compresses over his eyes every half hour or so, keeping him from reaching up to the burns with his hands. He slept, but even in sleep he groaned and writhed.

Long after dawn had turned the sky a delicate pink, Poletes's breathing suddenly quickened and he made a grab for the cloth covering his face. I was faster, and gripped his wrists before he could hurt himself.

"My lord Orion?" His voice was cracked and dry.

"Yes," I said. "Put your hands down at your sides. Don't reach for your eyes."

"Then it's true? It wasn't a nightmare?"

I held his head up slightly and gave him a sip of wine. "It is true," I said. "You are blind."

The moan he uttered would have wrenched the heart out of a marble statue.

"Agamemnon," he said, many moments later. "The mighty king took his vengeance on an old storyteller. As if that will make his wife faithful to him."

"Try to sleep," I said. "Rest is what you need."

He shook his head, and the cloth slid off, revealing the two raw burns where his eyes had been. I went to replace the cloth, saw that it was getting dry, and smeared more poultice on it from the bowl at my side.

"You might as well slit my throat, Orion. I'll be of no use to you now. No use to anyone."

"There's been enough blood spilled here," I said.

"No use," he muttered as I put the soothing cloth over the place where his eyes had been. Then I propped his head up again and gave him more wine. Soon he fell asleep again.

Lukka stuck his head into the tent. "My lord, King Odysseus wants to see you."

I ducked out into the morning sunshine. Commanding Lukka to have a man stand watch over the sleeping Poletes, I walked over to Odysseus's boat and clambered up the rope ladder that dangled over its curving hull.

The deck was heaped with treasure looted from Troy. I turned from the dazzling display to look back at the city. Hundreds of tiny figures were up on the battlements, pulling down its blackened stones, working under the hot sun to level the walls that had defied the Achaians for so long.

I had to step carefully along the gunwale to avoid tripping over the piles of treasure covering the deck. Odysseus was at his usual place on the afterdeck, standing in the bright sunshine, his broad chest bare, his hair and beard still wet from his morning swim, a pleased smile on his thickly bearded face.

Yet his eyes searched mine as he said, "The victory is complete, thanks to you, Orion." Pointing at the demolition work going on in the distance, "Troy will never rise again."

I nodded grimly. "Priam, Hector, Aleksandros—the entire House of Ilios has been wiped out."

"All but Aeneas the Dardanian. Rumor had it that he was a bastard of Priam's. We haven't found his body."

"He might have been burned in the fire."

"It's possible," said Odysseus. "But I don't think he's terribly important. If he lives, he's hiding somewhere nearby. We'll find him. Even if we don't, there won't be anything left here for him to return to."

As I watched, one of the massive stones of the parapet by the Scaean gate was pulled loose by a horde of men straining with levers and ropes. It tumbled down to the ground with a heavy cloud of dust. Moments later I heard the thump.

"Apollo and Poseidon won't be pleased at what's being done to their walls."

Odysseus laughed. "Sometimes the gods have to bow to the will of men, Orion, whether they like it or not."

"You're not afraid of their anger?"

"If they didn't want us to pull down the walls, we wouldn't be able to do it."

I wondered. The gods are subtler than men, and have longer memories. I knew that Apollo was angry with me. How would his anger display itself?

"It's your turn to select your treasure from the spoils of the city," Odysseus said. He gestured toward a large pile of loot at the stern of the boat. "Take one-fifth of everything you see."

I thanked him, and spent an hour or so picking through the stuff. I selected blankets, armor, clothing, weapons, helmets, and jewels that could be traded for food and shelter.

"The captives are down there, between the boats. Take one-fifth of them, also."

I shook my head. "I'd rather have horses and donkeys," I told Odysseus. "The children will be useless to us, and the women will merely cause fighting among my men."

Odysseus eyed me carefully. "You speak like a man who has no intention of sailing to Ithaca with me."

"My lord," I said, "you have been more than generous to me. But no man in this camp raised a hand to help my servant last night. Agamemnon is a cruel and vicious animal. If I returned to your land, I would soon be itching to start a war against him."

Odysseus muttered, "That would be foolish."

"Perhaps so. Better that our paths separate here and now. Let me take my men, and my blinded servant, and go my own way."

The King of Ithaca stroked his beard for several silent moments, thinking it over. Finally he agreed. "Very well, Orion. Go your own way. And may the gods smile upon you."

"And on you, noblest of all the Achaians."

I never saw Odysseus again. When I returned to my tent, I told Lukka to send the men to pick up the loot I had chosen, and to find horses and donkeys to carry it—and us. I saw questions in his eyes, but he did not ask them. Instead he went to carry out my orders.

As the sun began to sink behind the islands on the western horizon, and we gathered around the cook fire for the final meal of the day, a young messenger came running up to me, breathless.

"My lord Orion, a noble visitor wishes words with you."

"Who is it?" I asked.

The teenager spread both hands. "I don't know. I was instructed to tell you that a noble of the royal house will visit you before the sun goes down. You should be prepared."

I thanked him and invited him to share our meal. He seemed extraordinarily pleased to sit side by side with the Hatti soldiers. His eyes studied their iron swords admiringly.

A noble visitor from the royal house. One of Agamemnon's people? I wondered who was coming, and why.

As the long shadows of sundown began to merge into the purple of twilight, a contingent of six Achaian warriors marched toward our campfire, with a small, slim warrior in their midst. Either a very important person or a prisoner, from the look of it, I thought. The man in the middle seemed too small for any of the Achaian nobles I had met. He wore armor buckled over a long robe, and had pulled the cheek flaps of his helmet across his face, as if going into battle. I could not see his face.

I stood and made a little bow. The mini-procession marched right up to my tent before stopping. I went to the tent and pulled open the flap.

"A representative of the High King?" I asked. "Come to make certain that the old storyteller is truly blind?"

The visitor said nothing, but ducked inside the tent. I went in after him, feeling a seething anger rising in me. I had not slept in two days, but my smoldering fury at Agamemnon kept me awake and alert.

The visitor looked down at Poletes, lying on the straw pallet asleep, a greasy cloth across his eyes, the slits where his ears had been caked with dried blood. I heard the visitor gasp. And then I noticed that his hands were tiny, delicate, much too smooth to have ever held a sword or spear.

I grasped the visitor by the shoulders, swung him around to face me, and pulled off the helmet. Helen's long golden hair tumbled past her shoulders.

"I had to see . . ." she whispered, her eyes wide with fright.

I spun her around to face the prostrate old storyteller. "Then see," I said gruffly. "Take a good look."

"Agamemnon did this."

"With his own hand. Your brother-in-law blinded him out of sheer spite. Drunk with power and glory, he celebrated his victory over Troy by mutilating an old man."

"And Menalaos?"

"Your husband stood by and watched. His men held me at spear point while his brother did his noble deed."

"Orion, I wish I could . . . when I heard what had happened, I was so sick and angry . . ."

But there were no tears in her eyes. Her voice did not shake. The words she spoke had nothing to do with what she actually felt, or why she was here.

"What do you want?" I asked her.

She turned toward me. "You see how cruel they are. What barbarians they can be."

"You're safe now," I said. "Menalaos will make you his queen once more. Sparta may not be as civilized as Troy, but there is no Troy any longer. Be happy with what you have."

She stared at me, as if trying to decide if she could dare to say what was in her mind.

I felt my anger melting away under the level gaze of those exquisite sky-blue eyes.

"I don't want to be Sparta's queen or Menalaos's wife," Helen blurted. "Just one day in this miserable camp has made me sick."

"You'll be sailing back to Mycenae soon, and then to . . ."

"No!" she said, in a desperate whisper. "I won't go back with them! Take me with you, Orion! Take me to Egypt."

Chapter 24

I T was my turn to stand there in the tent gawking with surprise. "To Egypt?"

"It's the only really civilized land in the whole world, Orion. They will receive me as the queen I am, and treat me and my entourage properly. Royally."

I should have refused her point-blank. But my mind was weaving a mad tapestry of revenge. I pictured the face of Agamemnon when he learned that his sister-in-law, for whom he had ostensibly fought this long and bloody war, had spurned his brother and run off with a stranger. Not a prince of Troy who abducted her unwillingly, but a lowly warrior, recently nothing but a *thes,* with whom she ran off at her own insistence.

I had nothing much against Menalaos, except that he was Agamemnon's brother—and he did nothing to prevent Poletes's blinding.

Let them eat the dirt of humiliation and helpless anger, I said to myself. Let the world laugh at them as Helen runs away from them once again. They deserve it.

They would search for us, I knew. They would try to find us. And if they did, they would kill me and perhaps Helen also.

What of it? I thought. What do I have to live for, except to wreak vengeance against those who have wronged me? Apollo seeks to destroy me, now that I have helped to bring down Troy. What do I have to fear from two mortal kings?

I looked down at Helen's beautiful face, so perfect, her skin as smooth and unblemished as a baby's, her eyes filled with hope and expectation, innocent and yet knowing. She was maneuvering me, I realized, using me to make her escape from these Achaian clods. She was offering herself as my reward for defying Agamemnon and Menalaos.

"Very well," I said. "Poletes should be able to travel in two more days. We will leave on the second night from tonight."

Helen's eyes sparkled and a smile touched the corners of her lips. I took her tiny hand in mine and kissed it, and she understood fully what I did not need to say.

"The second night from tonight," she whispered to me. Then she stepped lightly to me and stood on tiptoes to kiss me swiftly on the lips.

She fastened the oversized helmet back on her head, tucking her hair well inside it, and left with her escorts. I watched them march back toward Menalaos's boats, then sent one of Lukka's men to fetch the healer. His women came and dressed Poletes's wounds before he himself arrived.

"Will he be able to travel in two days," I asked, "if he doesn't have to walk?"

The healer gave me a stern look. "If he must. He is an old man, and death will claim him anyway in a few years."

"Would traveling in a wagon harm him?"

"Not enough to make much difference," he said.

After they left, I stretched out on the pallet that had been freshly laid beside Poletes's. The old man tossed in his sleep and muttered something. I leaned on one elbow to hear his words.

"Beware of a woman's gifts," Poletes mumbled.

I sighed. "Now you utter prophecies instead of stories, old man," I whispered.

Poletes did not reply.

I fell asleep almost as soon as my head touched the straw. I willed myself to remain here, on the plain of Ilios, and not allow myself to be drawn to the realm of the Creators. I knew that danger beyond my powers awaited me there.

Whether my willpower was strong enough to keep me from being summoned to the Creators' domain, or whether Apollo, Zeus, and their company simply did not bother trying to reach me,

I cannot say. All I know is that I met no gods, angry or otherwise, in my sleep that night.

But I did dream. I dreamed of Egypt, of a hot land stretching along a wide river, flanked on either side by burning desert. A land of palm trees and crocodiles, so ancient that time itself seemed meaningless there. A land of massive pyramids standing like strange, alien monuments amid the puny towns of men, dwarfing all human scale, all human knowledge.

And *inside* the greatest of those pyramids, I saw my own beloved, waiting for me, as silent and still as a statue, waiting for me to bring her back to life.

The next morning I told Lukka that we would be leaving the camp and heading for Egypt.

"That's a far distance," he said. "Across hostile lands."

"That is where we're going," I insisted. "Will the men follow me?"

Lukka's brown eyes flicked up at mine, then looked away. "We've won three wagonloads of loot for a few days' work and a couple of hours of hard fighting. They'll follow you, never fear."

"All the way to Egypt?"

He made a humorless grin. "If we make it. The Egyptians hire soldiers for their army, from what I hear. They no longer fight their own wars. If we get to their borders, we will find employment."

"Good," I said, happy to have an excuse that would urge them onward toward my goal.

"I'll start the men gathering wagons for our supplies," Lukka said.

I took his shoulder in my hand. "I may bring a woman with me."

He actually smiled. "I was wondering when you'd unbend."

"But I don't want the men dragging along camp followers. Will they resent my bringing a woman? Will it cause trouble?"

Scratching at his beard, Lukka replied, "There've been plenty of women here in the camp. The men are satisfied, for now. We can move faster without camp followers, that's certain. And we'll probably find women here and there as we march."

I understood what he meant. "Yes, I doubt that our passage to Egypt will be entirely peaceful."

This time his eyes locked on mine. "I only hope that our leaving the camp is entirely peaceful."

I smiled grimly. He was no fool, this Hatti soldier.

Two nights later I bribed a teenaged boy to come with me to the camp of Menalaos. The area was not really guarded: the few armed men who stood watch knew that there were no enemies present. They were more intent on protecting their king's loot and slaves from thievery than anything else.

The youth and I found Helen's tent. Serving women loitered outside, eyeing me askance, as if they knew what was about to happen. One of them ushered me into her mistress's tent. It was large, and Helen was pacing in it nervously when we entered it.

Helen dismissed her servant, and with hardly a word between us, I knocked the startled youth unconscious, stripped him, and watched Helen pull his rags over her own short-skirted chemise. She pointed to a plain wooden chest, half as wide as the span of my arms, and as I hefted it she took up a smaller box.

Still wordless, we walked out of the tent, past the women, past the careless guards, and toward the riverbank, where Lukka and his men waited for us with horses, donkeys, and oxcarts.

We left the Achaian camp on the plain of Ilios in the dark of night, like a band of robbers. Riding on a thickly folded blanket that passed among these people for a saddle, I turned and looked for one last time at the ruin of Troy, its once-proud walls already crumbling and ghostlike in the cold silvery light of the rising moon.

The ground rumbled. Our horses snorted and neighed, prancing nervously.

"Poseidon speaks," said Poletes from the oxcart, his voice weak but discernible. "The earth will shake soon from his wrath. He will finish the task of bringing down the walls of Troy."

The old man was predicting an earthquake. A big one. All the more reason for us to get as far away as possible.

We forded the river and headed southward. Toward Egypt.

BOOK II

JERICHO

Chapter 25

AS Lukka had predicted, our journey was neither easy nor peaceful.

The whole world seemed in conflict. We trekked slowly down the hilly coastline, through regions that the Hatti soldiers called Assuwa and Seha. It seemed that every city, every village, every farmhouse was in arms. Bands of marauders prowled the countryside, some of them former Hatti army units just as Lukka's contingent was, most of them merely gangs of brigands.

We fought almost every day. Men died over a brace of chickens or even an egg. We lost a few of our men in these skirmishes, and gained a few from bands that offered to join us. I never accepted anyone that Lukka would not accept, and he took in only other Hatti professionals. Our group remained at about thirty men, a few more or less, from one month to the next.

I kept searching anxiously to our rear, every day, half expecting to see Menalaos leading his forces in pursuit of his wayward queen. But if the Achaians were following after us, I saw no sign. And I slept at nights without being visited by Apollo or Zeus or any of their kind. Perhaps they were busy elsewhere. Or perhaps whatever fate they had prepared for me was waiting in Egypt, inside the tomb of a king.

The rainy season began, and although it turned roads into quagmires of slick, sticky mud and made us miserable and cold, it also stopped most of the bands of brigands from their murderous marauding. Most of them. We still had to fight our way through a trap in the hills just above a city that Lukka called Ti-Smurna.

And Lukka himself was nearly killed by a farmer who thought we were after his wife and daughters. Stinking and filthy, the farmer had hidden himself in his miserable hovel of a barn —nothing more than a low cave that he had put a gate to—and rammed a pitchfork at Lukka's back when he went in to pick out a pair of lambs. It was food we were after, not women. We had paid the farmer's wife with a bauble from the loot of Troy, but the man had concealed himself when he had first caught sight of us, expecting us to rape his women and burn what we could not carry off.

He lunged at Lukka's unprotected back, murder in his frightened, cowardly eyes. Fortunately I was close enough to leap between them, knocking the pitchfork away with my arm.

The farmer expected to be killed by inches, but we left him trembling, kneeling in the dung of his animals. Lukka said little, as usual, but what he said spoke volumes.

"Once again I owe you my life, my lord Orion."

I replied lightly, "Your life is very important to me, Lukka."

I did not sleep with Helen. I hardly touched her. She traveled with us as part of our group, without complaining of the hardships, the bloodletting, the pain. She made her own bed at night, out of horse blankets, and slept slightly separated from the men. But always closer to me than anyone else. I was content to be her guardian, not her lover. If that surprised her, she gave no hint of it. She wore no jewels and no longer painted her face. Her clothes were plain and rough, fit for traveling rather than display.

Still she was beautiful. She did not need paints or gowns or jewelry. Even with her face smudged by mud and her hair tied up and tucked under the cowl of a long dirty cloak, nothing could hide those wide blue eyes, those sensuous lips, that unblemished skin.

Poletes gained strength and even some of his old cynical spirit. He rode in the creaking oxcart and pestered whoever drove the cart to tell him everything he saw, every leaf and rock and cloud, in detail.

Ephesus was the sole exception to our litany of warfare. We had spent the morning trudging tiredly uphill through a rainstorm, soaked and cold and aching. About half of the men were mounted on horses or donkeys. Helen rode beside me on a light dun-colored pony, wrapped in a dark blue hooded cloak, soggy and heavy with rain. I had sent three of our men on foot ahead as scouts. Several others trailed behind, a rear guard to warn us of bandits skulking behind us—or Achaians trying to catch up with us.

As we came to the top of the hill, I saw one of our scouts waiting for us beside the muddy road.

"The city." He pointed.

The rain had slackened, and Ephesus lay below us in a pool of sunlight that had broken through the gray clouds. The city glittered like a beacon of warmth and comfort, white marble gleaming in the sunshine.

We all seemed to gain strength from the sight, and made our way down the winding road from the hills to the seaport city of Ephesus.

"The city is dedicated to Artemis the Healer," said Lukka. "Men from every part of the world come here to be cured of their ailments. A sacred spring has water with magical curative powers." He frowned slightly, as if disappointed in his own gullibility. Then he added, "So I'm told."

There were no walls around Ephesus. No army had ever tried to take it or sack it. By a sort of international agreement, this city was dedicated to the goddess Artemis and her healing arts, and not even the most barbarian king dared to attack it, lest he and his entire army fall to Artemis's invisible arrows, which bring plague and painful death.

Helen, listening to Lukka explaining these things to me, rode up between us. "Artemis is a goddess of the moon, and sister of Apollo."

That made my heart quicken. "Then she favored Troy in the war."

Helen shrugged beneath her sodden cloak. "I suppose so. It did her no good, though, did it?"

"But she will be angry with us," Lukka said.

So is her brother, I knew, although they are not truly brother and sister. I made myself smile and said aloud to Lukka, "Surely you don't believe that the gods and goddesses hold grudges?"

He did not reply, but the expression on his dour face was not a happy one.

Whatever its patron deity, Ephesus was civilization. Even the streets were paved with marble. Stately columned temples of fluted white marble were centers of healing as well as worship. The city was accustomed to hosting visitors, and there were plenty of inns available. We chose the first one we came to, at the edge of the city. It was almost empty since the few who traveled in the rainy season preferred to be in the heart of the city or down by the docks where the boats came in.

The innkeeper was overjoyed at having some thirty of us as his guests. He kept rubbing his hands together and grinning as we unloaded our animals and carts.

"Your goods will be perfectly safe here, sir," he assured me, "even if they were made of solid gold. My own sons protect this inn and no thief will touch what is yours."

I wondered how certain of that he would have been if he had known that inside the boxes we carried to our rooms there *were* treasures of gold. We stacked all of the boxes in one room, the inn's largest. I chose to sleep in that room myself, with blind Poletes.

The city also had whorehouses. Lukka's men disappeared like a puff of smoke as soon as our horses were stabled and our goods safely stashed in our rooms.

"They'll be back in the morning," he told me.

"You are free to go, too," I said.

"You'll need someone to guard our goods," he said.

"I'll stand guard. You go see the city."

Lukka's stern face remained its impassive mask, but I knew he was debating within himself. Finally he said, "I'll come back at sunset."

I laughed and clapped him on the shoulder. "Come back at dawn, my dutiful friend. Enjoy the city and its delights. You've earned a night's entertainment."

"You're certain . . ."

Gesturing toward the boxes stacked next to my bed, I said, "I can guard our goods."

"Alone?"

"I have the innkeeper's ferocious sons." We had seen the sons. Two of them were big and burly, the other two slight and wiry, as if they had been born of a different mother. They hardly seemed dangerous to us, not after the fighting we had seen, but they appeared adequate to ward off sneak thieves.

"And I am here also," said Poletes. "Even without ears, I can hear better than a bat. In the dark of night, I will be a better guard than you and your two eyes."

Very reluctantly, Lukka took his leave of us.

Helen was in the next room. She had commandeered the innkeeper's two young daughters to serve her. I heard them chattering and giggling as they hauled steaming buckets of water up the creaking stairs and poured them into the wooden tub that the wife of the house had provided for Helen.

None of them knew who we were, of course. I knew there would quickly be talk about the beautiful golden-haired woman and the band of Hatti soldiers who were with her. But as long as no one associated us with the war at Troy or with the Achaians, we were safe enough.

"Tell me of the city," Poletes asked. "What is it like?"

I went to the balcony and began to describe what I saw: temples, inns, busy streets, a bustling port, sails out in the harbor, splendid houses up on the hills.

"There must be a marketplace in the heart of the city," Poletes said, cackling with glee. "Tomorrow one of the men can take me there and I will tell the story of the fall of Troy, of Achilles's pride and Agamemnon's cruelty, of the burning of a great city and the slaughter of its heroes. The people will love it!"

"No," I said softly. "We can't let these people know who we are. It's too dangerous."

He turned his blind eyes toward me. The scars left by the burns seemed to glower at me, accusingly.

"But I'm a storyteller! I have the greatest story anyone's ever heard, here in my head." He tapped his temple, just above the ragged slit where his ear had been. "I can make my fortune telling this story!"

"Not here," I said. "And not now."

"But I can stop being a burden to you! I could earn my own way. I could become famous!"

"Not while she's with us," I insisted.

He snorted angrily. "She has caused more agony than any mortal woman ever born."

"Perhaps so. But until I see her safely accepted in Egypt, where she can be protected, you'll tell no tales about Troy."

Poletes grumbled and mumbled and groped his way back to his

bed. I stayed at his side and steered him clear of the stacked boxes of loot.

As the old storyteller plopped down on the feather mattress, I heard a scratching at the door.

"Did you hear . . ."

Poletes said, "It's someone asking to come in. That's the way civilized people do it. They don't pound on the door as if they intended to break it down, the way you do."

I picked up my sword from the table between our two beds. Holding it in its scabbard, I went to the door and opened it a crack.

It was one of the innkeeper's daughters: a husky, dimpled girl with laughing dark eyes.

"The lady asks if you will come to see her in her chamber," she said, after a clumsy curtsy.

I looked up and down the hallway. It was empty. "Tell her I'll be there in a few moments."

Shutting the door, I went to Poletes's bed and sat on its edge.

"I know," he said. "You're going to her. She'll snare you in her web of allurements."

"You have a poet's way of expression," I said.

"Don't try to flatter me."

Ignoring his petulance, I asked, "Can you guard our goods until I return?"

He grunted and turned this way and that on the soft bedding and finally admitted, "I suppose so."

"You'll yell loudly if anyone tries to enter this room?"

"I'll wake the whole inn."

"Can you bar the door behind me and find your way back to the bed again?"

"What if I stumble and break my neck? You'll be with your lady love."

I laughed. "I may only be there a few minutes. I have no intention of . . ."

"Oh, no, not at all!" He hooted. "Just make sure you don't bellow like a mating bull. I'm going to try to get some sleep."

Feeling a little like a schoolboy sneaking out of his dormitory, I went to the door and bid Poletes a pleasant nap.

"I sleep very lightly, you know," he said.

Whether he meant that to reassure me that no sneak thief would be able to rob us, or to warn me to be quiet in Helen's room, next door, I could not tell. Perhaps he meant both.

The hallway was still empty, and I could see no dark corners or niches where an enemy could lurk in ambush. Nothing but the worn tiled floor, the plastered walls, and six wooden doors of rooms that my men had taken. Not that any of them would occupy them this night. On the other side of the hall was a railing of split logs, overlooking the central courtyard of the inn and its packed-dirt floor.

I clenched my fist to knock at Helen's door, then remembered Poletes's words. Feeling slightly foolish, I scratched at the smooth wooden planks instead.

"Who is there?" came Helen's muffled voice.

"Orion."

"You may enter."

I pushed the door open. She stood in the center of the shabby room, resplendent as the sun. Helen had put on the same robes and jewels she had worn that first time I had seen her alone, in her chamber in Troy. There, she had looked incredibly beautiful. Here, in this rough inn with its crudely plastered walls and uncurtained windows, she seemed like a goddess come to Earth.

I closed the door behind me and leaned my back against it, almost weak with the beauty of her.

"You have taken none of the treasures of Troy for yourself, my lord Orion," she said.

"I haven't wanted any of them. Until now."

She opened her arms and I went to her and swept her up and carried her to the soft, yielding downy bed. In the back of my mind I wept for a woman who was totally different from the golden, splendid Helen: a woman of lustrous dark hair and wondrous gray eyes, a tall and graceful goddess of truth and beauty. But she was dead, and Helen was warm fire in my arms.

The sun sank on the edge of the glittering sea and long violet shadows stole across the city of Ephesus as the cloak of night softly drew itself over all. The stars peeked through tattered clouds and Artemis's sliver of a moon came up while Helen and I made love and drowsed, half-woke and made love once more, then slept and woke and made love still again.

In the gray half light that precedes true dawn we slept in each other's arms, totally spent, unconscious with the sweet exhaustion of passion.

And I found myself in that other world of golden light so brilliant that it hurt my eyes.

"You think you can escape from me?"

I turned round and round, searching, straining for sight of the Golden One. Nothing. Only his voice.

"You have thwarted my plans for the last time, Orion. You cannot escape my vengeance."

"Show yourself!" I shouted. "Stand before me so I can throttle the life out of you!"

But I was sitting up in bed, my clawed hands clenching empty air, while Helen stared at me with wide frightened eyes.

That morning I took Helen and Poletes into the heart of the city, while Lukka—who had returned at dawn, true to his word —stood guard over our goods and dourly watched his men stagger back to the inn, one by one.

Ephesus was truly a city of culture and comfort, rich with marble temples and streets thronged with merchants and wares from Crete, Egypt, Babylon, and even far-off India.

Poletes was most interested in the marketplace. He was strong enough to walk now, and he had tied a scarf of white silk across his useless eyes. He carried a walking stick, and was learning to tap out the ground ahead of him so that he could walk by himself.

"Storytellers!" he yelped, as we passed small knots of people gathered around old men who squatted on the ground, weaving spells of words for a few coins.

"Not here," I whispered to him.

"Let me stay and listen," he begged. "I promise not to speak a word."

Reluctantly I allowed it. I knew I could trust Poletes's word. It with his heart that I worried about. He was a storyteller, it was in his blood. How long could he remain silent when he had the grandest story of all time to tell the crowd?

I decided to give him an hour to himself, while Helen and I browsed through the shops and stalls of the marketplace. She seemed deliriously happy to be fingering fine cloth and examining decorated pottery, bargaining with the shopkeepers and then walking on, buying nothing. I shrugged and accompanied her, brooding in the back of my mind over the Golden One's threat of the predawn hour.

He would destroy me if he could, I told myself. The fact that he hasn't shows either that the other Creators are restraining him, or that he needs me for some further tasks.

Or, I dared to think, that I am becoming powerful enough to protect myself.

The ground rumbled. A great gasping cry went up from the crowd in the marketplace. A few pots tottered off their shelves and smashed on the ground. The world seemed to sway giddily, sickeningly. Then the rumbling ceased and all returned to normal. For a moment the people were absolutely silent. Then a bird chirped and everyone began talking at once, with the kind of light fast banter that comes with a surge of relief from terror.

An earth tremor. Natural enough in these parts, I supposed. Unless it was a warning, a deliberate sign from those far-advanced creatures whom the peoples of this time regarded as gods.

The hour was nearly over. I could see Poletes, across the great square of the marketplace, standing at the edge of the crowd gathered around one of the storytellers, his gnarled legs almost as skinny as the stick he leaned on.

"Orion."

I looked down at Helen. She was smiling at me like an understanding mother smiles at a naughty son. "You haven't heard a word I've said."

"I'm sorry. My mind was elsewhere."

She repeated, "I said that we could live here in Ephesus very nicely. This is a civilized city, Orion. With the wealth we have brought, we could buy a comfortable villa and live splendidly."

"And Egypt?"

She sighed. "It's *so* far away. And traveling has been much more difficult than I thought it would be."

"Perhaps we could get a boat and sail to Egypt," I suggested. "It would be much swifter and easier than overland."

Her eyes brightened. "Of course! There are hundreds of boats in the harbor."

But when we went to the dock, all thoughts of boats fled from our minds. We saw six galleys stroking into the harbor, all of them bearing a picture of a lion's head on their sails.

"Menalaos!" Helen gasped.

"Or Agamemnon," I said. "Either way, we can't stay here. They're searching for you."

Chapter 26

WE fled Ephesus that night, leaving a very disappointed innkeeper who had looked forward to us staying much longer.

As we rode up into the hills and took the southward trail, I wondered if we could not have appealed to the city's council for protection. But the fear of the armed might of the Achaians who had just destroyed Troy would have paralyzed the Ephesians, I realized. Their city had no protective walls and no real army, merely a city guard for keeping order in the bawdier districts; it depended on the good will of all for its safety. They would not allow Helen to stay in their city when Menalaos and his brother Agamemnon demanded her surrender.

So we pushed on, through the rains and cold of winter, bearing our booty from Troy. A strange group we were: the fugitive Queen of Sparta, a blind storyteller, a band of professional soldiers from an empire that no longer existed, and an outcast from a different time.

We came to the city of Miletus. Here there were walls, strong ones, and a bustling commercial city.

"I was here once," Lukka told me, "when the great High King Hattusilis was angry with the city and brought his army to its gates. They were so frightened that they opened their gates and offered no resistance. They threw themselves upon the High King's mercy. He was magnificent! He slew only the city's leaders, the men who had displeased him, and would not allow us to touch even an egg."

We bought fresh provisions and mounts. Miletus would be the last major city on our route for some time. We planned to move inland, through the Mountains of the Bull and across the plain of Cilicia, then along the edge of the Mittani lands and down the Syrian coastline.

But the sounds and smells of another Aegean city were too much for Poletes. He came to me as we started to break our camp, just outside the city walls, and announced that he would not go on with us. He preferred to remain in Miletus.

"It is a city where I can tell my tales and earn my own bread," he said to me. "I will not burden you further, my lord Orion. Let me spend my final days singing of Troy and the mighty deeds that were done there."

"You can't stay by yourself," I insisted. "You have no house, no shelter of any kind. How will you find food?"

He reached up for my shoulder as unerringly as if he could see. "Let me sit in a corner of the marketplace and tell the tale of Troy," he said. "I will have food and wine and a soft bed before the sun goes down."

"Is that what you truly want?" I asked him.

"I have burdened you long enough, my lord. Now I can take care of myself."

He stood there before me in the pale light of a gray morning, a clean white scarf over his eyes, a fresh tunic hanging over his skinny frame. I learned then that even blinded eyes can cry. And so could I.

We embraced like brothers, and he turned without another word and walked slowly toward the city gate, tapping his stick before him.

I sent the others off on the inland road, telling them I would catch up later. I waited half the day, then entered the city and made my way to the marketplace. Poletes sat there cross-legged in the middle of a large and rapidly growing throng, his arms gesturing, his wheezing voice speaking slowly, majestically: "Then mighty Achilles prayed to his mother, Thetis the Silver-Footed, 'Mother, my lifetime is destined to be so brief that ever-living Zeus, sky-thunderer, owes me a worthier prize of glory . . .'"

I watched for only a few minutes. That was enough. Men and

women, boys and little girls, were rushing up to join the crowd, their eyes fastened on Poletes like the eyes of a bird hypnotized by a snake. Rich merchants, soldiers in chain mail, women of fashion in their colorful robes, city magistrates carrying their wands of office—they all pressed close to hear Poletes's words. Even the other storytellers, left alone once Poletes had started singing of Troy, got up from their accustomed stones and ambled grudgingly across the marketplace to listen to the newcomer.

Poletes was right, I reluctantly admitted. He had found his place. He would be fed and sheltered here, even honored. And as long as we were far away, he could sing of Troy and Helen all he wanted to.

I went back to the city gate, where I had left my horse with the guards there. I handed their corporal a few coppers, and nosed my chestnut mount up the inland trail. I would never see Poletes again, and that made me feel the sadness of loss.

But time and distance softened my sadness, blurred it into a bittersweet memory of the cranky old storyteller.

Lukka led us across a steep and snowy mountain pass and down into the warm and fruitful Cilician plain, where wine grapes, wheat, and barley grew and olive trees dotted the countryside.

The Cilician cities were tightly shut against all strangers. The collapse of the Hatti empire was felt here; instead of depending on imperial law and the protection of the Hatti army, each city had to look to its own safety. We bartered for what we needed with farmers and suspicious villagers, then headed eastward across the plain and finally turned south, keeping the sea always at our right.

I noticed that Helen looked over her shoulder often, searching as I did for signs of pursuit. We scanned the sea, as well, whenever we could see it. None of the sails we spotted bore a lion's head.

On the road we slept apart. It was better discipline for the men, I thought. I did not take her to bed unless we were in a town or city where the men could find women for themselves. I realized that my passion for Helen was controllable, and therefore not the kind of love that I had for my dead goddess.

Gradually, she began to tell me of her earlier life. She had been abducted when barely twelve, whisked away from the farm of an uncle on the saddle of a local chieftain who had taken a fancy to her newly budding beauty. Her father had bribed the grizzled old bandit and he surrendered her unharmed, but the incident convinced her father that he would have to marry off his daughter quickly, while she was still a virgin.

"Every princeling in Achaia sought my hand," she told me one night when we were camped in a little village ringed by a palisade of sharpened stakes. The village chief had decided to be hospitable to our band of armed men. Lukka and his men were being entertained by some of the local women. Helen and I had been offered a small hut of mud bricks. It was the first time we had been under a roof in weeks.

She spoke wistfully, almost sadly, almost as if all that had happened to her had somehow been her own fault. "With so many suitors, my father had to be very careful in his choice. Finally he picked Menalaos, brother of the High King. It was a good match for him; it tied our house to the most powerful house in Argos."

"You had no say in the matter?"

She smiled at such an absurd idea. "I didn't see Menalaos until our wedding day. My father kept me well protected."

"And then Aleksandros," I said.

"And then Aleksandros. He was handsome, and witty, and charming. He treated me as if I were a *person*, a human being."

"You went with him willingly, then?"

Again her smile. "He never asked. He never took the risk that I might refuse him. In the end, despite his wit and charm, he still behaved like an Achaian: he took what he wanted."

I looked deep into her bright blue eyes, so innocent, so knowing. "But in Troy you told me . . ."

"Orion," she said softly, "in this world a woman must accept what she cannot change. Troy was better for me than Sparta. Aleksandros was more civilized than Menalaos. But neither of them asked me for my hand: I was given to Menalaos by my father; I was taken from him by Aleksandros."

Then she added, almost shyly, "You are the only man I've had to pursue. You are the only one I've given myself to willingly."

I took her in my arms and there was no more talking for that night. But still I wondered how much of her tale I could believe. How true was her passion for me, and how much of it was her way to make certain that I would protect her all the way to distant Egypt?

The turmoil of our earlier travels eased after Cilicia. Robber bands and wandering contingents of masterless soldiery became rare. We no longer had to fight our way across the land. Yet each night Lukka had his men tend to their weapons and equipment as if he expected a pitched battle in the morning.

"Now we head toward Ugarit," Lukka told me as we turned south once again. "We sacked the city many years ago, when I was just a youngling squire clinging to my father's chariot as we charged into battle."

Past Ugarit we went. The once-mighty city was still little more than a burned-out shell, with shacks and shanties clinging to the blackened stumps of its walls where once mighty houses and fortified towers had stood. I saw the visible evidence of the power of the Hatti empire, strong enough to reach across mountains and plains to crush a city that defied its High King. And yet that power was gone now, blown away in the wind like the sands of a melting dune.

For the first time since I had been up in the hills above Troy, I saw a forest, tall stately cedar trees that spread their leafy branches high overhead, so that walking through them was like walking down the aisle of a living cathedral that went on for miles and miles.

And then, abruptly, we were in the rugged scorched hills of the desert. Bare stones heated by the pitiless sun until they were too hot to touch. Hardly any vegetation at all, merely little clumps of bushes here and there. Snakes and scorpions scuttled on the burning ground; overhead carrion birds circled waiting, waiting.

We cut far inland over the broken hilly terrain, avoiding the coast and the port cities. Now and again a band of marauders accosted us, always to their sorrow. We left many bodies for those patient birds to feast on, although we lost four men of our own.

The territory was a natural habitat for robbers: raw, lawless, a succession of broken barren hills and narrow valleys and defiles where ambush could be expected at every turn. The heat was like an oven, making the land dance in shimmering waves that sapped the strength from my men and their mounts.

Helen rode in the cart, shaded by tenting made of the finest silks of Troy. The heat took the energy from her, too, and her lovely face became wan and drawn; like the rest of us, she was caked with grimy dust. But not once did she complain or ask us to slow our southward pace.

"Meggido is not far from here," said Lukka one hot bright day,

as the sweat poured down his leathery face and into his beard.
"The Hatti and the Egyptians fought a great battle there."

We were skirting the shores of a sizable lake. Villages lay
scattered around it, and we had been able to barter some of our
goods for provisions. The lake water was bitter-tasting, but better
than thirst. We filled our canteens and barrels with it.

"Who won?" I asked.

Lukka considered the question with his usual grave silence, then
replied, "Our High King Muwatallis claimed a great victory
for us. But we never returned to that place, and the army came
back to our own lands much smaller than it was when it went
out."

Around the lake we traveled, and then down the river that
flowed southward out of it. Villages were sparse here. Farming,
even along the river, was difficult in the dry powdery soil. Most of
the villages lived on herds of goats and sheep that nibbled the
sparse grass wherever they could find it. These people also spoke
of Meggido, and told of the enormous battles that had been fought
for it from time immemorial. But they gave the city a slightly
different name: Armaggeddon.

The weather was getting so hot that we took to moving only in
the very early morning and again late in the day, when the sun had
gone down. We slept during the coldest hours of the night,
shivering in our blankets, and tried to sleep during the hottest
hours of midday.

One morning I walked on ahead, taking my turn as advance
scout. The day before we had beaten off an attack by a determined
party of raiders. They did not have the look of bandits about
them. Like us, they seemed to be members of an organized troop,
well armed and disciplined enough to back away from us in good
order once they realized we were professional soldiers.

I climbed a little rise in the rugged, barren ground and, with one
hand shading my eyes, surveyed the shimmering, wavering, hellish
landscape.

Rocks and scrub, parched grass turning brown under the sun,
except for the thin line of green along the banks of the river.

Up on the top of a rocky hill I saw a column of grayish-white
smoke rising. It looked strange to me. Not like the smoke of a fire
that curls and drifts on the wind, this was almost like a pillar,
densely packed, swirling in on itself, and rising straight up into the

bright, blinding sky. The smoke itself seemed to glow, as if lighted from within.

I scrambled across the rocky desert toward the column of smoke. As I trudged up the slope of the hill, I felt a strange tingling in my feet. It grew stronger, almost painful, as I neared the top.

The hilltop was bare rock, except for a couple of tiny outcroppings of bare brown dead-looking bushes. The column of smoke streamed directly from the rock toward the sky, with no apparent source. My legs were jangling as if someone were sticking thousands of pins into them.

"Better to take off your boots, Orion," came a familiar voice. "The nails in them conduct electrostatic forces. I have no desire to cause you undue pain."

Sullen anger flooded through me as I grudgingly tugged off the boots and tossed them aside. The tingling sensation did not disappear entirely, but subsided to the point where I could ignore it.

The Golden One stepped out of the base of the smoke column. He seemed somehow older than I had ever seen him before, his face more solemn, his eyes burning with inner fires. Instead of the robes I had seen him wearing when I had been on the plain of Ilios, he had draped himself in a plain white garment that seemed to be made of rough wool. It glowed softly against the swirling pillar of grayish smoke behind him.

"For your disobedience, I should destroy you." He spoke in a quiet, level, controlled tone.

My hands itched to reach his throat, but I could not move them. I knew that he controlled me, that he could stop my heart's beating with the flick of an eyebrow, could force me to kneel and grovel at his feet merely by thinking it. The fury within me rose hotter than the sun-baked stone on which I stood barefoot, hotter than the blazing cloudless sky that shone like hammered brass above us.

I managed to say, as I stood with my fists clenched helplessly at my sides, "You can't destroy me. The others won't let you. They opposed you at Troy, some of them. Blame *them* for your defeat."

"I do, Orion. I will have my vengeance against them. And you will help me to achieve it."

"Never! I won't raise a finger to help you. I'll work against you in every way I can."

He made a deep dramatic sigh and took a step toward me. "Orion, we must not be enemies. You are my creation, my creature. Together we can save the continuum."

"Once you killed her you made me your enemy."

He closed his eyes and bowed his head slightly. "I know. I understand." Looking at me with those intent eyes once more, he said softly, "I miss her too."

I tried to laugh in his face, but it came out like a snarl.

"Orion, I have been studying the situation carefully. There may—I say only *may,* mind you—be a way of restoring her."

Despite his controls I leaped forward and almost grasped him by the shoulders. But my hands froze in midair.

"Not so fast!" the Golden One said. "It's only a remote possibility. The risks are huge. The dangers . . ."

"I don't care," I said, my pulse roaring in my ears. "Bring her back to me! Restore her!"

"I cannot do it alone. And the others . . . those who opposed me at Troy, they will oppose me again. It will mean a deliberate change in the continuum of a magnitude that not even I have attempted before."

I heard his words, but I could not comprehend their full meaning. Nor was I certain that he was telling me the truth.

"I never lie, Orion," he said, reading my thoughts. "To restore her means tampering with the space-time continuum to such an extent that I could rip it apart just as surely as Ahriman once did."

"But you and your other Creators survived that," I said.

"Some of us did. Some of us did not. I told you that gods are not necessarily immortal."

"And that they are not necessarily just or merciful, too," I replied.

He laughed. "Just so. Just so."

"Will you try to restore her?" My voice was almost begging.

"Yes," he said. Before my heart could leap for joy he added, "But only if you obey me fully and completely, Orion. Her existence is in your hands."

There was no sense trying to resist or dissemble. "What do you want me to do?"

For an instant he did not reply, as if he were formulating his plans on the spot. Then he said, "You are heading south, toward Egypt."

"Yes."

"You will soon encounter a wandering band of people who are migrating out of Egypt. Whole families, hundreds of them, traveling together with their flocks and tents. They seek to occupy this territory, to make it their own . . ."

"*This* territory?" I gestured around at the barren rocks and dead scrub.

"Even this," replied the Golden One. "And they are opposed by the villagers and townspeople who already live here. You and your troop of soldiers will help them."

"Why them?"

He smiled at me. "Because they worship me, Orion. They believe that I am not merely the mightiest god of them all, but the only god that exists. And soon, with your help, they will be perfectly right."

Before I could ask another question, before I could even think, the Golden One disappeared and the pillar of smoke evaporated as if it had never been.

Chapter 27

W E pushed southward, down the river that flowed from one landlocked sea to another. There were villages dotted along its banks, protected by walls of dried mud bricks. Green farmlands fed by irrigation ditches stood in bold contrast to the bare browns and grays of the rocky hills. The people here were wary of strangers; too many wandering bands had come their way, anxious to take those green lands for themselves or, failing that, to pillage and loot the towns before moving on.

They traded with us, grudgingly, more in an effort to get us to leave their area as quickly as possible. I always kept Helen out of sight, inside the covered cart. And still I watched for signs of Achaians searching for us.

Then one hot afternoon, as the heat haze made a shimmering mirage out of a dry rocky canyon, we came across the advance scouts of the people the Golden One had told me about.

There were twenty of them, warriors, on foot, no two of them wearing the same kind or color of clothing or the same kind of weapons. A ragtag lot, at first glance. Smallish in stature, browned by the sun—just as we were, I realized.

They had arrayed themselves across the narrowest neck of the canyon as we approached them. I wondered if they thought they could stop us from passing through, if it came to a fight. Most of us were mounted on horses and donkeys. I thought we could punch through their thin screen if we had to.

But Lukka, scrutinizing them with a professional eye as we approached, said, "They're not fools, despite their shabby clothes."

"Do you recognize them?"

He shook his head the slightest distance it could move and still convey a negative. "They may be the Abiru that the villagers warned us against two days ago."

I nosed my horse forward. "I'll speak with their leader."

He rode up beside me. "I can translate, if they speak any language of the empire."

"I can understand their language," I said.

Lukka gave me a strange look.

"It's a gift from the gods," I explained. "The gift of tongues."

I rode slightly ahead and raised my hand in a sign of peace. One of the warriors walked up toward me, still holding his spear in his right hand. I slid down from my horse and stood on the dusty soil as he approached me. The heat beat down from the brazen sky and reflected off the scorching rocks. It was like standing in an oven. The only shade in sight was the sparse sliver along the canyon wall to my left. But this young warrior showed no interest in getting out of the hot sun.

His name was Ben-Jameen; he was the eldest son of a tribal chief. They called themselves the Children of Israel, he told me. Ben-Jameen was a youngster, his beard barely starting to sprout. But he was lean and hard-muscled; his eyes missed nothing as he scanned my two dozen men, the horses, donkeys, and oxcarts. He was tense and suspicious, gripping his spear tightly, as if prepared to use it at an instant's notice.

When I told him that we were Hatti soldiers, he used the term "Hittites," and seemed to relax slightly. He almost smiled.

"In whose service are you, then?" he asked.

"No one's. We have come from a great war, far to the north and west of here. We helped to destroy the kingly city of Troy."

His face went blank; he had never heard the name.

"Perhaps you know it as Ilium, by the straits called the Hellespont that lead into the Sea of Black Waters."

Still no gleam of recognition.

I gave it up. "It was a war, and these men helped to take the city after a long siege."

At that, something glimmered in his eyes. "Why are you here, then, in this land of Canaan?"

"We are traveling south, to Egypt, to seek service with the great king of that land."

He glared at me, then coughed up phlegm and spat on the parched ground. "*That* for the Pharaoh! It took my people four generations to escape the slavery of Egypt."

I made a shrug and replied, "We are a unit of professional soldiery. I have heard that the Egyptian king has need of soldiers."

Those suspicious eyes fixed on me. "You are not in anyone's service now?"

"No. The old empire has collapsed . . ."

"The God of Israel has smitten the Hittites," he murmured, and now he truly did smile.

I glanced at Lukka, still on his horse, off to one side, and was glad that he could not understand the Hebrew tongue.

"And now He will smite the evil worshipers of Baal who shut themselves up in their city." Ben-Jameen looked past me, at the men and their mounts, the carts, at Lukka sitting on his horse slightly behind me, and finally at me again. There was a new light in his eyes. "You will serve our God and our people and help us to take the city of Jericho, just as you took that northern city you spoke of."

"We are not seeking service here," I said. "We are traveling to Egypt."

"You will serve the God of Israel," Ben-Jameen insisted. Then, softening slightly, he said, "At least come and spend the night in our camp and meet our great leader Joshua."

I hesitated, sensing a trap.

The youngster smiled shyly. "He would never forgive me if I allowed you to leave without bringing you to him. I would be disgraced before my father's eyes."

It was difficult to argue with him.

"Besides," he added, the smile brightening slightly, "it will be impossible for you to go farther south without running into other groups of our people. We are a multitude."

I bowed to the inevitable and accepted his offer of hospitality as graciously as I could.

The Israelites were indeed a multitude, hundreds of families camped on a wide plain between the river they called Jordan and the worn, bare, baked-brown mountains. Their tents dotted the green plain, and their flocks stirred clouds of dust when they were driven from pasture to the rough fences of their nightly fold.

With the setting sun turning the western sky blood red, and the hot wind blowing down off those scorched mountains, the smell of those flocks was almost overpowering. No one seemed to notice it except us newcomers. Families were gathering before each tent, starting the evening cooking fires, chattering in their guttural language, children running, boys shouting at each other as they played with wooden swords and shields, girls screeching with high-pitched laughter.

But what caught my eyes, and Lukka's, was the walled city sitting atop a low hill in the middle of the plain. It dominated the region, just as Troy had dominated the plain of Ilios.

"That is Jericho," I told Lukka.

"It is known as the oldest city in the world," he said.

"Is it? The walls certainly seem high and thick."

"Stronger than Troy's."

"They want us to help them take it."

He made a coughing grunt.

"Can it be done?"

Lukka scratched at his beard. "My lord Orion, any city can be taken. It's only a question of time, and how many lives you can afford to lose."

We made our camp as far from the animal pens as possible. As the men pitched their tents, I brought Helen out from the covered cart. There was no sense trying to keep her hidden here.

"The men will want to mingle with the women here," Lukka told me.

I nodded, but warned, "Tell them to be careful and mind their manners. I doubt that these women are the kind who take to strangers."

He made a tiny smile. "They all seem to be well protected by family males," he agreed. "Still—no harm in being friendly."

"Just make certain that they're not so friendly they get their throats cut."

Ben-Jameen came back to us as the sun dipped below the western mountains and the long violet shadows crept across the plain.

"Joshua invites you to have supper with him in his tent." He seemed excited and pleased.

Just then Helen came out of my tent, freshly washed in water brought up from the distant river, clothed in a long pleated gown of crimson, a golden necklace and bracelet her only jewelry.

Ben-Jameen gaped at her.

"This is Helen, princess of the lost city of Troy," I said, deciding not to mention that she was Queen of Sparta. "She will accompany me at supper."

It took the youth several moments to get his mouth closed and his eyes off Helen. Finally he turned to me and said, "Among us, women do not eat with men."

"Your leader will have to make an exception in this case."

Ben-Jameen nodded dumbly and scrambled off to inform Joshua of this startling turn of events.

Helen stepped close to me. "I can stay here, Orion. It's not wise to cause trouble over me."

I disagreed. "It's necessary for you to come with me. I want this Joshua, whoever he is, to realize that he can't command me as if I were his servant."

"Ah, I understand," she said. Then, with a smile, "And I thought you couldn't bear the thought of taking a meal without me by your side."

I smiled back. "That, too."

Ben-Jameen returned with a guard of honor, six men in clean robes, armed only with short swords scabbarded at their sides, who escorted us to a wide, low tent of goat skins. I had to duck to get through the entrance flap.

Inside, the tent was spacious. Worn carpets covered the ground. A low table was spread with steaming bowls of meat and platters of olives, onions, and greens I could not identify. A dozen old men sat around the table, on brightly decorated cushions and pillows. At the center of the table sat a younger man, his long hair and beard still dark, his eyes bright with an inner fire.

It was Joshua's eyes that sent a warning alarm tingling along my nerves. They blazed with the light of a zeal that knew no bounds, as if he were so certain that what he was doing was the right thing that he never questioned any action that popped into his thoughts. He was an intense, dedicated man in his late thirties or early forties, I guessed, lean as a sword and as straight, unbent even by the burdens of leading his people as they struggled to find a homeland for themselves.

Ben-Jameen performed the introductions. None of the Israelites stood, but Joshua invited us to sit at the empty places around the table once we had been properly introduced to everyone. I sat directly across the table from Joshua, Helen on my left, Ben-Jameen on my right. The men ignored Helen so thoroughly that I knew her presence disturbed them no end.

There was no wine at the table, only a thin fermented goat's milk that tasted so sour I preferred the water. The food was plentiful, though. For a nomadic tribe on the march through a hostile land, they had plenty to eat. At least, these leaders did.

Joshua remained silent as we ate, but he watched me carefully, his eyes never leaving me. The old men asked me hundreds of questions about who I was, where I came from, were my men truly Hittite soldiers, had the God of Israel really destroyed the Hittite empire? I answered as truthfully as I could, and as we finished the meal with dates and melons, I complimented Joshua on the food.

"Yes," he said, "this is truly a land of milk and honey, just as the Lord our God promised it would be."

"Tell me of your god," I said. "What does he look like? What do you call him?"

A gasp went around the table. Several of the old men actually pushed away, as if afraid I would infect them. Even Ben-Jameen edged slightly away from me.

"His name is never spoken," said Joshua, his voice reedy, nasal, his words coming fast, as if he were angry. "He is the Lord God of Israel, the God of our fathers."

"The most powerful God of all," said one of the old men.

"The *only* God," Joshua insisted firmly. "All other gods are false."

"He is a golden, radiant figure?" I asked.

"No one has ever seen Him," said Joshua, "and it is forbidden to make images of Him."

"How does he communicate with you?"

"He spoke directly to Moses," said the elder on Joshua's right. "He led us through the wilderness and gave Moses the tablets of the law."

"He has led us here," said Joshua, tapping a blunt forefinger on the table. "To Jericho. We crossed the River Jordan dry shod, just as He led Moses and our people across the Sea of Reeds. He has promised us this land of Canaan for our own. But if we can't conquer Jericho we will be nothing but wandering beggars, strangers in our own land, outcasts forever."

"Jericho commands the plain here, that I can see."

"Jericho commands the entire region. He who holds Jericho holds all of Canaan," he said. "That is why we must take the city. That is why you must help us."

"We are only two dozen men."

"Two dozen Hittite soldiers," Joshua said. "The same Hittites who razed Ugarit. Soldiers who are expert at siege warfare."

"But with so few . . ."

Joshua's eyes blazed at me. "You have been sent by God to help us. To refuse would mean refusing the God of Israel. That would be an extremely unwise thing to do."

I smiled back at him. "It would be impolite of me to refuse your request, after the hospitality you have shown us."

"You will help us, then?" Despite himself, he leaned forward eagerly.

"My men and I will do what we can," I said, realizing that I was dealing with a fanatic and there was no way out.

They all smiled and nodded their heads and murmured about the will of God.

But I added, "Once Jericho falls, we will be on our way to Egypt."

"Egypt!" The word went around the table as if it were a blasphemy.

"Egypt is our destination," I said calmly. "We will help you in your siege of Jericho, and then go on our way to that land."

Joshua smiled thinly. "After Jericho falls, you can go to Egypt or anywhere else you choose." He made it sound as if he were saying, *You can go to hell, for all I care.*

Chapter 28

"THIS is madness," Lukka said.

We stood in the rising heat of morning, at the edge of the Israelite camp, studying the triple walls of Jericho. At sunrise we had ridden completely around the besieged city, as close as a bowshot. The walls were enormous, much higher than Troy's and undoubtedly much thicker. To make things worse, a deep trench had been carved out of the bedrock in front of the main length of the wall. A drawbridge crossed it, although the bridge was pulled up tight against the city gate now. The trench was partially filled with garbage and debris, but still it was steep-walled and an obstacle that looked all but impassable.

"We'll never be able to get siege towers against those walls," Lukka told me. I reluctantly agreed with him. Jericho stood atop a low hill, its main wall slanting from the bedrock floor of the valley plain up along the crest of the hill. Where the wall was set at the floor of the plain, the trench protected it. Where it wound up along the crest, smaller retaining walls stood before it, making a triple set of barriers. The hillside itself was too steep to roll siege towers up its sides, and the walls were studded with strong round towers from which archers and slingers could pelt an attacker with arrows and stones.

"No wonder Joshua needs help," I grumbled.

Lukka squinted against the sun glare. "The people of Jericho have had a hundred generations to perfect their defenses. No wandering band of nomads is going to bring those walls down."

I grinned at him. "That's why Joshua so kindly invited us to stay with him—until those walls *do* come down."

"We will be here a long time, then."

Through the morning we rode the circuit of the walls several times, looking for a weakness that simply was not there. The only thing I noticed was that some sections of the walls seemed older than others, their bricks grayer and less evenly aligned.

"Earthquakes," said Lukka. "The walls are made of mud bricks. Once they dry they become as hard as stone. But an earthquake can tumble them."

An earthquake. The glimmer of an idea stirred in the back of my mind.

Lukka was pointing. "See how the wall is built in sections, with timbers dividing one section from the next? That way, even when an earthquake damages one section of the wall, the rest can remain standing."

I nodded, but my mind was elsewhere.

That night, as we lay down together in my tent, Helen asked, "How long will we have to stay among these awful people?"

"Until they take the city," I answered.

"But they may never . . ."

I silenced her with a kiss. We made love, and she drifted to sleep.

I closed my eyes too, and willed myself to that other realm where the so-called gods played their games with destiny. Concentrating every particle of my being, I crossed the gulf of space-time that divided my world from theirs.

Once again I stood in that golden aura. But I could see their city through the shining mist, its towers and spires seemed clearer to me than ever before.

"Ahriman," I called, with my mind as well as my voice. "Ahriman, my one-time enemy, where are you?"

"Not here, creature."

I turned and saw the haughty one I thought of as Hera. She wore a golden gown that left one shoulder bare, gathered at her waist by a chain of glittering jewels. Her dark hair hung in ringlets, her dark eyes probed me. With a smile that seemed almost menacing, she said: "At least you are dressed better than the last time we met."

I made a slight bow. My makeshift uniform of tunic and leather vest was somewhat better than the rags I had worn at Ilium.

"Are you here to draw more of my blood?" I asked.

Her smile widened slightly. "Not really. Perhaps I can save the blood that's still in your body. Our golden Apollo has gone quite mad, you know."

"He no longer calls himself Apollo."

She shrugged. "Names are not important here. I speak only so that your pitifully limited mind can understand."

"I am grateful for such kindness," I said. "The Golden One has found a tribe that worships him as their only god."

"Yes. And he seeks to eliminate the rest of us. *And,*" she added, with an arch of her brows, "he is using you to help him."

I stood silently, digesting this news.

"Isn't he?" she demanded.

"I am helping the Israelites to conquer Jericho," I admitted. "Or, at least, I'm trying to . . ."

"That's part of his plan, I'm sure of it!"

"But I didn't know he is attempting to . . ." I recalled the word she had used, ". . . to eliminate you."

"You know now!"

"Does that mean he wants to kill you?"

She almost snarled at me. "He would if he could. But he'll never get that chance. We'll crush him—and you, too, if you continue to aid him in any way."

"But . . ."

Leveling an accusing finger at me, she warned, "There is no neutral ground, Orion. Either you cease your aid to him or you are our enemy. Do you understand?"

"I understand," I said.

"Then consider carefully the consequences of your actions."

"The one they call Athene," I said. "He promised me that . . ."

"His promises cannot be trusted. You know that."

"I want to revive her, to bring her back to life," I said.

"And he's offered you her life in exchange for your obedience." Hera shook her head angrily. "Leave your dead goddess to us, Orion. She is one of us, and not for the likes of you."

"Can she be revived?"

"That's not . . ."

"Can she be revived?" I shouted.

Her eyes widened, whether with anger or fear or something else, I could not tell. She took a deep breath, then replied calmly, evenly, "Such a thing is—possible. Just barely within the realm of possibility. But it's not for you to even dream of!"

"I do dream of it. I dream of nothing else."

"Orion, you poor worm, even if she could be revived, she would have nothing more to do with you. She is one of us, so far beyond you that . . ."

"I love her," I said. "That's the one advantage I have over you and your kind. I can love. So can she. But you can't. Neither you nor the Golden One nor any of the other gods. But she can, and she has loved me. And she died because of that."

"You are hopeless," Hera snapped. She turned away from me in a swirl of golden robes and disappeared into the shining mist.

I stood alone for several moments, then remembered why I had come here. To find Ahriman. The one the Achaians called Poseidon, the earth-shaker.

Closing my eyes, I visualized his hulking dark form, his heavy gray face, his burning eyes. I called him mentally, telling myself that if he would not come to me, then I must seek and find him.

I remembered, dimly, a forest of giant trees where Ahriman and his kind lived, in a continuum that existed somewhere, somewhen. Did it still exist? Could I find it?

A dark shadow passed over me. I sensed it even with my eyes closed. I opened them and found myself in a dark, brooding forest. Not a drop of sunlight penetrated the canopy of almost-black leaves far above me. The boles of huge trees stood around me like gray marble columns rising toward infinity. The ground between their trunks was cropped grass, as smooth and even as a park.

"Why are you here?"

Out of the darkness a darker shape took form: Ahriman, solid and massive, decked in clothes the color of the forest. But his eyes glowed like red-hot coals.

"To find you," I replied.

He stepped closer to me. In his harsh, labored whisper, he asked, "And why seek me?"

"I need your help."

He glared at me. It was like a volcano threatening to pour out lava. "I will not shake down the walls of Jericho for you, Orion. I will not help your golden madman in his wild schemes."

"It's not for him," I said.

"That makes no difference. It is enough for me to protect my own people in our own continuum. I will not become a party to the quarrels of the self-styled Creators. They did not create me or my kind. I owe them nothing."

"The Golden One promised he would revive Athene if I helped him," I said, ignoring his words. "He waits for me in the great pyramid in Egypt."

"He waits there to destroy you, once you have finished your usefulness to him."

"No," I said. "I will destroy him—somehow."

"And what of your dead goddess then?" he asked.

I had no answer.

Slowly Ahriman swung his massive head back and forth. "Orion, if you want an earthquake, you must make it for yourself."

I started to ask him what he meant, but the forest and Ahriman's dark, brooding presence slowly faded before my eyes, and I found myself sitting in the darkness of my tent, on the straw pallet next to Helen.

She was sitting up too, her eyes wide with terror.

"You were gone," she whispered, in a voice constricted by awe. "You were gone, and then you appeared beside me."

I put an arm around her bare shoulders and tried to calm her. "It's all right . . ."

"It's magic! Sorcery!" Her naked body was cold and trembling.

Pulling her close and wrapping both my arms around her, I said, "Helen, long ago I told you I was a servant of a god. That is the truth. Sometimes I must go to the gods, speak with them, ask them to help us."

She looked up at me. Even in the predawn shadows I could see the fear and wonder in her face. "You actually go to Olympos?"

"I don't know the name of the place, but—yes, I go to the home of the gods."

Helen fell silent, as if there were no words to express the shock she felt.

"They are not gods," I told her, "not in the sense that you believe. Certainly not in the sense that Joshua and his people believe. They care nothing for us, except to use us in their own schemes. They are not even immortal. The goddess that I once loved is dead, killed by one of her own kind."

"You loved a goddess?"

"I loved a woman who was one of the group whom you call gods and goddesses," I said. "Now she is dead, and I seek vengeance against the one who killed her."

"You seek vengeance against a god?"

"I seek vengeance against a madman who murdered my love."

Helen shook her lovely head. "This is all a dream. It *must* be a dream. Yet—dreams themselves are sent by the gods."

"It is no dream, Helen."

"I will try to understand the meaning of it," she said, ignoring my words. "The gods have sent us a message, and I will try to find its meaning."

It was her way of adjusting to what I had told her. I decided not to argue. Lying back on the pallet, I held her until she drifted back into sleep. My mind focused on Ahriman and his words to me: "Orion, if you want an earthquake, you must make it for yourself."

I thought I understood what he meant. With a smile, I went back to sleep.

Chapter 29

"TUNNEL under the wall?" Lukka seemed more amused than skeptical.

We were facing the western side of Jericho, where the main city wall climbed along the brow of the low hill. There were two smaller retaining walls at the base of the hill, one terraced a few yards above the other, but no defensive trench in front of them.

"Is it possible?" I asked.

He scratched at his beard. The hill on which Jericho stood was made from the debris of earlier settlements. Untold generations of mud-brick buildings had collapsed over the ages, from time, from the winter rains, from fire and enemies' destruction. Like all cities in this part of the world, Jericho rebuilt atop its own ruins, creating a growing mound that slowly elevated the city above the original plain.

"It would take a long time and a lot of workers," said Lukka, finally.

"We have plenty of both."

But he was still far from pleased. "Tunnels can be traps. Once they see that we are tunneling, they can come out from their walls and slaughter us. Or dig a counter tunnel and surprise us."

"Then we'll have to conceal it from them," I said glibly.

Lukka remained unconvinced.

But Joshua's eyes lit up when I explained my plan to him. "Once the tunnel is beneath the foundation of the main wall, we start a fire that will burn through the timbers and bring that section of the wall down."

He paced back and forth in his tent, his back slightly bent, his hands locked behind his back. Joshua was a surprisingly small man, but what he lacked in height and girth he made up in intensity. And although the Israelites seemed to be ruled by their council of elders, twelve men who represented each of their tribes, it was Joshua alone who made the military decisions.

Finally he wheeled toward me and bobbed his head, making his dark beard and long locks bounce. "Yes! The Lord God has sent us the answer. We will bring Jericho's wall down with a thundering crash! And all will see that the Lord God of Israel is mightier than any wall made by men!"

It was cosmically ironic. Joshua believed with every ounce of his being that I had been sent to him by his god. And truly, I had been. But I knew that if I tried to tell him that the god he adored was as human as he, merely a man from the distant future who had powers that made him appear godlike, Joshua would have blanched and accused me of blasphemy. If I told him that the god he worshiped was a murderer, a madman, a fugitive from his fellow "gods," a man I intended to destroy one day—Joshua would have had me killed on the spot.

So I remained silent and let him believe what he believed. His world was far simpler than mine, and in his own way Joshua was right: his god had sent me to help bring down Jericho's wall.

The secret of Jericho was its spring, a source of cool fresh water that bubbled out of the ground, from what Ben-Jameen had told me. That was why the city's eastern wall came down to the bedrock level: it protected the spring. Most of the towers were on that side; so was the trench and the main city gates.

Under the guise of tightening the siege around the city we put up a new group of tents on the western side of the hill and built a corral to hold horses, all out of bowshot range. One of the tents, the largest, was where we started digging. Joshua provided hundreds of men. None of them were slaves; there were no slaves in the Israelite camp. The men worked willingly. Not without complaining, arguing, grumbling. But they dug, while Lukka and his Hittites, as the Israelites called them, supervised the work.

Getting rid of the dirt became an immediate problem. We filled the tent with baskets of it by day, then carried the baskets a mile or so from the city and dumped them in the dark of night.

Timbers to shore up the tunnel were another problem, since trees were so scarce in this rocky desert land. Teams of men were sent northward along the river, to the land called Galilee, where they bartered for wood among the villagers who lived by that lake.

The ground was not too difficult for the bronze and copper pickaxes we had, so long as we stayed above bedrock. The layer of easy soil was barely deep enough to dig a tunnel. Our diggers had to work flat on their bellies. Later, I knew, when we reached the foundations of the two outer retaining walls, we would have real troubles.

I spent the nights with Helen, each of us growing edgier as the time dragged slowly by. She wanted to get away from this place, to resume our southward trek to Egypt.

"Leave now, tonight, right *now*," she exorted me. "Just the two of us. They won't bother trying to follow or bring us back. Lukka is handling the digging, that's all they really want of you. We can get away!"

I stroked her golden hair, glowing in the pale light of the moon. "I can't leave Lukka and his men. They trust me. And there's no telling what Joshua would do if we ran off. He's a fanatic. He might slaughter Lukka and the men once the tunnel is finished: sacrifice them to his god."

"What of it? They will die one day, sooner or later. They are soldiers, they *expect* to be killed."

"I can't do that," I said.

"Orion, I'm afraid of this place. I'm afraid that the gods you visit will take you away from me forever."

With a shake of my head I told her, "No. I promised you I would bring you to Egypt and that is what I will do. Only after that will I deal with the one I seek."

"Then let us go to Egypt now! Forget Lukka and the others. Tell the gods to bring us to Egypt now, tonight!"

"I don't *tell* the gods anything," I said.

"Then let me speak with them. I am a queen, after all, and a daughter of Zeus himself. They will listen to me."

"There are times," I said, "when you speak like a spoiled little child who is so totally self-centered that she deserves a spanking."

    She knew when she had reached the limit of my patience.
Winding her arms around my neck, she breathed, "I've never been
spanked. You wouldn't be so brutal to me, would you?"

    "I might."

    "Couldn't you think of some other punishment?" Her fingers
traced down my spine. "Something that would give you more
pleasure?"

    I played the game. "What do you have in mind?"

    She spent much of the night showing me.

    Although Helen and I usually took our meals with Lukka and
the men, at our own fire by our own tents, now and then Joshua or
Ben-Jameen would invite me to have supper with them. Me,
alone. They made it clear that women did not eat with the men. I
declined most of these invitations, but out of politeness I accepted
a few.

    Joshua was always surrounded by the elders or priests, with
plenty of servants and women bustling around his table. The talk
was always of the destiny of the Children of Israel, and how their
god rescued them from slavery in Egypt and promised them
dominance over this land they called Canaan.

    Ben-Jameen, his father, and brothers spoke of different things
when I ate with them. The old man recalled his days of slavery in
Egypt, laboring as a brickmaker for the king, whom he called
pharaoh. Once I hinted that Joshua seemed like a fanatic to me.
The old man smiled tolerantly.

    "He lives in the shadow of Moses. It is not easy to bear the
burden of leadership after the greatest leader of all men has gone
on to join Abraham and Isaac."

    Ben-Jameen chimed in, "Joshua is trying to make an army out
of a people who were slaves. He is trying to create discipline and
courage where there has been little more than hunger and fear."

    I agreed that it took an extraordinary man to accomplish that.
And I began looking at these Israelites with fresh eyes, afterward.
Unlike the Achaians at Troy, who were the topmost level of a
strictly hierarchical society, the warrior class, hereditary plunder-
ers, the Israelites were an entire nation: men, women, children,
flocks, tents, all their possessions, wandering through this sun-
blasted land of rocks and mountains seeking a place of their own.
They had no warrior class. The only special class I could see were
the priests, and even they worked with their hands when they had

to. I began to feel a new respect for them, and wondered if the promises of their god would ever be fulfilled.

Shortly after noon on the fourth day of the digging, Lukka came out of the big tent, squinted up painfully at the merciless sun, and walked toward me. As always, no matter heat or cold, he wore his leather harness and weapons. I knew that his coat of mail and his iron helmet were close to hand. Lukka was ready for battle at all times.

I was standing on a low rise, examining the distant wall of Jericho. Not a sign of activity. Not a sentry in sight. The city wavered in the heat haze as the sun blasted down on my bare shoulders and neck. I had stripped down to my kilt.

We had fired a few flaming arrows into the city that morning. Each day we made a small demonstration of force somewhere along the western wall, to make the city's defenders believe that we were there probing for a weak spot. But in the noonday sun no one stirred. Or, hardly anyone.

Lukka was dripping sweat by the time he reached me. I had tuned my body to accommodate the heat, opening up the capillaries just under the skin and adjusting my body temperature. Like any human being, I needed water to stay alive. Unlike ordinary humans, I could keep the water in my vital systems for a much longer time; I sweated away only a small fraction of it.

"You must be part camel," Lukka said, as I offered him the canteen I carried. He gulped at it thirstily.

"How goes the work?" I asked.

"We've reached the base of the outermost wall. I've given the workers some of our own iron spear points to attack the bricks. They're as hard as stone."

"How long will it take to break through?"

He shrugged his bare shoulders, making the leather harness creak slightly. "A day for each one. We could work the night through."

"Let me see," I said, striding toward the tent.

It was cooler under its shade, but the air inside the tent was close and confining. Dust hovered, thick enough to make me sneeze. Lukka ordered the workers to stop and leave the tunnel. I got down on my hands and knees, ducked into the darkness, and wormed my way forward.

The tunnel had been dug wide enough for two men to crawl

through, side by side. Lukka went in with me, slightly behind. We carried no lights, but every dozen feet or so the workers had poked a reed-thin hole up through the ground's surface. They provided air to breathe and a dim scattering of light that was barely enough to avert total darkness.

Quickly enough we came to the tunnel's end: a blank facing of stone-hard bricks. Two short poles lay on the ground, each with an iron spear point lashed to it. The bricks were scratched and gouged.

In the dim light I took one of the poles in my hands and jabbed it at the bricks. A dull chunking sound, and a few flakes of dried mud fell away.

"This is going to be slow work," I said.

"And noisy," Lukka pointed out. "Especially if we work at night, they'll hear us from inside the city."

He was right, as usual.

We scuttled out of the tunnel like a pair of rodents scrabbling through their lair. The bright sun and air of daylight seemed wonderful, despite the heat.

"No night work," I said to Lukka. "The time we might gain isn't worth the risk of being discovered."

"When we get close to the main wall, they'll hear us chipping away even in the daytime," he said.

"We'll have to think of something, then."

It was Joshua who thought of the solution. That night, when I told him we were getting close enough to be heard inside the city, he curled his fingers through his beard for several long moments, then looked up with a fierce smile.

"We will make so much noise that they will never hear your diggers at work," he said. "We will make a joyful noise unto the Lord."

I was not certain that his plan made any sense, but Joshua insisted that all would be well and told me to resume digging in the morning.

On my way back to my own tent that evening, as the sun dipped below the western mountains, turning them deep violet and the sky a blazing golden red, a stranger stepped in front of me.

"Orion," he whispered. "Come with me."

He was muffled in a long gray robe with a dark burnoose over it, the hood thrown over his head and hiding the features of his face.

But I knew who he was, and followed him wordlessly as he picked his way through the tents of the Israelite camp and out across the green field toward the distant river.

"This is far enough," I said at last. "We can stop here. Even if you glow like a star no one from the camp will notice."

He laughed, a low chuckle deep in his throat. "Not much chance of my putting out enough radiation for *them* to find me."

By *them,* I knew he did not mean the Israelites.

"You are helping these people to overcome Jericho. That pleases me."

"Will I be able to leave for Egypt once Jericho is taken?" I asked.

"Of course." He seemed surprised that I asked.

"And you will revive Athene?"

"I will try, Orion. I will try. I can promise nothing more. There are difficulties—enormous difficulties. *They* are trying to stop me."

"I know."

"They've contacted you?"

"I contacted them. They think you've gone mad."

He laughed again. Bitterly. "I struggle alone to uphold the continuum—*their* continuum—so that they can continue to exist. I stand between them and utter destruction. I protect the Earth and my creatures with every particle of my strength and wisdom. And they call that madness. The fools!"

"Hera told me that if I help you, she and the others will destroy me."

In the shadow of his hood I could not make out the features of his face. It was the first time I had met the Golden One that he did not radiate light and splendor.

When he failed to reply, I added, "And you have warned me that if I fail to help you, you will destroy me."

"And you have told *me,* Orion, that you want to destroy me. A pretty situation."

"Can you revive Athene?"

"If I can't, no one else can. No one else would even try, Orion. It takes a . . . madman, like me, to even attempt such a thing."

"Then I will continue to help you."

"And you will tell me *exactly* what they say to you, whenever they contact you again."

"If you wish," I said.

"I do not wish, Orion. I command. I can see your thoughts as clearly as words written across the sky in fire. You cannot hide anything from me."

"Then you see your own death."

He laughed, with genuine humor this time. "Ah, Orion, you truly believe that you can conquer the gods."

"You are not gods. You can delude ignorant nomads such as Joshua and his people, but I know you better."

"Of course you do," he patronized. "Now, get back to your Helen and let her try to wheedle you off to Egypt again."

There was nothing he did not know, I realized. He stood before me, and even in his disguise I could sense his condescending smile.

"Tell me one thing," I asked. "Why is Jericho so important? Why are these people of Joshua's so dear to your heart? Once you said that you are not so egocentric as to be pleased when people worship you. Is that still true?"

For a moment or two he did not answer. When he finally did, his voice was low and serious. "Yes, it is still true, Orion. It is pleasant to have my creatures adore me, I admit. But the real reason for Jericho, the real reason I will bring these people to rule this land of Canaan, is to humble those others who seek to thwart my plans. They stopped me at Troy, with your help. They will not stop me here!"

I had no reply to his words.

"They think me mad, do they? We shall see who is the true protector of the continuum. They will all bow to me, Orion. All of them!"

He turned and walked toward the river alone. I watched him in the deepening shadows of night, as the stars came out one by one, until his figure had disappeared into the darkness.

Chapter 30

"THIS could destroy all our plans, all our hopes."

Ben-Jameen's youthful face looked very grave. He stood in my tent alongside Lukka, with one of the Hatti soldiers behind, head hung low, two other soldiers flanking him, and a small angry crowd of Israelite men standing just outside in ominous silence.

Helen sat in the far corner of the tent, on a wooden chair that had been given to me by one of Ben-Jameen's brothers. One of the women had brought her a soft, feathered cushion, gaily decorated in bold stripes of red and blue.

But Ben-Jameen ignored her and said to me, "This Hittite soldier has had his way with one of the young women of my tribe, and now refuses to do the right thing by her."

I was surprised, almost stunned, at this. For weeks now we had lived in the Israelite camp without a hint of trouble. Hardly any of the women would have anything to do with men who were not of their own tribes. The few who did, young widows and the rare unmarried woman who did not worry about her virginity, had been enough to keep Lukka and his men reasonably happy.

But now one of the young women demanded marriage as the price of her lovemaking.

I looked at Lukka. His face was grimly impassive as he stood before me. I saw that his sword was at his side. Ben-Jameen, standing beside him, looked almost like a child: smaller, slimmer, his youthful face unlined, unscarred by battle. But he was representing the honor of his tribe.

"Bring the man before me," I said.

Lukka raised a hand. "With your permission, my lord, I will speak for the prisoner."

I raised an eyebrow.

"It is customary among us," said Lukka. "I am his commanding officer. I am responsible for his conduct."

So that was the way the game would be played, I said to myself. Lukka was standing between me and the accused man. If I wanted to mete out punishment, it would have to touch Lukka first.

Ben-Jameen glanced at the bearded soldier, and seemed to understand what Lukka's words implied.

"The young lady in question," I asked Ben-Jameen, "was she forced?"

He shook his head. "She does not claim so."

"Was she a virgin?"

Ben-Jameen's eyes widened. "Of course!"

I turned to Lukka. He shrugged slightly, "That is a matter of her word against the word of the accused."

Ben-Jameen's face went red. "Do you mean that you claim she was not?"

I held up both hands to stop the fight before it truly started. "There is no way to prove the point, one way or the other." Then I asked, "What does she want of this man?"

"Marriage."

"Does her father approve of this?"

"He demands it!"

I looked past them to the accused soldier, but his head was bowed so low I could not see his face. To Lukka, I asked, "Is the man willing to marry this woman?"

"Yes, he will marry her."

I thought I saw the soldier twitch, as if a hot needle had been jabbed into his flesh.

"Then what is the problem?"

"To marry into our tribe," Ben-Jameen said, "it is necessary to accept our religion."

"And that he will not do," said Lukka. "His god is Taru, the storm god, not some invisible spirit with no name."

I thought Ben-Jameen would burst. He turned flame red from the roots of his scalp all the way down his neck. If he had carried a weapon he would have attacked Lukka on the spot, I am sure.

I took him by the shoulders and made him face me. "Different men worship different gods, my friend," I said, as softly as I dared. "You know that."

He took a deep, shuddering breath. His face returned to something more like its normal color.

"Besides," Lukka added, "to join their religion he would have to be circumcised, and that he will not do."

"Is that necessary?" I asked Ben-Jameen.

He nodded.

I could hardly blame the man for refusing to allow himself to be circumcised. Yet he had picked the wrong woman to play with. She gave him sex and now expected her payment of marriage. The Israelites demanded that their women marry only men of their own faith, so he had to accept her religion. If he refused, we might well be overrun by her angry relatives who would slaughter us in the name of family honor and religious purity. Of course, we would take many of them to the grave with us, but it would end with all of us dead and Jericho still standing.

Almost, I wished that the Golden One was truly a wise and compassionate god who would descend upon us and bring the light of sweet reason to this thorny problem. Almost.

I looked Ben-Jameen in the eye and said, "My friend, it seems to me that if the man is willing to marry the young lady, that is sufficient. He did not go to her for religious revelation, but for love. You can't expect him to change his religion."

Before he could think of a reply, I added, "And, as you know, we have the sworn word of Joshua himself that once Jericho has fallen, we will be permitted to leave you and go on our way to Egypt. Is the young lady willing to accompany her husband to that land? Is her family willing to see her part from them?"

The youthful Israelite took a long time to consider his answer, frowning with thought as we all stood there, waiting for him to respond. He knew as well as I what was at stake here. Would he be willing to sacrifice this girl's honor for the sake of conquering Jericho?

It was Helen who broke the silence.

She rose from her chair and walked slowly toward me, saying, "You men cause such troubles! The poor girl, I understand how she feels."

Ben-Jameen stared at her. Helen wore a simple modest robe, but her golden hair and obvious beauty made even the simplest garments seem royal.

She came up beside me, and twisted the ring from her right index finger. It was a heavy circle of gold, set with a shining ruby.

"Give this to your kinswoman," Helen said, "and tell her it is a gift of a queen. She must be content with it, for the man she loves cannot marry her."

"But my lady . . ."

"Shush," said Helen. "What kind of a husband would she have, if he did marry her? An unwilling man who would blame her for every drop of rain that falls upon him. A soldier who knows nothing but violence, and who would run away from her the first chance he gets. Or drag her back to Egypt, the land of her slavery. Tell her father that he should be happy to be rid of him. After Jericho falls and we have left, let him consider her a widow. This ring will help her to find a fitting husband from among her own people."

"But her honor," said Ben-Jameen.

"Nothing can replace that. Yet she gave it away willingly enough, did she not? She has made a grievous mistake. Don't force her to compound it with an even greater one."

Ben-Jameen held the ring in one hand. He looked at Helen, then turned to me. Scratching his head, he finally said, "I will bring this to her father, and see if he agrees with your wisdom, my lady."

"He will," Helen replied.

Ben-Jameen walked slowly out of my tent, passing the guarded soldier like a man lost so deeply in thought that he barely sees where he is heading. The men outside babbled and muttered and chattered as they all headed back toward the tents of their tribe.

I smiled at Helen. "Thank you. That was very thoughtful of you, very wise. And very generous."

She made a haughty little smile back. "Any price is worth it if it speeds the day when we can leave this wretched place."

Lukka agreed. Waving a hand to tell his soldiers to get back to their tents, he said to me, "Maybe now we can get back to the business of bringing down that damned wall."

Chapter 31

JOSHUA'S "joyful noise unto the Lord" consisted of a marching band. He gathered together all the priests of his people in their most colorful robes and turbans, and had them march around the city's walls, carrying a beautifully crafted gold-plated wooden chest on a pair of long poles, preceded by seven men blowing on ram's horn trumpets and followed by more trumpets, drums, and cymbals.

The chest was a religious icon that Joshua called the ark of the covenant. I was never allowed to get close enough to see it in detail. In fact, Ben-Jameen insisted that merely to touch it would mean instant death. I wondered if it were some kind of equipment for communicating with the other realm in which the Golden One and his kind lived, but Ben-Jameen told me it contained two stone tablets bearing the laws given directly to Moses by their god.

I knew better than to argue religion, even with the youthful Ben-Jameen. The priests and their marching band made their joyful noise, circling the city walls all day long, fresh men coming up to replace tired ones as the day wore on.

Under cover of their music and chanting, we chipped away at the foundations of the main wall. Using Hittite iron spear points, we had broken through the two outer retaining walls, then tunneled fairly easily through the accumulated debris of thousands of years that made up Jericho's hill. There was room now for our diggers to make the tunnel high enough for a man to stand in.

When we hit the main wall's foundations, Joshua started his priests in motion.

At first they marched some distance away from the wall, and the soldiers up on the parapets eyed them very suspiciously, waiting for some kind of surprise attack. But even by the end of the first day, more and more women and children were up on the walls, watching this strange and colorful procession.

For six days they marched and played their instruments and chanted while we scraped and scratched at the massive foundation of the wall. The citizens of Jericho lined the parapets now, waving and jeering. Now and then some child would throw something, but no missile of war was directed at the marchers. Perhaps the people of the city thought it unwise to fire upon priests, or unlucky to risk incurring the wrath of a god. Perhaps they thought that the Israelites were trying to drive them all mad with the constant music and chanting.

That is what Helen thought. "I can't bear that horrid noise anymore! My ears ache from it!"

It was night, and the only sounds outside our tent were the drone of insects and the distant voice of a mother singing a soft lullaby to her children.

"If you truly visit the gods," she said, "why can't you ask them to topple the wall for you?"

I smiled. "I did. And they told me to do it myself."

Despite herself, Helen smiled back. "The gods are not always kind to us, are they?"

"Tomorrow will be the end of it," I said to her. "We've finished the digging. Now comes the fire."

I left Helen alone in our tent and went out into the darkness to supervise the preparations for tomorrow's assault. All the men who had been working so hard at the digging were now bringing brushwood from the fields, dragging it through the tunnel, and piling it up at the base of the main wall's foundation.

As I had expected, the wall's dried bricks were framed every few yards by stout timbers. Some of them were very ancient, dry as tinder. When they caught fire, the whole section of the wall would cave in. Or so I hoped.

Through the whole long night the men brought the brushwood to the tunnel and packed it against the wall's foundation. Lukka and two of his best men were down there, supervising the work and poking air holes along the base of the wall, so that the fire would not choke itself to death.

Finally it was finished. Lukka came out as the first hint of gray began to lighten the sky behind the mountains of Gilead and Moab, far across the Jordan.

I went in to make a final inspection, crawling along the first part of the tunnel on my belly in total darkness, feeling like an earthworm, blind and hemmed in on all sides. After what seemed like an hour, I felt the roof of the tunnel rising. I could get up and crawl on my hands and knees and, at last, stand like a man once more.

I carried a torch with me, and pieces of flint and iron to strike a spark that would light it. But not until the day was bright and Joshua's priests were parading around the walls again. We wanted to keep the attention of Jericho's defenders on the music and the marchers as long as possible, to let the fire get so good a start that there would be no way to put it out before the wall caved in. I also sensed that Joshua valued the public-relations aspect of making it appear as if the priests' noise-making brought down the wall.

He was keenly aware of the value of manipulating people's opinions. Time and again he compared their crossing of the Jordan River dry-shod with Moses's leading them across the Sea of Reeds in Egypt. And he kept insisting that the people of Canaan must see that the God of Israel was mightier than their own gods, whom he considered to be false and nonexistent.

I had also brought a small candle with me, and used the flint to light it once I had reached the tunnel's end. The brushwood seemed to be ready to burn: enough of it packed against and under the wall's foundation to ignite the timbers. I could smell the night air, slightly damp, coming through the holes Lukka had poked through to the surface. It seemed enough to feed the fire its needed oxygen. All was ready, I thought.

I doused the candle, but the light did not disappear. Instead, it grew and glowed all around me until I realized that I had been transported once again to the realm of the Creators.

Four of them faced me, against that featureless glow of gold that they used to keep their world hidden from my eyes. Yet, if I concentrated hard enough, I could make out the faint traces of strange shapes behind them. Equipment of some kind? Instruments? We seemed to be in a huge chamber, rather than outdoors. A laboratory? A control center?

I recognized the neatly bearded Zeus, with Hera standing beside him. The two others were male; I had seen them before. One was slim and wiry, although as tall as Zeus. His face was narrow, with a long pointed chin, and closely cropped jet-black hair that came to a V on his high forehead that exactly matched the angle of his chin. His smile was sardonic; his eyes mischievous. I thought of him as Hermes, the messenger of the gods, the trickster and patron of thieves. The other was burly, big in the shoulders and arms, with thickly curled red hair and eyes as tawny as a lion's. Ares, god of war. Obviously.

All of them wore identical suits of shimmering metallic fabric, almost like uniforms. The only differences among them were color: Zeus wore gold, Hera copper red, Hermes was clad in silver, Ares in bronze.

"You continue to assist our demented Apollo," said Zeus. It was a flat statement, neither accusatory nor questioning, like a court clerk reading a charge.

I replied, "I continue to do what I must to revive the one called Athene."

"You have been warned, Orion," said Hera, her dark eyes flashing.

I made myself smile at her. "Would you destroy me, goddess? Put an end to me, at last? That would be a relief."

"You could be a long time dying," she purred.

"No!" snapped Zeus. "We're not here to threaten or punish. Our purpose is to find Apollo and stop his mad scheming before he destroys us all."

"And this creature," said the dark-haired Hermes, "knows where to find him."

"I'm not his keeper," I said.

"He certainly needs one," said burly Ares, chuckling at his own wit.

"We can open your brain, Orion, and fish out all your memories," Hera said.

"I'm sure you can. And many of them you'll find to be very painful."

Zeus waggled one hand impatiently. "You say that you don't know where the Golden One is."

"Yes, that's the truth."

"But could you find him for us?"

"So that you can destroy him?"

"What we do with him is of no concern to you, Orion," said Hera. "Considering how he's treated you, I should think you'd be happy to see him put out of the way."

"Can you revive Athene?" I asked.

Her gaze faltered, shifted away from me. The others looked uneasy, even Zeus.

"We're not here to talk about her," snapped the redhead. "It's Apollo we're after."

Before I could think out all the implications of it, I said, "I can lead you to him—after he has revived Athene."

"No one can revive her," blurted Hera, annoyed.

Zeus and the others glared at her.

I said, "After he has failed to revive her, then."

With a malicious smile, Hermes asked, "How do we know we can trust you?"

I shrugged. "Apparently you can find me when you want to. If you become convinced that I'm not living up to my end of the bargain, then do whatever you want with me. If Athene can't be revived, I'm not all that interested in living any longer."

Real sympathy seemed to fill Zeus's eyes. But Hera sneered skeptically, "And what of your current love, the beautiful Helen?"

"She loves me just as I love her," I answered. "As long as we are useful to one another, and no further."

Zeus ran a hand across his beard. "You will deliver Apollo to us when you are satisfied that he cannot revive Athene?"

"I will."

"We can't trust the word of a creature," said Hera. "This is madness! The longer we wait the more danger we . . ."

"Be quiet," said Zeus. He spoke softly, but Hera stopped in midsentence. Turning his gray eyes back to me, he said, "I *will* trust you, Orion. The fate of the continuum depends on your word. If you are false to us, it will mean not only your own destruction, and not only our destruction, but the end of this continuum—the utter ruination of the entire space-time in which we exist."

"You're going to let the Golden One play out his game at Jericho?" Ares was wide-eyed with incredulity. "You're going to feed his madness?"

"I am going to trust Orion," replied Zeus. "For the time being."

All three of the others started to speak at once, but I never heard what they said. Zeus smiled and nodded at me, then moved his right hand slightly.

And abruptly I was in the utter darkness of the tunnel's end, under the foundation of the main wall of Jericho.

I stood there trembling for several minutes. The end was in sight, I knew. They might not be able to track down the Golden One, but they certainly could keep track of me. The instant our paths crossed, they would jump and seize him, kill him, before he had the chance even to try to revive the goddess I had loved.

I forced my body to calm itself. The bitter perversity of the situation was almost laughable. I wanted to destroy the Golden One. They wanted to destroy the Golden One. But I had to protect him until he had made his attempt to revive Athene. I doubted that I could do that. And the more I thought about it, the more I despaired of his ability to bring her back to me.

Yet—he was clever enough, powerful enough, to elude their grasp. They could not find him, even though they knew that he was at work here at Jericho. They were in fear of him, in fear for their lives. Perhaps he was truly the most powerful among them. And, while they were trying to find him and destroy him, he was scheming to destroy them. I was caught in the middle of their Olympian struggle.

A faint sound startled me. A hooting, bleating noise. The ram's horn trumpets! Blinking, I realized that thin gray pencils of morning light were angling down into the cavern where I stood. Joshua had started up his parade again. It was time for the final stroke against Jericho.

I struck the flint and lit the torch, then put it to the piles of brushwood stacked against the wall's foundation. Dry as the desert in this season of heat, the bare twigs and branches burst into flame instantly. I backed away from the sudden heat, then realized that I had better get out of the tunnel as quickly as I could.

I ducked into the lower part of the tunnel and scuttled along like a four-limbed spider, the heat glowing at my back, reaching for me. I wondered if the fire would take the timbers that shored up the tunnel roof, trapping me in its collapse. I was crawling on my belly now, much slower than I wanted to be going. Dimly I remembered other lives, other deaths: in the boiling fury of a volcano's eruption, in the blazing maelstrom of a runaway nuclear reactor.

Smoke was making me cough. I kept my eyes closed; not that I could have seen anything in the pitch-blackness of the tunnel. I snaked forward, driven by the heat behind me and the hint of fresh air ahead.

Suddenly a pair of strong hands grabbed my wrists and I felt myself being pulled along the scrabbly ground. I opened my eyes and saw Lukka, tugging, grunting, swearing as he pulled me into the daylight and safety.

We got to our feet, surrounded by the Hatti soldiers. They were fully armed now, with shields and armor ready for battle.

"Is it working?" I asked Lukka.

He smiled grimly. "Come see for yourself."

We went together outside the tent and looked toward the city. Thin spirals of smoke were rising from the base of the wall. As I watched, they went from whitish-gray to a darker, more ominous color. The smoke thickened.

"The timbers must have caught," said Lukka.

Off around the curve of the wall, the Israelite priests still blew their horns, thumped their drums, clanged their cymbals. They chanted the praises of their Lord, and the people of Jericho stood atop their doomed wall, watching the display, jeering or laughing as they pleased.

I turned my gaze back toward the tents of the main Israelite camp. The men were forming up in ranks. They wore no uniforms, had precious little armor among them, but every man carried some sort of shield and either a sword or a spear. They were ready for battle.

As the procession of priests rounded the curve of the wall, Joshua gave the order for his men to march. I estimated there were several thousand of them, from teenagers to graybeards. They marched in step with the priests, although their parallel circuit was much farther from the wall, out of bowshot range.

The priests came within sight of the smoke issuing from the base of the wall and turned away, heading back toward the camp. The armed men turned toward the wall, as if expecting it to fall at their feet.

And it did.

As the army of the Israelites approached the wall, the smoke became even thicker and blacker. I could hear strange groaning sounds, as if some creature trapped beneath the earth were moaning for release. The people up on the parapets were pointing and gesticulating now. I heard screams of sudden terror.

Then, with a great grinding, thundering groan, the whole section of the wall caved in, collapsed in on itself in a roar of falling bricks. Clouds of red-gray dust blotted out the smoke and rolled out across the plain toward us.

A single trumpet note rang piercingly clear through the shuddering thunder and screaming shouts from the city. With a roar that shook the ground, the army of Israel charged across the field and swarmed across the pile of rubble and through the breach in Jericho's wall.

Chapter 32

I held Lukka and his men back for half the day, not wanting to risk them in the fighting. We had done our job, the battle belonged to the Israelites.

But by the time the sun was overhead Jericho was in flames, and even the imperturbable Lukka was quivering to get in on the looting.

I stood by the tent where our tunnel began and watched as clouds of ugly black smoke spread across the cloudless sky. Lukka's men sat or stood in what little shade they could find, casting questioning looks his way. Finally he turned to me.

Before he could speak, I said, "Be back at our tents by nightfall."

He gave me one of his rare grins and motioned for his men to follow him. They sprang up like eager wolf cubs, happy to be on the hunt.

I went with them as far as the demolished section of the wall, to see for myself what our work had accomplished. The wall was more than nine meters thick, where it still stood. The pile of tumbled bricks and rubble on which I picked my way felt hot, even through the soles of my boots. The fire was not out, it still smoldered deep below. Thin gray smoke issued from the lower cross-timbers in the sections of the wall on the other side of our breach. The fire would burn away at them for hours more, perhaps for days, I realized. Other parts of the wall would fall.

Inside the city, it was Troy all over again. The Israelites were like the Achaians in one way: they slaughtered and raped and pillaged and burned just as the barbarians of Argos and Ithaca and the other Achaian kingdoms did, on the plain of Ilios. The frenzy of bloodlust was in them, and no matter which god they worshiped or what name they gave him, they behaved like beasts rather than men.

Perhaps Helen is right, I thought. Perhaps in Egypt we will find civilized human beings, order and peace.

I clambered back over the hot rubble and made my way to my tent. To my surprise, Helen was holding court there, sitting outside the tent surrounded by more than two dozen of the Israelite women. I got close enough to hear a few of her words: "They will be filthy and bloody and filled with lust when they return. You should have scented water prepared to bathe them and soothe their raging blood."

"Scented water?" asked one of the women.

"In a tub?" another wondered.

Helen replied, "Yes, and let your servants bathe your husband . . ."

"Servants?" They all laughed.

Helen seemed nonplussed.

"But tell us," said one of the older women, "how do you use kohl to make your eyes seem larger?"

"And what charms do you use to keep a man faithful to you?"

I walked away, out of earshot, shaking my head in wonderment. While the men were following their savage instincts, murdering, burning, looting, the women were following their instincts, too, learning how to subdue and tame their men.

For some time I walked aimlessly among the tents. The only men in the camp were children or grandfathers. The women clustered in little groups, like those with Helen, whispering among themselves and occasionally glancing at the burning city.

"Orion," a strong voice hailed me.

I turned and saw Joshua standing in the shade cast by the striped awning extended over the front of his big tent. A humid breeze bellied the awning slightly and made the woven wool fabric strain against its creaking ropes. I could smell moisture in the breeze, and the sweet fragrance of date palms. The fire from the city was sucking up air from the river valley.

Several of the older priests reclined around Joshua on benches or the ground. They looked tired, spent, slightly ashamed.

"You have Jericho," I said to Joshua.

"Thanks to the Lord our God," he said, then added, "and to you."

I bowed my head slightly.

"You have performed a great service for the God of Israel and His people," said Joshua. "You will be rewarded amply."

"I appreciate the gratitude of your people." Somehow I could not bring myself to say that I was happy to have helped them. "In a day or so my men and I will continue on our way . . . southward."

He knew I meant Egypt. "You are certain that you want to go in that direction?"

"Quite certain."

"It is what *she* desires, isn't it?"

"Yes."

"Orion, why spend your life as a woman's slave? Stay with me! Be my strong right arm. There are other cities to consider. The Philistines on the coast are powerful enemies."

I looked into his deep, glittering eyes and saw the same burning light that glowed in the eyes of the Golden One. Madness? Or greatness? Both, I thought. Perhaps the one cannot exist without the other.

"I have no quarrel with the Philistines or anyone else," I said. "And I have my own reasons for going to Egypt."

"You are tied to a woman's skirts," he taunted.

I replied. "I seek a god in Egypt."

"A false god," Joshua snapped. "There is only one true God . . ."

"I know what you believe," I said, before he could go further, "and perhaps you are right. Perhaps the god I seek in Egypt is the same one that you worship."

"Then why seek him in a land of slavery and tyranny?"

"Egypt is a civilized land," I countered.

Joshua spat at my feet. One of the old white-bearded priests who had been listening to us climbed arthritically to his feet and, leaning on a staff, pointed a bony finger at me.

"Egypt civilized? A land where the king orders the murder of every Israelite baby girl, simply because his ministers have told him that our numbers are growing too fast? That is civilization?"

His weak old voice trembled with anger. "A land where our whole nation was enslaved to build monuments to the tyrant who slaughtered our infants?"

I blinked at him, not knowing how to answer.

"We fled from Egypt," said Joshua, "with nothing but the clothes on our backs and what little goods we could carry. Their king sent his army to find us and bring us back. Only the miracle of our Lord God saved us and allowed us to escape. We spent years wandering in the wilderness of Sinai, willing to starve and go thirsty in the desert rather than return to slavery. No, Orion, do not think that Egypt is civilized."

"But I must go there," I insisted.

"To find the God who in truth resides among us? Stay with us, and God will bless you."

"The god I seek is worshiped by many peoples, in many ways. To some he is the god of the sun . . ."

"There is only one true God," the old priest intoned. "All other gods are false."

"He told me to seek him in Egypt," I blurted, nearing exasperation.

The old priest staggered back from me. Joshua's face went white.

"God spoke to you?"

"This god did."

"In a dream?"

I raised my arm to point at the distant riverbank. "There, by the river, a few nights ago."

"Blasphemy!" hissed the old priest, pulling at his long white beard.

Joshua shook his head, an almost smugly understanding expression on his face. "It was not the God of Israel you saw, Orion. It was a man, or a false vision."

By definition, as far as he was concerned. All very neat. I decided it was senseless to argue with them. If they knew that the god they worshiped was the one I had promised myself to kill, they would have torn me to pieces on the spot. Or tried to.

"Perhaps," I conceded. "Nevertheless, I must go to Egypt."

Joshua said, "That is a mistake, Orion. You will be better off staying with us."

"I can't," I said.

Joshua said nothing in reply. He merely spread his hands in a vaguely dismissive gesture. I took my leave of him and headed back toward my own tent, my insides churning with the realization that Joshua was not going to allow us to leave—willingly.

As night spread its dark cloak over the ruin of Jericho, the men came tottering back to camp, stained with blood and carrying the riches of the oldest city in the world. In twos and threes they made their way back to their tents, where their women waited for them. The men were silent and grim, the memories of their atrocities just beginning to burn themselves into their consciences. The women were silent, too, knowing better than to ask any questions.

Lukka brought his two dozen soldiers back in a group, each of them staggering under a load of silks, blankets, armor, weaponry, jewels, even precious carvings of ivory and jade.

"We will enter Egypt as rich men," he said to me proudly, once the loot was arrayed at my feet by the light of our campfire.

Softly, I said to him, "If we enter Egypt at all, it will be despite the efforts of Joshua and his people."

Lukka stared at me, his dour face half hidden in the flickering shadows thrown by the fire.

"Keep the men together, and be ready to move swiftly when I give the word," I told him.

He nodded curtly and immediately started the men packing up the loot and storing it in our wagons.

Helen was more impatient than ever to leave, and when I told her of my misgivings, she demanded, "Then we must flee now, this night, while they are drunk with their victory and sleeping without sentries posted."

"And what about the next morning, when they find we've left? They could easily overtake us and force us to return."

"Lukka and his soldiers could hold them off while we escaped," she said.

"And die giving us a few hours' head start on our pursuers?" I shook my head. "We'll leave, but only when I've convinced Joshua to let us go."

She grew angry, but realized there was no other way.

That night I slept without dreams, without visiting the realm of the Creators. But in the morning I had formed a plan for dealing with Joshua. It was simple, perhaps even crude. I hoped it would work.

All that day was given to ceremonies of thanksgiving and atonement, the priests singing hymns of praise to their god in melodies that sounded somehow mournful and melancholy. The people of Israel arrayed themselves in their finest garments, many of them taken from Jericho, and gathered in ranks, tribe by tribe, and joined in the singing. I saw that although the words of their hymns were directed at their invisible god, their eyes were directed toward Joshua when they sang words of praise. He stood before them, decked in a long robe of many colors, silently acknowledging their homage.

By sunset the people had split up into their tribal and family units, each gathering around their own fires, and the singing was lighter, happier, songs of the home and the people themselves. Dancing started here and there, men and women in separate circles, laughing and weaving around their fires as they stamped their feet on the dusty ground.

Ben-Jameen sent a boy to invite me to his family's tent, but I politely declined, since his invitation did not include Helen. Israelite men and women ate separately, of course, just as they danced.

I was waiting for Joshua's summons, and sure enough, as we were finishing dinner, a young man in a newly acquired bronze cuirass approached our fire and told me that Joshua wished to have words with me.

I told Helen and Lukka to be ready to leave, then followed the young Israelite to his leader's tent.

Joshua's tent was crammed with the spoils of Jericho: beautiful cypress chests inlaid with bone and ivory and packed to the brim with fine clothing, piles of draperies and blankets, tables sagging under loads of gilded plates and goblets, intricately engraved daggers, swords and armor, enamelware, pottery and wine jugs, heaps of jewelry and carvings.

I took it all in with one swift glance, then looked up to Joshua. He was sitting on a mound of pillows at the far end of the tent, dressed in splendid robes like an oriental potentate. With a wave of his hand, he dismissed the three serving girls, who ran past me on bare feet, leaving us alone in the tent.

"Take your pick," said Joshua, gesturing grandly toward the loot. "Whatever you want is yours. And take some jewelry for your beautiful companion."

I walked past the treasures, straight to him, and sat on the carpeting at his feet.

"Joshua, I neither want nor need any of this. I want you to live up to your promise, and let us go in peace now that we have helped you conquer Jericho."

There was no wine in sight. His hands were empty, his eyes clear. But he seemed almost drunk. Perhaps with victory. Perhaps with visions of future conquests.

"God has placed you in my hand, Orion," he said. "It would displease Him if I let you go."

"You speak for your god now?"

His eyes narrowed angrily. But he replied mildly enough, "Our next objective will be the Amalekites. They threaten our flank, and must be destroyed utterly."

"No," I said.

"You and your Hittite warriors are too valuable to give up," Joshua said. "Not while there are so many enemies around us."

"We must leave."

He raised a placating hand. "When we have made this region peaceful. When the Children of Israel can live here safely, without being threatened by their neighbors. Then you can leave."

"That could take years," I said.

He shrugged. "It is in God's hands, not mine."

I made myself smile at him. "Joshua, surely you of all men can understand the yearning of a man to be free. I have no desire to be a slave to you or your god."

"A slave?" He pointed toward the loot again. "Is a slave rewarded so handsomely?"

"A man who is not free to go where he wishes is a slave, no matter how many trinkets his master offers him."

He ran his fingers through the curls of his beard. "Then I'm afraid you will be a slave for a while longer, Orion. You and your Hittite soldiers."

"That cannot be," I insisted.

"If you resist," Joshua warned, his voice as mild as if he were discussing the weather, "your men will pay for your stubbornness. And your beautiful woman."

I had expected this so exactly that I was not even mildly surprised. Not even angry. I simply got to my feet and looked down at him.

"Ben-Jameen tells me," I said, "that your god struck the Egyptians with many plagues before their king would allow you to leave the land. I can't promise you plagues, but you will be sorry that you force us to stay."

Joshua's face turned deep red, whether from anger or shame I did not know. I left him sitting there and made my way back to my own tent.

Lukka and Helen both asked me eagerly if we were leaving.

"At dawn," I answered. "Now get some sleep. Tomorrow is going to be a hard day."

Chapter 33

HELEN was right about the Israelites' laxness that night. Jericho's men were slaughtered; the city's women and children cowered in the blackened remains of their burned and looted homes. There was no need for guards or sentries. The Israelites slept soundly after a day of ceremonies and celebration.

I picked my way silently through the darkness toward Joshua's tent. The only light came from the smoldering embers of campfires and the splendor of stars overhead. The hazy glow of the Milky Way split the heavens, and as I glanced upward I wondered once again which of those stars my love and I had been heading for when we died.

No time for memories. No time for bitterness. I reached Joshua's tent and stepped over the bodies of the servants sleeping just outside its entrance.

It was pitch-dark inside the tent. I felt my way toward Joshua, guided by the faint heat radiating from his body. Like a pit viper, I laughed to myself, although my heat-sensing abilities were mere vagaries compared to the refined sensitivities of a rattlesnake. Nonetheless, I sensed a faint emanation from the far end of the tent and groped toward it.

I made out Joshua's sleeping form when I was a few feet from him. He lay on his side, his back to me, stretched out on the pillows where I had seen him a few hours earlier, still wearing his splendid robes.

He slept alone. Good.

I reached out and clamped my left hand over his mouth. He awoke instantly and started to thrash out with his arms and legs. I leaned my right forearm against his windpipe and whispered: "Do you want the angel of death to visit this tent?"

His eyes went wide. He recognized me and became still.

Without taking my hand from his mouth I pulled him to his feet and said, "You and I are taking a little journey."

Then I concentrated on shifting to the realm of the Creators. I closed my eyes for a moment and felt that instant of piercing cold, then the warmth that glowed all around us. Joshua was still in my grasp, my left hand over his mouth, my right gripping his shoulder.

We stood on a height overlooking a vast domed city. The entire landscape was bathed in golden radiance, and I realized that for the first time I could see details of this realm with some clarity. The city spread out below us was a wonderland of graceful towers and spires, all within the protective curve of a huge transparent dome.

Joshua's eyes were bugging out of his head. I took my hand away from his mouth, but no words came from him. He simply stared, his jaw hanging open.

"Orion, really! This is too much!"

I turned to see the slim dark-haired Hermes.

"Now you're bringing other creatures along with you," he scolded. "If any of the others see this . . ."

"You mean you don't tell them everything?" I gibed back at him.

He grinned. "Not immediately. We have no secrets among ourselves, of course; information is shared whether we like it or not. But if I were you, I would get out of here before the others decide you're becoming too bold."

"Thank you. I will."

"See to it," he said, and disappeared.

Joshua's knees gave way and I had to prop him up. With a final glance around, to register every detail as firmly in my mind as I could, I closed my eyes again and willed us back to where we had come from.

I opened my eyes in the darkness of Joshua's tent. He was collapsed in my arms, trembling uncontrollably.

"When dawn comes," I said, "I and my people will leave your camp. We have served you faithfully, and I expect you to live up to your side of our bargain. If you try to hinder us in any way, I will come to you in the night and send you to that golden land once again—and leave you there forever."

I let Joshua sag back onto his pillows and strode out of his tent. That was the last time I saw him.

BOOK III

EGYPT

Chapter 34

HELEN was right: Egypt was civilization. Even Lukka was impressed.

"The towns have no walls around them," he marveled.

We had trekked across the rocky wilderness of Sinai, threading our way through mountain passes and across sands that burned beneath the pitiless sun, lured westward by the goal of Egypt. The scattered tribes of the Sinai were suspicious of strangers, yet their laws of hospitality were stronger than their fears. We were not exactly welcomed by the nomadic herders we came across, but we were tolerated, fed, given water, and wished heartfelt good-speed when we departed from their tents.

I always gave them some small token from our treasures: an amber cameo from Troy, a leaf-thin stone drinking cup from Jericho. The nomads accepted such trinkets solemnly; they knew their worth, but more, they appreciated the fact that we understood the obligations of a guest as well as those of a host.

Still, the heat and barrenness of that wasteland took their toll. Three of our men died of fever. The oxen that pulled our wagons collapsed, one after the other, as did several of our horses. We replaced them with hardy little asses and treacherous evil-smelling camels bought from the nomads in exchange for jewels and fine weapons. We left the lumbering carts behind and piled our possessions onto the donkeys and asses.

Helen bore the strain better than most of the men. She now rode atop a braying, barely tamed camel, in a swaying palanquin of silks that kept the sun off her. We all became bone-thin, parched of fat and moisture by the pitiless sun. Yet Helen kept her beauty; she needed no makeup or fine clothes. She never complained about the hardships of the desert; better than any of us, she realized that each step we took brought us closer to Egypt.

I did not complain, either. It would have done no good. And my goal was also Egypt and the great pyramid where I would meet the Golden One once more and make him return my beloved to me.

The morning finally came when our tiny band saw a palm tree waving on the horizon. To me it looked as if it were beckoning to us, telling us that our journey was nearly ended. We kicked our horses and camels to their best speed, the donkeys trailing behind us, and soon saw the land turning green before our eyes.

Trees and cultivated fields greeted us. Half-naked men and women bent over the crops, toiling amid an intricate network of narrow irrigation canals. In the distance I could see a river flowing.

"The Nile," said Helen, from the camel on which she rode. One of the Hittites was driving it, and she had made him pull it up beside me.

I turned in my makeshift saddle—merely a few blankets folded beneath me—and glanced back at her. "One of its arms, at least. This must be the delta country, where the river splits up into many branches."

The peasants took no notice of us. We were a band of armed men, too few to mean much to them, too many to question. We found a road soon enough and it led to the delta city of Tahpanhes.

Lukka was surprised at the lack of a defensive wall; I was surprised at how large a city it was. Where Troy and Jericho had huddled closely over a few acres, Tahpanhes sprawled nearly a mile across. I doubted that its population was much larger than Jericho's, but its people lived in spacious airy houses that dotted wide, straight avenues.

We found an inn near the edge of the town, a low set of dried-brick buildings arranged around a central courtyard where stately palms and willows provided shade against the constant sun. A grape arbor also stretched its trellises across one section of the courtyard. There was an orchard on the river side of the inn; the stables were on the other side. Depending on which way the wind blew, the atmosphere could be scented with lemons and pomegranates or with horse manure and the annoying buzz of flies.

The innkeeper was overjoyed at receiving two dozen travel-weary guests. He was a short, round, bald, jovial man of middle age who constantly held his hands clasped over his ample belly. His skin was as dark as Lukka's cloak, his eyes like two glittering pieces of coal—especially when he was engaged in his favorite pursuit, estimating how much he could charge for his services.

The innkeeper's staff was his family, a wife who was just as dark as her rotund husband and even fatter than he, and a dozen dark-skinned children ranging in age from about twenty to barely six. And cats. I counted ten of them in the courtyard alone, watching us with slitted eyes, padding silently atop the balcony rail or along the dirt floor. The innkeeper's children scampered sweatily, helping to unload our possessions, tend our animals, show us to our rooms. There was not an ounce of fat on any of the children.

I found that I could speak the language of Egypt as easily as any other. If Lukka marveled at my gift of tongues, he kept it to himself. Helen took it for granted, even though she could speak only her own Achaian tongue and the dialect of it spoken at Troy.

Once we were unpacked and comfortably settled in our rooms, I found the innkeeper at the outdoor kitchen, shouting orders to two teenaged girls who were baking loaves of round flat bread in the beehive-shaped oven. They wore only loincloths against the heat of the oven; their bare young breasts were firm and lovely, their lithe dark bodies covered with a sheen of sweat.

If the innkeeper objected to my seeing his daughters bare-breasted, he made no show of it. In fact, he smiled at me and tiltled his head toward them when he noticed me standing at the entrance in the wall that surrounded the open-roofed kitchen.

"My wife insists that they learn to cook properly," he said, without preamble. "It is necessary if they are to catch husbands, she says. I believe other skills are necessary, eh?" He laughed suggestively.

Apparently he was not opposed to offering his daughters to his guests, a fact that Lukka would appreciate. I ignored his insinuation, though, and said: "I have brought these men to your land to offer their services to the king."

"The mighty Merneptah? He resides in Wast, far up the river."

"My men are professional soldiers from the land of the Hittites. They seek service with your king."

The innkeeper's smile vanished. "Hittites? They have been our enemies . . ."

"The Hittite empire no longer exists. These men are without employment. Is there a representative of the king in this city? Some official or officer of the army that I can speak to?"

He bobbed his round bald head hard enough to make his cheeks bounce. "The king's overseer. He is here, in the courtyard, waiting to see you."

I said nothing, but allowed the innkeeper to lead me to the courtyard. The king's overseer was already here at the inn to look us over. The innkeeper must have sent one of his children running to him the instant we rode up to his door.

Several cats slinked out of our way as the fat innkeeper led me along a columned hallway and through a side entrance into the courtyard. Sitting in the shade of the grape arbor was a gray-haired man with a thin, hollow-cheeked face, clean shaven, as all the Egyptians were. He rose to his feet as I approached him. He was no taller than the innkeeper, the top of his gray head hardly reached my shoulder. His skin was a shade lighter, though, and he was as slim as a sword blade. His face was serious, his eyes unwaveringly studying me as I approached. He wore a cool white caftan so light that I could see through it to the short skirt beneath. He carried no weapons that I could see. His only emblem of office was a gold medallion on a chain around his neck.

Suddenly I felt distinctly grubby. I still wore the leather kilt and harness I had been wearing for many months, under a light vest. From long habit I still carried a dagger strapped to my thigh, beneath the kilt. My clothes were worn and travel-stained. I needed a bath and a shave, and I wondered if I should try to stay downwind from this obviously civilized man.

"I am Nefertu, servant of King Merneptah, ruler of the Two Lands," he said, keeping his hands at his sides.

"I am Orion," I replied.

There were two wooden benches beneath the arbor's twining vines. Nefertu gestured for me to sit. He is polite, I thought, or perhaps he simply feels uncomfortable stretching his neck to look up at me. My head grazed the grape vines.

Our genial host scuttled out of the kitchen area with a tray that bore a stone pitcher beaded with condensation, two handsome stoneware drinking cups, and a small bowl heaped with wrinkled black olives. He placed the tray down on a small wooden table within Nefertu's easy reach, then bowed and smiled his way back to the kitchen. Nefertu poured the wine and offered me a cup. We drank together. The wine was poor, thin and acid, but it was cold and for that I felt grateful.

"You are not a Hittite," he said calmly, putting down his cup. His voice was low and measured, like a man accustomed to speaking to those both below and above his station.

"No," I admitted. "I come from far away."

He listened patiently to my story of Troy and Jericho and Lukka's men who sought service with his king. He showed no surprise at the fall of the Hittite empire. But when I spoke of the Israelites at Jericho his eyes widened slightly.

"These are the slaves that our king Merneptah drove across the Sea of Reeds?"

"The same," I said, "although they say that they fled Egypt and your king tried to recapture them but failed."

The shadow of a smile flickered across Nefertu's thin lips. It passed immediately and he asked with some earnestness, "And now these same people have conquered Jericho?"

"They have. They believe that their god has given them the entire land of Canaan, and their destiny is to rule over it all."

Nefertu smiled again, slightly, like a man who appreciated an ironic situation. "They may form a useful buffer between our border and the tribes of Asia," he mused. "This news must be passed on to the pharaoh."

We talked for hours, there in the shaded corner of the courtyard. I learned that pharaoh, as Nefertu used the word, meant essentially "the government," the king's house, his administration. Egypt had been under attack for years now by what he called the Peoples of the Sea, warriors from the European mainland and Aegean islands who raided the coastal and delta cities from time to time. He considered Agamemnon and his Achaians to be Peoples of the Sea, barbarians. He saw the fall of Troy as a blow against civilization, and I agreed with him—although I did not tell him how I had defied the Golden One to bring about Troy's destruction.

Nor did I tell him that the woman who traveled with me was Queen Helen, nor that her rightful husband, Menalaos, was seeking her. I spoke only of the wars I had seen, and of my band's desire to join the service of his king.

"The army always needs men," Nefertu said. Our wine was long gone, nothing was left of the olives but a pile of pits, and the setting sun was throwing long shadows across the courtyard. The wind had shifted; flies from the stables were buzzing about us pesteringly. Still, he did not call for a slave to stand by us with a fan to shoo them away.

"Would foreigners be allowed in the army?" I asked.

His ironic little smile returned. "The army is hardly anything except foreigners. Most of the sons of the Two Lands lost their thirst for military glory long ages ago."

"Then the Hittites would be accepted?"

"Accepted? They would be welcomed, especially if they have the engineering skills you spoke of."

He told me to wait at the inn until he could get word to Wast, the capital city, far to the south. I expected to stay in Tahpanhes for many weeks, but the following day Nefertu came back to the inn and told me that the king's own general wanted to see these men from the Hittite army.

"He is here in Tahpanhes?" I asked.

"No, he is at the capital, at the great court of Merneptah, in Wast."

I blinked with surprise. "Then how did you get a message . . ."

Nefertu laughed, a gentle, truly pleased laughter. "Orion, we worship Amon above all gods, the glorious sun himself. He speeds our messages along the length and breadth of our land—on mirrors that catch his light."

A solar telegraph. I laughed too. How obvious, once explained. Messages could flash up and down the Nile with the speed of light, almost.

"You are to bring your men to Wast," said Nefertu. "And I am to accompany you. It will be my first visit to the capital in many years. I must thank you for this opportunity, Orion."

I accepted his thanks with a slight bow of my head.

Helen was overjoyed that we were going to the capital.

"There's no guarantee that we will see the king," I warned her. She dismissed such caution with a casual wave of her hand.

"Once he realizes that the Queen of Sparta and former princess of Troy is in his city he will *demand* to see me."

I grinned at her. "Once he realizes that Menalaos may raid his coast in his effort to find you, he may demand that you be returned to Sparta."

She frowned at me.

That night, though, as we lay together in the sagging down-filled bed of the inn, Helen turned to me and asked, "What will happen when you deliver me to the Egyptian king?"

I smiled at her in the shadows cast by the moonlight and stroked her golden hair. "He will undoubtedly fall madly in love with you. Or at least marry you to one of his sons."

But she was in no mood for levity. "You don't really think he would send me back to Menalaos, do you?"

Despite the fact that I thought such a move was possible, I answered, "No, of course he wouldn't. How could he? You come to him seeking his protection. He couldn't deny a queen. These people regard the Achaians as their enemies; they won't force you to return to Sparta."

Helen lay back on her pillow. Staring up at the ceiling, she asked, "And what of you, Orion? Will you stay with me?"

Almost, I wished that I could. "No," I said softly, so low that I barely heard my own voice. "I can't."

"Where will you go?"

"To find my goddess," I whispered.

"But you said that she is dead."

"I will try to revive her, to return her to life."

"You will enter Hades to seek her?" Helen's voice sounded alarmed, fearful. She turned toward me again and clutched at my bare shoulder. "Orion, you mustn't take such a risk! Orpheos himself . . ."

I silenced her with a finger against her lips. "Don't be frightened. I have already died many times, and returned to the world of the living. If there truly is a Hades, I have yet to see it."

She stared at me as if seeing a ghost, or worse, a blasphemer.

"Helen," I said, "your destiny is here, in Egypt. My destiny is elsewhere, in a domain where the people you call gods hold sway. They are not gods, not in the sense you think. They are very powerful, but they are neither immortal nor very caring about us humans. One of them killed the woman I love. I will try to bring her back to life. Failing that, I will try to avenge her murder. That is *my* destiny."

"Then you love her, and not me?"

That surprised me. For a moment I had no answer. Finally I cupped her chin in my hand and said, "Only a goddess could keep me from loving you, Helen."

"But I love you, Orion. You are the only man I have given myself to willingly. I love you! I don't want to lose you!"

A wave of sadness surged through me, and I thought how pleasantly I could live in this timeless land with this incomparably beautiful woman.

But I said, "Our destinies take us in different directions, Helen. I wish it were otherwise, but no one can outrun his fate."

She did not cry. Yet her voice was brimming with tears as she said, "Helen's destiny is to be desired by every man who sees her, except the one man she truly loves."

I closed my eyes and tried to shut out all the worlds. Why couldn't I love this beautiful woman? Why couldn't I be like an ordinary man and live out my years in a single lifetime, loving and being loved, instead of striving to battle against the forces of the continuum? I knew the answer. I was not free. No matter how I struggled, I was still the creature of the Golden One, still his Hunter, sent here to do his work. I might rebel against him, but even then my life was tied to his whim.

And then I saw the gray-eyed woman I truly loved, and realized that not even Helen could compare to her. I remembered our brief moment together and my mind filled with grief and pain. My destiny was linked forever with hers, through all the universes, through all of time. If she could not be brought back to life, then life meant nothing to me and I wanted the final death for myself.

Chapter 35

THE next morning we started our river journey to Wast, the capital. I felt drained, emotionally and physically. The long trek across the Sinai had taken its toll of my body, and now Helen's sad eyes and drooping spirits were assailing my spirit.

Once our broad-beamed boat pushed away from the dock, though, and its lateen sail filled with wind, we at least had the sights and sounds and smells of a new and fascinating land to occupy our minds. If Lukka was surprised at cities without walls to defend them, we were all constantly awed and delighted at what we saw of Egypt on our long trip up the Nile.

Nefertu was our host, our guardian, and our guide. The boat he had requisitioned had forty oars, and enclosed cabins for Helen and me, and for himself. A single lateen-rigged sail propelled us against the mighty river's current most of the time, driven by an almost constant northerly wind. The rowers were seldom needed. They were not slaves, I noticed, but soldiers who looked for commands not to the ship's captain but to Nefertu himself.

I smiled inwardly. This very civilized man had brought forty armed men along to make certain that we got where we were supposed to go, without fail. It was a subtle show of strength, meant to ensure that nothing went wrong during this journey, without alarming us or making us feel that we were under guard.

But if Nefertu was capable of subtlety, the land we saw from the boat's deck was just the opposite. Egypt was big, grand, imposing, awe-inspiring.

The Nile was its life stream, flowing a thousand miles from its headlands far to the south. On either side of the river we could see bare cliffs of limestone and granite, and desert beyond. But along the thin ribbon of the life-giving water, there were green fields and swaying trees and mighty cities.

It took a whole day to pass a typical Egyptian city, stretched out along the river's bank. We passed busy docks and warehouses, granaries where long lines of wagons unloaded the golden harvests of the land. Imposing temples stood at the water's edge, their stairs leading down to stone piers where many boats brought worshipers and supplicants.

"This is nothing," said Nefertu one afternoon as we glided past still another city. "Wait until we come upon Menefer."

We were eating a light dinner of dates, figs, and thin slices of sweet melon. Being civilized, Nefertu found it pleasant to have Helen dine with us. He spoke the Achaian tongue fairly well, and refrained from using his own language when Helen was present.

She asked, "What are the small buildings on the other side of the river?"

I too had noticed that the cities were invariably on the eastern bank, but there were small structures scattered along the opposite bank wherever a city existed, many of them carved into the rock face of the cliffs that lined the river valley.

"Are they temples?" Helen asked, before Nefertu could answer her first question.

"Of a kind, my lady," he replied. "They are tombs. The dead are embalmed and placed in tombs to await their next life, surrounded by the foods and possessions they will need when they awaken once more."

Helen's beautiful face betrayed her skepticism, despite what I had told her of myself. "You believe that people live more than one life?"

I kept my silence. I have led many lives, gone through death many times only to find myself revived in some strange and distant time. Not all humans lived more than once, I had been told. I found myself envying those who could close their eyes and make an end of it.

Nefertu smiled politely. "Egypt is an ancient land, my lady. Our history goes back thousands of years, to the time when the gods created the Earth and gave this gift of Mother Nile to our ancestors. Some of those tombs you see are a thousand years old; some are even older. You will find that our people are more concerned with death and the afterlife than with life itself."

"I should think so," Helen said, gazing back at the distant colonnaded buildings. "In Argos only the kings have such splendid tombs."

The Egyptian's smile broadened. "You have seen nothing of splendor as yet. Wait until Menefer."

The days passed easily. We drifted up the Nile, the steady north wind bellying our sail almost constantly. At night we tied up at a pier, but we slept aboard the boat. Lukka and his men were allowed to visit the cities where we stopped overnight, and Nefertu's guards introduced them to two of Egypt's most ancient entertainments: beer and prostitution. The men were becoming comrades, soldiers who would drink and whore together until they might be ordered to fall upon one another with naked swords.

Helen adopted the ship's cat, a pure white one that sauntered along the deck with a lordly air and permitted humans it especially favored to offer it food. The Egyptians regarded the cat as a mini-god; Helen was pleased that it allowed her to pet it —occasionally.

Then one morning I awoke just as the sun was rising above the cliffs to the east. Far in the distance I saw a glow on the western horizon. For an instant my heart stopped: I waited for the glow to expand and engulf me, to bring me face to face with the Golden One once more.

Yet it did not. It simply hovered on the horizon like a distant beacon. What its meaning was, I could not tell. I had not been summoned to the domain of the Creators since we had left the smoldering ruins of Jericho. I had not sought their realm. I knew I would meet them again in Egypt and either I would destroy the Golden One or he would destroy me. I was content to wait until that moment arrived.

But what was that strange beacon on the western horizon?

"You see it."

I turned, and Nefertu was standing at my side.

"What is it?" I asked.

He shook his head slowly. "Words cannot explain it. You will see for yourself."

Through the hours of early morning our boat sailed toward the light. We came upon the city of Menefer, a vast stretch of mighty stone buildings that towered along the Nile's eastern bank: temples and obelisks that reared into the cloudless sky, piers that dwarfed anything we had seen before, long colonnaded avenues lined with palms and eucalyptus trees, palaces with gardens and even groves of trees planted on their roofs.

All this we hardly noticed. One by one, every person on the boat turned eyes to the west and to the incredible sight that stood there.

"The great pyramid of Khufu," said Nefertu, in a whisper. Even he was awed by it. "It has stood for more than a thousand years. It will stand until the end of time."

It was an enormous pyramid of dazzling white, so huge and massive that it beggared all comparison. There were other pyramids nearby, and a great stone carving of a sphinx rested to one side, as if guarding the approach. Colonnaded temples flanked the road that led to the great pyramid; they looked like tiny doll houses next to its ponderous immensity.

The pyramid was faced entirely with gleaming white stone, polished so perfectly that I could almost make out the reflection of the sphinx in it. The cap, big enough to hold Priam's palace, but merely the tip of this awesome structure, blazed in the sunlight. It was made of electrum, an alloy of gold and silver, Nefertu told me. That is what had caught the morning sun when it had first arisen.

This was the place where I was to meet the Golden One. This is where I had to be to revive Athene. Yet our boat glided past.

As I watched, the dazzling white surface of the pyramid facing us slowly began to change. A great eye appeared, black against the white stones, and stared directly at us. A moan went up from everyone aboard, including me. Several of the Hittites fell to their knees. I felt the hairs on my arms standing on end.

Nefertu touched my shoulder, the first time he had put a hand on me.

"Do not be afraid," he said. "It is an effect caused by the sun and certain small stones that have been set out along the pyramid's face to cast a shadow when the sun is at the proper angle. It is like a sundial, except that it shows the Eye of Amon."

I tore my gaze away from the optical illusion and looked down at Nefertu. His face was grave, almost solemn. He was not laughing at the awe and fear he saw in the faces of his barbarian visitors.

"As I told you earlier," he said, almost apologetically, "there are no words that can explain the great pyramid, or prepare you for your first sight of it."

I nodded dumbly. It was difficult to find my voice.

The great Eye of Amon disappeared as quickly as it had opened, along about noon. Shortly afterward, the figure of a hawk manifested itself on the southward face of the pyramid. We spent the entire day watching the pyramid; not one of us could tear our eyes away from it for very long.

"It is the tomb of Khufu, one of our greatest kings, who lived more than a thousand years ago," Nefertu explained. "Within its mighty stones is the king's burial chamber, and other chambers for his treasures and retainers. In those bygone days, the king's household servants were sealed into the pyramid along with his embalmed body, so that they might serve him properly when he arose."

"The servants were sealed in alive?" I asked.

Nefertu said, "Alive. They went willingly, we are told, out of their great love for their master, and in the knowledge that they would be with him in the afterlife."

The expression on his lean face was difficult to read. Did he believe these stories, or was he merely transmitting the official line to me?

"I would like to see the great pyramid," I said.

"You have just seen it."

"I mean close up. Perhaps it is possible to enter . . ."

"No!" It was the sharpest word Nefertu had ever spoken to me. "The pyramid is a sacred tomb. It is guarded night and day against those who would defile it. No one may enter the tomb without the special permission of the king himself."

I bowed my head in silent acquiescence, while thinking to myself, I won't wait for the king's permission. I will enter the tomb and find the Golden One waiting for me inside it. And I will do it tonight.

Our boat finally docked at a massive stone pier on the southern end of the city. As usual, Lukka and his men went out into the city with Nefertu's guards. But I noticed that there were other guards from the city itself standing at the end of the pier. They would not allow anyone to pass unless Nefertu or some other official permitted it.

Helen, Nefertu, and I had dinner together aboard the boat: fish and lamb and good wine, all brought in from the city.

Nefertu told us many tales about the great pyramid and the huge city of Menefer. Once it had been the capital of Egypt —which he always referred to as the Kingdom of the Two Lands. Originally called the City of the White Wall, when Menefer became the capital of the kingdom its name was changed to Ankhtawy, which means "Holding the Two Lands Together." Since the capital had been moved south, to Wast, the city's name was changed to Menefer, meaning "Harmonious Beauty."

To Helen, speaking Achaian, the city's name was Memphis.

Impatiently I listened to their conversation as they dawdled over dinner. Finally it was finished and Nefertu bid us good night. Helen and I spent another hour or so simply staring at the city or, across the river, at the great pyramid and the other pyramids flanking it.

Khufu's massive tomb seemed to glow with hidden light even long after the sun had gone down. It was as if some eerie form of energy was being generated within those titanic stones and radiating out into the night.

"It must have been built by the gods," said Helen, whispering in the warm night as she pressed her body close to mine. "Mortal men could never have built anything so huge."

I put my arm around her. "Nefertu says that men built it, and the others. Thousands of men, working like ants."

"Only gods or titans could build such a thing," Helen insisted.

I recalled the Trojans and Achaians who believed that the walls of Troy had been built by Apollo and Poseidon. The memory, and Helen's stubborn insistence, put a slightly bitter tang in my mouth. Why do people want to believe that they themselves are not capable of great feats? Why do they ascribe greatness to their gods, who are in truth no wiser or kinder than any wandering shepherd?

I walked Helen across the width of the boat's deck, so that we were facing the city.

"And this mighty pier? Did the gods build this? It's far longer than the walls of Troy. And the obelisk at its end? The temples and villas we saw today? Did the gods build them?"

She laughed softly. "Orion, you're being silly. Of course not; gods don't stoop to building such mundane things."

"Then if the mortal men of this land could build such giant structures, why couldn't they build the pyramids? There's nothing terribly mysterious about them; they're just bigger than the buildings of the city—it took more manpower and time to build them."

She dismissed my blasphemy with bantering. "For a man who claims he serves a goddess, Orion, you certainly show scant respect to the immortals."

I had to agree. I felt scant respect to those who had created this world and its people. They felt scant respect for us, torturing and killing us for whatever strange purposes moved them.

Helen sensed my moodiness and tried to soothe me with lovemaking. For a few moments I forgot everything and allowed my body to blot out all my memories and desires. Yet when we clutched each other in the frenzy of passion I closed my eyes and saw the face of my beloved Athene, beautiful beyond human mortality.

Her bantering mood had changed, also. Whispering in my ear, Helen pleaded, "Don't challenge the gods, Orion. Please don't set yourself against them. Nothing good can come of it."

I did not reply. There was nothing I could say to her that would not either be a lie or cause her more worry.

For a while we slept wrapped in each other's arms. I awoke to the slight rocking of the boat and the subdued sound of men's muffled laughter. Lukka and the others were coming back. It must be nearly dawn.

Closing my eyes, I concentrated my mind on Khufu's great pyramid. Every particle of my being I attuned to that massive pile of stones and the burial chamber hidden within it. I saw it clearly, shining against the night, standing out before the dark starry sky, glowing intensely with a light that no mortal eye could see.

I stood before the great pyramid and it pulsated with inner energies, glowing, beckoning. Suddenly a beam of brilliant blue shot skyward from the very tip of the pyramid, a scintillating shaft of pure energy rising to the zenith of the bowl of night.

I was standing before the pyramid. My physical body was there,

I knew. Yet the guards standing evenly spaced along the edge of the great plaza before it did not see me. They did not sense the light radiating from the pyramid, did not see the corruscating shaft of brilliant blue energy that blazed skyward from its tip.

And I could approach no closer. As if an impenetrable wall stood before me, I could not get a single step nearer the pyramid. I stood out in the night air, straining until the sweat streamed down my face and chest, ran in rivulets down my ribs and legs.

I could not enter the pyramid. The Golden One had sealed himself inside, I realized, and would not let me reach him. Was he protecting himself against me, or against the other Creators who sought to eliminate him?

No difference, as far as I was concerned. Unless I could get inside the pyramid I could not possibly force him to revive Athene. I screamed aloud into the night, bellowing my anger and frustration at the stars as I collapsed onto the stone paving of the great plaza before Khufu's tomb.

Chapter 36

HELEN'S face was white with shock.

"What is it? Orion, what's the matter?"

I was in our bunk aboard the boat, soaked with sweat, tangled in the light sheet that we had thrown over ourselves.

It took two swallows before I found my voice. "A dream," I croaked. "Nothing . . ."

"You saw the gods again," she said.

I heard bare feet running and then a pounding at our door. "My lord Orion!" Lukka's voice.

"It's all right," I yelled through the closed door. "Only a bad dream."

Still ashen-faced, Helen said, "They will destroy you, Orion. If you keep trying this mad assault against them, they will crush you utterly!"

"No," I said. "Not until I've had my vengeance. They can do what they want to me after that, but I'll avenge her first."

Helen turned away from me, anger and bitter regret etched in every line of her.

I felt distinctly foolish that morning. If Nefertu wondered what had made me scream, he was too polite to mention it. The crew cast off and we resumed our journey upstream toward the capital.

All that morning I spent staring at the great pyramid as we slowly sailed upriver, watching its great Eye of Amon open and gaze solemnly back at me. The Golden One has turned it into his fortress, his refuge, I told myself. Somehow I will have to get inside it. Or die in the attempt.

For weeks we sailed the Nile, long empty days of sun and the river, long frustrating nights of trying to reach the Golden One or any of the other Creators. It was as if they had left the Earth and gone elsewhere. Or perhaps they were *all* in hiding. But from what?

Helen watched me intently. She seldom spoke of the gods, except occasionally at night when we were drowsing toward sleep. I wondered how much she really believed of what I had told her. I imagined that she did not know, herself.

Each day was much like every other, except for the changes in scenery along the riverbanks. One day we passed what looked like a ruined city: buildings reduced to rubble, stone monuments sprawled broken on the ground.

"Was there a war here?" I asked Nefertu.

For the first time, I saw him look irritated, almost angry. "This was the city of a king," he said tightly.

"A king? You mean this was once the capital?"

"Briefly."

I had to pull the story out of him, line by line. It was clearly painful to him, yet so fascinating that I could not resist asking him more questions until I had the entire tale. The city was named Akhetaten, and it had been built by the king Akhenaten more than a hundred years earlier. Nefertu regarded Akhenaten as an evil king, a heretic who denied all the gods of Egypt except one: Aten, a sun god.

"He caused great misery in the land, and civil war. When he at last died, his city was abandoned. Horemheb and later kings tore down his monuments and destroyed his temples. His memory brings great shame upon us."

Yes, I thought. I could see how uncomfortable the memory made Nefertu. Yet I wondered if Akhenaten's heresy had not been one of the Golden One's schemes run awry. Perhaps I had been there, in one of the lives that I could not remember. Perhaps I would one day be sent there by the Creators to do whatever mischief they wanted done.

No, I told myself. My days of serving them will be finished once I have brought Athene back to life. Or so I hoped.

We sailed on, and watched crocodiles slithering along the reed-choked banks of the river, and mountainous hippopotami splashing and roaring at one another, their huge pink mouths and stumpy teeth looking ludicrous and terrifying at one and the same time.

"Not a good place to go swimming," Lukka observed.

"Not unless you want to end up as their midday meal," I agreed.

Finally we neared Wast, the mighty capital of the Kingdom of the Two Lands. Along the eastern shore of the river, reedy swamps gave way to cultivated fields, and then to low whitewashed dried-brick buildings. Across the river we saw more tombs cut into the western cliffs.

As we sailed onward the buildings became larger, grander. Dried brick gave way to dressed stone. Farm houses gave way to handsome villas with brightly painted murals on their outer walls. Graceful date palms and orchards of citrus trees swayed in the hot wind. In the distance we began to see massive temples and public buildings, tall obelisks and gigantic statues of a standing man, magnificent in physique, his fists clenched at his sides, his face smiling serenely.

"They all have the same face," Helen said to Nefertu.

"They are all statues of the same king, Ramesses II, father of our current king Merneptah."

The colossal statues towered along the river's eastern bank, row upon row of them. The king must have quarried out whole mountains of granite and barged the rock along the river to put up such monuments to himself.

"Ramesses was a glorious king," Nefertu explained to us, "mighty in battle and generous to his people. He erected these statues and many more, even larger ones, farther upstream. They stand to remind our people of his glory, and to awe the barbarians to the south. Even to this day they are afraid of his power."

"'Look on my works, ye mighty, and despair,'" I said. The phrase sprang from my memory, and I knew it had been written for this egomaniac Egyptian king.

There were more tombs along the western cliffs, including one that was so beautiful it took my breath away when I first saw it. White, low, columned and proportioned in a way that would some day grace the Parthenon of Athens.

"It is the tomb of Queen Hatshepsut," Nefertu told me. "She ruled like a man—much to the unhappiness of the priests and her husband."

If Menefer was impressive, Wast was overwhelming. The city was built to dwarf human scale. Enormous stone buildings loomed along the water's edge, so that we tied our boat to a stone pier in their cool shadow. Avenues were paved with stone and wide enough for four chariots to run side by side. Up from the riverside rose many temples, massive columns of granite painted brightly, metal-shod roofs gleaming in the sun. Beyond them, up in the hills, handsome villas were dotted among groves of trees and wide cultivated fields.

We were greeted at the pier by a guard of honor, wearing crisply pleated uniforms of immaculately clean linen and chain mail polished so highly that it glittered. Their swords and spear points were bronze, and I noticed that Lukka took in their weaponry with a swift professional glance.

Nefertu was met by another official, dressed only in a long white skirt and gold medallion of office against his bare chest, who introduced himself as Mederuk. He led us, one and all, to the palace where we would await our audience with the king. Helen and I were put into a sedan chair carried by black Nubian slaves, while Nefertu and Mederuk took a second one. Lukka and his men walked, flanked by the glittering honor guard.

Helen was beaming with happiness. "This is truly the city where I belong," she said.

I belonged back at Menefer, I thought, at the great pyramid. The longer I remained here in Wast, the less likely my chances of destroying the Golden One and reviving Athene.

Looking through the curtains of our sedan chair as the Nubian bearers carried us up the rising avenue, I saw that Nefertu and Mederuk were chatting gaily like a pair of old friends catching up on the latest gossip. They were happy. Helen was happy. Even Lukka and his men seemed to be satisfied that they would soon be employed in the Egyptian army.

Only I felt restless and unsatisfied.

The royal palace at Wast was a vast complex of temples and living quarters, soldiers' barracks and grain storehouses, spacious courtyards and pens for meat animals. Cats roamed everywhere. The Egyptians revered them as sacred spirits and gave them free rein throughout the palace complex. I thought that they must be very useful against the mice and other vermin that inevitably infested granaries.

Our quarters in the palace were—palatial. Helen and I were given adjoining huge, airy rooms with high ceilings of cedar beams and polished granite floors that felt cool to my bare feet. The walls were painted in cool solid blues and greens, with bright reds and golds outlining the doorways and windows. The windows of my room looked out across tiled rooftops toward the river.

I saw that whoever had designed the room had a strict sense of balance. Exactly opposite the door from the hall stood the door to the terrace. The windows flanking it were balanced on the blank wall by paintings of window frames, exactly the same size and shape as the real windows, their "frames" painted the same bright colors.

Half a dozen servants were there to look after us. Slaves bathed me in scented water, shaved me, clipped and combed my hair, and dressed me in the cool, light linen fabric of Egypt. I dismissed them all and, once alone in my room, found my dagger amid the clothing I had left in a pile at the foot of my bed. I strapped it onto my thigh once more beneath my fresh Egyptian skirt; I felt almost naked without it.

Those false windows bothered me. I wondered if they hid a secret entrance to my room. But when I scanned them closely and ran my fingers across the wall, all I detected was paint.

A servant scratched timidly at the door, and once I gave him permission to enter, he announced that the lords Nefertu and Mederuk would be pleased to take dinner with my lady and me. I asked the servant to invite Nefertu to my room.

It was time for me to tell him the truth about Helen. After all, she wanted to be invited to stay in Wast. She wanted to be treated like the queen she had been.

Nefertu came and we sat on the terrace outside, under a softly billowing awning that kept the sun off us. Without my asking, a servant brought us a pitcher of chilled wine and two cups.

"I have something to tell you," I said, once the servant had left, "something that I have kept from you until now."

Nefertu smiled his polite smile and waited for me to continue.

"The lady with me, Helen: she was the Queen of Sparta, and a princess of the fallen Troy."

"Ahh," said Nefertu, "I was certain that she was no ordinary woman. Not only her beauty, but her bearing showed royal breeding."

I poured wine for us both, then took a sip from my cup. It was excellent, dry and crisp, cool and delicious. I took a longer swallow, savoring the best wine I had tasted since Troy.

"I had suspected that the lady was an important personage," Nefertu went on. "And I am happy that you have been honest with me. Actually, I was about to question the two of you rather closely. My lord Nekoptah will want to know everything about you and your travels before he grants you audience with the king."

"Nekoptah?"

"He is the chief priest of the royal house, a cousin to the king himself. He serves mighty Merneptah as first councillor." Nefertu sipped at his wine. He licked his lips with the tip of his tongue, and darted a glance over his shoulder, as if afraid that someone might be listening to us.

Leaning closer to me, he said in a lowered voice, "I am told that Nekoptah is not content merely to have the king's ear; he wants the king's power for himself."

I felt my eyebrows climb. "A palace intrigue?"

Nefertu shrugged his thin shoulders. "Who is to say? The ways of the palace are complex—and dangerous. Be warned, Orion."

"I thank you for the advice."

"We are to meet with Nekoptah tomorrow morning. He desires to see you and the lady."

"What about Lukka and his troops?"

"They are quartered comfortably in the military barracks on the other side of the palace. A royal officer will inspect them tomorrow and undoubtedly admit them to the army."

Somehow I felt uneasy. Perhaps it was Nefertu's warning about palace intrigues. "I would like to see Lukka before we go to dinner," I said. "To make certain he and his men are well taken care of."

"That is not necessary," said Nefertu.

"It is my responsibility," I said.

He nodded. "I'm afraid I have made you suspicious. But perhaps that is all to the good." Rising, "Come, then. We will visit the barracks and see that your men are happy there."

Lukka and his men were indeed comfortably quartered. The

barracks was nothing like the luxury of my own royal apartment, but to the soldiers it was almost heaven: real beds and a solid roof over their heads, slaves to fetch hot water and polish their armor, food and drink and the promise of a night's whoring.

"I'll keep them in check tonight," Lukka told me, a hard smile on his hawk's face. "Tomorrow we parade for the Egyptian officers; I don't want them hung over and disgracing you."

"I'll join you for the inspection," I told him.

Nefertu almost objected, but stopped himself before saying a word.

As we left the barracks and headed back toward our apartments I asked him, "Is there some problem with me being present at the parade ground tomorrow?"

He smiled his diplomat's smile. "Merely that the inspection will be at sunrise, and our meeting with Nekoptah is shortly afterward."

"I should be with the men when they are under inspection."

"Yes, I suppose that is right." But Nefertu did not seem overly happy about my decision.

We dined that evening in his apartment, a room about the same in size and decorations as my own. I got the feeling that Nefertu was delighted at his good fortune in finding us. It is not every day that a civil servant working in a small town far from the capital is invited to the royal palace and housed in such splendor.

Helen told her story to him and Mederuk, the official who had met us at the pier. She held them fascinated with her tale of the war between the Achaians and Trojans, and seemed quite proud to place herself at the center of it all.

Mederuk stared at her shamelessly all through the dinner. He was a man of middle age, his hair gray and thinning, his body overweight and soft. Like all the Egyptians, his skin was dark and his eyes almost black. He had a bland round face, virtually unlined, almost like a baby's. His life in the palace had left no traces of laughter or pain or anger on that chubby, insipid face. It was as if he carefully erased all evidence of experience each night and faced each new day with a freshly molded blankness that could not possibly offend anyone—nor give any hint of the thoughts going on behind that bland mask.

But he stared at Helen, beads of perspiration dampening his upper lip.

"You must speak to Nekoptah," he said, once Helen had finished her tale. The dinner was long finished; slaves had removed our plates and now nothing was on the low table at which we sat except wine cups and bowls of pomegranates, figs, and dates.

"Yes," agreed Nefertu. "I'm certain that he will advise the king to invite you to live here in Wast, as a royal guest."

Helen smiled, but her eyes went to me. I said nothing. She knew I would leave as soon as I could. Once I knew that she was safe, and that Lukka and his men were accepted in the army, then I could leave.

I said, "The lady brings a considerable treasure with her. She will not be a burdensome guest."

The two Egyptians saw the humor in my statement and laughed politely.

"A burden to the king," giggled Nefertu. He had drunk a fair amount of wine.

"As if the great Merneptah counted costs," agreed Mederuk with a well-trained smile. His wine cup had not been drained even once. I looked at him closely. His smooth plump face showed no trace of emotion, but his coal-black eyes betrayed the scheming that was going through his mind.

Chapter 37

I left Helen's bed before sunrise and silently padded through the door that connected to my own room. The sky was just starting to turn gray and the room was still dark, yet something made me halt in my tracks and hold my breath.

Just the faintest whisper of movement. The hairs on the back of my neck stood on end. I remained stock-still, my eyes searching the darkness, trying to penetrate the shadows. There was someone else in the room. I knew it. I sensed it. Still straining to see, I recalled exactly the layout of the room, the placement of the bed, the table, chairs, chests. The windows and the door to the hall . . .

A slight scraping sound, wood or metal against stone. I leaped at it, and banged painfully into the blank wall. Recoiling backward, I staggered a step or two and sat down on my rump with a heavy thud.

I had run against the wall precisely where one of the false windows was painted. Was it actually a hidden door, so cleverly concealed that I could not discern it?

I got slowly to my feet, aching at both ends of my spine. Someone had been in my room, of that I was certain. An Egyptian, not the Golden One or one of the other Creators. Sneaking around in the dark was not their style. Someone had been spying on me—on us, Helen and me. Or going through my belongings.

A thief? I doubted it, and a swift check of my clothes and weapons showed that nothing had been taken.

I dressed quickly, wondering if it was safe to leave Helen alone and sleeping, wondering if the intruder wanted me to wonder about her and stay away from Lukka and the parade ground. Nefertu had warned me about palace intrigues, and I was thoroughly puzzled.

A scratching at my door. I yanked it open and Nefertu stood there, dressed and smiling the polite meaningless smile that served as his way of facing the world.

After greeting him, I asked, "Is it possible to place a guard at Helen's door?"

He looked genuinely alarmed. "Why? Is something amiss?"

I told him what had happened. He looked skeptical, but strode off down the hall to find the guard corporal. A few minutes later he returned with a guard, a well-muscled black man dressed in a zebra-hide kilt with a sword belted around his middle.

Feeling somewhat better, I went off to the parade ground outside the barracks.

Lukka had his two dozen men arrayed in a double file, their chain mail and armor glistening with fresh oil, their helmets and swords polished like mirrors. Each man also held an iron-tipped spear rigidly erect, at precisely ninety degrees to the ground.

Nefertu introduced me to the Egyptian commander who was to inspect the Hittites. His name was Raseth, a swarthy, heavyset, blustery old military man, bald and blunt as a bullet, with arms that looked powerful despite his advancing years. He limped slightly, as if the years had added too much weight to his body for his bandy legs to carry.

"I've fought against Hittites," he said to no one in particular as he turned toward the troops lined up for him, "I know how good they are."

Turning toward me, he tugged at the collar of his robe, pulled it down off his left shoulder to reveal an ugly gash of a scar. "A gift from a Hittite spearman at Meggido." He seemed proud of the wound.

Lukka stood at the head of his little band, his eyes staring straight ahead at infinity. The men were like ramrods, silent and unblinking in the early sun.

Raseth walked up and down the two ranks, nodding and muttering to himself while Nefertu and I stood off to one side, watching.

Finally Raseth turned abruptly and limped back toward us.

"They fought where?" he asked me.

I briefly described the sieges at Troy and Jericho.

Raseth nodded his head knowingly. He did not smile, he was not the type of officer who smiled in front of troops.

"Engineers, eh? Well, we don't engage in many sieges," he said. "But they'll do. They'll do fine. The king's army welcomes them."

That was the easiest part of the day.

From the barracks Nefertu led me across a wide empty courtyard. The morning sun was just starting to feel hot against my back, throwing long shadows across the smoothed dirt floor. Along the back wall of the courtyard I saw a cattle pen, and a few humpbacked brahmas shuffling around, their tails flicking at flies. The breeze was coming off the river, though, and I smelled jasmine and lemon trees in the air.

"The royal offices," Nefertu pointed toward a set of buildings that looked to me like temples. I noticed that he looked nervous, tense, for the first time in all the long weeks I had known him. "Nekoptah will see us there."

We headed up a long, slowly rising rampway, flanked on either side by statues of Ramesses II, all of them larger than life, each of them the same: a powerfully muscled man striding forward, fists clenched at his sides, a strangely serene smile on his handsome face. Not a flaw in body or face, perfectly symmetrical, utterly balanced. The pink granite of the statues caught the morning sun and looked almost like warm flesh.

I felt as if a living giant were gazing down at me. Or a god. One of the Creators. Despite the sun's warmth, I shuddered.

At the end of the statue-lined ramp we turned left and passed a row of massive sphinxes: reclining lion's bodies with the heads of bulls. Even reclining, the sphinxes were as tall as I.

"The lion is the symbol of the sun," Nefertu explained. "The bull is Amon's totem. These sphinxes represent the harmony of the gods."

Between the forepaws of each sphinx was a statue of—who else? At least these were merely life-size.

"Are there no statues of Merneptah?" I asked.

Nefertu nodded his head. "Oh, yes, of course. But he reveres his illustrious father as much as any man of the Two Kingdoms. Who would want to tear down statues of Ramesses to replace them with his own? Not even the king would dare."

We approached a huge doorway, flanked on either side by two more colossal statues of Ramesses: seated, this time, his hands filled with the staff of office and the sheaf of wheat that symbolized fertility. I began to wonder what it must be like to ascend to the throne after the reign of such a monarch.

"Merneptah and Nekoptah," I asked as we entered, at last, the cool shade of the temple, "are they related by blood?"

Nefertu smiled tightly, almost grimly, I thought. "Yes. And they both revere Ptah as their guardian and guide."

"Not Amon?"

"They revere Amon and all the gods, Orion. But Ptah is their special patron. The city of Menefer was Ptah's special city. Merneptah has brought his worship here, to the capital. Nekoptah is the chief priest of Ptah."

"Is there a statue of Ptah that I can see? What does he look like?"

"You will see soon enough." He said it almost crossly, as though irritated by my questions, or fearful of something I did not understand.

We were striding through a vast hallway of tremendous columns, so tall that the roof above us was lost in shadows. The floor was marble, the gigantic columns themselves granite, as wide around as the mightiest tree. Guards in gleaming gold armor stood spaced every few yards, but it seemed to me they were there for ceremony and grandeur. There had been no need for armed men in this temple for a thousand years. This huge chamber had been designed to dwarf human scale, to overpower mere mortal men with its grandeur and immensity. It was a ploy that haughty, powerful men used up and down the ages: utilizing architecture to bend men's souls, to fill them with wonder, and admiration, and fear of the power that had raised these mighty pillars.

A pair of glittering eyes stared at me from the deep shadows. I almost laughed. Another of the palace's innumerable cats.

At the end of the awesome court we climbed up steps of black marble. Down another corridor, this one lined with small statues of various gods bearing heads of animals: a hawk, a jackal, a lion, even an anteater. At the end of the corridor a giant statue stood in a special niche, its head almost touching the ceiling.

"There is Ptah," said Nefertu, almost in a whisper.

The god's statue loomed before us, almost as huge as the colossi of Ramesses outside the temple. A skylight in the roof far above us cast a shaft of sunlight along the length of the statue's white stone. I saw a man's face, his body wrapped in windings like a mummy, except that his hands were free and clasping a long, elaborately worked staff. A skullcap covered his head, and a small beard dangled from his chin. The face looked uncannily like that of the slim, sarcastic Hermes I had last seen when I had briefly transported Joshua to the Creators' realm.

Nefertu stopped at the foot of the giant statue, where incense smoldered in a pair of braziers. He bowed three times, then took a pinch of something from the golden pan between the braziers and threw it onto the embers at his left. The stuff made a small burst of flame and sent white smoke spiraling toward the distant ceiling.

"You must offer a sacrifice, also, Orion," he whispered to me.

Straight-faced, I went to the railing and tossed a pinch of incense onto the brazier to my right. Its smoke was black. Turning back to Nefertu, I saw his eyes following the dark billow. His face was not pleased at all.

"Did I do something wrong?" I asked.

"No," he said, his eyes still on the drifting smoke. "But sacred Ptah is apparently not entirely happy with your offering."

I shrugged.

As he led me down a narrower corridor, past another pair of golden-armored guards and to a massive door of ebony set into a deep, stone doorway, Nefertu seemed distinctly nervous, filled with an anxiety he could not hide. Was he apprehensive about meeting Nekoptah, or was it something I had done? Or had failed to do?

Another guard stood before the door. Without a word he opened it for Nefertu.

We stepped through the doorway into a sizable room. Morning sunlight slanted through three windows on our right. The room was absolutely bare of decorations: the stone walls were as blank as a prison cell's. The floor was empty and uncovered. Far at the other end of the room, next to its only other door, was a long table heaped with rolled-up writing scrolls. Two huge silver candlesticks stood at each end of the table, the candles in them unlit.

Behind the desk sat an enormously fat man, his head shaved

bald, his huge globulous body covered with a gray sleeveless robe that went to the floor. His arms, flabby, thick, hairless, and pink as a baby pig, rested on the polished wood of the table. Every finger and both his thumbs bore jeweled rings, some of them so buried in flesh that they could not have been taken off in years. His jowls were so huge that they cascaded down onto his chest and shoulders. I could barely make out a pair of eyes embedded in that grossly corpulent face, studying us as we crossed the long empty chamber to stand before his desk. His face was painted: eyes lined with black kohl and daubed with green shadow above and below them, his cheeks pink with rouge, his lips deep red.

Nefertu threw himself onto the floor and pressed his forehead against the bare tiles. I remained standing, although I bowed slightly from the waist to show my respect.

"O great Nekoptah," intoned Nefertu, from the floor, "high priest of dreaded Ptah, right hand of mighty Merneptah, guide of the people, guardian of the Two Lands, I bring you the barbarian Orion, as you commanded."

The high priest's fleshy painted lips curled in what might have been a smile. "You may rise, Nefertu my servant. You have done well." His voice was a clear sweet tenor. It sounded strange, such a lovely voice coming from such a gross, ugly face. Then I realized that Nekoptah was a eunuch, one who had been dedicated to the god's service in childhood.

Nefertu slowly climbed to his feet and stood beside me. His face was red, whether from pressing it against the floor or from embarrassment at having done so, I could not tell.

"And you, barbarian . . ."

"My name is Orion," I said.

Nefertu gasped at my effrontery. Nekoptah merely grunted.

"Orion, then," he granted. "My general Raseth tells me that your two dozen Hittites will make a passable addition to our all-conquering army."

"They are fine men."

"I am not so easily satisfied, however," he said, his voice rising slightly. "Raseth is of an age where he dwells in the past. I must look toward the future, if I am to protect and guide our great king."

He eyed me carefully as he spoke, waiting for a reaction from me. I remained silent.

"Therefore," he went on, "I have thought of a test that these recruits can undertake."

Again he waited for a reply. Again I said nothing.

"You, Orion, will lead your men to the delta country, where the barbarian Sea Peoples are raiding our coastal cities once again. One particularly troublesome set of raiders flies a lion's-head emblem on their sails. You will find them and destroy them, so that they will trouble the Lower Kingdom no longer."

Menalaos, I realized. Searching for Helen and ravaging the coastal cities, looting as much as possible while he searches. Possibly with Agamemnon alongside him.

"How many of these ships have been seen?" I asked.

Nekoptah seemed delighted that I had finally spoken. "Reports vary. At least ten, possibly as many as two dozen."

"And you expect two dozen soldiers to conquer two dozen shiploads of Achaians?"

"You will have other soldiers with you. I will see to that."

I shook my head. "With all respect, my lord . . ."

"Your holiness," Nefertu whispered.

It took an effort to get the words past my gag reflex. "With all respect—your holiness—I did not intend to stay with the Hittites once they were accepted into your army."

"Your intentions are of little interest," said Nekoptah. "The needs of the kingdom are paramount."

Ignoring that, I continued, "I came here as escort to the Queen of Sparta, the lady Helen . . ."

"Escort?" He smirked. "Or consort?"

I could feel the blood rising in me. With a deliberate effort I calmed myself, constricted capillaries that would have colored my face.

Softly, I said, "So someone was spying on us in our rooms."

Nekoptah threw his head back and laughed. "Orion, do you think the king's chief minister will allow strangers into the palace without keeping watch on them? Every breath you take has been observed—even the dagger you carry hidden beneath your kilt was seen and reported to me."

I nodded acquiescence of the fact, knowing that there were armed guards standing on the other side of the door behind the priest's desk, ready to defend their master or slay us at the slightest word from him. Yet there was one thing that Nekoptah did not know, for he had never observed me in action: I could tear out his throat before the guards could open that door. And I could kill three or four armed men, too, if I had to.

"I've been carrying it for so long now that it seems a part of my body," I said meekly. "I'm sorry if it causes offense."

Nekoptah waved a fleshy hand, the rings on his fingers glittering in the morning sunlight. "The chief priest of almighty Ptah is not afraid of a dagger," he said grandly.

Nefertu shuffled his feet nervously, as if he wished he were somewhere else.

"As I was saying," I resumed, "I came here as escort to the lady Helen, Queen of Sparta, princess of the fallen Troy. She wishes to reside in the Kingdom of the Two Lands. She has wealth enough so that she would not be a burden on the state . . ."

Nekoptah waggled a fat hand impatiently, a movement hard enough to make his mountainous jowls quiver like ripples in a lake.

"Spare me the dull recitation of facts I already know," he said impatiently.

Again I struggled to keep my anger from showing.

Pointing a stubby thick finger at me, Nekoptah said, "This is what the king wishes you to do, Orion. You will take your men downriver to the delta, seek out these barbarian raiders, and destroy them. That is the price for accepting your Queen of Sparta into our city."

Kill Helen's husband in return for her safety in Egypt's capital. I thought it over for a moment, then asked: "And who will protect the lady while I am away?"

"She will be under the protection of the all-seeing Ptah, Architect of the Universe, Lord of the Sky and Stars."

"And mighty Ptah's representative here among mortals is yourself, is it not?" I asked.

He dipped his chins in acknowledgment.

"Will the lady be allowed to meet the king? Will she live in his house, protected by his servants?"

"She will live in my house," Nekoptah said, "protected by me. Surely you don't fear *my* intentions toward your—queen."

"I promised to deliver her to the King of Egypt," I insisted, "not the king's chief minister."

Again Nefertu drew in his breath, as if expecting an explosion. But Nekoptah merely said mildly, "Do you not trust me, Orion?"

I replied, "You wish me to lead troops against the Achaian invaders of your land. I wish my lady to meet the king and dwell under his protection."

"You speak as if you had some power of bargaining. You have none. You will do as you are told. If you please the king, your request will be granted."

"If I please the king," I said, "it will be because the king's chief minister tells him to be pleased."

A wide, smug smile spread across Nekoptah's painted face. "Precisely, Orion. We understand one another."

I tacitly acknowledged defeat. For the moment. "Will the lady Helen be permitted to see the king, as she wishes?"

His smile even broader, Nekoptah answered, "Of course. His royal majesty expects to sup with the Queen of Sparta this very evening. You yourself may be invited—if we are in complete agreement."

For Helen's sake I bowed my head slightly. "We are," I said.

"Good!" His voice could not boom, it was too high. But it rang off the stone walls of the audience chamber, nonetheless.

I glanced at Nefertu out of the corner of my eye. He seemed immensely relieved.

"You may go," said Nekoptah. "A messenger will bring you your invitation to supper, Orion."

We started to turn toward the door.

But the high priest said, "One thing more. A small detail. On your way back from crushing the invaders, you must stop at Menefer and bring me the chief priest of Amon."

Nefertu paled. His voice quavered. "The chief priest of Amon?"

Almost jovially, Nekoptah replied, "The very same. Bring him here. To me." His smile remained fixed on his fleshy lips, but both his hands had squeezed themselves into fists.

I asked, "How will he know that we represent you?"

Laughing, he answered, "He will have no doubt of it, never fear. But—to convince the temple troops who guard his worthless carcass . . ."

He wormed a massive gold ring off his left thumb. It was set with a blood-red carnelian that bore a miniature carving of Ptah. "Here. This will convince any doubters that you act by my command."

The ring felt heavy and hot in my hand. Nefertu stared at it as if it were someone's death warrant.

Chapter 38

OBVIOUSLY, Nefertu had been shaken by our meeting with the king's chief minister. He was silent as we were escorted back to my apartment, far across the complex of temples and palaces that made up the capitol.

I remained silent, also, trying to piece together the parts of the puzzle. Like it or not, I was in the middle of some sort of convoluted palace conspiracy; Nekoptah was using me for his own purposes, and I doubted that they coincided with the best interests of the Kingdom of the Two Lands.

One glance at Nefertu told me he would offer no hint of explanation. He was ashen-faced as we walked between the gold-armored guards down the long corridors and lofty colonnaded courts of the capitol, with their cats skulking in the shadows. His hands trembled at his sides. His mouth was a thin line, lips pressed together so hard that they were white.

We reached my apartment and I invited him inside.

He shook his head. "I'm afraid there are other matters I must attend to."

"Just for a moment," I said. "There's something I want to show you. Please."

He dismissed the guards and entered my room, his eyes showing fear, not curiosity.

I knew we were being watched. Somewhere along the walls there was a cunningly contrived peephole, and a spy in the employ of the chief priest of Ptah observing us. I took Nefertu out onto the terrace, where a pair of rope-sling chairs overlooked the busy courtyard and rustling palm trees.

I needed to know what Nefertu knew, what was in his mind. He would not tell me willingly, I could see that. So I had to pry into his mind whether he wanted me to or not. Perhaps somewhere beneath the surface of his rigid self-control I could reach the part of his mind that was searching for an ally against whatever it was that was frightening him.

The poor man sat on the front inch of his chair, his back ramrod straight, his hands clasped on his knees. I pulled my chair up close to his and put my hand across his thin shoulder. I could feel the tenseness in the tendons of his neck.

"Try to relax," I said softly, keeping my voice low so that whoever was watching could not hear.

I kneaded the back of his neck with one hand while staring deeply into his eyes. "We have known each other for many weeks, Nefertu. I have come to admire and respect you. I want you to think of me as your friend."

His chin dipped slightly. "You are my friend," he agreed.

"You know me well enough to realize that I will not harm you. Nor will I knowingly harm your people, the people of the Two Lands."

"Yes," he said drowsily. "I know."

"You can trust me."

"I can trust you."

Slowly, slowly I forced his body and his mind to relax. He was almost asleep, even though his eyes were open and he could speak to me. His conscious mind, his willpower, were allayed. He was a frightened man, and he badly needed a friend he could trust. I convinced him not only that he could trust me, but that he must tell me what it was that was frightening him.

"That's the only way I can help you, my friend."

His eyes closed briefly. "I understand, friend Orion."

Gradually I got him to talk, in a low monotone that I hoped could not be overheard by Nekoptah's spies. The story he unfolded was as convoluted as I had feared. And it spelled danger. Not merely for me: I was inured to danger and it held no real terror over me. But Helen had inadvertently stepped into a trap that Nekoptah had cunningly devised. Loathe him though I did, I had to admire the quick adroitness of his mind, and respect the strength and speed with which he moved.

It had been whispered up and down the length of the kingdom —so Nefertu told me—that King Merneptah was dying. Some said it was the wasting disease; others whispered that he was being poisoned. Be that as it may, the true power of the throne was being wielded by the king's chief minister, the obese Nekoptah.

The army was loyal to the king, not a priest of Ptah. But the army itself was weak and divided. Its days of glory under Ramesses II were long gone. Merneptah had allowed the army to erode to the point where most of the troops were foreigners and most of the generals were pompous old windbags living on past victories. Where the army had slaughtered the Sea Peoples who raided the delta in Ramesses's time, now the barbarians sacked cities and terrified the Lower Kingdom, and the army seemed unable to stop them.

Nekoptah did not want a strong army. It would be an obstacle to his control of the king and the kingdom. Yet he could not allow the Sea Peoples to continually raid the delta country; the Lower Kingdom would rise up against him if he could not defend them adequately. So the chief priest of Ptah hit upon a brilliant plan: send the newly arrived Hittite contingent against the Sea Peoples, as part of a new army expedition to the delta. Let the barbarian leaders see that the man who stole Helen from the Achaian victors at Troy was now in Egypt. Let them know that, just as they suspected, Helen was under the protection of the Kingdom of the Two Lands.

And let them know, by secret messenger, that Helen would be returned to them—if they stopped their raids on the delta. Even more: Nekoptah was prepared to offer Menalaos and his Achaians a part of the rich delta country as their own, if they would guard the Lower Kingdom against attacks from other Peoples of the Sea.

But first Menalaos had to be certain that Helen actually was in Egypt. For that, Orion and his Hittites would be sent into the delta as sacrificial lambs, to be slaughtered by the barbarians.

And more.

Unrest against Nekoptah's usurpation of power was already being felt in the city of Menefer, the ancient capital, where the great pyramids proclaimed the worship of Amon. The chief priest of Amon, Hetepamon by name, was the main plotter against

Nekoptah. Should Orion get out of the battles of the delta alive, he was to bring Hetepamon back to Wast with him. As a guest, if possible. As a prisoner, if necessary.

Of course, if Orion should be killed by the Sea Peoples, as seemed likely, someone else would be sent to pluck Hetepamon from his temple and bring him to the power of Nekoptah.

A neat scheme, worthy of a cunning mind.

I leaned back in my chair and relaxed my mental grip on Nefertu's mind. He sagged slightly, then took in a deep breath of revivifying air. He blinked, shook his head groggily, then smiled at me.

"Did I fall asleep?"

"You drowsed a bit," I said.

"How odd."

"It was a very tense meeting this morning."

He got to his feet and stretched. Looking out over the courtyard below us, he saw that the sun was nearly setting.

"I must have slept for hours!" Turning to me, he looked genuinely puzzled. "How boring that must have been for you."

"I was not bored."

With a testing, tentative shake of his head, Nefertu said, "The rest seems to have done me good. I feel quite refreshed."

I was pleased. He was too honest a man to carry the burden of Nekoptah's scheming within his mind, without a friend to share the problem.

But Nefertu still looked slightly puzzled when he took his leave of me. I asked him to meet me for breakfast the next morning, so I could tell him about our royal evening.

Supper with the King of Egypt, the mightiest ruler of the world, the pharaoh who had driven the Israelites out of his country, was a strange, disquieting affair.

Helen was tremendously excited about meeting the great king. She spent the entire afternoon with female servants running about, bathing and scenting her, tying her hair in piles of golden curls, making up her beautiful face with kohl for her eyes and rouge for her cheeks and lips. She dressed in her finest flounced skirt of golden threads and tinkling silver tassels, decked herself with necklaces and bracelets and rings that gleamed in the lamplight as the last rays of the sun died against a violet western sky.

I wore a fresh leather kilt, a gift from Nefertu, and a crisp white linen shirt, also provided by the Egyptian. I strapped my dagger to my thigh as a matter of course.

Helen opened the door that connected our two rooms and stood in the doorway, practically trembling with anticipation.

"Do I look fit to meet the king?" she asked.

I smiled and replied truthfully, "The proper question would be, is the King of Egypt fit to meet the most beautiful woman in the world?"

She smiled back at me. I went to her, but she held me at arm's length. "Don't touch me! I'll smudge or wrinkle!"

I threw my head back and laughed. It was the last laughter to come from me.

An escort of a full dozen gold-clad guards took us through narrow corridors and flights of stairs that seemed to have no pattern to them except to confuse one who did not know the way by heart. Thinking back to my morning's meeting with Nekoptah, and to what Nefertu had unknowingly revealed to me, I realized that Helen and I were truly prisoners of the chief priest, rather than guests of the king.

Instead of a magnificent dining hall filled with laughing guests and entertainers who regaled the company with song and dance while servants carried in massive trays heaped high with food and poured wine from golden pitchers, Merneptah's supper was a quiet affair in a small windowless chamber.

Helen and I were brought by the guards to a plain wooden door. A servant opened it and beckoned us into the smallish room. We were the first there. The table was set for four. A chandelier of gleaming copper hung above the table. Serving tables stood flat against the walls.

The servant bowed to us and left by the room's only other door, set in the farther wall.

Once again I felt the hairs on the back of my neck rise. We were being watched, I knew. There were paintings on the walls, scenes of royal hunts with the king—drawn much larger than everyone else—spearing lions and leopards. I saw the glint of coal-black eyes where a lion's tawny ones should be.

"Is hospitality in Sparta so cold that the king would leave his guests alone in a room without food or drink or entertainment?" I asked Helen.

"No," she said, in a small voice. She seemed vastly disappointed.

The door from the hall opened and fat Nekoptah waddled through, covered by a white floor-length robe that looked like a tent. He was decked in almost as many jewels as Helen and the paint on his face was much heavier. I had warned Helen about his appearance, and my estimation of him. He had heard every word I had spoken, I could tell from the nasty expression he gave me.

"Forgive the informality of this evening," he said to us. "Later, we will arrange a proper state dinner for the Queen of Sparta. Tonight, the king merely wishes to meet you and welcome you to the Kingdom of the Two Lands."

He reached for Helen's hand and brought it to his lips. She kept herself from cringing, but just barely.

Nekoptah clapped his hands once, and a servant immediately came from the farther door with a tray of wine goblets.

We had barely tasted the wine, a sweetish red that Nekoptah said was imported from Crete, when the hall door opened again and a guard announced: "His royal majesty, King of the Two Lands, beloved of Ptah, guardian of the people, son of the Nile."

Instead of the king, though, six priests in gray robes entered the room, bearing copper censers that filled the room with smoky, pungent incense. They chanted in an ancient tongue and made a mini-procession around the table three times, praising Ptah and his servant on Earth, Merneptah. As they left, six guards in golden armor marched in and lined themselves along the wall, three on each side of the doorway, and froze into blank-faced immobility. Each of them held a spear that almost touched the ceiling. Then came two harpists and four beautiful young women bearing peacock-plume fans. In their midst walked the King of Egypt, Merneptah.

He was a man of middle years, his hair still dark. Slim of body and small in stature, he walked slightly bent over, as if stooped with age or cares—or pain. He wore a sleeveless robe of white decorated with gold embroidery around its border. His skin was much lighter than any Egyptian I had met. Unlike his chief minister, the king wore no adornments except for a small golden medallion bearing the symbol of Ptah on a slim chain about his neck, and copper bracelets on his wrists.

It was his eyes that troubled me. They seemed clouded, unsteady, almost unseeing. As if his thoughts were turned almost totally inward. As if the world around him was not important, an annoyance, an impediment to what he considered truly important.

I glanced down at Helen, standing beside me. She had caught it too.

The two harpers and the fan-bearing women bowed low to their king and left the room. One of the guards out in the hall closed the door and we were alone, except for the six guards lining the wall like statues. I knew that I would be seated with my back to them, and that did not please me.

Introductions were polite but perfunctory. Helen curtsied prettily for the king, who seemed completely indifferent to her beauty—even to her presence. I bowed and he mumbled something to me about the barbarians from the sea.

We sat at table and servants brought us a cold soup and platters of fish. The king ate almost nothing. Nekoptah ate enough for all four of us.

Conversation was desultory. Nekoptah did most of the talking, and most of it was about how the worship of Ptah was being resisted by fanatics who were trying to reinstate the madness of Akhenaten.

"Especially in Menefer," complained Nekoptah, while gobbling a morsel of fish. "The priests there are trying to bring back the worship of Aten."

"I thought it was Amon they glorified," I said, "rather than Aten."

"Yes," said Helen. "We saw the Eye of Amon on the great pyramid there."

Nekoptah frowned. "They say it is Amon they reverence, but secretly they are trying to bring back Akhenaten's heresies. If they are not stopped, and stopped soon, they will plunge the Two Lands into turmoil once again."

The king nodded absently, picking at his food.

With me translating for her, Helen tried to engage him in conversation, asking about his wife and children. The king merely stared past her.

"His majesty's wife died last year in childbirth," said Nekoptah.

"Oh, I'm sorry . . ."

"The baby died also."

"How awful!"

The king seemed to make an effort to focus his eyes on her. "I have one son," he muttered.

"Prince Aramset," interjected Nekoptah. "A comely lad. He will make a fine king, one day." But his face clouded, and he added, "Of course, his royal majesty has many other fine sons by his royal concubines, as well."

Merneptah lapsed into silence again. Helen glared at the fat priest.

And so it went through the whole supper. At last it was finished and the king bade us good night and left. I noticed that Nekoptah barely bowed to his king; not that he could have gotten far, as fat as he was.

As the guards escorted us back to our quarters, I asked Helen, "Do you think the king is ill?"

Her face showed how troubled she felt. "No, Orion. He is drugged. I have seen it before. That fat beast is keeping him drugged so that he can control the kingdom for himself."

I was glad that she spoke only Achaian and the guards could not understand her. At least, I hoped that they could not.

The situation was painfully clear to me. Nekoptah was in control of the capital and the king. He was using me to set up a deal that would trade Helen for the security of the delta country against the Sea Peoples. For good measure, he was going to remove the chief priest of Amon and tighten his hold on the entire kingdom.

To guarantee that I do as he wished, Nekoptah would hold Helen hostage in the capital, not realizing that I knew he intended to hand her back to Menalaos.

And the Golden One had made a fortress for himself inside the great pyramid.

It all looked hopelessly snarled. Until I saw that with one stroke I could cut the knot. Like a message sent by some god, a plan took shape in my mind. By the time Helen and I had returned to our apartments, I knew what I had to do.

Chapter 39

I had not expected the prince of the realm to join our expedition downriver.

As Lukka and his men marched aboard the boat that would take us to the Lower Kingdom, a sedan chair flanked by a guard of honor was carried by six sweating Nubians slowly down the stone pier and stopped at our gangplank. A young man pushed the curtains aside and stepped lithely from the chair, slim, well muscled, and as light of skin as Merneptah and the priests I had seen.

His name was Aramset: the only legitimate son of the king. He was barely old enough to have a bit of down fuzzing his chin. He was a handsome lad, a good indication of what his father must have looked like as a teenager. He seemed eager to take part in a war.

The nominal leader of our expedition, the limping, overweight General Raseth, bowed low to the prince and then introduced me to him.

"We're going to slaughter the barbarians," Aramset said, laughing. "My father wants me to learn the arts of war, so that I will understand them when I rule."

He seemed pleasant enough. But inwardly I knew that Nekoptah had arranged this royal addition to our expedition. If the prince happened to get himself killed in battle, and there was no other legitimate heir to the throne, it strengthened his grip on the power of the kingdom even further.

Again I had to admire Nekoptah's cunning.

I had taken leave of Helen that morning, trusting her safety to the care of Nefertu. She did not fully understand all the machinations swirling around us, but she sensed that schemes within schemes were taking me away from her.

"Menalaos still seeks me," she said, as I held her in my arms.

"He is hundreds of miles away," I said.

She leaned her golden head against my chest. "Orion, sometimes I think that it is my destiny to return to him. No matter what I do, he still pursues me, like the hounds of fate."

I said nothing.

"He will kill you if you do battle against him," she said.

"No, I don't think so. And I don't really want to kill him, either."

She pushed away from me slightly and gazed up into my eyes. "Will I ever see you again, my protector?"

"Of course."

But she shook her head. "No. I don't think so. I think this is our final farewell, Orion." There were tears in her eyes.

"I will come back," I said.

"But not to me. You will seek your goddess and forget about me."

I was silent for a moment, thinking to myself that she was right. Then I said, "No one could ever forget you, Helen. Your beauty will live through all the ages."

She tried to smile. I kissed her one last time, knowing that someone was watching us, and then bade her good-bye.

Nefertu accompanied me to the docks, and I asked the slim old man to watch over Helen and protect her against the intrigues of the palace.

"I will, my friend," he said. "I will guard her honor and her life."

So, as our boat pushed off from the dock with the early morning sun slanting through the obelisks and monumental statues of the capital, I waved a final salute to Nefertu, knowing in my heart that one gray-haired minor functionary would never be able to protect anyone—even himself—against the growing power of Nekoptah. My only hope was to do what I had to do quickly, and get back to the capital to deal with the fat chief minister before he could cause harm to Helen or my newfound Egyptian friend.

I scanned the palace buildings as our boat glided out into the Nile's strong current, looking for a terrace where a golden-haired woman might be waving to me. But I saw no one.

"So we begin to earn our pay."

I turned abruptly and saw Lukka standing beside me, his dour face set in a tight smile. He was glad to be away from the palace and heading toward battle, where a man knew who his enemies were and how to deal with them.

Aramset turned out to be a pleasant young man who laughed to hide his nervousness. General Raseth bustled about the boat constantly, hovering over the royal heir until the prince made it clear he would rather be treated as one of the regular officers.

Strangely, Lukka and the prince seemed to get along very well. The youngster genuinely admired the battle-scarred professional soldier, and seemed eager to learn all he could from him.

One hot afternoon, as the oarsmen paddled us past the ruins of Akhetaten, I heard Lukka telling the prince, "All that I have spoken to you in the past days means nothing, compared to the experience of battle. When the enemy comes charging at you, screaming their war cries and leveling their spears at your chest, then you'll find out whether your blood is thick enough for war. Only then."

Aramset stared at Lukka with great round eyes and followed the Hittite soldier around the boat like a faithful puppy.

Our boat carried fifty soldiers, and it was powered by sixty oarsmen: slaves, many of them black Nubians. Since we were sailing downriver, the Nile's own powerful current did the heaviest work for us.

Dozens of other boats joined us as we headed for the delta. At each city where we tied up overnight there were more soldiers waiting to join our expedition, and boats to carry them. I began to see the true power of Egypt, the organization that could bring together a fleet carrying the men and materiél for a mighty armed force that could strike over distances of hundreds of miles.

But I wondered which of the men on our own boat were spies for Nekoptah? Which were assassins? How many of the troops on the other boats had been ordered to fall back, once battle had begun, and let me and my Hittites be cut to pieces by the barbarian raiders? I knew I could trust no one except Lukka and, through him, his two dozen soldiers.

Over those long hot days and dark warm nights I got to know Prince Aramset. There was much more to him than a laughing, nervous youngster.

"I want Lukka and his Hittites to be my personal guard, once we return to Wast," he told me one evening, as we dawdled over the remains of supper.

We were tied to the pier of one of the cities that dotted the riverbank, rocking gently in the eddies of the main current. It was an oppressively hot, still night, and we ate on the open afterdeck of the boat, desperate to catch any stray breeze that might waft by. A slave slowly swept a palm-leaf fan over our heads to keep the mosquitoes away. General Raseth had fallen asleep at the table, drowsing over his empty wine cup. The prince never took wine; he drank clear water only.

"You couldn't pick a better, more loyal man, your highness," I said.

"I will pay you handsomely for them."

He had pride, this teenager. But I answered, "My prince, allow me to make you a gift of them. I know that Lukka would be pleased to serve you, and it would please me to make the two of you happy."

He nodded slightly, as if he had expected no less. "Yet, Orion, I shouldn't accept such a valuable gift without offering something in return."

"The friendship of the crown prince of the Two Lands is a gift beyond price," I said.

He smiled at that. Deliberately, I poured a cup of wine from the little Raseth had left and offered it to him.

He refused with a slight wave of his hand.

"To seal our bargain," I suggested.

"I never drink wine."

"You don't like its taste?"

His face turned sour. "I have seen what wine has done to my father. Wine—and other things."

"He is not sick, then?"

"Only in his soul. Since my mother died, my father wastes away within himself."

There was bitterness in his voice. He was out to prove to his father that he could be a worthy heir.

As delicately as I could, I asked about Nekoptah.

Aramset eyed me carefully. "The high priest of Ptah and the chief minister to the king is a very powerful man, Orion. Even I must speak of him with great respect."

"I understand his power," I said. "Will you keep him as *your* chief minister when you become king?"

"My father lives," the prince said flatly. No trace of anger at my presumption. No trace of rancor toward Nekoptah. He had learned to hide his emotions well, this young man.

"Yet," I pressed, "if your father should become unable to rule, through sickness or melancholy—would you be appointed to rule in his place, or would Nekoptah act for him?"

For long moments Aramset said nothing. His dark eyes bored into me, as if trying to see how far he could trust this stranger from a distant land.

Finally he said, "Nekoptah is perfectly capable of administering the kingdom. He is doing so now, with my father's approval."

There was no sense pressing him further. He was wise enough not to say anything against Nekoptah that might be overheard. But I thought he did not like the fat chief minister very much. His hands had balled themselves into fists at my first mention of him and remained tightly clenched until he bade me good night and walked off to his cabin.

We reached the delta country at last, rich with green farmlands, crisscrossed by irrigation canals, lush with beautiful long-legged birds of snowy white and delicate pink. The local garrison commanders conferred with General Raseth and told him that the Sea Peoples had taken several villages near the mouth of a western arm of the river. They estimated the number of barbarian warriors at more than a thousand.

That evening, the general, Prince Aramset, and I took supper together in the small cabin atop the boat's afterdeck. Raseth was in a jovial mood as he dug into the stewed fish and onions.

"Make allowance for the local troops' natural exaggerations," he said, reaching for the wine pitcher, "and we have nothing more than a few hundred barbarians to deal with."

"While we have more than a thousand trained men," said the prince.

Raseth nodded. "It's simply a matter of finding the barbarians and hitting them before they can scatter or get back to their ships."

I thought of the Achaian camp along the beach at Troy. I wondered if Odysseus or Big Ajax would be among my enemies.

"The horses and chariots are coming up on the supply ships," Raseth was muttering to no one in particular. "In a few days' time we will be ready to strike."

I looked at him from across the supper table. "Strike where? Are you certain the barbarians will still be in the villages where they were seen several days ago?"

Raseth scratched at his chin. "Hmm. They could move off elsewhere in their ships, couldn't they?"

"Yes. Using the sea, they could move quickly across the breadth of the delta and strike a hundred miles away before we know they've pulled out."

"Then we need scouts to keep watch on them," said Aramset.

The general beamed at his young prince. "Excellent!" he roared. "You will make a fine conquering general one day, your highness."

Then they both turned to me. Raseth said, "Orion, you and your Hittites will scout the villages where the barbarians were last seen. If they have gone, you will return here and tell us. If they are still there, you will keep them under observation until the main body of our army arrives."

Before I could say anything, Prince Aramset added, "And I will go with you!"

The general shook his blunt, bullet-shaped head. "That is far too great a risk to take, your highness."

Especially if I'm betrayed to Menalaos by one of Nekoptah's spies, I thought. Was Raseth working for Nekoptah? What secret orders did he carry in his head?

Prince Aramset was not pleased at being balked. "My father sent me on this expedition to learn of war. I will not sit in the rear safely while others are doing the fighting."

"When the fighting commences, your highness, you will be by my side," General Raseth said. "Those are my instructions." He added, "From the king's own lips."

Aramset was taken aback. But only for a moment. "Well, in the meantime, I can accompany Orion and his men on this scouting mission."

"I cannot allow that, sir," the general replied.

The youngster turned to me. "I'll stay beside Lukka. He won't let any harm come to me."

As gently as I could, I replied, "But what harm may come to Lukka, when he has you to look after and neglects his other duties?"

The prince stared at me, his mouth open to answer, yet no words coming forth. He was a goodhearted youth, and he genuinely loved Lukka. His only problem was that he was young, and like all young men, he could not visualize himself being hurt, or maimed, or killed.

Raseth took advantage of the prince's silence. "Orion," he said, his voice suddenly deep with the authority of command, "you will take your men overland to the villages where the barbarians were last seen, and report their movements to me by sun-mirror. You will leave tomorrow at dawn."

"And me?" the prince asked.

"You will stay here with me, your highness. The chariots and horses will soon arrive. There will be battle enough to satisfy any man within a few days."

I nodded grim agreement.

It was a two-day march from the riverbank where our boat had tied up to the coastal village where the black-hulled Achaian ships lay pulled up on the beach.

The land was flat and laced with irrigation canals, but the fields were broad enough to allow chariot warfare, if you did not mind tearing up the crops growing in them. Lukka had the men camp along the edge of one of the larger canals, by a bridge that could easily be held by a couple of determined men or, failing that, burned so that pursuers would have to either wade across the canal or find the next bridge, a mile or so away.

Then he and I crossed the bridge and made our way through the fields of knee-high wheat, tossing in the breeze, until we came to the edge of the village. It lay along the beach, and I saw dozens of small fishing boats tied up to weathered wooden piers. The Achaian warships were up on the sand, tents and makeshift shacks dotted around them, smoke from cook fires sending thin tendrils of gray toward the sky.

Despite the breeze coming in from the sea, the morning was hot, and the sun burned on our backs as we lay at the edge of the wheat field and watched the activity in the village. None of the ships bore the blue dolphin's head of Ithaca, and I found myself happy that Odysseus was not there.

"There's only eight ships here," said Lukka.

"Either the others have moved on to other villages, or they've returned to Argos."

"Why would some of them return and leave the others here?"

"Menalaos seeks his wife," I said. "He won't return without her."

"He can't fight his way through all of Egypt with a few hundred men."

"Perhaps he's waiting for reinforcements," I said. "He may have sent his other ships back to Argos to bring the main body of Achaian warriors here."

Lukka shook his head. "Even with every warrior in Argos he wouldn't be able to reach the capital."

"No," I admitted, speaking the words as the ideas formed in my mind. "But if he can cause enough destruction here in the delta, where most of Egypt's food is grown, then he might be able to force the Egyptians to give him what he wants."

"The woman?"

I hesitated. "The woman—for his pride. And something more, I think."

Lukka gave me a quizzical look.

"Power," I said. "His brother Agamemnon has taken control of the straits that lead to the Sea of Black Waters. Menalaos seeks to gain similar power here in Egypt."

It sounded right to me. It *had* to be right. My whole plan depended on it.

"But how do you know those are Menalaos's ships?" the ever-practical Lukka asked. "Their sails are furled, their masts down. They might be the ships of some other Achaian king or princeling."

I agreed with him. "That is why I'm going into the Achaian camp tonight—to see if Menalaos is truly there."

Chapter 40

F Lukka objected to my plan, he kept his doubts to himself. We returned to our camp by the canal, ate a small meal while the sun set, and then I started back to the village and the Achaian camp.

The villagers seemed to be living with the invading barbarians without friction. They had little choice, of course, but as I picked my way through the darkness I sensed none of the tenseness of a village under occupation by a hostile force. None of the mud-brick houses seemed burned. There were no troops posted to guard duty anywhere. The villagers seemed to have retired to their homes for a night's rest without worrying about their daughters or their lives.

There were no signs of a battle having been fought, nor even a skirmish. If anything, the Achaians seemed to have set up a long-term occupation here. They had not come for raping and pillaging. They had something more permanent in mind.

Good, I thought. So did I.

- I made my way down the shadowy streets of the village, twisting and twining under the cold light of a crescent moon. The wind was warm now, blowing from landward, making the palms and fruit trees sigh. Somewhere a dog barked. I heard no cries or lamentations, no screams of terror. It was a quiet, peaceful village—with a few hundred heavily armed warriors camped along the beach.

Their campfires smoldered in front of each ship. A line of chariots, their yoke poles pointing starward, rested on the far side of the camp, near the rude fencing of the horse corral. A few men slept on the ground, wrapped in blankets, but most of them were inside their tents or the rude lean-tos they had constructed. A trio of guards loafed at the only fire that still blazed. They seemed relaxed rather than alert, like men who had been posted guards as a matter of form, rather than for true security.

I headed straight toward them.

One of them spotted me approaching and said a word to his two companions. They were not alarmed. Slowly they picked up their long spears and got to their feet to face me.

"Who are you and what do you want?" the leader called to me.

I came close enough for them to recognize my face in the firelight. "I am Orion, of the House of Ithaca."

That surprised them.

"Ithaca? Has Odysseus come here? The last we heard he had been lost at sea."

They lowered their spear points as I came to within arm's reach of them. "The last I saw of Odysseus was on the beach at Ilios," I said. "I have been traveling overland ever since."

One of them began to remember. "You were the one who had the storyteller for a slave."

"The blasphemer that Agamemnon blinded."

An old anger rose inside me. "Yes," I replied. "The one Agamemnon blinded. Is the High King here?"

They looked uneasily at one another. "No. This is the camp of Menalaos."

"Are there no other Achaian lords with him?"

"Not yet. But soon there will be. Menalaos is mad with rage since his wife ran away from him after Troy fell. He swears he won't leave this land until she is returned to him."

"If I were you, Orion," said the third one, "I'd run as far from this camp as I could. Menalaos believes you took Helen from him."

I ignored his warning. "How does he know she is in Egypt?"

The leader of the trio shrugged. "From what I hear, he's had a message from some high and mighty Egyptian, telling him that the lady Helen has come here. They're holding her in some palace someplace."

"That's what they say," another of the guards agreed.

The story that Nefertu had unknowingly revealed to me was

stunningly accurate. Nekoptah must have sent word to Menalaos as soon as Nefertu had reported Helen's presence in Egypt, months ago. Of course Nefertu had recognized that she was an important woman of the Achaian nobility; he had finally told me as much. And Nekoptah, wily scoundrel that he was, immediately saw how he could use Helen as bait to bring Menalaos and the other warlords of the Sea Peoples into his own service.

I said, "Take me to Menalaos. I have important news to tell him."

"The king is asleep. Wait until morning. Don't be in such a hurry to get yourself killed."

I debated within myself. Should I insist on waking Menalaos? They were giving me a chance to escape his anger. Should I go back to Lukka and our camp, then return in the morning? I decided to wait here at the beach and get a few hours' sleep. Menalaos's wrath seemed of little consequence.

They looked at me askance, but found a blanket for me and left me to sleep. I stretched out on the sand and closed my eyes.

To find myself in a strange chamber, surrounded by machines with blinking lights and screens that showed colored curving lines pulsing across them. The entire ceiling glowed with a cool light that cast no shadows.

I turned and saw the sharp-featured Creator I had dubbed Hermes. As before, he was clad in a glittering silver metallic uniform from chin to boots. He dipped his pointed chin once in greeting.

Without preamble he asked, "Have you found him yet?"

"No," I lied, hoping that he could not see my mind.

He arched a brow. "Really? In all the time you've been in Egypt, you have no idea where he's hiding?"

"I haven't seen him. I don't know where he is."

With a thin smile, Hermes said, "Then I'll tell you. Look into the great pyramid. Our sensors here detect a power drain focused on that structure. He is obviously using it as his fortress."

I countered, "Or he is allowing you to think so, while actually he's somewhere—or some*when*—else."

Hermes's eyes narrowed. "Yes . . . he is clever enough to decoy us. That's why it is vital that you get inside the pyramid and see if he's actually there."

"I am trying to do that."

"And?"

"I am trying," I repeated. "There are complications."

"Orion," he said, making a show of being patient with me, "there is not much time left. We must find him before he brings down this entire continuum. He's gone quite mad, and he's capable of destroying us all."

What of it? I thought. Perhaps the universes would be better off with all of us dead.

"Do you understand me?" Hermes insisted. "Time is running out for us. There is only a matter of days!"

"I'm doing the best I can," I said. "I tried to penetrate the great pyramid, and it didn't work. Now I must enter it physically, and for that I need the cooperation of the king, or possibly the chief priest of Amon."

Hermes gusted a great impatient sigh. "Do what you must, Orion, but for the love of the continuum, do it *quickly*!"

I nodded, and found myself blinking at the first streaks of dawn in the clouded sky of the Egyptian shore.

Half a dozen armed guards were standing around me, one of them poking the butt of his spear into my ribs.

"On your feet, Orion. My lord Menalaos wants to roast your carcass for breakfast."

I scrambled to my feet. They grabbed my arms and held me fast as they marched me off toward the king's tent. I had no chance to reach for my sword, still laying on my blanket. But the dagger that I kept strapped to my thigh was still there, beneath my kilt.

Menalaos was pacing like a caged lion as the guards brought me before him. Several of his nobles stood uneasily before the tent, swords already at their sides, although they wore no armor. Menalaos was clad in an old tunic, and had a blood-red cloak over his shoulders. He was quivering with fury so that his dark beard trembled.

"It *is* you!" he bellowed as the guards brought me to him. "Light the fires! I'll roast him inch by inch!"

The nobles—all of them younger than Menalaos, I noticed —looked almost frightened at their king's rage.

"What are you waiting for?" he snapped. "This is the man who stole my wife! He's going to pay for that with the slowest death agonies anyone has ever suffered!"

"Your wife is well and safe in the capital of Egypt," I said. "If you will listen to me for a . . ."

Enraged, he stepped up to me and smashed a backhand blow across my mouth.

My temper snapped. I shrugged off the two men pinning my arms, then smashed them both with elbows to their middles. They fell gasping. Before they hit the ground I had whipped out my dagger and, clutching the startled Menalaos by the hair, I jabbed its point to his throat.

"One move from any of you," I growled, "and your king dies."

They all froze: the nobles, some of them with their hands already on their sword hilts; the other guards, their eyes wide, their mouths hanging open.

"Now then, noble Menalaos," I said, loudly enough for them all to hear, even though my mouth was next to his ear, "we will discuss our differences like men, or face each other as enemies in a fair duel. I am not a *thes* or a slave, to be bound and tortured for your pleasure. I was a warrior of the House of Ithaca, and now I am the leader of an army of Egypt, an army that's been sent here to destroy you."

"You lie!" Menalaos snarled, squirming in my grasp. "The Egyptians have welcomed us to their shores. They are holding my wife for me, and have invited me to sail to their capital to reclaim her."

"The chief minister of the Egyptian king has built a lovely trap for you and all the Achaian lords who come to this land," I insisted. "And Helen is the bait."

"More lies," said Menalaos. But I could see that I had caught the interest of the other nobles.

I released my grip on him and threw my dagger onto the sand at his feet.

"Let the gods show us which of us is right," I said. "Pick your best warrior and have him face me. If he kills me, then the gods will have shown that I am lying. If I best him, it will be a sign from the gods that you should listen to what I have to say."

Murderous anger still flamed in Menalaos's eyes, but the nobles crowded around eagerly.

"Why not?"

"Let the gods decide!"

"You have nothing to lose, my lord."

Seething, Menalaos shouted, "Nothing to lose? Don't you understand that this traitor, this abductor—he's merely trying to gain a swift clean death instead of the agony he deserves?"

"My lord Menalaos!" I shouted back. "On the plain of Ilios I begged you to intercede on behalf of the storyteller Poletes from the anger of your brother. You refused, and now the old man is blind. I'm not begging you now. I *demand* what you owe me: a fair fight. Not some young champion who rushes foolishly to his death. I want to fight *you*, mighty warrior. We can settle our differences with spears and swords."

I had him. He took an inadvertent step back away from me, remembering that I had fought so well at Troy. But there was no way he could back out of facing me; he had told them all that he wanted to kill me. Now he had to do it for himself, or be thought a coward by his followers.

The entire camp formed a rough circle for the two of us while Menalaos's servants armed him. This would be a battle on foot, not with chariots. One of the guards brought me my sword; I slung the baldric over my shoulder and felt its comforting weight against my hip. Three nobles gravely offered me my choice from several spears. I picked the one that was shorter but heavier than the others.

Menalaos came forward out of a cluster of servants and nobles, armored from helmet to feet in bronze, carrying a huge figure-eight shield. In his right hand he bore a single long spear, but I noticed that his servants had placed several others on the ground a few paces behind him.

I had neither shield nor armor. I did not want them. My hope was to best Menalaos without killing him, to show him and the other Achaians that the gods were so much with me that no man could oppose me successfully. To accomplish that, I had to avoid getting myself spitted on Menalaos's spear, of course.

I could feel the excitement bubbling from the Achaians circled around us. Nothing like a good fight before breakfast to stimulate the digestion.

An old man in a ragged tunic came out of the crowd and stepped between us. His beard was long and dirty-gray.

"In the name of ever-living Zeus and all the mighty gods of high

Olympos," he said, in a loud announcer's voice, "I pray that this combat will be pleasing to the gods, and that they send victory to he who deserves it."

He scuttled away and Menalaos swung his heavy shield in front of his body. With his helmet's cheek plates strapped shut, all I could see of him was his angry, burning eyes.

I stepped lightly to my right, circling away from his spear arm, hefting my own spear in my right hand.

Menalaos pulled his arm back and flung his spear at me. Without an instant's hesitation, he dashed back to pick up another.

My senses quickened as they always do in battle, and the world around me seemed to slow down into the languid motions of a dream. I watched the spear coming toward me, took a step to the side, and let it thud harmlessly into the sand by my feet. The Achaians "oohed."

By this time Menalaos had grasped another spear. He pivoted and hurled this one at me, also. Again I avoided it. With his third spear, though, Menalaos came charging at me, screaming a shrill war cry.

I parried his spear with my own and swung the butt of it into his massive shield with a heavy *thunk,* hard enough to knock him staggering. He tottered to my left, regained his balance, and came at me again. Instead of parrying, this time I ducked under his point and rammed my own spear between his legs. Menalaos went sprawling and I was on top of him at once, my legs pinning his arms to the ground, my sword across his throat, between the chin flaps of his helmet and the collar of his cuirass.

He stared at me. His eyes no longer glared hate; they were wide with fear and amazement.

Sitting on the bronze armor of his chest, I raised my sword high over my head and proclaimed in my loudest voice: "The gods have spoken! No man could defeat one who is inspired by the will of all-powerful Zeus!"

I got to my feet and pulled Menalaos to his. The Achaians swarmed around us, accepting the judgment of the duel.

"Only a god could have fought like that!"

"No mortal could face a god and win."

Although they crowded around Menalaos and assured him that

no hero in memory had ever fought against a god and lived to tell the tale, they kept an arm's length from me, and looked at me with undisguised awe.

Finally the old priest came up close and stared nearsightedly into my face. "Are you a god, come to instruct us in human form?"

I took a deep breath and made myself shudder. "No, old man. I could feel the god within my sinews when we fought, but now he has left, and I am only a mortal once more."

Menalaos, bareheaded now, looked at me askance. But being defeated by a god was not shameful, and he allowed his men to tell him that he had done something very brave and wonderful. Yet it was clear that he held no love for me.

He invited me into his tent, where he watched me silently as servants unstrapped his armor and women slaves brought us figs, dates, and thick spiced honey. I sat on a handsomely carved ebony stool: of Egyptian design and workmanship, I noticed. It had not come from this fishing village, either.

Menalaos sat on a rope-web chair, the platter of fruit and honey between us. Once the servants had left us alone, I asked him, "Do you truly want your wife back?"

Some of the anger returned to his eyes. "Why else do you think I'm here?"

"To kill me and serve a fat hippopotamus who calls himself Nekoptah."

He was startled at the chief minister's name.

"Let me tell you what I know," I said. "Nekoptah has promised you Helen *and* a share of Egypt's wealth if you kill me. Correct?"

Grudgingly, "Correct."

"But think a moment. Why would the king's chief minister need an Achaian lord to get rid of one man, a barbarian, a wanderer who stumbled into Egypt in company of a royal refugee?"

Despite himself, Menalaos smiled. "You are no ordinary wanderer, Orion. You are not so easy to kill."

"Did it ever occur to you that Helen is being used as bait, to lure you to *your* death—you, and all the other Achaian lords who come to Egypt with you?"

"A trap?"

"I didn't come alone. An Egyptian army is waiting barely a

day's ride from here. Waiting until they can snare all of you in their net."

"But I was told . . ."

"You were told to send word back to your brother and the other lords that they would be welcomed here, if you did as the king's chief minister asked," I said for him.

"My brother is dead."

I felt a flash of surprise. Agamemnon dead!

"He was murdered by his wife and her lover. His prisoner Cassandra, also. Now his son seeks vengeance, against his own mother! All of Argos is in turmoil. If I return there . . ." His voice choked off and he slumped forward, burying his face in his hands.

Cassandra's prophecy, the tales that got old Poletes blinded —they were true. Clytemnestra and her lover had murdered the High King.

"We have nowhere to turn," Menalaos said, his voice low and heavy with misery. "Argos is upside-down. Barbarians from the north are pushing toward Athens and will be in Argos after that. Agamemnon is dead. Odysseus has been lost at sea. The other Achaian lords who are coming here to join me are coming out of desperation. We've been told that the Egyptians will welcome us. And now you tell me that it's all a trap."

I sat on the stool and watched the King of Sparta weep. His world was collapsing on his shoulders and he had no idea of where to turn.

But I did.

"How would you like to turn this trap into a triumph?" I asked him.

Menalaos turned his tear-filled eyes up toward me, and I began to explain. It would mean giving Helen back to him, and deep inside me I hated myself for doing that. She was a living, breathing woman, warm and vibrantly alive. Yet I bartered her like a piece of furniture or a gaudy ornament. The anger I felt within me I directed against the Golden One; this is *his* doing, I told myself. His manipulations have tangled all our lives; I'm merely trying to put things right. But I knew that what I did I did for myself, to thwart the Golden One, to bring me one step closer to the moment when I could destroy him—and revive Athene. Love and hate were fused inside me, intermingled into a single white-hot force boiling and churning in my mind, too powerful for me to resist. I could barter away a queen who loved me, I could sack cities and slay nations to gain what I wanted: Athene's life and Apollo's death.

So I went ahead and told Menalaos how to regain his wife and win a secure place in the Kingdom of the Two Lands.

Nekoptah's scheme was a good one. Practically foolproof. He had thought of almost everything. All I had to do was turn it against him.

Chapter 41

I moved through the next several weeks like a machine, speaking and acting automatically, my inner mind frozen so that the bitter voices deep within me could not catch my conscious attention. I ate, I slept without dreams, and I brought my plans closer to fruition, day by day.

There was a measure of bitter satisfaction in turning Nekoptah's treacherous scheme against its creator. The fat priest had taken one step too far, as most schemers ultimately do. By sending Prince Aramset on this expedition, he had hoped to eliminate his only possible rival for kingly power. But Aramset was the key to my counter scheme. I followed Nekoptah's plan to the letter except for one detail: Menalaos and the other Achaians would offer their loyalty to the crown prince, not the king's chief minister. And Aramset would treat the Achaians honestly.

Vengeance against the chief minister gave me a taste of gratification. But only the ultimate vengeance, triumph against the Golden One, would bring me true pleasure. And I was moving toward that final moment when I would crush him utterly.

It was strange, I reflected. I had entered this world as a *thes,* less than a slave. I had become a warrior, then a leader of soldiers, then the guardian and lover of a queen. Now I was preparing to create a king, to decide who would rule the richest and most powerful land in this world. I, Orion, would tear the power of rulership from the bejeweled fingers of scheming Nekoptah and place it where it belonged: in the hands of the crown prince.

Aramset at first listened to my plan coolly when I brought Menalaos to his boat, moored a day's march upriver from the coast. But once its implications became clear to him, once he realized that I was offering him not only a solution to the problem of the Sea Peoples, but a way to remove Nekoptah, he warmed to my ideas quickly enough.

Nekoptah's spies still infested the army and the prince's retinue, but with Lukka's Hittites protecting him, Aramset was safe enough from assassination. And gruff old General Raseth was loyal to the prince, in his blustering way. The overwhelming majority of the army would follow him if a crisis arose. Nekoptah's spies were few in number and powerless against the loyalty of the army. The king's chief minister depended on stealth and cunning to achieve his ends; his weapons were lies and assassins, not troops who fought face-to-face in the sunshine.

The young prince received the King of Sparta with solemn dignity. None of his usual laughter or youthful nervousness. He sat on a royal throne set up on the afterdeck of his royal boat, under a brightly striped awning, dressed in splendid robes and wearing the strange double crown of the Two Lands, his face set in an expression as stonily unchanging as the statues of his grandfather.

For his part, Menalaos gave a splendid show, his gold-filagreed armor polished until it blazed like the sun itself, his dark beard and curled hair gleaming with oil. Fourteen other Achaian lords were ranked behind him. With their glittering armor and plumed helmets, their dark beards and scarred arms, they looked savage and fierce alongside the Egyptians.

The boat was crammed with men: the prince's retinue, soldiers, dignitaries from the coastal towns, government functionaries. Most of them wore long skirts and were bare to the waist, except for their medallions of office. Some of them were spies for Nekoptah, I knew, but let them report back to their fat master that the crown prince had solved the problem of the Sea Peoples without bloodshed. My only regret was that I could not see the chief minister's painted face twist in anger at the news.

Official scribes sat at the prince's feet, recording every word spoken. Artists perched atop the boat's cabins, sketching madly on sheets of papyrus with sticks of charcoal. Many other boats were ringed around us, also thronged with people to witness this momentous occasion. The shore was crowded, too, with men and women and even children from many towns.

Lukka stood behind the prince's throne, slightly to one side, his lips pressed firmly together to keep himself from grinning. He enjoyed standing higher than Menalaos.

I stood to one side of the assembly and listened to Menalaos faithfully repeat the lines I had told him to speak. The other Achaian lords, newly arrived from their troubled lands with their wives and families, shuffled uncomfortably in the growing heat of the rising sun. The converse between the Egyptian prince and the dispossessed King of Sparta took most of a long morning. What it amounted to was simply this:

Menalaos pledged the loyalty of all the Achaians present to Prince Aramset and, through him, to King Merneptah. In return, Aramset promised the Achaians land and homes of their own—in the name of the king, of course. Their land would be along the coast, and their special duty would be to protect the coast from incursions by raiders. The Peoples of the Sea had been absorbed by the Land of the Two Kingdoms. The thieves had been turned into policemen.

"Do you think they will do an honest job of protecting the coast?" Aramset asked me, as servants removed his ceremonial robes.

We were in his cabin, small and low and stuffy in the midday heat. I felt sweat trickling down my jaw and legs. Somehow the young prince seemed perfectly comfortable in the sweltering oven.

"By giving them homes in the kingdom," I said, repeating the argument I had made many times before, "you remove the reason for their raids. They have nowhere else to go, and they fear the barbarians invading their land from the north."

"My father will be pleased with me, I think."

I knew he was expressing a hope more than a certainty.

"Nekoptah will not," I said.

He laughed as the last windings were taken off his torso and he stood naked except for the loincloth around his groin.

"I will deal with Nekoptah," the prince said happily. "I have my own army now."

The dressers departed and other servants brought chilled water and bowls of fruit.

"Would you prefer wine, Orion?"

"No, water will do."

Aramset took up a small melon and a knife. As he began to slice it, he asked, "And you, my friend. You worry me."

"I?"

He slouched on the bunk and looked up at me. "You are willing to give up that beautiful lady?"

"She is Menalaos's lawful wife."

Aramset smiled. "I have seen her, you know. *I* wouldn't give her up. Not willingly."

Feeling distinctly uncomfortable, I said nothing. How could I explain to him about the Creators and the goddess I hoped to restore to life? How could I speak of the growing unhappiness within me, the reluctance to give up this woman who had shared my life for so many months, who had offered me her love? Silence was my refuge.

With a shrug, Aramset said, "If you won't talk about women, what about rewards?"

"Rewards, your highness?"

"You have done me a great service. You have done this kingdom a great service. What reward would you have? Name it and it is yours."

I barely gave it an instant's thought. "Allow me to enter the great pyramid of Khufu."

For a moment Aramset said nothing. Then, pursing his lips slightly, he replied, "That might be difficult. It's actually the province of the chief priest of Amon . . ."

"Hetepamon," I said.

"You know him?"

"Nekoptah told me his name. I was to bring him back to Wast with me, if I survived his trap with Menalaos."

Impulsively, Aramset jumped to his feet and went to the chest on the other side of the tiny cabin. He flung open its lid and pawed through piles of clothes until he found a small, plain bronze box. Opening it, he lifted out a gold medallion on a long chain.

"This bears the Eye of Amon," he told me. I saw the emblem etched into the bright gold. "My father gave me this before . . . before he became devoted to Ptah."

Before he became hooked on the drugs that Nekoptah administered, I translated to myself.

"Show this to Hetepamon," said the prince, "and he will recognize it as coming from the king. He cannot refuse you then."

Our mighty armada unfurled their sails and started up the Nile two days later. The army that the Egyptians had gathered was now augmented by Menalaos and a picked complement of Achaian warriors, bound by oath to Aramset. The main strength of the Achaians remained on the coast, with Egyptian administrators to help settle them in the towns they would henceforth protect. The prince headed back for the capital, with his bloodless victory over the Peoples of the Sea.

I paced the deck each day, or gripped the rail up at the bow, trying to make the wind blow harder and the boat move faster against the current on the strength of sheer willpower. Each morning I strained my eyes for the first glimpse of the gleaming crown of Khufu's great pyramid.

Each night I tried to reach inside that ancient tomb by translocating my body. To no avail. The Golden One had shielded the pyramid too well. Mental exertion could not penetrate his fortress. My only hope was that the high priest of Amon could lead me physically through an actual door or passage into that vast pile of stones.

That would be the ultimate irony, I thought, as I lay on my bunk sheathed in the sweat of useless exertion, night after night. The Golden One may be able to prevent his fellow Creators from entering his fortress, but could he stop a pair of ordinary humans from merely *walking* in?

The day finally came when we sailed past the outskirts of Menefer, and the great pyramid's polished white grandeur rose before our eyes.

I summoned Lukka to my cabin and told him, "No matter what happens at the capital, protect the prince. He is your master now. You may never see me again."

His fierce eyes softened; his hawk's face looked sad. "My lord Orion, I've never thought of a superior of mine as a . . . a friend . . ." His voice faltered.

I clapped him on the shoulder. "Lukka, it takes two to make a friendship. And a man with a heart as strong and faithful as yours is a rare treasure. I wish I had some token, some remembrance to give you."

He broke into a rueful grin. "I have memories enough of you sir. You have raised us from dirt to gold. None of us will eve: forget you."

A lad from the boat's crew stuck his head through the oper cabin door to tell me a punt had tied up alongside and was waiting to take me to the city. I was glad of the interruption, and so wa: Lukka. Otherwise we might have fallen into each other's arms anc started crying like children.

Aramset was waiting for me at the ship's rail.

"Return to me at Wast, Orion," he said.

"I will if I can, your highness."

Despite his newfound dignity at being a true prince with ar army at his command, his youthful face was filled with curiosity. "You have never told me why you seek to enter Khufu's tomb."

I made myself smile. "It is the greatest wonder in the world. I want to see all its marvels."

But he was not to be put off so easily. "You're not a thief seeking to despoil the royal treasures buried with great Khufu. The marvel you seek must be other than gold or jewels."

"I seek a god," I replied honestly. "And a goddess."

His eyes flashed. "Amon?"

"Perhaps that is how he is known here. In other lands he has other names."

"And the goddess?"

"She has many names too. I don't know how she would be called in Egypt."

Aramset grinned eagerly, the youngster in him showing clearly through a prince's seriousness. "By the gods! I'm half tempted to come with you! I'd like to see what you're after."

"Your highness has more important business in the capital," I said gently.

"Yes, that's true enough," he said, with a disappointed frown.

"Being the heir to the throne is a heavy responsibility," I said. "Only a penniless wanderer is free to have adventures."

Aramset shook his head in mock sorrow. "Orion, what have you done to me?" The sorrow was not entirely feigned, I saw.

"Your father needs you. This great kingdom needs you."

He agreed, reluctantly, and we parted. I saw Menalaos peering over the gunwale as I clambered down the rope ladder to the waiting punt. I waved to him as cheerfully as I could. He nodded somberly back.

One advantage of a mammoth bureaucracy such as administered Egypt is that, once you have it working for you, it can whisk you to your goal with the speed of a well-oiled machine. The bureaucrats of Menefer had been given orders by the crown prince: convey this man Orion to Hetepamon, high priest of Amon. That they did, with uncommon efficiency.

I was met at the pier by a committee of four men, each of them in the long stiff skirt and copper medallion of minor officials. They showed me to a horse-drawn carriage and we clattered across the cobblestoned highway from the riverfront to the temple district in the heart of the vast city.

I was ushered by the four of them, who hardly said a word to me or to each other all that time, through a maze of courtyards and corridors until finally they showed me through a small doorway and into a modest-sized, cheerfully sunlit room.

"The high priest will be with you shortly," one of them said. Then they left me alone in the room, shutting the door behind them.

I stood fidgeting for a few moments. There were no other doors to the room. Three smallish windows lined one wall. I leaned over the sill of the center one, and saw a forty-foot drop to a garden courtyard below. The walls were painted with what I guessed to be religious themes: animal-headed human figures accepting offerings of grain and beasts from smaller mortal men. The colors were bright and cheerful, as if the paintings were new or recently redone. Several chairs were grouped around a large bare table that appeared to be made of polished cedar. Other than that, the room was empty.

The door finally opened, and I gasped with shock as the hugely obese man waddled in. Nekoptah! I had been led into a trap! My pulse thundered in my ears. I had left my sword, even my dagger, on the ship in Lukka's care. All that I carried with me was the medallion of Amon around my neck and Nekoptah's carnelian ring, tucked inside my belt.

He smiled at me. A pleasant, honest-seeming smile. Then I noticed that he wore no rings, no necklaces, no jewelry at all. His face was unpainted. His expression seemed friendly, open, and curious—as though he was meeting me for the first time, a stranger.

"I am Hetepamon, high priest of Amon," he said. Even his voice sounded almost the same. But not quite.

"I am Orion," I said, feeling almost numb with surprise and puzzlement. "I bring you greetings from Crown Prince Aramset."

He was as fat as Nekoptah. He looked so much like the high priest of Ptah that they might be . . .

"Please make yourself comfortable," said Hetepamon. "This is an informal meeting. No need for ceremony."

"You . . ." I did not know how to say it without sounding foolish. "You resemble . . ."

"The high priest of Ptah. Yes, I know. I should. We are twins. I am the elder, by a few heartbeats."

"Brothers?" And I saw the truth of it. The same face, the same features, the same hugely overweight body. But where Nekoptah exuded dark scheming evil, Hetepamon seemed at peace with himself, innocent, happy, almost jovial.

Hetepamon was smiling at me. But as I stepped closer to him, he peered at my face, squinting hard. His pleasant expression faded. He looked suddenly troubled, anxious.

"Please, move away from the sun so that I can see you better." His voice trembled slightly.

I moved, and he came close to me. His eyes went round, and a single word sighed from his slack mouth.

"Osiris!"

Chapter 42

HETEPAMON dropped to his knees and pressed his forehead on the tiles of the floor.

"Forgive me, great lord, for not recognizing you sooner. Your size alone should have been clue enough, but my eyes are failing me and I am not worthy to be in your divine presence . . ."

He babbled on for several minutes before I could get him to rise and take a chair. He looked faint: His face was ashen, his hands shaking.

"I am Orion, a traveler from a distant land. I serve the crown prince. I know nothing of a man named Osiris."

"Osiris is a god," Hetepamon panted, his chubby hands clutched to his heaving chest. "I have seen his likeness in the ancient carvings within Khufu's tomb. It is your face!"

Gradually I calmed him down and made him realize that I was a human being, not a god come to punish him for some self-imagined shortcomings. His fear abated, little by little, as I insisted that if I resembled the portrait of Osiris, it was a sign from the gods that he should help me.

But he talked to me, too, and explained that Osiris is a god who takes human form, the personification of life, death, and renewal.

Osiris was the first king of humankind, Hetepamon told me, the one who raised humans from barbarism and taught them the arts of fire and agriculture. I felt old memories stirring and resonating within me: I saw a pitiful handful of men and women struggling against the perpetual cold of an age of ice; I saw a band of neolithic hunters painfully learning to plant crops. I had been there. I had given them fire and agriculture.

"Osiris, born of Earth and Sky, was treacherously murdered by Typhon, the lord of evil," said Hetepamon, his voice flat and softly whispering, almost as if he were in a trance. "His wife Aset, who loved him beyond all measure, helped to bring him back to life."

Had I lived here in an earlier age? I had no memory of it, yet it might have happened.

Forcing myself to appear calm, I said to Hetepamon, "I serve the gods of my far-distant land, who may be the same gods you worship here in Egypt, under different names."

The fat high priest closed his eyes, as if still afraid to look at my face. "The gods have powers and hold sway far beyond our ability to comprehend."

"True enough," I agreed, silently adding that I would one day comprehend them in their entirety—or die the final death.

Hetepamon opened his eyes and took a great, deep, massively sighing breath. "How may I help you, my lord?"

I looked into his dark, dark eyes and saw honest fear, real awe. He would not argue when I told him that I was mortal, but he remained convinced that he was being visited by the god Osiris. Maybe he was.

"I must go into the great pyramid. I seek . . ." I hesitated. No sense giving him a heart attack, I thought. "I seek my destiny there."

"Yes," he said, acceptingly. "The pyramid is truly placed at the exact center of the world. It is the site of destiny for us all."

"When can we enter the pyramid?"

He gnawed on his lower lip for a moment. His resemblance to Nekoptah still unsettled me, slightly.

"To go to the great pyramid would mean a formal ceremony, a procession, prayers and sacrifices that would take days or weeks to prepare."

"Isn't there a way we could get inside without such ceremony?"

He nodded slowly. "Yes, if you wish it."

"I do wish it."

Hetepamon bowed his head in acquiescence. "We will have to wait until after the sun sets," he said.

We spent the day slowly gaining confidence in one another. I gradually got over the feeling that he was Nekoptah in disguise and, bit by bit, Hetepamon grew easier in the presence of a person whom he still suspected might be a god in disguise. He showed me through the vast temple of Amon, where the great columned halls soared higher than trees and the stories of creation and flood and the relationships between gods and men were carved on the walls in pictures and elaborate hieroglyphs.

One of the things that convinced me he actually was a twin of Nekoptah was his foolish habit of chewing on small dark nuts. He carried a small pouch on a belt around his ample waist and constantly dug his hamlike fists into it to feed himself. His teeth were badly stained by them. Nekoptah, despite his other short-comings, was not a nibbler.

From Hetepamon I learned the history of Osiris and his beloved wife/sister Aset, whom the Achaians called Isis. Osiris had de-scended into the netherworld and returned from death itself to be with her, such was the love between them. Now the Egyptians saw Osiris in the disappearance of the sun at the end of each day and the turning of the seasons each year: the death that is followed inevitably by new life.

I had died many times, only to return to new life. Could I bring my Athene back to life? The legend said nothing about her death.

"These representations are not accurate portraits of the gods," Hetepamon told me as we stood before a mammoth stone relief, carved into one entire wall of the main temple. His voice echoed through the vast shadows. "The human faces of the gods are merely idealized forms, not true portraits."

I nodded as I gazed at the serene features of gods and—smaller —kings long dead.

Leaning close enough for me to smell the nuts on his breath, he whispered confidentially, "Some of the gods' faces were actually drawn from the faces of kings. Today we would consider that blasphemy, but in the old days people believed the kings were themselves gods."

"They don't believe that now?" I asked.

He shook his fat wattles. "The king is the gods' representative on Earth, the mediator between the gods and men. He becomes a god when he dies and enters the next world."

"Why does your brother want you under his power?" I asked suddenly, sharply, without preamble.

"My brother . . . ? What are you saying?"

Taking Nekoptah's carnelian ring from my waistband and showing it to him, I said, "He commanded me to bring you to the capital. I doubt that it was for a brotherly visit."

Hetepamon's face paled. His voice almost broke. "He . . . commanded you . . ."

I added, "He is telling the king that you are trying to bring back Akhenaten's heresy."

I thought the priest would collapse in a fat heap, right there on the stone floor of the temple.

"But that's not true! I am faithful to Amon and all the gods!"

"Nekoptah sees you as a threat," I said.

"He wants to establish the worship of Ptah as supreme in the land, and himself as the most powerful man in the kingdom."

"Yes, I believe so." I said nothing about Prince Aramset.

"He has always felt badly toward me," Hetepamon muttered unhappily, "but I never thought that he hated me enough to want to . . . do away with me."

"He is very ambitious."

"And cruel. Since we were little boys, he enjoyed inflicting pain on others."

"He controls the king."

Hetepamon wrung his chubby hands. "Then I am doomed. I can expect no mercy from him." He gazed around the huge, empty temple as if seeking help from the stone reliefs of the gods. "All the priests of Amon will come under his sword. He will not leave one of us to challenge Ptah—and himself."

He was truly aghast, and seemed about to blubber. I saw that Hetepamon was neither ambitious nor ruthless. How he became chief priest of Amon I did not know, but it was clear that he had little political power and no political ambition.

I was certain now that I could trust this man who looked so like my enemy. So I calmed him down by telling him how Aramset was returning to the capital with power, and the burning ambition to protect his father and establish his own place as heir to the throne.

"He's so young," Hetepamon said.

"A prince of the realm matures quickly," I said. "Or not at all."

We left the great temple and climbed a long flight of stone steps, Hetepamon puffing and sweating, until we reached the roof of the building. Under a swaying awning I could see the sprawling city of Menefer and, across the Nile, the great gleaming pyramid of

Khufu standing white and sharp-edged against the dusty granite cliffs in the distance.

Servants brought us chairs and a table, while others carried up artichokes and sliced eggplant, sweetmeats and chilled wine, figs and dates and melons, all on silver trays. I realized that we had never been truly alone, never unobserved, all through our wanderings through the temples. I felt sure, though, that no one had dared come close enough to overhear us.

I was amused to see that Hetepamon ate sparingly, almost daintily, nibbling at a few leaves of artichoke, avoiding the meats, taking a fig or two. He must eat something more than those nuts he carries with him, I realized, to keep that great girth. Like many very overweight people, he did most of his eating alone.

We watched the sun go down, and I thought of their Osiris, who died and returned just as I did.

Finally, as the last rays of sunset faded against those western cliffs and even the gleaming pinnacle of the great pyramid at last went dark, Hetepamon heaved his huge bulk up from his chair.

"It is time," he said.

I felt a trembling through my innards. "Yes. It is time."

Down the same stairs we went, through the vast darkened main temple, guided only by a few lamps hanging from sconces in the gigantic stone columns. Behind a colossal statue of some god, its face lost in shadows, Hetepamon went to the wall and ran his stubby forefinger against the seam between two massive stones.

The wall opened, the huge stone pivoting noiselessly, and we stepped silently into the chamber beyond. A small oil lamp burned low on a table next to the door. Hetepamon took it, and the stone slid back into place.

I followed the fat priest through a narrowing corridor, our only light the small flicker of the lamp he held.

"Careful here," he warned in a whisper. "Stay to the right, against the wall. Don't step on the trapdoor."

I followed his instructions. Again, farther down the corridor, we had to keep to the left. Then we went down a long, long flight of stairs. It seemed interminable. I could barely make them out in the flickering lamp's flame, but they seemed barely worn, although heavily coated with dust. The walls of the stairwell pressed close; my shoulders grazed against them as we descended. The roof was so low that I had to keep my head bent forward.

Hetepamon stopped, and I almost bumped into him.

"It becomes difficult here. We must skip over the next step, touch the four after that, then skip the one after those four. Do you understand?"

"If I miss?"

He puffed out a long breath. "At the least, this entire stairwell will fill with sand. There may be other punishments that I am not aware of; the old builders were very careful, and very devious."

I made certain to follow his instructions to the inch.

Finally we reached the bottom of the stairs and started along a slightly wider corridor. I was starting to feel relieved. The worst was over. No more warnings about trapdoors or steps to avoid.

We stopped and Hetepamon pushed against a door. It creaked open slowly and we stepped past it.

Suddenly light glared all around us, painfully bright. I threw an arm over my eyes, waiting to hear the mocking laughter of the Golden One.

Then I felt Hetepamon's hand tugging at me. "Have no fear, Orion. This is the chamber of mirrors. This is why we could not approach the tomb until after sundown."

I lowered my arm and, squinting, saw that we were inside a room covered with mirrors. On the walls, on the floor, on the ceiling, nothing but mirrors. They were not flat, but projecting outward at all sorts of weird angles, everywhere except for one zigzag path across the floor. The light that had shocked me was merely the reflection of Hetepamon's lamp, dazzling off hundreds of mirrored facets.

Pointing upward, the fat priest said, "There are prisms above us that focus the light of the sun. During daylight hours this chamber would kill anyone who stepped into it."

Still squinting, I followed him across the polished, slippery path, through another creaking door, and back into a dark narrow corridor.

"What next?" I growled.

He replied lightly, "Oh, that's the worst of it. Now all we must do is climb a short staircase and we will be in the temple of Amon, beneath the pyramid itself. From there it is a long climb to the king's burial chamber, but there are no more traps."

I felt grateful for that.

The temple was a tiny chamber, buried deep underground,

barely large enough for an altar table, a few statues, and some lamps. Three of the walls were rough-hewn from the native rock; the fourth was covered with faint carved reliefs. The ceiling seemed to be one enormous block of dressed stone. I could sense the tremendous weight of the massive pyramid pressing down upon us, oppressive, frightening, like a giant hand squeezing the air from my lungs. A shadowed alcove hid the flight of almost vertical steps that led upward to the king's burial chamber.

Wordlessly, Hetepamon lifted his lamp over his head and turned toward the wall of carved pictures.

He pointed with his free hand. "Osiris," he whispered.

It was my portrait. And beside it stood the picture of my Athene.

"Aset," I whispered back.

He nodded.

So it was true. We had both been in this land a thousand years ago, or more. And she was here now, waiting for me to restore her to life. I knew it. I was close to her. The thought made me tremble inside.

"I will remain here, Orion, while you go up to Khufu's tomb," said Hetepamon.

I must have flashed him a fiercely questioning glance.

"I cannot climb the steep ascent, Orion," he apologized hastily. "I assure you that there are no further dangers to be wary of."

"Have you ever been in the king's burial chamber?" I asked.

"Oh, yes, each year." He guessed my next question. "The procession enters the pyramid from its outer face, where a hinged stone serves as a door. The ramp leading to the tomb is much easier to climb than the shaft you must go through tonight. Even so," he smiled, "I am carried along by eight very strong slaves."

I nodded understanding.

"I will await you here, and offer prayers to Amon for your destiny, and for the safety of Prince Aramset."

I thanked him and, after lighting one of the altar lamps from his, started up the steep winding stairs.

It must have taken an hour or more, although I lost all sense of time as I plodded up the steep steps, winding around and around and around. They seemed to be cut into the walls of the shaft, some of them little more than narrow clefts in the native stone. My lamp provided a little pocket of fitful light against the darkness, and as I climbed I began to feel as if I was not actually going anywhere, as if I was on a vertical treadmill, trudging achingly, painfully forever. It was almost like being in sensory deprivation: no sound except my own breathing and the scuffling of my boots against the stone steps; nothing to see except the dusty walls in the dim light of the lamp. The world might have dissolved outside or turned to ice or burned to a cinder and I would never have known it.

But I plodded on, and at last came to the end.

I climbed up through a hole in the floor and found myself in a large chamber where a great stone bier bore a magnificent sarcophagus, at least ten feet long, made of beautifully worked cypress inlaid with ivory, gold, lapis lazuli, porphyry, turquoise, and god knows what else. Splendid implements filled the chamber: bowls bearing sheafs of grain and vases that were filled, I was certain, with fine wines and clear water. Probably they were renewed each year, as part of the ceremonies Hetepamon had told me about. Tools and weapons were neatly stacked against the walls. Stairs led upward, toward other storehouse chambers. Everything the king needed in life was here or nearby, ready for his use in his next life.

But there was no sign of the Golden One.

Chapter 43

I stood before Khufu's dazzling sarcophagus, surrounded by the finest implements that human hands could make, and clenched my fists in helpless anger.

He was not here! He had lied to me!

Neither the Golden One nor the body of Athene was in this elaborate burial chamber. I wanted to scream. I wanted to smash everything in sight, rip open the dead king's sarcophagus, tear down the entire pyramid, stone by giant stone.

Instead I merely stood there, dumb as any animal, feeling tricked and defeated.

But my mind was working. The Golden One had made this pyramid his fortress, protecting it with energies that not even the other Creators could penetrate. It took an ordinary mortal to physically penetrate the passages built into the pyramid to reach this far. Trying to translocate oneself from outside the pyramid would not work, the energy defenses would prevent it.

So why did the Golden One defend this pyramid? As a decoy? Perhaps.

Or—perhaps this chamber was in reality a jumping-off spot to his actual hiding place. He is protecting the pyramid because it contains some clue to his true whereabouts. Some clue, or some device for making the transition.

I knew that the Creators were not gods. They did not shift their presences from one realm of the continuum to another by mystical *fiat*. They did not generate energy by divine willpower. They used machines, devices, technologies that were godlike in their power but the offspring of human brains and hands, just as the weapons and implements in this tomb were.

I thought to myself, If the Golden One has such a device hidden in this titanic pile of stones, it must be emitting some kind of energy. Could I sense it?

I closed my eyes and tried to shut off my conscious mind. With a gut-wrenching effort of will I disconnected all my five normal senses: I was blind, deaf, totally alone in a universe of nothingness.

For how long I remained that way, I have no idea. But eventually a tiny thread of sensation wormed its way into my awareness. A gleam, a tendril of warmth, a faint, faint buzzing, like the hum of electrical equipment far off in the distance.

Very slowly I opened my eyes and revived my other senses, careful not to snap the connection with the energy leak I had found. I made my way, almost like a sleepwalker, toward a carved panel in the wall of the tomb. It opened at my push and revealed another upward-winding passage. I climbed.

Through several other chambers and along more dark passageways I went, always pulled along by that faint hint of energy.

Finally I found it: a small chamber up near the very top of the pyramid, so low and cramped that I had to bend over to get into it. My upraised hand touched smooth metal that was warm and vibrating with energy. The electrum cap of the pyramid: a good conductor of electricity and other forms of energy, I realized.

Hunched in the middle of the tiny chamber, taking up almost all its space, was a dome of dull black metal, squatting there like the egg of some gigantic robot bird. It was humming to itself. I put my hand on its smooth surface. Warm.

My hand seemed to stick slightly as I pulled it away, as if I had touched paint that had not yet dried. I put my hand back on the dome, pressed it flat, and felt the surface yield slightly. I leaned on it harder, and my hand seemed to penetrate the surface, sink through it. It was cold, freezingly, painfully cold.

But I could not pull my hand back. Something inside the dome was drawing me forward, forcing me deeper into its cryogenic innards. I yelled and dropped the lamp I had carried all this way as my whole body was sucked into the deathly cold beyond the surface of the dome.

I felt death again, the cold breath that brings agony to every cell,

very nerve in my body. I was falling, falling in absolute darkness
s my body froze and the last flashes of life in my brain succumbed
o pain and darkness. My final thoughts were of love and hate:
ove for my dead Athene, hate for the Golden One, who had
eaten me once again.

But when I opened my eyes I was lying on soft grass. A warm
un beat down on me. A pleasant breeze sighed. Or was that my
wn breath returning to my lungs?

I sat up. My heart thundered in my chest. My eyes stared. This
vas not Earth. The sky was vivid orange. There were two suns
hining, one huge enough to cover almost half the sky, the other a
mall diamond-bright pinpoint shining *through* the orange ex-
oanse of its swollen companion. The grass on which I sat was a
Jeep maroon color, tinging off to blackish brown. The color of
dried blood. It felt spongy, soft, more like a mold or a layer of flesh
than like real grass and ground. There were hills in the distance,
strangely shaped trees, and a stream.

"We meet again, Orion."

I turned and saw the Golden One standing behind me. Scrambling to my feet, I said, "Did you think you could hide from me?"

"No, of course not. You are my Hunter. I built those instincts
into you."

He was wearing a loose flowing shirt of gold with long billowing
sleeves, and dark trousers that hugged his lower torso and legs
closely and were tucked into thigh-length boots. He seemed more
relaxed than ever before, smiling confidently, his thick mane of
golden hair tousled by the wind. But when I looked into his tawny
eyes I saw strange lights, hints of passions and tensions that he was
trying hard to control.

"I have delivered Helen to the Egyptians. I have brought down
the walls of Jericho for you. Agamemnon, Odysseus, and most of
the other Achaian warlords have been swept away. New invaders
are conquering their lands. They've paid for their conquest of
Troy."

His eyes glittered. "But you haven't."

"I've done what you asked. Now it's your turn to live up to your
end of the bargain."

"A god does not bargain, Orion. A god commands!"

"You're no more a god than I am," I snapped. "You have better
tools, that's all."

"I have better *knowledge,* creature. Don't mistake the toys fo
the toymaker—or his knowledge."

"Perhaps so," I said.

"Perhaps?" He smiled tolerantly. "Do you have any idea o
where you are, Orion? No, of course not. Do you have any idea o
what my plans are leading to? How could you?"

"I don't care . . ."

"It makes no difference whether you care or not," he said, hi
eyes brightening. "My plans go forward despite your petty anger
and pouts. Even despite the opposition of the other Creators."

"They are trying to find you," I said.

"Yes, of course. I know that. And they asked you to help them
didn't they?"

"I haven't."

"Haven't you?" He was suddenly suspicious, eyeing me warily
almost angrily.

"I've served you faithfully. So that you will revive Athene."

"Faithfully, yes. I know."

"I've done what you asked," I insisted.

"Asked? Asked? I never *ask,* Orion. I told you what must be
done. While the others dither and discuss and debate, I *act.*" His
breathing quickened, his eyes took on a look of madness. "They
don't deserve to live, Orion. I'm the only one who knows what to
do, how to protect the continuum against our enemies. They don'
realize it, but they're actually serving the enemy. The stupid fools,
they're working for the enemy! They deserve to be destroyed.
Wiped out. Utterly."

I stared at him. He was raving.

"I'm the only one worthy of existence! My creatures will serve
me and me only. The others will be destroyed, as they deserve to
be. I will be alone and supreme! Above all others! Forever!"

I grew tired of his ranting. "Apollo, or whatever your name is,
it's time for you to revive Athene . . ."

He blinked at me. More soberly, he replied, "Her name is
Anya."

"Anya." I remembered. "Anya."

"And she is quite thoroughly dead, Orion. There will be no
reviving."

"But you said . . ."

"What I said is of no matter. She is dead."

My fingers twitched at my sides. He stared at me, and I could
eel the forces he commanded engulfing me, drowning me, freez-
ng my body into stillness even though he chose to leave my mind
wake.

With a scream that shook the heavens I broke free of his
ypnotic commands and sprang for his throat. His eyes went wide
nd he tried to raise his hands to defend himself but he was far too
low. I grabbed him and the momentum of my spring tumbled us
prawling to the blood-colored grass.

"You built strength and killing fury into me too, didn't you?" I
ellowed as I squeezed the life out of his throat. He made terrified
trangling noises and batted at me ineffectually with his hands.

"If she can't live, then neither can you," I said, tightening my
;rip, watching his eyes bulge, his tongue swell. "You want to wipe
ut the others and reign supreme? You won't even last another
minute!"

But powerful hands pulled my arms away and lifted me to my
eet. I struggled against them, uselessly, and then realized who was
olding me.

"That's enough, Orion!" said Zeus sharply.

I glared at him, blood-fury still pounding along my veins. Four
other male Creators held my arms tightly. Still more of them,
women as well as men, stood grouped around the fallen Apollo
and me, dressed in an assortment of tunics, robes, glittering
metallic uniforms.

Zeus waited until I stopped struggling. The Golden One lay
gagging and coughing on the dried-blood ground, leaning on one
elbow, his other hand touching his throat. I saw the purple
imprints of my fingers there and I was only sorry that I hadn't
been allowed to finish the job.

"We asked you to find him for us, not murder him," Zeus said,
his sternness struggling against a satisfied little smile.

"I found him for myself," I said. "And when he refused to
revive Ath . . . Anya, I knew he deserved to die."

Shaking his head at me, Zeus said, "No one deserves to die at
the hands of another, Orion. That is the ultimate lie. Can't you see
that he's mad? His mind is sick."

New fury surged through me. "And you're going to help him?
Try to cure him?"

"We will cure him," said the lean-faced Hermes. "Given time."

He knelt over the fallen Apollo and touched him with a sho
metal rod that he had taken from his tunic pocket. The wel
around the Golden One's neck faded and disappeared. H
breathing returned to normal.

"Physical repairs are the easiest," Hermes said, rising to hi
feet. "Repairing the mind will take longer, but it will be done."

"He wanted to kill you—all of you," I said.

Hera replied, "Does that mean we should kill him? Only
creature thinks that way, Orion."

"He killed Anya!"

"No," said the Golden One, climbing slowly to his feet. "Yo
killed her, Orion. She became mortal for love of you, and sh
died."

"I loved her!"

"I loved her too!" he shouted. "And she chose you! Sh
deserved to die!"

I strained against the men holding me, but they were too man
and too strong. Even so, Apollo dodged backward, away from me
and Zeus stepped between us.

"Orion!" he snapped. "To struggle against us is pointless."

"He said he could revive her."

"That was his madness speaking," said Zeus.

"No it wasn't!" the Golden One taunted. "I *can* revive her! Bu
not for him. Not so that she can give herself to this . . . this . .
creature!"

"Bring her back to me!" I screamed, straining uselessly agains
the four who held me.

Hera stepped before me, her taunting smile gone; instead he
face was grave, almost sympathetic. "Orion, you have served u
well and we are pleased with you. But you must accept what mus
be accepted. You must put all thoughts of Anya out of your mind."

She reached up and touched my cheek with the tips of her
fingers. I felt all the fury and tension drain out of me. My body
relaxed, my rage subsided.

To Hera I said, "Put all thoughts of her out of my mind? That's
like teaching myself not to breathe."

"I feel your pain," she said softly. "But what's done cannot be
undone."

"Yes it can!" the Golden One snapped. He laughed and glared at
me. Zeus nodded at Hermes, who gripped him by the shoulders.

The burly redhead I called Ares also stepped close to the Golden One, ready to restrain him if necessary.

"I could do it," he said, his eyes wild. "I could bring her back. But not for you, Orion! Not so that she can embrace a creature, a worm, a thing that I made to serve me!"

"Take him back to the city," said Zeus. "His madness is worse than I thought."

"I'm not the mad one!" Apollo ranted. "I'm the only sane one here! The rest of you are crazy! Stupid, shortsighted crazy fools! You think you can control the continuum and save yourselves? Madness! Nothing but madness! Only I can save you. Only I know how to keep your precious necks out of the noose. And *you,* Orion! You'll never see Anya again. Never!"

The murderous rage was gone from me. I felt empty and useless.

Hermes began to lead the Golden One away, with brawny Ares following behind. Zeus and the others began to fade, shimmering in the double sunlight like a desert mirage. I stood alone on the strange world and watched them slowly dissolve from sight.

Just before he disappeared, the Golden One turned and shouted over his shoulder. "Look at you, Orion! Standing there like a forlorn puppy. No one's going to bring her back! There's only the two of us who could, and I'm not going to, and you don't know how!"

He howled with laughter as he faded out and disappeared with the others, leaving me alone on a strange and alien world.

Chapter 44

I T took several moments for the meaning of the Golden One's words to sink home.

"No one's going to bring her back! There's only the two of us who could, and I'm not going to, and you don't know how!"

I could return Anya to life. That's what he had said. Was it merely a taunt, a final cruel slash intended to tantalize me? I shook my head. He is mad, I told myself. You can't believe anything he says.

Yet he had said it, and I could not get it out of my mind.

I gazed around the alien landscape and realized that if I was to have any chance at reviving Anya, I had to be back on Earth to do so. Closing my eyes, I willed myself to return. I thought I heard the Golden One's mad laughter, ringing in the farthest distance. Then it seemed that Zeus spoke to me: "Yes, you may return, Orion. You have served us well."

I felt an instant of cold as sharp as a sword blade slicing through me. When I opened my eyes I found myself back in the great pyramid, in the burial chamber of Khufu.

Drenched with sweat, I lurched against the gold-inlaid sarcophagus. Every part of me was exhausted, body and mind. Somehow I dragged myself down the spiraling stone stairway to the underground chamber where Hetepamon waited.

The fat priest was kneeling before the altar of Amon. He had lit all the lamps in the tiny chamber. Pungent incense filled the room

s he murmured in a language that was not the Egyptians' current
ongue.

"... for the safety of the stranger Orion, O Amon, I pray.
Mightiest of gods, protect this stranger who so resembles your
beloved Osiris ..."

"I am back," I said, leaning wearily against the stone wall.

Hetepamon whirled so quickly that he lost his balance and went
down on all fours. Laboriously, he lifted his ponderous bulk to his
feet.

"So quickly? You've barely been gone an hour."

I smiled. "The gods can make time flow swiftly when they want
to."

"You accomplished your mission?" he asked eagerly. "You have
fulfilled your destiny?"

"This part of it," I said.

"Then we can leave?"

"Yes, we can leave now." I glanced up at the statue of Amon
standing above the altar. For the first time I noticed how much it
resembled the Creator I knew as Zeus, without his trim little
beard.

For the next several days we sailed up the Nile, Hetepamon and
I, heading for the capital. Prince Aramset expected me there.
Menalaos and Helen were there; they would be reunited before I
returned. At least, I thought, she will live in the comforts of Egypt.
Perhaps she will be able to teach her husband some of the arts of
civilization and make her life more bearable.

Nekoptah awaited us, too. I had no idea of how Aramset would
deal with him. The king's chief minister would never give up his
power willingly, and the prince seemed terribly young for this
game of court politics. I was glad that Lukka headed his personal
guard.

But thoughts of them merely buzzed somewhere in the back of
my mind as we sailed up the busy river. My eyes saw towns and
cities glide by, monuments towering along the water's edge, farms
and orchards being worked by naked slaves. But my thoughts were
of Anya and the Golden One's taunting words.

Did I have the power to revive her? If so, how could I learn to do
it when none of the other Creators knew how?

Or did they? I felt an icy anger grip me in its merciless clutche
Were they telling me the truth, Zeus and Hera and the others? (
was Anya the victim of a power struggle among them, the loser i
a battle among the Creators? They said they did not kill on
another, but the Golden One had caused Anya's death, an
perhaps none of them *chose* to help me bring her back.

Each night I tried to make contact with the Creators, to reac
their golden-shimmering domed city somewhere in the far futu
of this time. But they refused me. I lay on my narrow bunk in th
creaking boat and saw nothing but the reflections of the rive
against the low wooden ceiling, heard nothing except the drone o
insects and the distant faint voice of an occasional song from th
shore.

Our reception at Wast was very different from the day whe
Helen, Nefertu, and I had first arrived. The prince himself awaite
us, with an honor guard of brightly polished soldiery that line
both sides of the stone pier from end to end. Thousands of peopl
thronged the waterfront, drawn by the sight of Prince Aramse
young and dashing in his purple-hemmed skirt and golden pecto
ral.

I saw Lukka and his men, wearing Egyptian armor now
standing proudly in the first rank, nearest the prince.

And no sign of Nekoptah or any priest from his temple.

We were welcomed quite royally. Aramset walked right up to m
and greeted me with both hands on my shoulders, to the tumultu
ous cheers of the crowd.

"The lady Helen?" I asked him, over the noise of the cheering

Grinning, he shouted in my ear, "She has had a happy reunio
with her husband, and is now allowing him to court her in th
Egyptian manner—with gifts and flowers and serenades by min
strels in the evening."

"They aren't sleeping together?"

"Not yet." He laughed. "She's making him learn the ways o
civilization, and I must say that he seems eager to learn—so tha
he can bed her."

I had to smile to myself. In her own way Helen would cultivate
Menalaos. Still, I felt more of a pang of regret than I had expected
to.

Aramset greeted Hetepamon with regal solemnity, then showed
us to chariots drawn by quartets of matched white stallions. Our

arade moved up the streets of the capital at a stately pace; the
rince was giving the crowds plenty of time to admire him. He
1ay be young, I thought, but apparently he knows a thing or two
bout politics. He must have spent his few years closely observing
1e mechanics of power. I was impressed.

Once we reached the palace, I saw old Nefertu standing at the
9p of the stairs that led into its main entrance. I was glad to see
im alive and safe from Nekoptah's machinations.

We alighted from the chariots, and Aramset came to me. "I
1ust make a fuss over the chief priest of Amon; he is a much more
mportant personage than a mere friend, Orion."

"I understand."

"In three days there will be a majestic ceremony, to seal the new
lliance between the Achaians and the Kingdom of the Two
ands. My father will preside, and Nekoptah will be at his side."

"What is happening . . ."

"Later," the prince said, his youthful face beaming. "I have
1uch to tell you, but it must wait until later."

So he went to Hetepamon while I fairly ran up the steps to greet
Jefertu, realizing as I pranced toward him that it was the prospect
f news about Helen that was really exciting me.

All that afternoon and well into the evening Nefertu filled me in
n what had transpired during my absence. News of our peaceful
uccess in the delta country had, of course, been flashed to
Jekoptah by sun-mirror almost as soon as it had happened. He
eemed furious at first, but put a good face on it for the king. He
ad made no overtures against Helen, realizing that his "hostage"
ad been turned into the prize for the alliance with Menalaos.

As the sun cast lengthening shadows across the city, we sat in
ny apartment, I on a soft couch covered in painted silk, Nefertu
n a wooden stool where he could look past me to the terrace and
he rooftops beyond.

"Nekoptah has been strangely silent and inactive," said the
ilver-haired bureaucrat. "Most of the time he has remained shut
ip in his own quarters."

"He won't give up the power of this kingdom without a
truggle," I said.

"I believe the sudden emergence of Prince Aramset as a force to
e reckoned with has stunned him and upset all his plans,"
Jefertu said. "And for that, we have you to thank, Orion."

"Meaning that Nekoptah blames me for it."

He laughed—a soft chuckle, actually, was all that Nefer would allow himself.

"And the lady Helen?" I asked.

Nefertu's face took on that blank, expressionless look of professional bureaucrat who wishes to reveal nothing. "She well," he said.

"Does she want to see me?"

Turning his eyes away from me slightly, he replied, "She has n said so."

"Would you tell her that I wish to see her?"

He looked pained. "Orion, she is allowing her husband to wo her all over again. The husband that *you* sent to her."

I got up from the couch and walked toward the terrace. He w right, I knew. Still, I wanted to see Helen one final time.

"Take my message to her," I said to Nefertu. "Tell her that I w be leaving for good once the ceremony with the king is finished would like to see her one last time."

Rising slowly from his chair, the old man said tonelessly, "I w do as you ask."

He left, and I stayed on the terrace, watching the evening tu from sunset red to deep violet and finally to black. Lamps winke on all across the city, matched by the stars that crowded the cle dark sky.

A servant from the prince arrived with a set of packages and a invitation to supper. The packages contained new clothes: not a Egyptian-style tunic or skirt of white linen, but a leather kilt an vest similar to what I had been wearing for so many months. laughed to myself. This outfit was handsomely tooled and worke with silver. It included a cloak of midnight blue and boots as so as a doe's eyes.

Aramset was becoming a true diplomat. I wondered how m stained old outfit smelled to him. Servants answered my clappir hands and prepared a bath for me. Finally, bathed, perfume decked in my new kilt, vest, and cloak—with my old dagger sti strapped to my thigh—I was escorted to Aramset's quarters.

We dined quietly, just the two of us, although I saw a quartet (Lukka's men standing guard just outside the door to the prince chambers. Servants brought us trays of food, and the prince ha them sample everything before we tasted it.

"You fear poison?" I asked him.

He shrugged carelessly. "I have surrounded the temple of Ptah
ith soldiers, and given them orders to keep the chief priest
side. He's in there brooding, and hatching schemes. I have
uggested to my father that Nekoptah and his brother officiate at
he ceremony three days from now, the two of them together."

"That should be interesting," I said.

"The people will see that the priests of the two gods are as alike
s peas in a pod." Aramset smiled. "That should help to get rid of
ny plans Nekoptah may have about setting up Ptah above the
ther gods."

I bit into a melon and thought to myself that Aramset was
andling court politics rather well.

"Your father is . . . well?" I asked.

The prince's youthful face clouded. "My father will never be
ell, Orion. His sickness is too advanced, thanks to Nekoptah.
he best that I can do is to make him comfortable and allow the
eople to continue believing in their king."

Aramset seemed in total control of the situation. There was
othing left for me to do here. Within three days I could take up
ny quest to find Anya, wherever that would take me. Still, I
hought, it would be good to see Helen one more time.

A servant came rushing into the room and fell to his knees,
kidding on the polished floor and almost bumping into the
rince.

"Your royal highness! The high priest of Ptah is dead! By his
wn hand!"

Aramset leaped to his feet, knocking over the chair behind him.
By his own hand? The coward!"

"Who shall tell the king?" the servant asked.

"No one," snapped Aramset. "I will see this suicide first." He
tarted for the door.

I went with him, and motioned the Hittite guards to accompany
s. One of them I sent for Lukka, with orders to bring the rest.

We crossed the starlit courtyard and entered the vast temple of
tah. Up the stairs and along the corridor to the same office where
urly Nekoptah had first received me.

He lay on his back, a huge mound of flesh with a deep red gash
cross the rolls of fat of his throat. In the flickering light of the
lesk lamp we saw his painted face with eyes staring blankly at the

dark wooden beams of the ceiling. His golden medallion lay ov
one shoulder, blood already caking on it. The rings on his stub
fingers glinted in the lamplight.

I stared at the rings.

"This is not Nekoptah," I said.

"What?"

"Look." I pointed. "Three of his fingers have no ring
Nekoptah's fingers were so swollen that no one could have take
the rings off without cutting off the fingers themselves."

"By the gods," Aramset whispered. "It's his brother, made up
look like him!"

"Nekoptah murdered him, and he's roaming free in the pala
right now."

"My father!"

The prince bolted off toward the door. The Hittite guards ca
me a confused glance, but I motioned for them to go wi
Aramset. He was right: His first duty was to protect his fathe
Nekoptah could go anywhere in the palace, disguised as his tw
brother. I doubted that he intended to harm the king, but Arams
was right to go to him.

I knelt over the dead body of poor Hetepamon for a fe
moments, and then suddenly realized where Nekoptah wou
strike next.

I got to my feet and ran for Helen's quarters.

Chapter 45

I understood the high priest's murderous plan. His goal was to undo the alliance between the Achaians and the Egyptians, to show the king that Prince Aramset had brought the barbarian menace into the very capital of the land. Who knows, I thought as we raced through the palace toward Helen's apartment, perhaps he will get Menalaos to kill the prince.

If he has Helen he has control of Menalaos, I knew. Even if he doesn't murder the prince, if he can get Menalaos to run amok in the palace, Prince Aramset's newfound influence with his father is gone. Nekoptah returns to power with a haughty "I told you so."

Past startled guards I ran, guided by my memory of the palace's layout. But there were no guards at Helen's door. It was slightly ajar. I pushed it open.

Nefertu lay sprawled on the floor, a jeweled dagger sticking out of his back.

I rushed to him. He was still alive, but just barely.

"I thought . . . chief priest of Amon . . ."

His eyes were glazed. Bright red blood flowed from his mouth.

"Helen." I asked, "Where did he take Helen?"

"The underworld . . . to meet Osiris . . ." Nefertu's voice was the faintest whisper. I could feel his pain. He tried to breathe, but his lungs were filled with blood and agony.

I had no time to be gentle. He was dying in my arms.

"Where did Nekoptah take Helen?"

"Osiris . . . Osiris . . ."

I shook the poor old dying man. "Look at me!" I demanded. '
am Osiris."

His eyes widened. Feebly, he tried to reach for my face with on
limp hand. "My lord Osiris . . ."

"Where has the false priest Nekoptah taken the foreig
woman?" I demanded.

"To your temple . . . at Abtu . . ."

That was what I needed to know. I lay Nefertu's gray head dow
on the painted tiles of the floor. "You have done well, mortal. Res
in peace now."

He smiled and sighed and stopped his breathing forever.

The temple of Osiris at Abtu.

I went to Prince Aramset and told him what had happened.

"I cannot leave the palace, Orion," he said. "Nekoptah's spie
and assassins may be anywhere. I must remain here with m
father."

I agreed. "Just tell me where Abtu is and give me the means t
get there."

Abtu was a two-day chariot drive north of the capital. "I ca
have fresh horses ready for you every ten miles," the prince sai
Then he offered me Lukka and his men.

"No, they are your personal guard now. Don't strip yourself o
their loyalty. A charioteer and relays of fresh horses will be all
need."

"Nekoptah won't be alone at Abtu," warned Aramset.

"That's right," I said. "I will be there."

Before the sun rose I was standing in a war chariot, light an
tough, beside a nut-brown Egyptian who lashed the four powerfu
chargers along the royal road northward. I carried nothing but th
clothes I had been wearing and an iron sword, Lukka's own, give
to me by the Hittite captain as I took my leave of him. And th
dagger had been my companion for so long that it had left it
imprint on my right thigh.

We raced furiously along the road, kicking up a plume of dus
behind us, the horses thundering along the packed earth, m
charioteer grunting and puffing with the exertion of controllin
the four of them.

We stopped at royal relay posts only long enough to chang
horses and take a bite to eat and a sip of refreshing wine.

By dawn of the second day my charioteer was exhausted. He :ould hardly drag his stiff and sore body from the chariot when we stopped at the halfway point. I left him at the relay post there. He protested. He begged me to let him continue, saying that the prince would have him flogged to death for abandoning me. But here was no sense taking him farther.

I took the reins in my own hands. I had watched him long enough to know how to handle the horses. Fatigue clawed at my body, too, but I could consciously damp down its warning signals and pour more oxygen into my bloodstream by hyperventilating as I drove four fresh animals pell-mell into the brightening morning.

The river was on my left, and I passed many boats floating downstream on the Nile's strong current. Not fast enough for this mission. I cracked my whip over the horses' ears and they strained harder in their harnesses.

At a bend in the road I happened to turn and glance back behind me. Another rooster tail of dust rose behind me, far back at the horizon. Someone was following me in just as mad a hurry as I was. Had the prince sent troops to back me up? Or could it be Menalaos rushing to rescue his wife? Either way, it would be help for me. Then another thought struck me: Could it be followers of Nekoptah, rushing to back *him*?

As the sun set, I drove madly through a village of small houses, scattering the few people and children on the main road, and past a mile or so of precise formal gardens bordered by rows of trees and gracefully laid-out ponds. The temple of Osiris stood in their midst, facing a long rampway that led to the river. A single boat was tied up at the pier.

A half-dozen guards in bronze armor stood before the temple's main gate as I pulled up my lathered horses and jumped from the chariot.

"Who are you and what are you doing here?" demanded their leader.

I was willing to fight them if I had to, but it would be quicker and easier if I could avoid it.

"On your knees, mortals!" I boomed, in my deepest voice. "I am Osiris, and this is my temple."

They gaped at me, then laughed. I realized that I was caked with dust from the road, and hardly the glorious radiant figure of a god.

"You are one of the foreigners that my lord Nekoptah told u
would try to enter the sacred temple," said the guard leader. H
drew his sword and the others moved to surround me. "For you
blasphemy alone, you deserve to die."

I took a deep breath. There were six of them, wiry littl
Egyptians with deep-brown skins and even darker eyes, thei
chests protected by armor, conical bronze helmets on their head:
and swords in their hands.

"Osiris dies each year," I said, "and each time the sun goe
down. I am no stranger to death. But I will not be killed at th
hands of mortals."

Before he could react I snatched the sword from his hand an
threw it toward the river in a high arc. Its bronze blade caught th
last rays of the dying sun. They stared as it arced high overhead
Before they could react I threw their leader to the ground an
reached the next man. He went down with a blow to his head. B
the time their leader had risen to his hands and knees I had decke
all the rest of them.

I pointed at their leader, recalling the imperious tones that th
Golden One had often used on me. "Stay on your knees, morta
when you face a god! And be glad that I have spared your lives.'

All six of them pressed their foreheads to the dust, tremblin
visibly.

"Forgive me, O powerful Osiris . . ."

"Stand watch faithfully and you will be forgiven," I said
"Remember that to tempt the wrath of the gods is to court painfu
death."

Into the temple I strode, wondering in the back of my mind if
god ever ran. Not in front of worshipers, I supposed. Not bad for
man sent to this time as a mindless tool, a servant bereft o
memory. I had risen to a maker of kings and a pretender o
godhood.

Now I was bent on vengeance once more, this time not fo
myself but for an innocent fat priest and a faithful old bureaucrat
both murdered because they stood between Nekoptah and th
power of the kingdom. I drew my sword and hunted the chie
priest of Ptah in the temple of Osiris.

Through courtyards lit by the newly risen moon and pas
colonnaded halls lined with statues of the gods I strode, sword i

and. I came upon a row of small chambers, sanctuaries for various gods. Nekoptah was not in the shrine of Ptah, where I looked first. Then I saw that the shrine of Osiris had a small doorway at its rear. I went to it and pushed it open.

The three of them were there, standing beside the altar of Osiris, lit by the flames of lamps set into the walls: Nekoptah, Helen, and Menalaos.

The erstwhile King of Sparta was in full bronze armor, his heavy spear gripped tightly in his right hand. Helen, in a shimmering gown of silver-blue, stood slightly behind him.

"I told you!" shouted Nekoptah. "I told you he would come seeking the woman."

The priest's face was unpainted and his resemblance to Hetepamon was uncanny. Yet where the brother was smiling and amiable, Nekoptah was snarling and vicious. I noticed that his hands were bare, except for the three fingers where rings were imbedded too deeply in flesh ever to come off.

"Yes," I said, more to Menalaos than Nekoptah. "I seek the woman—to return her to her husband."

Helen's eyes flared at me, but she said nothing.

"You took her away from me," Menalaos growled.

"He slept with her," said Nekoptah. "They have made a cuckold of you."

I answered, "You drove her away, Menalaos, with your brutal ways. She is willing to be your wife now, but only if you treat her with love and respect."

"You make demands of me?" he snapped, hefting his spear.

I sheathed my sword. Softly, I said, "Menalaos, we have faced each other in combat before . . ."

"The gods will not always favor you, Orion."

I took a quick glance at the intricate carvings on the temple walls. Sure enough, there was Osiris, and Aset—my Anya, I realized—and all the other gods and goddesses of the Egyptian pantheon.

"Look at my likeness, Menalaos." I pointed to the portrait of Osiris. "And you, too, false priest of Ptah. See who truly faces you."

The three of them looked up to the carving of Osiris. I watched Menalaos's eyes widen, his mouth drop open.

"I am Osiris," I said, and I felt it to be the absolute truth. "Th gods will always favor me, because I am one of them."

Helen was gaping, but Menalaos was goggle-eyed. Onl Nekoptah saw through my words.

"It's not true!" he screamed. "It's a trick! There are no gods an there never have been. It's all a lie!"

I smiled at his twisted, enraged face. So in his heart of heart Nekoptah had no belief at all. He was the worst kind of cynic.

"Helen," I said. "Menalaos is your husband, and no matte what has transpired between us, it is to him that you must nov cling."

Nodding, she answered, "I understand, Orion . . . or should call you Lord Osiris?"

She asked with a slight smile that made me wonder how mucl she believed me. No matter; she saw what I was trying to accomplish and she accepted it. We both knew we would never see each other again.

Ignoring her question, I turned to her husband. "And you Menalaos. You have torn down the walls of Troy and searched hal the world for this woman; she is yours now, won by the valor of your arms. Cherish her and protect her. Forget about the past."

Menalaos straightened to his full height and glanced at Helen almost boyishly.

"Fools!" spat Nekoptah. "I'll have you all slaughtered."

"Your troops will not raise their swords against a god, fat priest," I told him. "Whether you believe me or not, they do."

He knew that I intended to kill him. His tiny pig's eyes darted wildly back and forth as I stepped toward him.

Suddenly Nekoptah threw a fat arm around Helen's neck. A slim dagger appeared in his other hand, and he raised it to her face.

"She dies unless you do as I say!" he screeched.

He was too far away for me to reach him before he could slice her throat open the way he had killed his twin. Menalaos stood frozen beside them, his spear gripped in his right hand.

"Kill him!" Nekoptah commanded Menalaos. "Drive your spear through the dog's heart."

"I cannot kill a god."

"He's no more a god than you or I. Kill him, or she dies."

Menalaos turned toward me and lifted his spear. I stood unmoving. In Menalaos's eyes I saw confusion, fear, not hate or even anger. Nekoptah's face was a seething map of hatred, his eyes burning. Helen stared at her husband, then looked at me.

"Do what you must, Menalaos," I said. "Save your wife. I have died many times. A final death does not frighten me."

The Achaian king raised his long spear high above his head, then whirled and sank it into the fat neck of the priest. Nekoptah gave a strangled grunt; his body spasmed, the knife fell from his numbed fingers, and he released Helen as he clawed at the spear haft with his other hand.

His face contorted in a fierce frown, Menalaos yanked the spear from Nekoptah's neck and the fat priest collapsed in a heap on the stone floor of the temple, blood gushing over his huge body.

Throwing the spear to the floor, Menalaos reached for Helen. She fled to his arms gladly and rested her head against his chest.

"You saved me," she said. "You saved me from that horrible monster."

Menalaos smiled. In the flickering light from the wall lamps, it seemed to me that his swarthy face reddened slightly.

"You have done well," I said to him. "That took courage."

He ran a finger across his dark beard, a gesture that made him seem almost shy. "I am no stranger to battle, my lord. Many times I have seen what happens when a spear strikes a man's flesh. The body freezes with shock."

"You have rid this kingdom of its greatest danger. Take your wife and return to the capital. Serve Prince Aramset well. The burdens of the kingdom will be on his shoulders now. And one day he will be king in fact, as well as in duty."

His arm around Helen's shoulders, Menalaos started for the door. She turned to say a last good-bye to me.

"Orion, behind you!"

I wheeled and saw the bleeding Nekoptah on his feet, staggering, clutching Menalaos's long spear in both his hands. He lurched and drove its bloody point into my chest with all his weight behind it.

"Not . . . a god . . ." he gasped. Then he fell face down on the stone flooring, finally dead.

The shock of sudden pain flooded my brain with unwanted memories of other deaths, other agonies. I stood transfixed, the spear hanging from my chest. Every nerve in my body screamed excruciatingly. I felt my heart trying to pump blood, but it was torn apart by sharp bronze.

I sank to my knees and saw my own blood spilling to the floor. Helen and Menalaos stood frozen, staring in horror.

"Go," I told them. I meant it as a command. It came out as a whisper.

Helen took a step toward me.

"Go!" I made it stronger, but the effort sent waves of giddiness through me. "Leave me! Do as I say!"

Menalaos pulled her to him once more and they fled through the open doorway, into the night, toward the capital and a life together that I hoped would be bearable, perhaps even happy.

I sat heavily, all the strength gone from my body, leaning forward until the spear propped me from falling any farther, its butt wedged against Nekoptah's obese corpse.

The final death, I thought.

"If I can't be with you in life, Anya, then I will join you in death," I said aloud.

I toppled over onto my back as the black shadows of death swirled and gathered about me.

Chapter 46

I lay on my back, waiting for the final death, knowing that neither the Golden One nor any of the other Creators would revive me again. Nor would they revive Anya. They were glad to be rid of us both, I knew.

A wave of anger crested over the pain that throbbed through my body. I was accepting their victory over me, over *her*, their victory over us. They were tenderly nursing the Golden One back to sanity so that they could continue their mastery over the human race and its ultimate destiny.

Memories of other lives, other deaths, flooded through me. I began to understand what they had done to me and, more important, how they had done it.

With the last ebbing bit of strength in me, I slowly reached up and clasped the spear imbedded in my chest. Bathed in cold sweat, I closed off the receptor cells that shrieked with pain, willed my body to ignore the agony flaming through me. Then, weakly, slowly, I pulled the spear out of me. The bloody barbs of its point tore great gouges of flesh, but that no longer mattered. I pulled it free and let it fall clattering to the stone floor.

The world was swimming giddily about me now, the very walls of the temple shimmering, their carvings shifting and undulating almost like living creatures in an intricate, eerie dance.

I propped myself up on my elbows and watched the walls, saw my own image and that of Anya facing each other, wavering, moving, fading from my sight.

The secret of time is that it flows like an ocean, in vas
enormous currents and tides. Humans see time as a river, like th
Nile, always moving linearly from *here* to *there*. But time is a wid
and beautiful sea that touches all shores. And in the many lives
had led, I had learned a little about navigating on that sea.

It takes energy to move across time. But the universe is fille
with energy, drenched with the radiant bounty of uncounted stars
The Creators knew how to tap that energy, and my memories o
their actions taught me how to tap it also.

The walls of Osiris's temple faded before my eyes, but did no
disappear. The carvings melted away. The dancing, shimmerin
pictures slowly dissolved until the walls were blank and smooth
as if newly erected.

I rose to my feet. The wound in my chest was gone. That existe
in another time, thousands of years away.

Through the open doorway I saw not the columned court of the
main temple, but a lush garden where fruit trees bent their heavil
laden branches to the grassy ground and flowers were openin
their colorful petals to the first welcome rays of the morning sun

The temple I was in was small, plain, virtually undecorated. A
rough stone altar stood against one wall, with a single small statue
atop it. It was the figure of a man with the head of a beast I coul
not recognize: a sharply curved beak, almost like a hawk's, but the
rest of the face had no birdlike qualities to it.

No matter. I saw that there was another doorway in the opposite
wall, and that it led into a smaller, inner shrine. It was dark in
there, but I stepped through the doorway without hesitation.

Through the dim shadows I saw her lying on the altar, dressed in
a long gown of silver. Her eyes were closed, her hands lay by her
sides. She was not breathing, but I knew she was not dead. Merely
waiting.

I looked up at the low ceiling, barely above my head. It was
made of wooden beams covered with planks and sealed with
pitch. I reached up and, sure enough, the section of roof just over
the altar was hinged. I pushed it open and let the morning sun
shine down on Anya's recumbent figure.

The silver of her robe gleamed like a thousand tiny stars. Color
returned to her cheeks.

I stepped to the altar, leaned over her, and kissed her on the lips.
She felt warm and alive. Her arms twined around my neck and

he sighed deeply and kissed me back. My eyes filled with tears
nd for many long minutes we said nothing at all, merely held
ach other so closely that neither time nor space could separate us.

"I knew you would find me," Anya said at last, her voice low
nd warm and filled with love.

"They said you couldn't be revived. They told me you were gone
orever."

"I was here. Waiting for you."

Anya sat up slowly, and then I helped her to stand. Her eyes held
he depths of the universes in them. She smiled at me, the same
radiant smile I remembered from so many other existences.

But as I held her in my arms, rejoicing, the memory of our death
ogether sent a chill shudder through me.

"What is it, my love?" she asked. "What's wrong?"

"The Golden One murdered you . . ."

Her face grew grave. "He is mad with jealousy of you, Orion."

"The other Creators have taken him. They're trying to cure his
madness."

She looked at me with new respect. "And you helped to capture
him, didn't you?"

"Yes."

"I thought so. They couldn't have done it without you, just as
they couldn't have revived me without you."

"I don't understand," I said.

She touched my cheek with her soft, wonderful fingertips. "It
will take time to teach you, my brave Orion, but you already know
much more than you realize."

A new question rose in my mind. "Are you human now, or
a . . . goddess?"

Anya laughed. "There are no gods or goddesses, Orion. You
know that. We have much more knowledge than earlier human
species. We have much more powerful capabilities."

Much more powerful than I, I thought.

As if she could read my mind, Anya said, "Your own powers are
growing, Orion. You have learned much since the Golden One first
sent you to the Ice Age to hunt down Ahriman. You are becoming
one of us."

"Can you be killed?" I blurted.

She understood my fear. "Anyone can be killed, Orion. The
entire continuum can be destroyed, and everything in it."

"Then there's no place for us to be at peace? No time when v can rest and live and love as ordinary human beings do?"

"No, my darling. Not even ordinary mortals have that luxur The best we can hope for is to be together, to face the joys an dangers of each moment side by side, through all time, across a the universes."

I took her in my arms once more and felt not merely conten but supernally happy. "That will be good enough. To be with yo no matter what, is all I desire."

Epilogue

WITH Anya beside me, I walked out of the ancient temple into the warming sunshine of the new day. All around us, a lush green garden grew: flowering shrubs and bountiful fruit trees as far as the eye could see.

Slowly we walked toward the river, the mighty Nile, flowing steadily through all the eons.

"Where in time are we?" I asked.

"The pyramids have not been started yet. The land that will someday be called the Sahara is still a wide grassland teeming with game. Bands of hunting people roam across it freely."

"And this garden? It looks like Eden."

She smiled at me. "Hardly that. It is the home of the creature whose statue stood on the altar."

I glanced back at the little stone temple. It was a simple building, blocks of stone piled atop one another, with a flat wooden slat roof.

"Someday the Egyptians will worship him as a powerful and dangerous god. They will call him Set."

"He is one of the Creators?"

"No," Anya said. "Not one of us. He is an enemy; one of those who seek to twist the continuum to their own purposes."

"As the Golden One does," I said.

She gave me a stern look. "The Golden One, power-mad as he is, at least works for the human race."

"He created the human race, he claims."

"He had help," she replied, allowing a small smile to dimple he cheeks.

"But this other creature . . . the one with the lizard's face?"

The smile vanished. "He comes from a distant world, Orion and he seeks to eliminate us all from the continuum."

"Then why are we here, in this time and place?"

"To find him and destroy him," said Anya. "You and I together Hunter and warrior, through all space-time."

I looked into her glowing eyes and realized that this was m destiny. I am Orion the Hunter. And with this huntress, thi warrior goddess, beside me, all the universes were my huntin, grounds.

Author's Afterword

THE distant past has always been just as exciting to me as the distant future, and seems an equally fascinating domain for science fiction.

The novel you have just read is science fiction, not an historical novel. Obviously this is so, for the novel deals with the gods and goddesses of the ancients, and attempts to portray them as advanced human beings from a far distant future who have the ability to travel through time at their whim.

Yet the historical parts of this novel are as accurate as careful research can make them—with some deliberate deviations from "known" history.

It is agreed among most students of ancient history that the siege of Troy celebrated in Homer's *Iliad* and the fall of Jericho described in the Old Testament's Book of Joshua both happened sometime around the middle of the twelfth century B.C. To the novelist, this presents the opportunity of placing the same character(s) at both events; both could have happened within the lifespan of a human being. Perhaps they happened within a few years, or even a few months, of each other.

Once I realized that this was so, the temptation to examine the fabled Trojan Horse and the true cause of the "tumbling down" of Jericho's walls simply overpowered me.

Thus the historical backbone of this novel—the Achaian siege of Troy, the Israelite invasion of Canaan, the collapse of the powerful Hittite empire, and the troubles of Egypt during the

attacks of the Sea Peoples—are faithful to modern historic
scholarship.

In classic Greek legend there is no certainty about Helen's fa
after the Achaians sacked Troy. Some tales claim that she went
Egypt and spent the remainder of her days there. If she were th
kind of woman I think she was, she would surely have preferre
civilized, peaceful Egypt to the semi-barbaric rigors of Achaia
Sparta.

I have taken a few liberties with the canons of history. Sever
scholars have pointed out that the Trojan Horse might have been
siege tower covered with horse hides. It could not have been bui
by the Achaians, however, who have left absolutely no evidence
such sophisticated military technology. But siege towers had bee
used in the Middle East for centuries before Troy. Certainly th
Hittites knew of them, and thus I bring a Hittite contingent to th
service of Odysseus and the House of Ithaca.

The cause of the collapse of Jericho's walls is more speculativ
but I believe it is consistent with the archaeological evidence an
the record from the Book of Joshua.

In this novel, I have it that while the Hebrews were slaves i
Egypt, pharaoh commanded every *female* infant to be killed. Th
contradicts the Biblical telling of the murder of every male bab
Biblical scholars and historians agree that the Egyptians appare
ly carried out the slaughter as a means of controlling the Hebrew
population growth; the Jewish slaves were out-populating th
native Egyptians. To my mind, the Egyptians were intellige
enough to realize that killing male children would not alter th
Jewish birthrate; killing female children would. Thus the slaug
ter of the baby girls. I assume that later generations of Jewis
scribes were so thoroughly male-oriented that they change
the story to agree with their concepts of male importance an
dominance.

These speculations are perfectly in accord with the traditiona
science-fiction axiom that the author is free to invent *anything,* s
long as no one can prove him wrong. The Egyptians slaughtere
baby girls, and Troy and Jericho were both toppled by Hittit
engineers.

The most fantastic elements in the novel are, of course, Orio imself and the pantheon of advanced human time-travelers who resent themselves as gods and goddesses to the ancients.

Does this mean that the novel is fantasy, rather than science ction? To be science fiction, a story must deal fairly with le known laws of science, and reasonable extrapolations there-f.

Time travel is clearly impossible, almost. Physicists have specu-ated that black holes representing collapsed stars or even col-apsed galaxies must have gravitational fields about them that are ⊃ intense they warp space-time. Space and time are bent so rastically that modern physics cannot predict what happens nder such circumstances. Such black holes may represent, len, natural time machines. What nature can do, the human lind can eventually duplicate or even improve upon. Time ma-hines are clearly impossible today, but they may not always be ⊃, especially if you allow plenty of millennia for them to be eveloped.

Thus the novel is, to my way of thinking, science fiction. Again, he axiom is that an author can use anything that cannot be *proven* ⊃ be wrong. Time travel is reasonable material for a science ction novelist to use in his speculations. Even more fascinating re the consequences of time travel.

If one grants the possibility of time travel, then the need for a upernatural being, a god, as the cause of the universe—and of umankind—goes out the window. Consider a very advanced uman civilization, thousands of years in our future. Their :nowledge is so great that they discover the means to travel hrough time; past and future are like different currents in a vast ▸cean, to them. They could go back to an earlier eon on Earth and reate the human race, their own ancestors. In fact, *they would ave to.*

To those earlier people the creators would seem like gods. It is ▸lear that the ancient gods were not the benificent moralists that ve believe our modern gods to be. In fact, to any rational mind, he concept of a god who is perfectly just and perfectly merciful is lot only illogical, it is decidely out of tune with the observable acts of the world around us.

Now then—if the "gods" are as human as you and I but possess

enormously greater powers than we do, and if power truly do
corrupt the human spirit, imagine how wildly malevolent a
all-powerful god must be!

The result of such ratiocinations is the novel you have ju
finished reading, and its predecessor, *Orion*.

There will be more.

Ben Bo
West Hartford, Connectic

BEN BOVA

]	53200-7	AS ON A DARKLING PLAIN	$2.95
]	53201-5		Canada $3.50
]	53217-1	THE ASTRAL MIRROR	$2.95
]	53218-X		Canada $3.50
]	53202-3	BATTLE STATION	$3.50
]	53203-1		Canada $4.50
]	53212-0	ESCAPE PLUS	$2.95
]	53213-9		Canada $3.50
]	53221-X	GREMLINS GO HOME (with Gordon R. Dickson)	$2.75
]	53222-8		Canada $3.25
]	53215-5	ORION	$3.50
]	53216-3		Canada $3.95
]	53210-4	OUT OF THE SUN	$2.95
]	53211-2		Canada $3.50
]	53223-6	PRIVATEERS	$3.50
]	53224-4		Canada $4.50
]	53219-8	PROMETHEANS	$2.95
]	53220-1		Canada $3.75
]	59406-1	STAR PEACE: ASSURED SURVIVAL	$7.95
]	59407-X		Canada $9.95
]	53208-2	TEST OF FIRE	$2.95
]	53209-0		Canada $3.50
]	53206-6	VOYAGERS II: THE ALIEN WITHIN	$3.50
]	53207-4		Canada $4.50
]	53225-2	THE MULTIPLE MAN	$2.95
]	53226-0		Canada $3.95

THE BEST IN SCIENCE FICTION

☐ 53125-6   DRAGON'S GOLD by Piers Anthony and Robert E. Margroff $3.9?
☐ 53126-4   Canada $4.9?

☐ 53103-5   SHADE OF THE TREE by Piers Anthony $3.9?
☐ 53104-3   Canada $4.9?

☐ 53172-8   BEYOND HEAVEN'S RIVER by Greg Bear $2.9?
☐ 53173-6   Canada $3.9?

☐ 53206-6   VOYAGERS II: THE ALIEN WITHIN by Ben Bova $3.5(
☐ 53207-4   Canada $4.5(

☐ 53257-0   SPEAKER FOR THE DEAD by Orson Scott Card $3.95
☐ 53258-9   Canada $4.95

☐ 53308-9   THE SHADOW DANCERS: $3.95
☐ 53309-7   G.O.D. INC. NO. 2 by Jack L. Chalker   Canada $4.95

☐ 54620-2   THE FALLING WOMAN by Pat Murphy $3.95
☐ 54621-0   Canada $4.95

☐ 55237-7   THE PLANET ON THE TABLE by Kim Stanley Robinson $3.50
☐ 55238-5   Canada $4.50

☐ 55327-6   BESERKER BASE by Fred Saberhagen, Anderson, Bryant,
    Donaldson, Niven, Willis, Velazny $3.95
☐ 55328-4   Canada $4.95

☐ 55796-4   HARDWIRED by Walter Jon Williams $3.50
☐ 55797-2   Canada $4.50

Buy them at your local bookstore or use this handy coupon:
Clip and mail this page with your order.

Publishers Book and Audio Mailing Service
P.O. Box 120159, Staten Island, NY 10312-0004

Please send me the book(s) I have checked above. I am enclosing $_____
(please add $1.25 for the first book, and $.25 for each additional book to
cover postage and handling. Send check or money order only — no CODs.)

Name _____

Address _____

City _____ State/Zip _____

Please allow six weeks for delivery. Prices subject to change without notice.